Herbert Kastle was born and brou
an English teacher, an editor, an a
devotes his time to writing. M
successful novels including *The M*
Squad, *Dirty Movies* and *Sunset P*

By the same author

HERBERT KASTLE

Little Love

GRAFTON BOOKS
A Division of the Collins Publishing Group

LONDON GLASGOW
TORONTO SYDNEY AUCKLAND

Grafton Books
A Division of the Collins Publishing Group
8 Grafton Street, London W1X 3LA

Published by Grafton Books 1974
Reprinted 1982, 1984, 1986

First published in Great Britain by
W. H. Allen & Co Ltd 1973

ISBN 0-583-12228-0

Printed and bound in Great Britain by
Collins, Glasgow

Set in Linotype Granjon

For TERI

'All's fair in love and war.'

ONE

It was the end of winter, and the end of me, I guess, as a business-man and a lot of other things. I was on a trip to eight cities, ostensibly to visit district wholesalers and pitch them on discount items, but what I was doing was simply wandering. Like the kids with long hair you sometimes see on the roads. Only I had a Porsche six and matched cowhide luggage, instead of a thumb and a bedroll.

I'd reached my sixth stop, St Louis, and was staying at the Forest Park Hotel. Two days, and I'd used up the business excuse. I figured I'd head for Chicago. Chicago has some nice girls, and one of them could have meant something to me, and I must have been feeling the need for someone to mean something to me. Three years of living alone begins to hurt a man.

It was a mild morning. I was packed by nine-thirty and down-stairs in the coffee shop by ten. I had eggs and bacon and took my vitamins, all twelve tablets. That's my programme, worked out with the help of Carlton Fredericks and Ron Levine – Ron being a friend and an unorthodox MD. I was on my way to the desk to check out, and then I saw how clear and bright it looked outside. So I went for a walk.

Which was mistake Number One.

There's a broad avenue, a block from the hotel, called Lindell. I walked there, away from the park that gives the hotel its name. I was wearing a topcoat over my sports jacket and slacks, and that came off as the sun got to me. I began to feel good, tasting spring in the air, even though back in New York there was still four inches of snow on the ground. I looked around, at apartment houses and a motel and a supermarket closed by a strike and restaurants and a Cinerama movie and people. I reached a men's clothing store and looked in the window. Nothing that would threaten King's Road, but they had some suède that interested me.

Mistake Number Two – I went inside. It was a small shop, and at first no one seemed to be there. Then I saw the doorway behind the counter which held the register and fronted the shelves of shirts, socks, and underwear.

I walked over, leaned on the counter and looked through the door into an office. A girl sat at a desk, doing her nails. I couldn't see her too well; she was sitting with her side to me. I made out long blonde hair and what appeared to be a rather plump figure.

7

When she finally turned her head, I got the impression of youth –
maybe eighteen or nineteen, and the sort of piggish good looks that
some wide-nosed, wide-faced Polish broads have.

'Yes?' she said, and went back to her nails.

'Good morning. Could you tell me when the people who run the
shop will be back?'

She looked up again. 'What shop?'

'*This* shop.'

She waved a hand back and forth to dry it, and swung her chair
around to face me.

I was about to go on with my gag, flashing a quick smile to
distinguish the make-out as opposed to the critical approach. But I
said nothing. She said, 'In a minute,' that piggy blonde face sullen
as hell. But that wasn't what had stopped me. I'd simply forgotten
my wise-guy line. She'd planted both feet firmly on the floor, a most
unladylike distance apart, and I was looking right up her skirt
between sweet round thighs to a dark joining. And I was attacked
by uncharacteristic appetite. Uncharacteristic because I hadn't been
that horny of late.

She waved her hand a few more times, looked up at me, caught
the direction of my eyes, and closed her legs with an almost audible
snap.

'Spring fever,' I said.

She put her head down and laughed; a giggly, little-girl laugh.
Then she came out to the counter, shorter than she'd looked sitting,
no more than five-three, and said, 'What can I do for you?' She had
an uncultured, somewhat Southern way of speaking ... and I
thought of the Ozarks not too far away. I said, 'You'd better re-
phrase that so I don't get thrown out of here.' She smiled, and there
was a dimple in her left cheek. She leaned on the counter, close to
me, a very lovely girl, all the piggish quality gone with that smile
and that gleam of greyish-green eyes and that sweet, little-girl voice.
'All right,' she said. 'Is there anything you'd like to see?' and even
before I raised my eyebrows, playing the old double-meaning game
to the hilt, she was laughing. 'Is there anything you'd like to *buy*?'
she said, and as I nodded quickly, excessively, she turned away,
shoulders shaking, bending far over, and that mini gave me a flash
of upper thighs and the beginning of buttocks.

When she turned back to me, she said, 'I pass.'

I've tried to remember time and again exactly what I felt then,
whether there was some stirring other than the sexual, some sign of
what was to come. But I honestly can't recall anything except a
stirring in the pants and the certainly that I could make this ob-

vious little sexpot if I stuck around St Louis just one more night.

And so I didn't waste time. 'I came in for a suède vest, but before anyone interrupts us, I'd also like to have lunch and dinner with you.'

'I eat lunch in. I have a date for dinner.' She came around the counter. 'This way to the vests.'

She was wearing a checkered suit, mini as I've said, and she wasn't very big on top and her legs were on the plump side ... but my sense of disappointment, of loss, was sharp. And this despite the fact that she continued to seem a rather cheap little piece to me. I walked with her, deliberately brushing her side with my own. 'Are you *sure*?'

'Goddam right I'm sure,' she said, moving away.

Quick revision of estimate of how long it would take to make her. She was sullen again, and cold. I murmured, 'Sorry, just pressed for time,' and we stopped at the suède rack. I tried on some vests, and said it wasn't common to find a sales*girl* in a shop catering exclusively to men. She said, 'I've outsold every sales*man* Mr Alexis ever had.' I said I could understand why, and only wished I were staying longer in St Louis ... now.

She asked if I wanted the vest I was wearing. I said yes, and we returned to the counter where she boxed it, accepted my credit card, and said, 'Well, thank you, sir. If you ever visit St Louis again ...'

'What about tomorrow night?'

'I'm dated through Saturday. I'm off Sunday, and free for dinner.'

It was Tuesday. She didn't really think I'd stick around for five days?

I said, 'Couldn't you switch tonight's date, or tomorrow's, to Sunday?'

'Why?'

I said goodbye, and by the time I reached the door she was back in the office. I walked further along Lindell for about an hour, but the good feeling, the springtime feeling, was gone. I was on the make. I wanted that blonde. I wanted her more than I'd wanted any woman I'd met in ... well, I'd have said months, but the truth was I wanted her more than anyone I'd *ever* met, even then. It had begun to happen. The chemistry. The obsession.

I made Mistake Number Three, and went into a deli and bought four different kinds of sandwiches and bean salad and potato salad and coffee and Coke and milk and pastry. I asked where I could buy some champagne, and they carried that too, unlike New York where anything alcoholic except beer is in a separate store. And for good measure, I took a jar of Romanoff caviar.

9

Lugging my coat, the boxed vest, and that big bag of food, I returned to the clothing store. There was a man behind the counter, and I thought I'd be eating all this stuff while driving to Chicago, but then the blonde came out of the office and said, 'Oh, forget anything?'

I didn't like the man being there, but it was either speak up or chicken out. I said, 'Brought lunch.'

The man stared at me. He was about fifty-five, maybe a little more; short and slight and sour looking, and the sourness increased by the second. I knew right away he had an interest in his salesgirl, whether active or passive.

She hesitated, then smiled and said, 'Great,' and spoke to the man, calling him Mr Alexis, saying we'd arranged to eat together because she hadn't known he'd be in before three.

'But I *said* I might,' he muttered, looking like a disappointed little boy ... until she put her hand on his arm and murmured something too low for me to hear.

He came around the counter. I said, 'Nice store you have.' He said, 'Thanks, got three more, all doing well,' which was bragging and made me feel ashamed for him. And when I glanced at the girl, she was smiling a mocking little smile. He said, 'I'll be back at three, Ellie,' and went out.

I put my packages on the counter. 'He likes you, Ellie.'

'Everyone likes me. I'm so intelligent.'

That mocking little smile was still there, and that sweet voice seemed to have an edge to it, and I began to think that a pass might run into heavy opposition.

She took the bag and carried it into the office. 'C'mon in.' She drew a second chair from against the wall to the desk and began emptying the bag. 'Wow. You expecting more girls?'

'Didn't know exactly what this one liked.'

She took out the champagne. 'Last of the big-time spenders.' But the edge was gone from her voice. The little jar of caviar came last. 'Is it good?'

'I like it. Some people say it's just salty fish eggs.'

We sat down, me with my back to the door. She spread everything out and took paper cups from a drawer and said, 'I want the caviar first.'

We used a letter opener to pry up the lid, and plastic spoons to spread it over pieces of toast torn from a sandwich. She tasted and said, 'You don't get any more,' and began to eat it straight from the jar.

I opened the champagne, a reasonably dry New York State, and she sipped and nodded. I said, 'Do I get any more of *that*?'

'Yes. Because I'm so nice.' Smile and dimple, and something clutched my chest. What the hell was wrong with me?

We ate a lot and talked a little. She ate a *hell* of a lot, and said she knew she shouldn't. A couple of young guys came in and she went out to them. They looked around and played cute with her and she finally said, 'Keep looking. I'll be right back.' She returned to the office and we ate and she watched the store through the door and the guys finally left.

She lit a cigarette. 'May be dangerous for your health,' I said.

'And stains your fingers and makes your breath smell bad. That's why I smoke maybe three a week.'

'Why now?'

She looked at it and took another puff and put it out. 'Celebration.'

I took her hand. 'Is it?'

She looked at our hands. Hers were very small, very soft. I never could go for girls with big, strong hands. She said, 'Yes. Hello and goodbye.' She took away her hand. 'Thanks for lunch. It was special.'

My insides were in turmoil. I was turned on far beyond what this little scene called for.

She cleaned up the desk and repacked the uneaten food. 'Want it?'

'No.'

'I'll take it home.'

I poured the last of the champagne into both our paper cups. She said, 'No more for me or I'll be balling the customers.'

It shocked me; and then I realized she was watching me closely.

'You really think I'd do it too, don't you?' she asked.

'Of course not.'

'I *look* it, don't I? The type, I mean?'

I stood up. 'You look beautiful. You look so damned good...'

I took her by the arms. She said, 'Don't,' and she meant it. I walked out to the store and picked up my coat and my package. She said, 'Goodbye, Nick.' I said, 'Goodbye, Ellie.' I walked out the door and started for the hotel. Damned nonsense! I had all the sex I could handle back home, all ages and some far better looking than the blonde. I'd get enough in Chicago, too. It wasn't as if I were the hungry old man. So why the sick feeling...

I turned back. She was standing in the open door. I said, 'There's just one thing I'd like to do before leaving St Louis.'

'What's that?'

'Kiss you goodbye.'

She turned away, and I felt I'd struck out. Then she said, 'Yes, I'd like that too.'

I followed her into the office and dropped my things on the desk. She closed the door. I put my hands on her arms again and drew her toward me very carefully, afraid she'd change her mind. I bent my head and touched her lips. For a moment that was it; a touching of lips. Then she moved, almost imperceptibly, but *toward* me. The next minute we were up against each other, I was hard, her tongue pushed into my mouth, I ran a hand over her bottom.

She broke free and turned away. I took her around from behind. She moved her bottom into me. I cupped a breast. I kissed her neck. I said, 'Ellie, so very sweet, so very sweet.' She said, 'All right.' She was breathing hard. 'No more.'

I surprised myself by letting her go. '*Please* see me again.'

'Why?' But the attempt at coldness failed.

'Because . . . we're fun together.'

'Oh yes, fun and games.' Still, she was turned on, I could see it.

'See me tomorrow, if not tonight.'

'I told you . . .'

'*After* your dinner date.'

She thought a moment. 'I'll try. No promises.'

I gave her the number of the Forest Park and my room and said I'd wait for her to call from nine on.

'From *eleven* on.'

I began to argue the point. I was spoiled, then. I'd had it my own way with the chicks for quite a while, then. But I shut myself up. I was *afraid* of arguing with this one.

I touched her face, and felt good doing it, and felt *great* when she smiled. And then thought of something. 'Don't get mad,' I said – and I was beginning to do something I wouldn't become aware of for a while; I was falling into *her* pattern of speech, similar to the old pattern of my Brooklyn boyhood – 'but do you eat breakfast?'

'Coffee, sometimes sausages.'

'Eat them with me tomorrow?'

'I never get up in time to eat *out*.'

'Just this once?'

'Okay. Just this once. You know where the Pancake House is?'

'I passed one on the way from the hotel . . .'

'That's it. Nine o'clock. I have to open the shop at ten.'

I said, 'Great.' I smiled and she smiled and she kissed me quickly on the cheek. Again I grabbed her and again we came together and this time my hands went under her dress and inside her pants and stroked that full backside and I don't know how long it was but I was almost ready to try for it right then and there and she seemed to want the same thing ... and someone came into the store.

'You get out of here,' she whispered, staring at me. 'I just don't *do* these things!'

I got out of there. Later, I thought of her boss, Mr Alexis, and wondered if she meant she didn't do 'these things' with *customers*. And what about all those dates, right up until Sunday? And damned if I wasn't upset, and even more upset at myself for feeling that way.

At eight I called Teaneck and spoke to Seth. I asked about his sister and he said she'd called from school earlier in the evening and everything was going well, grades and boyfriend and health. I asked about his mother and he said she was out with Ralph, who appeared to be her big hope for remarriage. Which meant he was alone in the house, and even though he was a very self-sufficient and sensible twelve-year-old, I didn't like it. I wanted to be there with him, checking his homework or kidding around or mocking old movies on TV with him.

I said, 'Hey, man, we'll soon be out at Shea seeing the Mets clobber all comers.' He said, 'You mean getting clobbered,' and we were off, that screwy little Montreal fan and his Mets-crazy old man. Where he'd ever picked up his feeling for the Canadians, I don't know, but it was always good for a laugh or two between us.

I hated to say goodnight to him that night. I missed him very much that night. And by nine I was uptight, so I put on the plaid Edwardian suit and went down to the bar, thinking to find a little action. There was a leggy waitress with a good face and ink-black wig and she looked bored with the two or three square-type mid-Western males giving her the hot-eye. I took a table and ordered a vodka gimlet on-the-rocks and talked to her and by the third drink she was asking me where I'd bought the suit. I said, 'Would you believe Sweden?' and made my World-Traveller pitch. She said she got off at midnight.

I left at ten-thirty, nodding at her as if I'd be back, but I was through for the night. I was down. I was bored with my business and bored with the Good Life and it was time to escape with exercise and sleep ... which I used to be able to do easily enough.

I did a set of situps and a set of pushups and used my hand-grippers and wished I could run a few miles and instead ran-in-place for five minutes.

Just as I was turning off the shower, I thought I heard the phone ringing. When I got into pyjamas, I checked the switchboard. There was a message for me: 'Call Ellie,' and a number.

My heart began to bang away. I told myself to play it cool, not to call until tomorrow morning, say I'd been out...

I asked the operator to get me the number.

I loved it when Ellie said, 'Hello?' and that voice came through to me in all its sweetness. I loved it when she said, 'I'm bored. You want to do something about it?' I loved it when she said, 'No, I'll come to the hotel. I haven't cleaned my place in a month.'

She had my room number, and she hadn't asked me to meet her in the lobby, but I dressed in record time and was out in front of the hotel when she drove up in a cab. Her smile as I opened the door for her was the most radiant thing I'd ever seen. She wore an open black raincoat over a pale blue pants outfit, and her hair was brushed gold and it didn't make any difference that I'd noticed the dark roots earlier today. It didn't make any difference that she was at least ten pounds overweight; the extra pounds were all in the right places. It didn't make any difference that I saw a blemish or two under her makeup; she was still the most beautiful girl I'd ever met.

Poets, sing your songs. No song can tell my joy at walking into that lobby with her. I felt that the bellhop leaning against the desk was dying for her. I felt that the elevator operator, at least sixty, could barely hide his lust and envy. I felt ... a teenager with the school beauty queen. But better. Because I was going to make love to this beauty.

I did, but not until five that morning. I had a bottle of Scotch in the room and a kitchen unit for ice and water. We drank and she asked questions about my work.

I manufacture and sell toys in partnership with a man who was once an acquaintance, became a friend after I saved his ass from a loan shark, and now would like to see me drop dead because of a gradual withdrawal from unnecessary work. I'd been taking less of a cut for almost a year on threat of legal action, but Harold wasn't really satisfied. What he wanted was for me to sell out; sell my share in the golden goose, which I wasn't about to do. But I told Ellie none of that; simply that I made the kids happy with the greatest toys and games this side of Santa Claus's North Pole operation. She was delighted.

'Toys! Got any samples?'

I did. She immediately appropriated a Raggedy Anne doll for a younger sister. Then we played with something called Flip-Chip, one of my brainchildren, a combination of tiddlewinks and the old carnival game of throwing balls through holes (painted up as eyes and mouths) in canvas.

14

The players face each other, sitting across a table, or on the floor, a clown-faced target between them, the opening being the clown's mouth. Each receives ten plastic chips, and a spring lever to flip them at and, hopefully, through the mouth-opening into the opponent's territory. The first to rid himself of all chips on his side of the target, including those his opponent manages to flip through the opening, shouts, 'Flip-Chip!' and wins.

We sat on the floor. Despite the fact that I couldn't keep my eyes off her, and missed far more often than I do when I play with a buyer, or with Seth, I was the one to call, 'Flip-Chip!' She shoved ten chips back at me and said, 'This time I'll get you!'

I began to crawl around to her side of the clown. She said, 'Get back there! I'm going to *win*!'

She meant it. I said I'd play, if she gave me a kiss. She smiled, but only a little, and pecked me on the cheek, and began to flip at the target before I was really in position.

I concentrated a little more, and beat her again.

Another kiss, this time on the lips, and she was again flipping away at the target long before I was in position.

I gave it my full attention, and beat her; and did it twice more for a total of five straight games. She then kicked over the clown, shouting, 'Not fair! You're a goddam expert!' She was red in the face, caught by sudden anger ... and lovelier than ever. I tried for my sixth straight kiss. She lost some of her anger, but squirmed away and said, baby-style, '*No!* Wanna *play*!'

We tried a word game on the style of anagrams. No contest, as her vocabulary wasn't up to it. We switched to *Treasure Trove*, which depended upon casts of the dice. Here she had better luck, and here I was able to catch her hand and kiss it, and draw her toward me and kiss her lips, and finally come around to her side of the board and press her down on the carpet. But she rolled away and jumped up. She went to my sample case and said, 'What else?'

She took out several wind-up cars and trains for the pre-school child and set them to darting about the floor. She made me sit facing her, and catch them, and send them back to her. And when I again tried to get her down on the carpet, she said, 'All finished!' and ran back to the couch.

I began putting the toys away. She watched me, then laughed her squealing little laugh. I asked what was so funny. 'You,' she said. 'What a look on your face!'

I concentrated on packing my samples. She laughed and laughed. I tried to look cool, above-it-all, at ease ... and knew I wasn't succeeding. After a while, I laughed too.

I mixed fresh drinks and we sat together on the couch and I took her hand. We sipped and our fingers moved, stroking, entwining. Then she took her hand away and touched her face. 'Shit,' she muttered, and got up. She took her bag and headed for the bathroom. I said, 'Your skin bother you?' She kept going. When she came out, the makeup was reapplied. She said, 'Mr Alexis thinks you're too old for me. How old are you?'

'How old is Mr Alexis?'

'Mr Alexis can be ninety. I don't date Mr Alexis. I don't do anything with Mr Alexis. He gets shots – *looks* at me when I'm not careful with my legs, or when I bend over. He never gets *me*.'

'And it's different with us?'

She sat down beside me. 'What do you think?'

I took her hand. I kissed her cheek. She said, 'I'm twenty.'

I'd never worried about my age with chicks. I was suddenly worried. I said, 'I'm over twenty-one.'

She shrugged. 'And married, right?'

'Wrong.'

She shrugged again. 'Anyone who looks like you, dresses like you, smooth like you, money like you, he's married.'

'I *was* three years ago.'

'Yeah, who knows?'

'Want my address? My phone number? Want to visit me in New York? Meet my friends? Check me out?'

She laughed. 'If I said yes, you'd faint.'

She *should* have been right. But she wasn't.

I showed her a picture of Seth, when he was four. It's a picture I always carry; the cutest he's ever taken. I didn't show her the other one, taken when he was eleven. I showed her a picture of Denise, when she was eight. Another cute one, and again I didn't show the other, taken at high school graduation.

She said, 'They look like you.'

'Thanks.'

'*They* should say thanks.'

I put away the pictures and kissed her and tried to start it moving, to get it back to where it had been in the clothing store. She didn't exactly fight. She just got away, time and again. But she didn't mind the action, and I didn't mind her getting away. It was good, all of it.

She told me she'd worked for Alexis for two years. He paid her well, gave her much freedom, 'likes me a lot'.

I asked if she *used* his liking.

A moment's hesitation. 'Yes. I keep him looking, wanting . . . but

16

he's never tried a real heavy make. He'll pat when I don't move fast enough. He'll take me to lunch; sometimes close up the store. If I'm late he doesn't yell. He doesn't report all my income. I get away with murder. He's asked me out a few times, but he knows I won't go for the bed bit.'

'You *never* go for the bed bit?'

She laughed. 'Less than you think.'

'How many men have had the honour?'

She kept laughing. 'You expect me to tell you?'

I was sweating now. I wasn't having any fun now. A sign, a portent of things to come. 'Why not? I'll tell you ...'

'C'mon, you'd need all night.'

We were quiet a while.

'Seven,' she said.

I winced.

She laughed. 'You should see your face. Like my mother's, if I told her that. And seven isn't a lot, is it?'

'For anyone your age it is.'

She sighed. 'What are you, some sort of priest?'

She was annoyed with me. I didn't blame her. I didn't understand it myself; why this should be of so much importance to me.

I mixed another two drinks, and by the time we finished we were holding hands and smiling again. Then she kicked off her shoes and said she wanted to lie down. My nod must have been rather eager. She laughed and went through the archway to the big double bed. I said, 'At least take off the jacket.' She took it off and threw it toward a chair. It landed on the floor. I hung it up for her. She said, 'Come snuggle.'

We lay together, dressed, and she turned her back on me and put her ass into my crotch and took my hand and brought it around to her breast and sighed and said, 'Just a little nap.' And was asleep in about a minute.

I moved a little against her rear. I caressed her breast. I kissed her neck and hair. I closed my eyes and inhaled her fragrance. And damned if I wasn't happy, just lying there with her.

I must have dozed off. I awoke and she was on her stomach, breathing heavily. I undressed, and began undressing her. I got her blouse and brassiere off. I got her blue bell-bottoms off. And then I saw her in dark pantyhose; no panties. Then I felt a terrible appetite. I use the word terrible because it actually hurt.

Lust is lust, right?

Wrong. This wasn't the same as anything I'd ever felt. I lusted, yes. I also hurt with longing. It was the first time I'd ever wanted

17

to own someone completely, and therefore the beginning of my being owned.

She sighed as I straddled her and lifted her hips and drew down the blue hose. I fingered her. She grew wet, and she grew awake, and she mumbled, 'Nickie,' using the diminutive for the first time. She moaned and tried to turn over, and I held her there, tonguing and fingering until she began to heave up and cry out; until she grew still. Then I turned her over. Then I kissed her breasts; small but beautiful breasts. Then I kissed her belly. Then she drew me up and we kissed, kissed, and her hand slid down to me; that erotic little hand. I didn't have to say softer or harder or anything. She knew just what I was feeling. She took the pulse of my passion through my penis. And when I was leaking, and when I was saying her name endlessly, and when I couldn't stand another second without her, she drew up her knees and put me in her and we made love for a short time because I was so far gone with need.

It had always ended for me then. I would come back occasionally for a second go, if the girl was really good, but at forty-five and for some years before, I hadn't remained hard after an orgasm.

I remained hard now. I felt I'd never made love before. Her smell. Her taste. No hangups and everything so good that it frightened me a little. I must have known I was going to be hooked.

I was still hard and I was still in her but I wasn't moving. 'Fuck me,' she said in that baby voice, looking into my face. 'C'mon, Nickie, fuck me,' and she smiled and she tugged me by the hair down to her mouth, and we kissed and kissed all the while I fucked her.

Okay, the pornography. It's always the same, right? There's the petting and the fucking and the language. Always the same.

Not for me. I'd never described it that way, not for myself and not for anyone else. The petting and the fucking and the language was what I began to live for. It was the love I'd been waiting for without knowing I'd been waiting for it. It was being born. It was coming alive. It was understanding how happy my body could be.

I wanted to tell her I loved her, but how could I? How could it be between this little blonde, this twenty-year-old St Louis woman, and the forty-five-year-old World Traveller? Between the highschool graduate who'd barely graduated, and the Masters in Psychology who'd used his profession to sell and to build a business and then to drift away from the business to freedom from drudgery? And even if all that hadn't been so, how could it be this *fast*, this very first night?

But her body and my body said they loved each other.

I forgot about love ten minutes after we finished making love that first night. I asked when she'd begun taking the pill.

'Well,' she said, and got out of bed and headed for the bathroom. I followed. 'You use something else? Diaphragm?' (But she hadn't put it in, unless when she'd gone to apply her makeup.)

She tried to close the bathroom door. I held it open. She said, 'Listen, I think I'd better make. It helps wash it out, doesn't it?'

I stared at her. 'You've had *seven men* in your life?'

She said, 'It was really just two, and one was almost rape.'

'But ... didn't you use *anything*? I mean, you're twenty years old and you've heard of conception, dammit, and you must know ...' I was enraged at her naivety, her ignorance, and even though I didn't know it at the time my rage was at least partly at myself for becoming more and more involved with a girl who knew so little, even about her own body. But I tried hard to control my anger. We'd just made love, and it had been the best love I'd ever experienced, bar none. I said, 'You *didn't* use anything?'

'Well.' Her eyes fell.

My control slipped. 'Why the hell didn't you tell me?'

'Don't yell. I was going to. I just ... forgot.'

'A douche. We've got to buy ...'

I checked my watch. A quarter to six. There was a drugstore across the street from the hotel. But a quarter to six in the morning ...

I told her to put enough water in the tub to cover her crotch and get into it and spread wide and try to wash everything out. She said, 'It's only three, no wait, maybe four, maybe five days after my period.'

'Maybe six?'

'Seven at the most.'

I turned on the tub and ran for the phone. The desk said the drugstore opened at nine. No, they didn't know of any that were open all night ... but if it was an emergency, Jewish Hospital was only a few blocks away.

Jewish Hospital. My Jewish mother was only a thousand miles away, and I'd as soon go to *her* with a request for a douche!

She was in the tub, splashing water into her. She looked at me, and smiled. I was going to tell her what a damn fool she was ... but instead I kissed her and washed her back and her titties and dried her and took her hand and led her to the bed and held her in my arms. She said, 'Don't worry. I've never been pregnant.' I said, 'Perfect reasoning,' and I was ready to go again. 'Ahm *tahred*,' she said, exaggerating her accent and rolling over on her side. She put that sweet ass into my groin and tugged my hand under her neck and onto her breast and said, 'Don't forget to wake me at nine, for breakfast.'

'Ahm tahred too,' I said. 'I'd better tell the switchboard to give us a ring.'

'No. You'll wake up on time. Don't move. It's so nice.' And she turned her head and smiled in my direction. 'You're so nice. I'm so glad you came along. I was beginning to think no more would ever come along.'

I closed my eyes. The talky Jewish salesman was speechless.

I didn't get up until ten-fifteen. I shook her and it took a long time to get her awake, and then I told her. 'Shit,' she said, and began to get out of bed, and then just sank back. 'He'll call the store. He'll come down by ten-thirty and open up himself. I'll say I was sick.'

What sort of girl *was* this? (And yet I knew. The irresponsibility touched a responsive chord in me ... harked back to the *original* Nick Leib.)

I got her up, and she took almost an hour to wash and brush out her hair and dress. I got my car from the parking lot and she sat slumped in the seat, muttering, 'Nice wheels,' eyes at half mast. I said, 'It's another lovely day. Spring, baby.'

'Fuck spring.'

I laughed. She didn't. I stopped for a traffic light and looked at her. The most beautiful girl in the world ... but she was *down* to the floor.

'What's wrong?'

'I hate mornings. I could die mornings.'

'Will I see you tonight?'

'We'll talk later.'

She was dozing when we pulled up in front of Alexis Fashions for men. I said, 'Last stop.'

She crawled out and went to the door and fumbled in her bag, and the door opened. Alexis was standing there. He looked past her at me. I waved, and got out to add some credence to her story. She simply walked past him into the store.

'She wasn't feeling well,' I said.

He nodded, as sour as month-old yogurt. He went inside and closed the door.

I didn't like leaving her here ... with him. Laugh, but I didn't. She was mine.

I went to the Pancake House and had pancakes. I ordered two coffees and pastries to go and drove the few blocks to the clothing store. When I walked in, she was saying, '... you want to fire me, go ahead. You want me to stay, let me alone.' That sweet voice was thin and shrill.

'You can't continue this way, Ellie. You need some discipline, some order in your life.' His voice was a whine.

They were in the office. No bell rang to announce my entrance. I stood quietly. She said, 'You're right. But not now, please.'

There was movement. She said, '*Charlie* ...'

I walked very quietly, and there he was stroking her arm, and there she was, smiling and moving away. 'It's too early for touch tackle,' she said.

I moved back and called, 'Hello?'

She came out. I said, 'Breakfast.'

She smiled. 'I never did thank you for stopping by and giving me a lift. That car of mine, deadsville.'

Alexis came out. I put the bag on the counter. He said, 'Do you want to buy anything?'

She said, '*Charlie!*' just as if speaking to a child. He looked down. He said, 'Well, he really shouldn't ...'

I took out the coffees and pastries. 'Sorry. I run a business myself. I understand.'

'Toys,' she said, and opened one of the coffees. 'Tell Mr Alexis about your toys, Nickie.'

I wasn't exactly getting the little-boy treament, but I didn't like whatever I *was* getting. However, I wasn't in a position to argue; not with Alexis giving me the fish-eye. I told him about my toys.

He muttered a thanks for the coffee and they both stood behind the counter sipping, and then he said he had to get over to his Ladue store. He hesitated as if hoping I'd walk out with him, but I said I wanted to try on a pair of suède pants to go with the vest I'd bought yesterday.

He looked at Ellie. 'You really got to discipline yourself,' he said.

'I know. You're right. Don't worry.' She spoke to me. 'He's like a father. If it wasn't for Charlie, I'd starve.'

I thought he'd react badly to that, but instead he smiled, and even turned a little of that smile on me. He went out. She said, 'He was going for feels this morning. If I'm late, he figures it gives him an edge.'

I felt terrible. 'If that's the way it works, you're something like a whore, aren't you?'

Her face hardened; the sullen, piggish look was back. 'The way I figure it, I was more like a whore last night.'

'I apologize. What I said was uncalled for.'

She drank her coffee. I asked where she lived. She said about ten minutes from the store, on Forest Park Boulevard. I asked for the address and phone number.

'To use from New York?'

'I'm staying in St Louis a while.'

'And *then* you'll use it from New York?'

'Yes. I will.'

Her smile was back. I began to come around the counter. She said, 'Hold it.' I stopped. She said, 'Take out your little black book.'

I wrote down the information. 'What about tonight?'

'I said I'd call you about eleven, didn't I?'

'But that was before ...'

'I've got things to do. Goodbye.'

I must have paled. I know I was raging. I went to the door. She said, 'Nickie, I liked you, but I don't know anything about anything.'

I didn't understand ... but I did know her voice had changed, and that when I looked at her she was solemn and sweet, and that she didn't want me walking out angry. I said, 'I'll wait for your call.'

But I didn't. I called her at the store at three. I said I was going out to buy the greatest steaks and champagne.

'Try Straub's,' she said. 'And don't forget the caviar. But I don't know what time I can make it. And I've got a store full of people and Charlie's back.'

The line clicked. I went out and found the quality supermarket and bought everything for a good dinner. I stopped at the drugstore for a can of contraceptive foam and an applicator. I thought of how I would teach her to use it. I went to a florist and bought a bouquet of roses. Then I returned to my room ... and waited until one-thirty in the morning, at which time I lay down and told myself to go to sleep. Instead, I got up and tried her home phone. Nothing. I wondered if her date had Emko Contraceptive Foam. I wanted to kill him.

I lay down again. I tried counting backwards, and forwards, and thought longingly of a sleeping pill, and at that time I never used them. And there was a knock at the door.

I tried not to run. She came in and said, 'What a drag. He took me to his aunt's birthday party and we had to blow out candles ...'

I said, 'Bullshit,' and took her in my arms and kissed her. She murmured, 'Honest,' with no conviction whatsoever, and put her tongue in my mouth.

I told her how to use the foam injector. She was embarrassed. I did it for her, and took a while, moving the tube around in her. Then she muttered, 'Lost your own?' and we were off.

TWO

At the end of our first week together, Ellie and I drove to the Pancake House and I finally showed her the latest pictures of Denise and Seth. 'They've aged ten years in a week,' she said, and laughed and pinched my cheek so that the waitress looked away embarrassed I suppose at the young girl and middle-aged man playing it up so blatantly. But by then, if Ellie had said to, I'd have fucked her in Busch Stadium on Ladies Day.

It was actually eight days I spent in St Louis that first trip. I saw Ellie every night, and expected to spend all day Sunday with her but didn't, and later found out she was seeing Harv Cohen, her 'other Jew' as she once put it, and someone far more important in her life than I suspected for quite a while. Harold was screaming at me by phone and telegram, and so I said I would skip Chicago and come directly to New York. I told Ellie to try and arrange for a week's vacation, and when she said it didn't look too good I said a long weekend would do. I wanted to give her the air fare, but she refused and said, 'You're lucky to have such a young girlfriend. I got a youth card. About sixty dollars round trip to New York.'

I drove off, sick about leaving her, and then relieved, and by the time I hit the turnpikes convinced I'd been cunt crazy for a while but was well out of it by now. She was always late and always hell in the mornings and undereducated and certainly nothing for the long haul, and it was time I stopped being alone so much and stopped falling into such basically debasing affairs and started thinking of finding myself another wife, young and beautiful, sure, but Quality . . .

It was in Pennsylvania, a little after midnight, that I decided to give her a call. After all, we'd been together so much the past week and the poor kid was probably feeling a little blue and here I was at a service station and the phones just inside.

She answered on the second ring. Her voice sliced right through to my insides. One, 'Hello?' and it was as if we were back at the Forest Park with me waiting for her to come, late as usual.

'It's Nick.'

'Hey, whatcha doing?'

'Driving. What're *you* doing?'

23

'Reading. Setting my hair.'

I heard a voice in the background. A male voice.

'Listening to the radio,' she added. And then, 'Could you hold on a minute?'

I just wouldn't think another guy was there. Not at this hour – after eleven in St Louis. Then she was back on the phone. 'Turned down the radio.' Was her voice hushed, or was it my imagination? 'Miss you, honey,' she said. 'Miss your big old thing. Miss our steaks and caviar. Miss our talks. Miss my Nickie-boy.'

'I miss you too,' I said. 'I want you to come to New York. Soon.'

'I will, honey. Real soon.'

Noise in the background. That voice again, or banging?

'What's that?' I asked.

'You mean you can hear it?' she laughed. 'Neighbours.'

I said it. I had to. 'You have a boyfriend over. Don't say anything. I didn't expect to become your one-and-only in a week. Let's keep it adult, shall we?'

She did just as I asked; she didn't say anything. And it killed me. I laughed. 'Well, I won't delay your action.'

'There's no action.' Flat, cold voice. 'He's hung up about you. We've been arguing all night. We just got home from dinner. He's knocking on the bathroom door, where I went in with the phone. He's going to leave if I don't come out in a minute.'

'Then I'd better say goodbye.'

'If you want. I wore his ring once. I thought I was going to again . . . but the toy maker from New York came to town.'

'Well, if the man's important . . .'

'He's not . . . anymore. Nothing's important. Just fun and games, right, Nickie-boy?'

I felt she was going to hang up then, and I said, quickly, 'You're not Fun-and-games. Didn't I say I wanted to see you again?'

'That means something? Besides bed, that is?'

'Yes.' I was afraid to say more, and said, 'It means something. At least let's find out.'

Two weeks later we found out, or began to. I dated a few times, especially my orally-inclined married friend. Her kick, at least with me. She used the word love, but she wasn't willing to risk her comfortable home in Westchester or the 'psychic health' of her eight-year-old daughter. She 'loved' me, once or twice a week, and rushed away to her real life afterwards. Which suited me fine . . . though after Ellie I began to see that it had been years since *I'd* had a real life; perhaps I'd never had one.

There was a twenty-two-year-old actress who was brilliant, good in bed, and in love with a beach bum in Hawaii. But I was a very close second, she assured me, and it couldn't possibly work with him in the 'final analysis' and, most important of all, I was *here* and he was *there*.

And there was one serious contender, in Chicago, who was too neurotic at the present, and probably forever, to continue what had begun to look like the real thing about a year ago. Her analysis came first, and so we'd faltered badly.

And there were other prospects – teachers and models and divorcees and stuff wandering around the teaming streets of Manhattan. New York is a make-out paradise, once you earn the dough and get a little free time and learn the trick of *meeting* people. I'd learned that trick long before my divorce.

So really, what was special about Ellie? What could happen with Ellie except more of what had happened in bed at the Forest Park Hotel? I mean, there wasn't an eighteen-year-old secretary who couldn't speak better English than she could, didn't have more polish than she had, and didn't come off more like a lady than she did ... and couldn't, if convinced she should, do as much as Ellie could sexually. In fact, what woman couldn't?

Surprise answer: *no* woman. Because Ellie had taken hold upstairs, in my head, not just downstairs where any woman can take hold. Ellie was IT. Not that I was convinced, even after I'd met her at LaGuardia and felt my insides jumping outside as she strolled lazily from the ramp to where I was waiting. Not even while walking with her to the luggage pickup and holding her hand and seeing some airport workers eyeing her and feeling again, again and always, that this was the most beautiful little chick in all the world.

In the car I kissed her. In the car she held to me, murmuring, 'I'm so happy to see you,' and I said, still the makeout king and still unconvinced that it was anything but a ball – an intense ball but it would end; it had to; we were just too mismatched – 'Me too, baby,' my hand under her skirt because that was it, that was the locus of the feeling. And there was nothing wrong with that either. She was hot for me and I was hot for her and what could be better, what could be more fun?

We went directly to the apartment. She took a bath and I scrubbed her back and we had champagne and caviar and went to bed. And fucked until I felt it was going to fall off.

Then she looked around. Then she stepped onto the terrace and said, 'God, New York City!' looking toward the East River, which is a clear shot from my sixteenth-floor terrace and windows, though the entrance to the Towers, as they call the complex, is on Second Avenue.

I have three rooms – big bedroom, nice living room, small eat-in kitchen, big foyer – and garage space, and being on the downtown side of Forty-second Street makes the rental just a little less painful, though five hundred and eighty plus sixty for parking isn't exactly featherweight.

That first visit, two weeks after I'd left St Louis, was all bed and champagne and caviar. The three days went and it was a ball, I told myself. Just a ball. Unusually active; and no doubt about it, I wanted to be with her every minute, but still, under the classification of good screwing, period. Except that on Monday morning I was the one who couldn't get up.

The alarm went off at six and I saw that she could move when she had to. She began to pack and when I groaned and said just a few more minutes she said, 'You can rest until just before we have to leave. I'll get you up. You've had a rough three days, Nickie-boy,' and she laughed and kissed me and said, 'Ugh! You need a mint,' and gave me a mint and kissed me again. I began to beg her to call Alexis and say she'd missed the eight a.m. jet that would get her to St Louis by nine-twenty (because of the gain of an hour) and to her job by ten; begged her to stay until the six p.m. plane. And when she hesitated and sat down at the edge of the bed and touched my face, I begged her to say she had to stay another day and would be in *Tuesday* morning. 'Why?' she asked, but not as she had in St Louis; now she was soft. Now she was touching me and I was touching her and I said, 'Because I can't let you go; not just yet.'

You'll notice I didn't say, 'Because I love you.'

She lay down beside me and I held her and after a while she got under the covers and said, 'I'll call him at nine, at home.'

That was ten o'clock New York time, and she made me leave the bedroom, but I listened at the door, not risking picking up the kitchen extension and heard the wheedling, far-from-businesslike way she spoke to him. 'Don't be silly, Charlie, my cousin is sick.' She went on, playing the man shamelessly ... but hell, that was her business literally. How else could a girl like that make a decent living, or even hold on to a job? At least she wasn't a cocktail waitress in a bunny outfit, as her older sister had been.

I'd begun to get more information about Ellie McBaren, her life and times, but I was also beginning to know that she held a great deal back from me. I'd also begun to *give* more information to Ellie McBaren, but we didn't really open up with each other until she'd been raped. At least I *think* she was raped. That's one of the things about Ellie; the never being sure what had actually happened to her or where to reach her or what the hell she was doing, *ever*.

The rape was after her *second* three-day visit, that stretched into five fantastic days. (This time we both used the word love, but only during or approaching orgasm, and it doesn't really count then, does it?) The section of Lindell on which the clothing store was located was in a bad neighbourhood, and her apartment, which I'd never seen, was only six blocks away. 'Bad neighbourhood.' You know what that means, don't you?

You'll have to forgive my latent and antiquated liberalism – at least of a year ago – but it bothered me when she would describe black crime infiltrating from the ghetto a few blocks away. Not that she spoke the usual mid-West, poor-white, racist shit. Far from it. She *rejected* racism, violently, because it was part of her class and neighbourhood and family, and she hated all three, and despised her Catholic upbringing; and rejection, violent rejection of everything that had come her way until she broke free as an adult, was a big part of her personality.

Anyway, brought up on the *New York Times*, you become un-comfortable if anyone identifies a crime as *black* as opposed to simply *human*. I mean, identification by colour is important to cops, but not to civilians. Or so we used to say. Things are changing now, and not for the better.

Okay, I'm relaxing in the apartment with a beer and the aftertaste of a good dinner at the Japanese steak house and thinking that my date with Ledya had been fine, just fine, even though I'd grown unaccountably tired and our brief session in bed had been unaccount-ably blah and that I'd rushed the girl out and put her in a cab instead of driving her home and that she'd sensed something . . .

Anyway, I was thinking of Ellie, whom I hadn't seen in almost three weeks. It was Saturday, not quite midnight, and I wanted to call her and speak to her, but she was a tough girl to catch in, even then. Besides, it was foolish to call. We'd spoken only Thursday; make that Friday, since she'd phoned at two a.m. She'd been sweet and loving and said she missed me and wanted to visit me again but she couldn't because Mr Alexis was 'very upset'. I didn't want to talk about Mr Alexis. I asked how come I hadn't been able to get her in at midnight, Tuesday, and at one a.m. the next night? 'Well, I was at my sister's . . .' and away she went, with what *might* and might not have been the truth. She'd already admitted that she still saw a good deal of her ex-fiancé, Harv Cohen, twenty-five and her first real love and doing well as general manager of papa's two hardware stores. She'd also admitted that she slept with him occasionally, and said she felt he 'deserved it' for his 'generosity' (that was one big word she had down pat!) and kindness and so on.

No sweat, right, since everyone slept with everyone else nowadays and she was simply being honest ... the bitch!

So it was foolish to call Saturday, especially since I'd also received a letter this morning, a very lovely letter despite the misspellings and slips of grammar. The ending had really reached me.

'I adore you, Nick Leib. Thank you for making me believe in love again.'

I took the letter from the dresser and read it again and felt an ache, a good feeling and a bad feeling, and figured what-the-hell, I'd call, but not now, because it was only eleven in St Louis and she couldn't expect to be home at eleven, not a groovy little chick like that. I'd wait until twelve, or one. I'd watch television ...

The phone rang. At first I thought it was Ellie, the voice was so similar; so much the soft, high, sweet, sexy voice I identified only with Ellie. It gave me the hots, instantly. Then she identified herself as Gina, the older sister; and then she was crying.

That's when it all changed. Because I almost passed out, I was so frightened that something had happened to my girl. That's the way I thought of her from then on; as 'my girl'.

'What is it?' I asked, sinking to the edge of the bed. It was still rumpled and there was still an odour of woman and it made me sick. Because Ellie's sister was trying to tell me something about Ellie and crying so hard she couldn't get it out, and here I'd been betraying her ...

Betrayal. That too became an important word, a *deadly* word in our relationship. Betrayal, an outdated concept in today's flesh market ... but let it grab hold of you and you're lost.

Gina finally managed some speech. Ellie had been attacked outside her apartment house last night. 'Black bastard...' sobs ... 'grabbed her and she fought him...' wailing ... 'and then someone came and we don't think...' sobs ... 'but she just walked away after the cops talked to her...' a series of Dear-Christs ... 'and now Harv, do you know him, anyway he called and said she was at his folks' home and they'd had a doctor in and she was hysterical and the doctor gave her something and she kept saying your name.'

Later, I learned he'd called the sister and Gina had driven over with her husband and only then Gina had heard, from Ellie herself, that she'd been wandering around all last night and most of today, crying and trying to pull herself together (and, I still suspect, wondering whether she'd *asked* for that attack from a man she *knew*

28

and knew well, not a strange ghetto black), and examining her life and thinking of how to get away from that life ... but remember, I got all this, not from the sister, but from Ellie, and only as part of other conversations, over a long period of time. Anyway, the sister had spoken to Ellie privately and then had called me.

But at the time, I felt a sudden burst of affection, and respect, for Harv Cogen, because I thought *he'd* told the sister to call me. I asked the sister if I could speak to Ellie now.

'Yes. She's still at Harv's place, but you can call. She wants you to call.' I took the number and thanked her and dialed so quickly after hanging up that I didn't have a dial tone. I did it again, and a woman answered. I asked for Ellie, and the woman hesitated and said, 'I don't think she's really able to speak now.' A nice Jewish Momma, protecting her *zeindela's* girlfriend, even though a *shiksa*. I said, 'Ellie will want to speak to me. At least tell her it's Nick Leib.'

And then Ellie was on the phone. Her voice was very dull. She said, 'Nick, I'm so ... damned tired. I'm sick of St Louis. Men looking at me ... thinking all the time ... maybe you too ... I'm so sick of everything. I'm dumb and maybe my mother was right and I'm no use to anyone.'

She frightened me, and I also have to admit she offered me something I wanted. To have her with me, and for more than the few days' visits. To get her away from Alexis and Harv Cohen and whoever else was able to get his hot male hands on her.

That's the way I felt, and I'm not proud of it, but it's important that I understand exactly how I felt because it all added up to the destruction of something, and the building of something else.

'Come here,' I said.

'Are you sure? I'm such a mess ...'

'Come here. Rest. Stay as long as you want. Stay forever.' (But I didn't mean 'forever' – I meant for as long as we could enjoy each other, which wouldn't be forever or even close to it, right?)

She took a deep breath. She whispered, 'Thank you, honey. But ... it isn't *pity*, is it? Because if I thought it was ...'

'Pity? I'd stock the place full of Vietnamese orphans if pity moved me to invitations.'

She laughed a little. 'Then ... what is it?'

'I care, Ellie.' I was still hedging, but I was also beginning to move into the true feeling, the heavy feeling. 'I care very much, and we'll decide what we want to do about it when you come here.'

'But ... for how long? Mr Alexis ...'

'That's part of what you're sick of, and you know it.' Now I was cutting out the feel-happy old bastard! 'That's using yourself in a way you suspect, isn't it?'

Weak, whispery, 'Yes.'

'Tell him you're sick and you have to get away and you don't know when you'll be back.'

'I'll lose my job.'

'You won't need a job.' And I wouldn't need dates. I'd have the best thing ever, here in my bed, my arms, my own exclusive property. And no one was talking marriage, right? 'I'll take care of everything for a while. And if you want a job later, I can get you one in New York.'

She began to say something, and I cut in quickly with, 'Or I'll take you back to St Louis and help you there. I know people, honey. Trust me.'

She asked what to do about her apartment, and I said I'd pay the rent until she made a final decision, and she replied with sudden anger, 'I don't mean the money. I have a little money. You think too much about money, Nick.'

She was right. I thought a *lot* about money. But that's the way it is when you grow up hearing your parents fight to the death about a few bucks to pay off the loans and the grocer and assorted Brooklyn relatives who are doing better than you are.

I said I didn't mean to insult her. I merely wanted her to forget everything except packing a bag and getting away from St Louis, to me.

And that's what she did. She arrived early the next evening, grey of face, limping, and still the most beautiful girl in the world. I took her home, and she wanted to go right to bed, but I had to have the story of the attack and I had to see the physical evidence, the developing bruises on her thighs and calves ... and I wanted to lay her. I controlled it and we went to bed and I held her and rocked her and she said, 'I'm so lucky to have you, Nickie. So very lucky,' and fell asleep.

I turned off by turning away, and waited until early Monday morning for my jollies. She still wasn't too keen about it, but my explanation that she could withdraw from sex, have an unhealthy fear of it, if she allowed too much time to pass between the attack and a truly loving encounter, impressed her, and my story of how I'd been made to fly again as soon as I got out of the Army hospital after my crackup, and how it had helped conquer my developing fear of flying, impressed her, and so she gave in. I was slow and I was gentle, but I was getting mine and loving it and the fact that the girl was nuts about me, and began to say it, over and over, was the only reason it worked for her.

Try to remember one thing, while you're thinking what a bastard I am, or was. The sex kick was there, yes, but it was *out-sized*. Remember that I'd had sex before, a good deal of it, and that it had never been this good, even when I was younger and more sensitive. Remember that whatever motives I *gave* myself, my true feelings were something else again.

Ellie stayed two weeks. Those weeks were among the happiest of my life. We saw movies and plays and, once, attended the opera, which I'd never really cared for and which she had never seen before, but which we were wild about together. *Madame Butterfly* at the Met, watched and listened to with hands and eyes and smiles entwined.

Afterward, we had dinner and got into a bit of an argument. Ellie felt there was a great deal of truth and reality in *Madame Butterfly*, and I lectured her on plot being opera's weakest point. She said, 'I don't know about other operas – we'll have to get a book on librettos so I can check – but this one wasn't that way. I think lots of men treat lots of women the way Pinkerton treated Butterfly.'

I laughed. 'Sure. Every day Americans take Japanese mistresses, give them children, then marry American...' I stopped, as I began to think of Korea and Vietnam.

Ellie nodded, reading my thoughts. 'Sure. But I don't even mean that – Americans or English or Europeans, with gooks, Chinks, you know, coloured types. I mean right here in the States among whites, where there are rich and poor, or educated and uneducated, or smart and dumb.'

I began to grow uncomfortable. I assured myself I saw no parallel between what she was saying, and what I was living ... yet I wanted to change the subject. She read my thoughts again ... but this time she backed off a bit.

'See?' she said, and laughed briefly and shrugged and didn't look quite as pleased with herself as she had a moment ago. 'You don't like to think of it, Nickie. I'm not saying you're treating *me* like that, but...' Again she shrugged. 'Maybe someone who didn't know how we are together, maybe strangers, maybe *they* would say it had to come to that, had to turn out bad...'

At that point I took her hand and kissed it and said I wanted to buy my Madame Butterfly a bottle of champagne. She smiled. 'I didn't mean us, honest I didn't, Nickie. If I thought it was that way...' She leaned across the table, and we kissed, and then we ate and drank. And afterward home to bed and, as always, glorious, stupendous, magnificent fucking.

31

We didn't miss a night. We came *close* to missing the next-to-the-last night of her stay. That was when we returned from the cottage exhausted after a day of cutting grass on the front and lakeside lawns, playing two hours of badminton, visiting three State Parks, and chasing each other around in continuous childish horseplay. In addition, I'd demonstrated how I run by putting in two fast miles at James Baird Park. So we were both inclined to sleep rather than make love, and I figured tomorrow morning would be soon enough. But as I was lying in bed, Ellie stopped undressing to say, 'Hey, forgot to show you something. A picture. At least I *think* I put it in the flap of my suitcase.' She rummaged around. My eyes were beginning to close when she said, 'Wasn't I a goofy looking kid?'

It was a tinted photograph of her, taken when she was in Junior High, '...oh, maybe thirteen years old. Maybe younger.' She handed it to me.

Ellie-the-child's face had much about it that was present now; especially in the subtly sensual smile and the deep dimple and the smoky eyes.

She lay down beside me and put her head against mine and we looked at the photograph together, and she told me that shortly before it had been taken she'd begun masturbating, at home and in school bathrooms and anyplace else she could seclude herself for a few minutes. And telling me this she put her hand under her dress and murmured, 'Since you're too tired,' and began to squirm and sigh. Watching her excited me and so as I stroked myself she watched. We masturbated, and finished while looking into each other's eyes. And then played and petted ... and fucked.

Those two weeks were perfect. I still avoided the word 'love', but I was hers and she was mine. I still didn't introduce her to any of my friends ... though later I tried to make her see that I didn't really have friends, or numbers of acquaintances; at least not since my divorce. I didn't introduce her to Ron, and I didn't bring her up to the office ... but of course I was on vacation (Harold said I'd taken a *permanent* vacation) and her stay was only fifteen days, and the pressure of our isolation from both our worlds couldn't mount very high in so short a time.

At the end of the two weeks we decided she was to go home, get rid of her apartment and possessions, say goodbye to her family, friends and Harv, and that I would then join her in St Louis, rent a station wagon, load up whatever she wanted to take with her, and we would have a sweet, leisurely trip back. She nodded, her face alight with joy. I reminded myself that we still had not mentioned

32

marriage; and equally important, I told no one but Dr Ron Levine what was happening. Not my mother and not my ex-wife and not my children and not my business partner. No one but my old bumming partner, and he congratulated me with just a little too much twinkle, and I then admitted feeling more for this hot little chick than I'd expected to feel. He grew serious. 'Well, play the Pygmalion bit. Educate the girl. Take care of her and do her some good and when it's ended, you'll be even.'

I liked the concept. Right. Pygmalion, not Madam Butterfly. And when it ends, no one gets hurt, we both gain. Beautiful!

Ron and I talked a good deal about Ellie, in person and on the phone, before I went to get her in St Louis. I guess I was feeling the need to justify the whole thing. I guess I was fighting a sense of wrong-doing, and also one of impending involvement – heavy, emotional involvement. So I talked and talked, and Ron listened and threw me comforting lines. I'm sure he got a little sick of it, but of course he owed me. I'd listened to him talk endlessly, and this for months, not days, when he'd had his one heavy affair six years ago and was considering leaving his wife. What stopped him more than anything else, I believe, was he couldn't see breaking up his beautiful investment portfolio. Good old Ron. Solid old Ron. Comfortable old Ron ... at least on the ouside. But miserable, actually. Wanting love, wanting passion, and settling for a beautiful investment portfolio and an occasional night out with a fast chick.

Maybe it's more than that. Maybe he was practising what he preached. He once said, 'The worst thing that can happen to you is to get what you want.' He was trying to comfort a twenty-year-old patient who had gone into a state of depression, a near nervousbreakdown, when the girl he loved married another man. What Ron meant was that reaching any goal, including marrying a woman, is the end of striving toward that goal, which is the death of desire, and the death of desire is in effect the end of life or the best part of life.

That might have been what happened when Ellie came to live with me. But other things happened to preface it.

Ellie flew home to St Louis on a Monday. She called me that night to say she'd arrived safely and was going to stay at her mother's because the apartment depressed and frightened her since the rape. She would speak to me Wednesday night and tell me when to come out.

Great. Except that I didn't hear from her on Wednesday, and when I called her mother's I got this cold, hard voice saying that Ellie hadn't been there since Monday and hadn't slept there *at all* and she didn't know or care where she was. Click Dead line.

I sat staring at the phone. But the girl was crazy about me, and coming to live with me. Where could she be?

I tried her apartment. A recording came on, saying the number was no longer in operation.

No sweat. She was busy selling things and packing things. She must be at her married sister's place. I didn't have the number. When I'd asked, she'd said they'd just moved and she didn't have the new number and she would give it to me when she got it. And I didn't have Gina's last name.

I actually did some work; at least I went to the office. I was home every night at five, and waited for her call until one, and then drank myself to sleep. And had nightmares. She called Sunday at midnight.

'Hi, it's Ellie! Watcha doing?'

'Going crazy,' I replied calmly. And then, 'Why the fuck didn't you call when you said you'd call! Where've you been!'

Her voice went from joy to surprise, hurt surprise, and almost instantly I began to feel a loss of justification for my anger. Which was ridiculous.

'Why are you screaming, Nickie? When did I say I'd call ... in five or six days, right?'

'You damn well know you said you'd call on Wednesday! You said that on Monday. And you said you'd be staying at your mother's. And I've been waiting, sweating...'

'I'm sorry, honey. Did I really say I'd call on Wednesday? I can't remember. I'm not too good about time, Nickie. But I've missed you. Did you miss me?'

'No, I'm yelling my head off because I don't give a damn!'

She giggled. 'I know what you miss.'

I began to feel a stirring. 'Yeah, so where were you?'

'You miss my sweet smile and cute dimple ... and what else, Nickie?'

I wanted to know where she'd been, and at the same time I began to grow hot and wanted to play her little game. I said nothing.

'You miss fucking me, baby, that's what you miss. Well, get on a plane and come down here tomorrow morning and fuck me.'

I was ready to fly there that second. And I wondered at myself. I wondered what the hell was wrong with me to want this girl so much even as she was evading an important question. If we were going to be together, we had to be reasonably honest with each other. (I said 'reasonably', didn't I! So it covers the not wanting

34

marriage and a few others things. But it *doesn't* cover disappearing for almost a week and not saying where you've been.)

'Where were you, Ellie?'

'Uh-oh. Our first big fight's coming up, right?'

'Where were you? You didn't stay at your mother's. Were you with Harv?'

'Oh, sure. He just loves me now that I'm coming to live with you.'

'Then where were you?'

She sighed. I waited. She said, 'Don't you trust me?'

'Should I?'

Her voice changed again; grew dim, dull. 'Maybe not.'

'I can barely hear you.'

'You sure you still want me to come back?'

'Of course I do. I simply want to know where you were. You asked if I trusted you. Trust is built on experience. Let's start building that experience right now.'

Another moment of silence, and then she said, 'I couldn't take my mother. And I couldn't stand my apartment – being alone there at night. It scared me. So I went to Gina's, my sister's. And I went to Old Missou to see my friend Claire. And now I'm back and I've gotten my things packed and given away what I'm not taking and I'm all set and waiting for you to come and get me. Do you want to come and get me, Nickie?'

'I'll be on the eight a.m. TWA flight. What did Harv say when you told him you were going to live with me?'

She hesitated what seemed like a long time. 'He got pale. And then he wished me luck. He's ... a nice guy, Nickie.'

I didn't like her voice. 'You had to *see* him to notice that pale face. When did you see him?'

'Look, this call is costing a fortune, and I'll have to pay my sister. I'll tell you at the airport tomorrow, all right?'

It wasn't all right. She was evading again. But I said, 'Give me a kiss,' and the little lip-popping sound came. I gave her two and we said goodbye and hung up.

And then I wanted to ask exactly what she had told Harv – if she had really admitted to coming to live with me. And I couldn't quite see her doing that; felt she would cover, would hold to him in some way. Because I was doing the same thing with a few girls, saying I would be out of touch for a while. Because we were both not sure it would work out. Because, in a way, I was *waiting* for the time it would stop working, waiting to be free of something I feared and mistrusted – the relationship between me and Ellie McBaren.

35

From the air, St Louis is flat and brown and somehow raw looking. It isn't much better on the ground. It can be nasty and cold in
the winter, and it's always hot as hell in the summer. This day,
however, was bright and perfect ... except for the fact that Ellie
wasn't there when I walked from the plane. I looked around a few
minutes, and just waited a few minutes, and then went to a phone.
And heard her call my name.

She was wearing something I'd never seen before – a white
knit mini-dress with red vertical stripes. I loved the way it hugged
her body, and I loved the way it just about covered her panties ...
but I also saw a guy in coveralls looking back at her and, as she
smiled and held out her arms, I saw the skirt rise a little and saw
the guy in coveralls stop for a better look at her ass. I began to
tighten up, wondering what the hell was wrong with her, wearing
such a turn-on outfit in public.

She ran into my arms and hugged me and that guy was still
looking and I tried to fix him with my eyes over her shoulder, but
his eyes were busy elsewhere. I swung her up and around, blocking
his view. She kissed me, and I tried to forget other men, tried to
enjoy what I had in my arms ... but last night's questions were still
bugging me, plus the dress, and I said, 'Let's sit down a moment
and talk.'

'They've got a nice coffee shop ...'

'Right here, honey.' I didn't want any more men looking at her.
And this too bothered me – I mean, *knowing* I was so uptight, so
insecure with this girl. And was I also a little *ashamed* of her?

We sat down in the now-empty waiting area of Gate 6. She took
my hand and smiled at me. I couldn't help smiling back; that
dimple and those teeth and those eyes, all adding up to a happy girl,
a girl who in the next moment said, 'I love you, Nickie. Kiss me,
honey.'

'When did you see Harv?'

'Let's go to the car.'

'Why are you afraid to answer?'

'I'm not afraid.' She faced forward, not looking at me. 'I just
don't see what difference it makes. I said goodbye, didn't I? I'm
leaving him and coming to you, right? So what difference does it
make? You want details? You want to know if I was sad and he
was sad?' She was angry now. 'Okay, we were sad.'

I took her hand. 'I can understand that, honey. I just ... well,
when you didn't call ...'

'I don't keep a calendar in my head, Nick. You might as well know
I'm lousy at writing on time and calling on time and being on time.

But I said goodbye to him and he accepted it and that's that.'

'Did you tell him you were going to live with me?'

She got up and walked a few steps away. 'Why hurt him even more than he's been hurt?'

'Then you *didn't* tell him?'

'I'm sure he knows.'

'But you didn't actually say...'

She turned on me. 'Look, if you don't want me to come to New York, say so now. If you're looking for things to fight about so you can get out of it...'

I went to her and took her by the arms. I kissed her forehead. 'I'm sorry. I want you to be honest with yourself, with him. If not, then maybe it's *you* who're having second thoughts.'

She dropped her eyes. I knew what was coming, and wished I hadn't pushed her into it. She said, 'Yes, well, I've been thinking a little. He begged me not to go. He said he loved me. He said I was giving up my job and home and friends and family – though we both don't care a damn about my family, except for Liz, my baby sister. Anyway, he said he would marry me if I could love him. And I said I couldn't.'

'Not now,' I muttered.

'Not now,' she repeated, nodding. 'I said I was going away to school, finally. To college to New Jersey ... that school you mentioned.'

'The Saturday School at Fairleigh Dickenson?'

'I didn't give him the name. He might check. I told my mother the same thing, but she didn't believe me. I talked to Liz about you, and my mother pumped her and she's sure I'm going to live with some dirty old man who'll use me and throw me away. She said I'm just like my grandmother.'

I felt myself going white, and forced a laugh. 'That grandmother might be the McBaren for me.'

'I told Gina the truth, and gave her your number so I can be reached in case of emergencies. But I want to wait a while before I tell *everyone*. Don't you?'

She had me there.

I muttered something about telling my closest friends, and introducing her soon to Seth, and planning on introducing her to Denise when she came home from school, but she said, 'See? It makes sense to wait, Nickie. We don't know what'll happen. And what about those phone calls you got when I walked out of the room? Don't tell me they were all business?'

I said they were unimportant, and that only she counted, and that once we were living together, everyone would find out.

'Okay, once we're living together and you feel we *always* will live together, then I'll tell Harv and the whole world. Until then, *please* don't push me. Play fair, Nickie.'

I nodded. We walked to the baggage area and got my suitcase. Her car was a beat-up 1967 Mustang with practically no brakes. I held my breath as she sped to the Forest Park Hotel ... where I had the same suite as before, and where we made long, satisfying love. Then she said she had to go and I couldn't come with her.

I was getting into my shorts and looked up. 'Why?'

'Harv is taking some stuff from my apartment. I tried to get it all done before you arrived, but I visited my grandma and I had to talk to Charlie – Mr Alexis – and it ate up time.'

'Dammit! You had a full week...'

'*Stop it!*'

It was a real scream, and it shocked me. I said, 'Take it easy.'

'You're pushing me, Nick, and I can't be pushed! You're like my mother – why don't I do this and why don't I do that! I don't do *anything* right, Nick. I do what I do my own way, the only way I can. If you don't like it...' She grabbed up her clothes and ran for the bathroom. By the time I got there, the door was locked.

'Ellie, open up.'

No answer.

'Ellie, please.'

There was a click. I pushed the door open. She was sitting on the toilet, head down, the clothes in a pile at her feet. I picked them up. She laughed. 'Hang them up neatly, Nicky.' I threw them at her head and she ducked and then my hand was flying at her face. I stopped in time, but she stared at me and said, voice shaking, 'If you ever hit me... If you ever hit me, Nickie, it's all over. Right then, it's all over.'

'You're not the only one with a temper. You can't mock...'

'I can mock and I can *say* anything. I won't hit you, Nickie, and you'd better not hit me. My mother hit me too much. And pushed me too much. I can't take it, Nickie.'

I backed off then. I picked up the clothing and brought it into the bedroom and began to hang it in the closet ... then threw it on the bed. But I straightened out the dress. *My* mother. *My* training. 'Hang your things up neatly, Nickie.' And a shot in the face if I didn't. Well, it was *good* training. I wished to hell Ellie had picked up a little of it.

I went back to the bathroom. She was still sitting on the toilet.

'C'mon, honey, get up.'

'Why? I'm trying to shit.'

When I finished laughing, she said, 'I'm always constipated. From dieting so much, I guess. And laxatives hurt my guts.'

'We'll get you on fruit-juice cocktails, with a solid base of prune juice. Soon as we get home, we'll start straightening out all your problems and hangups.'

'Think you can do the job?'

I nodded.

She got up from the toilet and came to me.

'All finished?' I asked, and cupped her rear in both hands.

'Never got going,' she said, and put her tongue in my mouth.

We made love again, and by then it was twelve-thirty and she said, 'Christ, I said I'd meet him at the store at twelve. I'll have to call.'

'The phone's just where it was the last time.'

She went to it, still nude, then looked at me. I didn't move. She said, 'Could I have some privacy?'

'But we're . . .'

'Didn't I leave the bedroom when you got calls in New York?'

'I didn't ask you to.'

'Once you waited and looked at me. And once you murmured you couldn't talk.'

Both times were Ledya, my little actress. But she didn't turn me on a tenth as much as Ellie. And I'd drop her in a second if it came to a showdown. And yet I didn't want to lose her completely, in case this nutty St Louis broad disappeared in a few weeks. I got up and went into the bathroom. 'Turn on the water,' Ellie called. 'Please, honey.'

'That's *horny*,' I cracked, not knowing what else to say. God, to be banished from the room by my lover, the woman who was going to live with me, while she called an ex-boyfriend! Or *was* he ex?

She giggled. I turned on the water, hot and cold, and waited and then turned them back a bit and put my ear to the keyhole. I just about could hear her voice. She was whispering. I opened the door and walked in, whistling. She was saying, '. . . can't promise anything, hon.' She looked at me, and shook her head slowly. Then she said, 'I'll see you at the store,' and hung up.

I said, 'You've probably given him plenty this week, so why not a last fuck?'

She went to the bedroom and her clothes. I followed, sweating, trembling, wanting to hit someone, to hurt someone as I'd been hurt.

She dressed, her back to me. As she bent to pull her panties over a

39

foot, I slapped her bottom, perhaps a little harder than I'd planned. She whirled on me. 'I gave him *nothing,* though I spent Wednesday and Thursday with him. He drove me around both days ... took off from work to help me bring stuff to Gina and Liz and my mother. Helped me sell my car to a friend and we'll deliver it today. Helped me leave his life, and all the time he had a bump in his pants and let me tell you that Harv's bump is about a third bigger than yours. And I *am* going to give him what he wants now. I *am* going to give him a fuck, or maybe half a dozen because he can go on and on and when he's hot. Because you hit me. And maybe he'll be able to convince me I shouldn't leave.'

I laughed as hard as I could, hatred choking my throat. 'You're proving to be just what you appear.'

'And what's that?'

'Look in the mirror, baby. Ever see anything closer to a whore?'

She nodded, dressing like mad. 'My mother again.'

'What about your father? Didn't he spot it too? You never mention your father. Is he some goddam pimp ...'

'He's a goddam jailbird. He's in stir in California, for life.'

My anger, based on fear of Harv Cohen, on jealousy of any man who might touch my girl, began to weaken. 'I'm sorry. You should have told me. We have to tell each other things like that.'

She picked up her shoulder purse. 'Why? I'm a whore and whores have to keep their mouths shut when they meet decent people. Or else they lose out, as I did with you. Now I'll just have to go back to fucking for Harv and Charlie ...'

'Did you?'

My anger had returned, tenfold. I was moving toward her, and I must have looked like death because she suddenly sat down on the bed. 'Please, Nickie. I never let Charlie touch me. Harv was going to marry me. Harv loves me. He begged me and begged me not to leave. He almost cried. Try to understand I loved him – or thought I did – and he's been so good to me and I don't want to hurt him. My life hasn't been that great, honey. He was the best thing in it, until you came along. And maybe ...'

She stopped. I knew she'd been about to say, 'And maybe he's *still* the best thing in it.' And maybe she was right.

I sat down beside her. 'What time will you be back?'

'I don't know.'

'But you *will* spend tonight with me?'

She smiled then. 'Tonight and every night, honey, for as long as you want me.'

My heart leaped. I pulled her face to me. I kissed her. I almost said, 'I love you.' But I didn't. I wasn't sure. She was a child; a wild, sexy, crazy child. Perhaps a sick child. How could I entrust my life, my future, to such a girl? Of course, I could have lied – said 'I love you' anyway. But that is the worst crime in the world, the ultimate obscenity. To me, at least.

I said, 'Please come back as early as you can.'

'I will. Another kiss, Nickie?'

It was a long one, a strong one, and I wanted her again. She said, 'Hey, you're too much.'

'For a dirty old man, you mean. Harv goes five and six times, right?'

She laughed. 'At his best, he never went as much as you, as long as you, as beautiful as you.' She pinched my cheek so hard I yelled, then ran for the door.

My smile lasted a few minutes; the good feeling behind it, a few hours. Both were long gone, and forgotten, by nightfall. Ellie wasn't even back by eleven, by twelve, by one a.m., and I'd run out of meals and walks and things to do to kill time and thought – images of her and Harv in bed together. Once the phone rang, and I leaped at it muttering, 'Thank God.' It was the desk, wanting to know if I was checking out tomorrow.

The hour between one and two a.m. was so long, so bad, I handled it the only way I could, in bed with my head under the pillow.

She walked in at two-ten, smelling of booze.

'Don't tell me you were delivering furniture until two a.m.?'

'We had a farewell dinner and a few drinks.' She was solemn, almost sullen. 'I got confused.'

'About what?' I knew, of course.

'About us. And Mr Alexis offered me a raise.'

'I know what kind.'

'Funny man. He offered me plenty, and that too if I want it, and with that would come everything I need. I mean a new car and clothes and plenty more. And Harv wouldn't know and wouldn't drop out of my life and wouldn't yell and wouldn't smack me around. And I'm leaving my home and friends. And for what? So you can say you *want* me?'

I returned to the bed and she sat down on the couch. We looked at each other through the archway. I lay back. A moment later, she began to move around. I knew she was getting her bag and a few things she'd left here this morning. I knew she was going to leave, or was testing to see if I would stop her. And I wanted to stop her, on my knees if necessary, because being together and fighting was one thing, but losing her was something else again. I just couldn't stand the thought of losing her. Not yet.

But I said nothing. She moved around some more and then a door closed. I didn't know if it was the bathroom or the hall door.

There was silence. After about five minutes, I got up and went to the bathroom. It was empty. I said, 'Oh God.' I went to the hall door and opened it and looked out. No one. I closed it and dropped into the chair near the desk. I looked at the phone. I didn't even know where to reach her. I still didn't have her sister's number or last name.

Quite suddenly my life was empty. There was nothing to look forward to. I knew Ellie had begun to mean a lot to me, physically. But why this terrible fear, this frightening nothingness?

I got up and went to the bed and then couldn't tolerate lying down. I had to get out of here!

'Ellie,' I said, hearing my voice tremble, and went to the closet. Why the hell had I bugged her so? She was right – she was leaving everything and everyone for me, and I didn't allow her the right to say goodbye to the man who'd been closest to her. And even if she *had* fucked him one last time, and I believed her when she said she hadn't, what right did I have to criticize her, to call her a whore? What right did I have to question her at all? She was coming to me with no guarantees...

I was opening the closet door. A hand came out and smacked me lightly across the face. I gave a choked scream and leapt backward. Out of the closet stepped Ellie, saying, 'Let that be a lesson to you, Mr Leib.'

I said, 'You nut!' and lunged for her. She shrieked at the top of her lungs and I thought the people in the next room and upstairs and downstairs would be calling the cops by now, but who cared? She was laughing and I was laughing and I caught her and she said, 'No hitting, Nickie!' and I said, 'Just a little spanking.'

Over my knees she went and up went that mini-dress and I began a playful spanking ... and then I realized she was wearing panty-hose and no panties. When she'd left the suite she'd been wearing panties and no pantyhose.

I let her go. She turned her head, looking at me in surprise. 'Don't I get it warmed up?'

'You've had it warmed up.'

'Not *that* again?'

I moved, and she got off me and sat beside me on the bed. 'Now don't tell me they left something in there?' She grinned and tried to

42

pinch my cheek. I pushed her hand away, brusquely.

'For Chrissakes,' she muttered. 'I'm going to bed.'

'When you left, you had panties. Now you have pantyhose.'

Did she hesitate for a second, or was she simply ingesting what I'd said? 'Do you know where Harv and I were before dinner? At my apartment, getting some things. Will you admit that it's possible I own a few pair of pantyhose? Will you admit it's possible I decided to change from panties to pantyhose?'

'Why?'

'Shit! Because I like pantyhose at night! Because it gets cooler at night. Because how many times have you seen me in pantyhose without panties, you goddam detective you!'

She jumped up. I grabbed her arm. 'In that dress, honey, you should *always* wear panties.'

'Not when I'm saying goodbye to Mr Alexis. Because he deserves a last look at my ass. Because he's got to have something to remember so when I run away from you, from your goddam picking and pushing, I'll have a job to come back to.'

I remained seated, but held her arm. I cooled it by smiling and saying, 'Did he like it?'

'He kissed it for a half an hour.'

I pulled her closer, looking up at her. 'I'll bet he wanted to.'

'You're goddam right. When Harv went out to the car for a minute, he put his hand under my dress and squeezed it. And just tonight I let him.'

'But he didn't kiss it. It needs kissing.'

'Nickie . . .'

'I don't give a damn about Harv and Charlie and whoever else is in your life. *Was* in your life. Tomorrow we drive to New York, right?'

Her voice grew quiet. 'Right.'

'Tomorrow we load up the car – where *are* your things?'

'In the apartment, all packed and ready. We'll get them in the morning.'

'Okay. Tomorrow we drive home. Tomorrow we start a new life. So everything before tomorrow is ancient history, right?'

'Right.'

She was looking over her shoulder at me. Our eyes locked. 'And tomorrow there are only two people in the world, you and me, right?'

'Right.'

I reached up to touch her face. 'And those two people won't ever look at any other men and women, right?'

'Right ... but whatever happened to your original idea?'

I was lost in her eyes, her soft voice, her dimpled smile. 'What?'

'You were going to kiss my ass, weren't you, Mr Leib?'

I was laughing as I got the pantyhose down. I stopped laughing as the appetite gripped me, not only in the crotch but in the chest and guts.

She was wild for a fucking, but first she devoured *me*. I protested I hadn't washed, but she wouldn't stop. Her tongue went everywhere ... she was a quick study, and I came without meaning to.

'Now see what you've done,' I muttered, sinking back exhausted.

'Tastes like walnuts,' she said, and I realized she'd swallowed it. It thrilled and touched me, and I stroked her head.

'And what are *you* going to do?' I asked.

She took my hand and brought it to her. I said, 'Not tonight.' She looked disappointed, until I began to kiss her small, hard breasts, and then her belly, and then her nest. It took quite a while, and the next morning my tongue was actually sore at the base, at the muscle. She said it was the first time ever for her, to a conclusion. I joked that Harv had a lot to learn.

We were lying in each other's arms. She said, 'Yes, he does.' She stroked my face. 'I love you, Mr Leib.'

I kissed her so as not to have to answer. I just couldn't say the words, yet. She turned her back on me, pushing her ass into my crotch, drawing my hand under her neck and onto her breast. Her favourite position, and she was asleep in moments.

It took me a while longer.

I had it all under control, didn't I? I would make her happy and she would make me happy. The Pygmalion bit. Maybe I could never really *love* her. You had to respect a woman before you could love her, right? And whatever I felt for Ellie McBaren, respect wasn't part of it. Also, you had to trust the woman you loved, and Ellie was just too ... well, perhaps not promiscuous, but certainly vulgar. Of course I was at least as vulgar as she was. In fact, she was the first woman who matched my vulgarity, and I loved it. With others, I'd always had to hide it, the language and the thoughts. Not with Ellie.

Actually, I felt she hadn't fucked around nearly as much as some of the well-educated, successful, socially-oriented women I knew. What I mistrusted in her wasn't so much her loyalty as her ability to resist a clever ploy, a sharp makeout artist.

Anyway, Ellie was sleeping and I was trying to sleep. I was satisfied and I was happy, but I wasn't hopeful for the future. How could I be hopeful, given Ellie's screwy ways? And given my own built-in snobbishness – built in by dear old Mum with her 'fine' girls and 'not-so-fine girls'? Guess how she would classify Ellie! And guess how at least part of her loving son classified Ellie.

I fell asleep, knowing one thing. I'd been bored for years. I wasn't bored now.

The next day, the rental station wagon was delivered to the hotel. Ellie and I drove to her apartment, where the first thing she said was, 'Christ, I forgot to take my pill last night.' I'd gotten her a six-month supply from Ron during her two-week visit, but getting her to take it six *days* in a row was another matter. She rushed into the bathroom, as if another ten seconds might prevent pregnancy, and gulped one down. Meanwhile, I began moving some of her things to the car. She had five battered suitcases, a large portable TV, a portable stereo record player, and an incredible pile of clothing on hangers. Later, the clothing filled both my bedroom closets (and I have *huge* closets), relegating me to the closet in the foyer. And those suitcases also held mostly clothing, underclothing, nighties, accessories.

The trip back was a ball – roads reasonably empty, this last week in May, weather clear and mild. We should have made it in two days. We took five. We went up side roads and explored small towns and stopped at motels at four o'clock and made love until seven and drove miles for good dinners and further for drive-in movies, where we petted wildly, shamelessly. On the fourth day, she began to talk about her life – family and friends and love affairs. Mentioned offhandedly was Russ Doon. I knew the name; had read of the man, once a fine professional football player who'd become a compulsively obscene extension of his penis. He'd been brought up on criminal sexual charges no less than five times in the past two years. She said, quickly, 'Yes, but he wasn't that way with me and you know how much crap there is about blacks.' I was glad to accept it, though later I remembered her averted eyes and how quickly she went on to the next, totally-unrelated point.

When she finished, I was horrified, hurt, wanted to run from her, wanted to hold her close where she'd be safe, didn't know what the hell I wanted to do ... because of what she'd experienced in her brief twenty years. But her story, and it was far from complete then, had certainly intensified my fears, my lack of respect and trust, my lack of hope in our future. Not because it was strange and objectionable to me, but because I recognized so much of the natural Nick Leib in her; so much of what I'd *almost* been as a youth. And so I determined to eradicate the past from her life, her mind; to change her into a reasonably organized, controlled and educated person, one

45

who might make me comfortable and happy. Perhaps then I could begin to think of a future with her.

One more thing. There was something in me that responded to the painful and sordid aspects of her life, not only with natural sympathy but with unnatural and intense sexuality. I was more turned-on than ever after our trip from St Louis.

THREE

Ron Levine is small, has sallow skin, wears thick glasses and a sour expression ... and thinks he's Rock Hudson. I'm about twice his size and never had the kind of trouble he's had with girls, but I sometimes feel the way he looks.

I guess it's all in the childhood. Ron's parents were middle-class and reasonably fond of each other, the father a successful real estate agent. My parents were always broke, hated each other, and my father didn't succeed at anything except dying quickly. Which perhaps explains why Ron once said, 'No one dies of a broken heart any more; the times are just not Byronesque enough.' And why I replied, 'Bullshit, we've simply localized the affected area scientifically – it's the *brain* that breaks, and it can kill and maim easily.'

The way I see it, the potential to be killed or maimed is determined by the outcome of love affairs; more specifically, that *first* love affair between you and your parents. If the affair is unsuccessful, you acquire that awful potential that Ron doesn't have and I do have. And that Ellie has in spades.

' I must've been eleven,' she said that day in the car, 'when Dad went to Los Angeles to find a job in construction. Man, what he found! Trouble, even more than he'd had in St Louis.' She tried to laugh. 'Well, he was always a loser. So he became a *big* loser. At least he got his picture in the LA papers.' Another forced laugh. 'He really tried to be nice. And he ends up being called a *murderer*.'

Lonnie McBaren was a drinker and a brawler, but also, according to Ellie, a rather gentle and innocent man, always getting into fights because of a feeling for the underdog. 'He'd cry at movies and TV,' she said. 'The parts where kids were hurt by grownups, or where some poor cowboy got pushed into a gunfight and was killed by a professional gunman. I think he was always trying to turn around those movies in real life ...'

Lonnie interfered in a fist fight in a North Hollywood bar, taking on the bigger man. He was arrested for homicide when the man he hit fell, cracked his head on the bar, and died. Even considering

Lonnie's long record of minor arrests and convictions, the court was unaccountably harsh. 'Unaccountably' to me, but not to Ellie.

'What can you expect? He had a lousy charity lawyer. You know, one of those court-appointed jerks they make such a big deal about on TV. But man, they're usually bad news! You ask anyone in a poor neighbourhood about free lawyers. If you went to a student doctor and he experimented with you, what do you think your chances of walking out would be? So this jerk experimented and made the judge mad, and fouled up the appeal, and Dad got life.'

It wasn't actually life; an indeterminate sentence, with a *possibility* of life imprisonment. And that was the end of Lonnie as father. But it wasn't the end of him as a factor in Ellie's life. He remained the half-remembered hero, the champion of the underdog, the gentle and innocent victim of a vicious social and legal system that operated to the advantage only of those with education and money.

At the same time, she knew he was the direct cause of almost everything bad that had happened in her life. If he hadn't been a drinker, her mother would not have been the near-psychotic she became. 'Anyway, not as *bad*, Nickie, because she did have a rough time, I've got to admit that, and with a real husband I think she'd have been a lot better. I can remember, as a baby, how she'd rock me and sometimes kiss me. Then I got older, and it got worse and worse. . . .'

If Lonnie had not been incapable of supporting his family, the McBarens would not have experienced the grinding poverty of their South St Louis slum neighbourhoods, and Ellie would not have been sent away from home twice. Both she considered banishments, and both were traumatic experiences.

In fact, Ellie's life was *full* of trauma. That she'd turned out as well as she had was something of a miracle.

Taking it from the top, she was born in July, twenty years before I met her, the second of Lon and Mary McBaren's three children. There were five miscarriages. From the time she was able to remember anything, she remembers Lon coming home drunk and Mary screaming at him. 'Not because he was bombed – he was always kind of quiet and happy when he was drunk – but because he'd spent his pay, and we needed every dime.' She also remembers that her mother spoke of herself as coming from 'a good St Louis family' and of her father as being 'a low Ozarks hillbilly'. Yet her mother's mother was the scandal of both families, the scarlet lady, the beautiful woman of no morals whatsoever, who alone of all the Guerneys and McBarens had managed to escape poverty. 'She was always coming out of some marriage, some affair, with money. I give her credit for it! She was married four times, and you couldn't count her love affairs. All kinds and ages of men, but they had to have one thing. Money! 'Course, now she's almost sixty and she's alone and kind of bitter ... and I guess she's the reason Mum's so hung up about sex.'

The Guerneys were pure Irish. The McBarens were a mixture of just about everything found in the mid-West. 'I'm not sure about *all* the blood in me, but I know I have Irish, French, Scottish, German, English and Cherokee Indian. And this should make you happy, Nickie, I've even got a little Jew in me. My great grand-mother on my father's side was one-quarter Jewish.'

I didn't say it, but I thought she was the best advertisement mongrelization had ever produced.

The Catholic Church played a major role in her life. She was forced to attend Sunday Mass until the day she left home, and from the first found it empty and meaningless. 'Whenever me and Gina would come in the house, we'd say, "Back to the Holy Family." And whenever we'd leave the house, we'd say, "Praise be to God." But it was no joke, all that dumb crap. Okay, if you believe it and want it ... but when you're *forced*, then it's worse than nothing. I still can't look at a nun ...'

She was sent to parochial school, and hated it. Later, she was sent to public school to save the tuition, and hated it slightly less. 'At least no one slapped you around, like those goddam nuns. But I'd already learned all my bad habits, and I couldn't even make myself read a story in the English book – a story I would like if I read it on my own – because they said I *had* to read it. I guess I was taking too much ordering around and slapping around in my house to take more of it in school. Anyway, school in my neighbourhood was a place where mothers sent their kids to get them out of their hair. Church was a place they sent the girls hoping they wouldn't get knocked up by fourteen, and the boys praying they wouldn't be in jail by sixteen.'

With a new baby on the way, Mary McBaren sent six-year-old Ellie to stay with her paternal grandmother in a small Ozark community Ellie called 'Bley', but which we couldn't find on the map. She remembers little of this stay. 'I guess I just wiped it out of my mind, because Gina was allowed to stay home. I was younger than her by almost three years, the baby of the family, and yet I was sent away and she stayed. Gina was always my mother's favourite, and you know why? Because she didn't look as much like my father as I did! I can tell you, I *hated* Gina for a while ...'

Favourite or not, Gina was included in the almost daily beatings and 'groundings', being kept in for minor infractions, such as leaving a piece of clothing on the bed or floor. But the mother was particularly and progressively more cruel to Ellie for 'looking just like that drunken hillbilly', and Ellie received her first beating with a belt the very day she left for Bley.

I asked what her mother looked like.

'She's kind of goodlooking. If she would smile sometimes ... but even so, she's got big boobs and a good figure and even now she's only forty-three years old and the men look at her. But she's really fucked up. She hates everything in pants.'

She then tried to skip over the Ozark stay, but I pressed her with questions. Finally, she said, 'I told you, I don't really remember much. Well, a few things, like from L'l Abner.' She quickly threw them at me:

An enormous family with aunts and uncles and their offspring living together in the widowed grandmother's large, ramshackle house.

The house loaded with 'crap furniture, mostly beds'.

A truck farm out back, a good-sized corn field on one side, an outhouse on the other, with a dump-yard of old cars, rusting bed-springs, and rotting farm implements beyond the privy.

'A hundred dirty kids piling into the oldest pickup truck you ever saw, when we went to town.'

Town being one street with a half-dozen stores and a movie house.

Hating her dresses, which were hand-me-downs and much too large for her.

Liking her grandmother who cooked well and was kind to her, when she had the time to notice her. 'Those were the best meals I ever had, until I left home.

'Grandma's home-made beer, which I'd get to sip sometimes and which was damned good. And some moonshine brewed by an uncle, which burned like hell and made me cough and made the dumb sonofabitch say, "That can't be old Lonnie's kid. He could put away a *gallon*!" '

Being ashamed of her cousins when they went to town together, 'because they all had buck teeth and yelled at the tops of their lungs'. And because they began handling each other sexually at a very early age, and this led to many of the girls becoming pregnant at an early age. (Ellie's not-quite-joking definition of a virgin in the Ozarks: 'A five-year-old who can outrun her brothers and cousins, and outfox her uncles.')

49

After Elizabeth's birth, and Lonnie landing a new job as a plasterer, Ellie returned hime, where the father soon began drinking again and the mother soon began beating her again. Kindergarten hadn't been bad, but first ·grade in parochial school gave her a lifelong antipathy for formal education. She daydreamed continuously, avoiding the realities of home and classroom. 'So the nuns slapped me around even more to make me pay attention, and so I hated them more and daydreamed more. I'd sit in a dark place behind the staircase at home, or in an empty lot next door, or in the toilet at school, any place I could be by myself, and I'd make up stories in my mind. I'd think how my father would stop drinking and own his own construction business. How my mother would kiss him and say things about him. How we'd all be happy together in restaurants and in cars. How all the relatives from my mother's side would come to visit at our new house and envy us, even Grandma Guerney. I built this house up in my mind so I could really see it. It was a big white house in the country; not the country like Bley, but *rich* country, with lawns and swimming pools and fences and maids. It had a long porch, and a big tree in the front yard with a wagon wheel under it all planted around with flowers. I dreamed about Christmas in that house, with presents, and Mum and Dad going crazy over me and Gina and Liz. Maybe that's because Christmas was always such a drag, with Dad getting drunk for days and then Christmas Eve with my mother saying we had rotten presents because he'd drunk up all the money. And still, he always managed to get us *something*.'

She began to care for Liz, first as a play object, an animated doll that her mother encouraged her to feed and change, then as a playmate, and finally as a person ... a person she feared for. Liz too resembled the father, and as such came in for heavy punishment.

After Lon's disaster in California, before he went to trial, the family had to move to even meaner surroundings, where Ellie was subjected to the worse element St Louis had to offer, black as well as white, though as in most slum areas there was little contact between the races, except in violence.

'No one went to California to see Dad. My mother wouldn't have, even if she'd been able to raise the money, and his brothers just didn't think of it. My Uncle Brett wrote to him and to the lawyer, but that was it. And that neighbourhood, wow! Yet there were nice kids there too. I remember one black boy about my age who used to talk to me, and who made up stories just the way I did ... but then my mother saw us talking and she chased him away and beat the hell out of me, and would you believe what she called me, her own little girl? A nigger lover, and she said more too, about my growing up worse than the tramps in the neighbourhood because they only did it with whites. I can see now she was really crazy! But I didn't see it then, and it made me think I was somehow dirty, and what made me feel even worse was I didn't understand what I was doing wrong.'

With the approach of full sexuality, Ellie entered what she termed 'one hell of a life. I mean, she made me out a whore from eleven on, and I didn't even know what to do with that thing between my legs! She just didn't want me to *have* a cunt! No matter how I tried to please her, it was no use. If it was bad before, it was *murder* afterward.'

Home became prison. The mother kept her three daughters indoors as much as possible. But the prisoners, at least the two older ones, began to escape at night. Ellie and Gina took to climbing out their bedroom window and joining the fun at 'the Jute Joint', a club the kids built in an empty store on the next street. 'Sometimes we'd have a soda, if a boy would buy it for us, at Shaw's Garden on Cleveland Avenue, and man that seemed like heaven to me! But at the club we didn't drink sodas.'

There she learned to drink whisky from the bottle, to curse with the best of them, and to act as if she could fight and take on a boy in bed. 'But I was scared shitless of fighting. I hate hitting, you know that. And I didn't know which end was up when it came to sex. But no one else knew it, not even Gina. I had an act . . .'

Accused of pinching an older girl's boyfriend, she stalked up to the girl, said, 'You wanna fight it out?' and made her back down. 'But my knees were shaking so bad I thought I'd fall on my face!'

As for sex, 'I got a real break, and it kept my reputation without losing me my cherry.' Invited by a fifteen-year-old with a rep as a skin merchant to join him on the cot in back, she played a hunch about the boy, an instinct that said he was as big a phony as she was, and swaggered into the room ahead of him. Everyone watched from the main clubroom as the boy rubbed his hands together, followed her, and with a big grin, shut and locked the door. She lay down, beginning to doubt her instinct, beginning to tremble, but remained outwardly calm. He said, 'Ellie, hey, you're real young, so let's go slow,' and lay down beside her and took her hand. Despite his words, she felt the moment of truth was fast approaching, when she would either have to come across and be what her mother said she was or run out and lose the approval of her peers. But he did nothing more; simply held her hand and lay looking up at the

51

ceiling. And she realized he was shaking worse than she was. Finally, she kissed his cheek and murmured, 'Think we can go back now, Bill?' He nodded, and they returned to the main clubroom, where everyone stared at them admiringly, and where she heard Bill say, 'Wow!' in reply to a question from another boy. And so, at the ripe old age of eleven, she achieved notoriety, and a nickname – Hellie-Ellie.

For a while, Bill became her steady and protected her from the advances of boys who might *not* have been phonies. In fact, one used a very straightforward approach on a night Bill was absent. He said he had 'something interesting' to show her, and when they were alone in the alley beside the store, he produced it. 'I got to admit, it *was* interesting. I'd never seen one before. But I said, "*That* little thing?" and laughed, and he went down. I'll bet I gave him a lifelong hangup!'

Bill's protectorship weakened when he was whipped in a fight by another, bigger boy, who then began courting Ellie by putting her into corners for hugs and kisses and 'feels all over my body'. She ran from him once in tears, but he wasn't the type to give up easily. What might have happened had she remained in the neighbourhood at this time she didn't know, but her second trip to Bley came along.

After a four-month wait, her father was brought to trial. Instead of being freed to return home, as he and his attorney had assured the family he would be, he was convicted. The mother reacted by shipping Gina to *her* mother, Ellie to Bley, and taking herself and Liz off to Kansas City and a sister's, 'where I had something like a nervous breakdown. It lasted three months, and they were the longest months of my life. It was summer and I should have been able to have some fun at Grandma's, but what with everyone talking about Dad, and not knowing what was happening with Gina and Liz, or whether we'd ever be together again, I was always scared and always crying. And remember, I was now eleven, going on twelve, and that's ripe for a girl in the Ozarks.' She paused. 'Sex. Always the goddam sex. I think I hated it, Nickie. I think I'd have been happy to be sexless. I mean, part of me wanted to enjoy it, play with it as a kid and use it as a woman, but most of me blamed it for everything bad in my life. It seems that whenever my mother hated anyone, including me, it had to do with men, with sex.'

Her second night at Grandma McBaren's, a male cousin named Evan came to the bed she shared with a female cousin named Lottie, and plumped himself down between the two girls. He then proceeded to masturbate Lotttie, who was thirteen, and to have Lottie masturbate him; he was approaching fifteen. 'He was a big, skinny, *mean* boy with dirty yellow hair. He had big hands, big feet and big everything else. Yes, that too.

'He put his hand on my leg, high up, when I tried to get out of the bed. I sat up anyway, and he *squeezed*, those big fingers digging into my flesh. Man, I lay down fast! Then he looked at me and looked at me while Lottie yanked up and down on him. It was the first time I ever saw how a man's thing worked, and I guess it got to me – Lottie's hand pulling and that big thing getting redder and redder, and then the way his chest heaved and the way he gasped and the way he spurted all over. A little even got on me. And then Lottie came, and even though she was quiet about it, I could see how her body moved and how she loved it. Evan began talking to me, asking me wouldn't I like some fun too, and I kept saying no, I was tired, I wanted to sleep. Know what he did? He put his finger right into me, and he said, "You ain't so tired, Ellie. It's nice and wet." I guess it was, after all I'd seen!'

But she was still very much the product of her mother's violent rejection of sex and talk of bad women, and was determined to become what Mary McBaren could love and respect. Equally important, she was still too young to have received the full onslaught of her own bodily demands. So she pushed him away. He then hit her a few times, in the side and in the belly, and threatened to 'change yore face aroun' so you won't much like it, heah me?' She heard, and learned to let him play with her ... and also learned that despite hatred of him, it felt good.

'He came to the bed every night, and he didn't hit me again, and he gave up trying to make me kiss him or touch him. And then he began playing with me *before* he touched Lottie.'

He would work himself up with Ellie, fingering her while kissing her half-formed breasts, her belly and her rounding thighs, telling her all the while she was the prettiest girl he'd ever seen and when she was older they would become lovers and he would give her presents. 'He didn't know it, and maybe I didn't either, but a few times he got me so I almost wanted to kiss him. But later, I'd remember he was forcing me, and I'd hate him. And he got me in trouble with Lottie.'

The older girl grew jealous, and waited her chance at revenge. It came when she saw Ellie enter the outhouse just before the family was to leave for town one afternoon. She locked her in by putting a board across two large, bent nails strategically placed in an earlier demonstration of Ozark humour.

'You ever been in an outhouse? No matter how much chemical

they drop down the hole every week, it still stinks like hell. And it's dark, even in the daytime, because the window thing they cut in the door has to be small so's people can't look in. Like a crescent moon, you know? And this little place was handling a family of God-knows-how-many people; I think it was about twenty! I always tried to hold my breath in there, or take as few breaths as I could. I once almost fainted, doing that. And I hated the newspaper they used for toilet paper. Well, I heard the truck starting up and the kids yelling, but that didn't worry me. I'd much rather have stayed at the house by myself. So I sat there until the truck was gone. Then I tried to open the door.

'I can't tell you what happened to me when I saw I wasn't going to be able to get out. The family would be gone two or three hours. And I was alone in that darkness and stink. And everything I hated was wrapped up in that goddam shithouse. And I think I must have gone a little crazy, because I began to scream and I kept screaming and I thought my head would come off. And then the door opened and Grandma was there and she was hugging me and saying it was only a damn fool joke...' The grandmother had taken a head count through the cab window, and realized Ellie was missing from among the dozen some-odd children in the bed of the truck.

As much as Ellie was comforted by her grandmother, and as much as the other kids said it was nothing to bawl about, and even with Lottie's apology (brought on by a few hard smacks to the bottom), Ellie remained terrified of the outhouse, and this developed into a generalized fear of being locked in toilets. As I'd seen, she often left the bathroom door open and, when she locked herself in, it generally meant some sort of trouble.

There was one other traumatic incident during that second visit to Bley. A young aunt who had supposed renewed a childhood affair with her half-brother was knifed by her husband. 'She was a real pretty girl, about nineteen or twenty, with two little boys, one an infant and the other maybe a year older. The cousins were always whispering about her and this half-brother, and not only about that. She was always laughing it up with whatever man happened to be around, or even with some of the older kids. Evan said she'd pulled him off twice, and that if she hadn't been stabbed he was sure she'd have done him in another week or two. But he could've been lying.

'I was in the kitchen that night, playing checkers with Grandma. This aunt, Cleo, was standing around watching us and talking and filing her nails. I remember she was wearing low-slung shorts cut down from old blue jeans and a halter top that left most of her belly bare. Then in walked her husband, I forget his name, and Grandma suddenly yanked me away from the table. Because he was liquored up and he'd grabbed the bread knife off the counter. He said something like, "You dirty whore, you and that bastard brother," and he stuck the knife into Cleo, between her shorts and her halter. She screamed, and Grandma pulled me out of the kitchen to the road. I looked back. Cleo was leaning against the table, the knife sticking out of her belly and the blood running down into her shorts. Her husband was at the sink, vomiting. Grandma was saying, "Lord, Lord, that's what comes of playing the whore of Babylon. You remember that, girl. You remember that." '

Cleo survived, and remained with her huband, and no one reported anything to the law.

The law was the enemy. In this, Ellie was adamant. The law was at least as bad as the criminals. 'Fucking pigs! They beat up on poor people and try to force any girl they catch alone.'

When I protested that not *all* police could be that way, she said, 'Okay, maybe not all, but *most*.'

Again I protested. She then said, 'When was the last time you were poor or a girl?'

End of argument, especially as I'd begun remembering police harassment as boy in Brooklyn.

On her return home from Bley, she learned that the Jute Joint had been broken up due to neighbours' complaints, that the police had found some stolen items there, and that five of the boys, including Bill and her would-be seducer, were serving time in a youth house.

School continued to be a disaster, though she was passed on from grade to grade. But at the age of twelve and a half, Ellie was suddenly mature and the boys began to come around in droves. She had found her one area of complete success ... and her mother being what she was, she now entered her period of greatest agony at home. 'I got my first period and went to her, crying, and you can't believe what a fit she threw. She acted as if I'd *made* it happen, just so I could play around. I got the belt almost every day. I got it for sure if a boy came to the house, so I told them not to come there. But I wanted to talk to them, and be with them. I wanted anything that wasn't my mother's screaming and hitting! They all tried to make out with me. That's because they were normal. I wasn't. I wouldn't let them touch anything but my hand.'

She hadn't yet been kissed on the lips by thirteen, an age by which all her friends were well into petting, and several into fucking. But she couldn't forget her cousin's finger, and began masturbating. 'I think I came the first time I tried it, in bed at home after Gina fell asleep. I did it a lot, sometimes two and three times a day, in the bathroom in school, and in the library, and at home. It was the only real pleasure I had. It was a way of forgetting the crap at home and at school. And shit, I *liked* it! It was sex, without the boys my mother hated!'

At fourteen, she was as tall and developed as she was now. The boys – some seventeen and eighteen – kept trying, and failing. A middle-aged neighbour named Otto Shermer had better luck. He caught her alone when she came to visit his daughter one Sunday afternoon and showed her a few pornographic pictures. She was stunned, but fascinated. Then he whispered that she was the prettiest girl in the neighbourhood, and the 'sweetest and most decent' (she remembered those words until today). He stroked her arms, her shoulders, her breasts, and then his hand went under her dress.

He was 'fat and old' but he kept talking and somehow she found that she couldn't move ... didn't *want* to move. After all, he was a father, good to his wife and daughter, sober and kind, with a steady job in the telephone company. His hand drew down her panties and stroked the bare cheeks and then slipped between to touch the smooth flesh of her inner thighs ... and to brush at the sparse bush of pubic hair. He was sitting on a kitchen chair and she was standing beside him, held close by one arm around her waist. But she admitted she didn't struggle; never even voice a complaint.

His hand returned to her rear and his head bent and he kissed her thighs and then, just a brushing of the lips, her cunt. And all the time he murmured soft things, flattering things, loving things. Her eyes closed. She remembered hearing her breath, so very loud in the quiet kitchen. And the next thing she knew she was on his lap, her back to him, her dress up round her waist, her pants at her ankles, his 'thing' pressing between her thighs. She felt the heated flesh touch her vulva, but he didn't try to enter. He humped up and down, begging her to press her thighs close together, something she was doing anyway to prevent any true consummation. She heard *his* breath mounting, and then he gasped, *'Leiber kindt!'* and spurted over her thighs. She began to cry ... and so did he.

'I ran. I never went back to his apartment, not even when his daughter asked me to her birthday party. But I never said anything about it either. I'd see him in the street sometimes, coming home from work, and he'd look at me, his face so sad and so soft, and I just couldn't dislike him or think of him as dirty or evil, as my mother and maybe others would.' She sighed. 'But two years ago I was in the old neighbourhood and went with a friend to the park and he was there in the playground. Yeah, watching the little girls on the swings.

'Boy, that neighbourhood! I don't know how we managed to draw all the nuts and perverts, but we did.' She laughed. 'It was a game for me and my friends, trying to avoid them on the way to school each morning. Maybe they knew the cops wouldn't roust them as hard as they would in a rich neighbourhood. Whatever it was, we'd go by the long path, and sure enough some nut with a raincoat would be waiting behind a tree and jump out and open the coat and we'd run, but not before we'd seen his thing sticking out at us.' Another laugh. 'I don't know why, but the biggest cocks I've ever seen belonged to those creeps!

'I remember once I was late and figured I'd cut right across the park; leave the path I mean. I was coming over this little hill, and walked smack into a creep in a long raincoat. Soon as I saw him, I knew what he was. And there I was alone with him. But he was as shocked as I was. The main rush of girls was over and he was probably on his way home, or to work. I always figured they were cops or priests! Anyway, he froze and I froze, and then he tried to open his coat, but he'd already buttoned it. I ran. I looked back, and he was running after me, the coat finally open, trying to unzip his fly. He was yelling, "Wait a minute! For the love of God...!"'

At fifteen, she took a summer job with a man who owned three lunch wagons, positioning them outside factories and selling sandwiches, hot dogs and cold drinks to the workers. Ellie ran one of the wagons, and came in for a good deal of sex-banter from the younger workers. She didn't mind it. She was good at ignoring it. Each morning Morrie would pick her up in the lunch wagon and drive her to the factory. Each afternoon at four he would drive her home. Always he would talk to her about work, about finding a way to live well 'without knocking yourself out', and toward the end of summer he revealed himself as not only a purveyor of food but also of women. He was a pimp, supplying several 'real quality houses and a few call-girl operations' around St Louis.

At first she laughed, not believing him. 'He was a small, neat, quiet guy about thirty – nothing like I imagined a pimp.' But a few days later he brought along one of his girls. She was a pretty redhead, not dyed and painted looking like they show whores in the movies, and maybe eighteen years old. She told me she made between five and seven hundred a week, and had been hooking since she was fifteen – my age. She said I could live at home, and go to school, and make a hundred and fifty a week on just four or five dates. Morrie said he would get me started by buying me clothes and help me with cover stories during the school year by saying I was

57

working part-time for him. If I gave my mother fifty a week, she'd *want* to believe me, wouldn't she?

'He was right. And the girl said why should I give it away for nothing, or get myself knocked up and then slave for some husband who'd run around on me anyway? She said to just look at the young marrieds in the neighbourhood and how they lived. She was right too. I agreed with both of them. The only thing was, they thought they were talking to Hellie-Ellie, and they were talking to a scared-shitless virgin. All I could say was that I'd think about it. The next day, Morrie offered me a hundred dollars – my first trick, he called it – if I'd fuck him. He said it flat out, not touching me – he never tried to touch me – but I got so red in the face I thought I was going to bust. He said to forget it and I knew where to find him if I ever wanted to, and I stopped working for him that same day. And I *did* know where to find him. A few months later, *everyone* knew where to find him, because he was busted for pimping and sent up for two years. A cop came to the house to ask me did I know anything about him, and I said no, and the goddam pig tried to grab me because Mum wasn't there. . . .'

That term, she fell madly in love . . . with the best student in her high school, a boy her own age, who seemed to return her feelings. I figured with a boy as nice as Leonard, a boy with his reputation for clean living and hard work, I could finally have someone come to my home. So I let him, and as soon as he left I got not only the belt but the broom handle . . . even though Mum was in the apartment the whole time! You know what she said? Something like this: "You don't think I saw when you slipped into the bathroom with him, you filthy little whore?" and she wacked me with the belt. I was yelling, trying to explain that I'd only brought him a fresh towel, and anyway, how could anything happen in a few seconds? She said, "Dirty minds find ways – touches and all sorts of rotten things to do!" and bam, I got the broom handle over my back. I couldn't go to school the next day, I was so sore. But this time I *cared* for the boy, and I wasn't going to stop seeing him, even if she killed me!'

She began to meet Leonard outside, most often at the baby-sitting jobs she took to help with the grim finances at home – especially grim since Gina had graduated and taken a job, and an apartment of her own. Only then did Ellie enter the kissing and petting stage most of her friends had entered two and three years before.

After about three months, she and Leonard began playing at coitus. 'We'd dry-hump, but I wouldn't allow any clothing to be removed. He'd get on me, both of us fully dressed, and rub and grind until he came. I never could come that way, but I'd go into the bathroom – to wash up, I'd say – and masturbate, thinking of him and wanting him, but still scared that I might turn out to be what my mother thought I already was.

'We were the talk of the school. He called me his sweetheart, and everyone thought I was laying him for regular like clockwork. I guess he didn't do anything to stop the kids from thinking that, even though they wouldn't have believed him no matter what he said. And I guess he'd have been ashamed to admit he wasn't getting Hellie-Ellie when so many other guys said they'd had her. But I didn't care what anyone said or thought. I was in love, and it was all beautiful.'

She graduated, for the same reason she'd been promoted every year – a school system that refused to keep back any but those who didn't attend class, were near idiots, or who were actually criminal in their behaviour. Leonard was the valedictorian, and his parents chatted with her and sympathized over her mother being ill and unable to attend.

'Mum just wouldn't come. She said I'd never done anything to deserve graduation and it was all a farce. She was right ... but it really shocked me. I didn't feel like her daughter after that.'

Leonard took her to the prom, and her mother beat her for coming home half an hour later than her deadline of midnight. 'I barely felt it, I was so upset by what Len had told me that night.' He'd accepted a scholarship at the University of Illinois, Chicago campus, instead of Washington University in St Louis, where he'd always intended to go. And he was leaving the following week for a summer job in Chicago, and then his freshman year. Would she see him next Saturday night for their 'farewell date'?

All that week she was in a fog, though she answered half a dozen want ads in an attempt to get her first full-time job. 'I didn't do very well. I was so confused about Len. What was he planning to do about *us*? I mean, if we were in love, he couldn't just leave me ...'

Saturday afternoon her mother accused her of not really trying to land a job, and grounded her for the night. Ellie went to bed early, and climbed out the window as she had when she'd gone to the Jute Joint. She'd reasoned that Len was going to surprise her by asking her to come along with him to Chicago. She could get a job and maybe even try evening classes at the University. She would live with him, give herself to him, and after he graduated they would get married. And her mother could scream as much as she liked!

'I was seventeen, Nickie, and ready to become a real woman, at

59

least with Len. I'd been dating him for two years, and I'd told him I loved him a hundred times. Once in a while he said the same, but mumbling it, like a boy *would*, I figured. I just couldn't believe he was going away, bang, like that!'

They met on the corner and walked toward Shaw's Garden, holding hands. He described his summer job with a law firm, and how his scholarship would cover almost all his tuition, and his impressions of Chicago during his three-day visit there a week ago. He was bubbling over with enthusiasm, but he said absolutely nothing about Ellie. 'If I never see this dump again,' he said as they walked through the neighbourhood, 'it'll be too soon. Fact is, you can keep all of St Louis. From now on it's Chicago, New York, maybe Los Angeles, for *my* stomping grounds!'

She forced a smile and a nod, and began to realize something.

'This boy had never felt anything for me but what all the other boys had felt – an itch in the balls. But I made myself stop thinking that. It couldn't be ... not after two whole years together! I had to let him talk about his career. Once he got it all out, he'd begin talking about *us*.'

Leonard talked on and on, and revealed much about himself that night. Money and education and power, these were what he was after. *Okay*, she thought. *Why not?* Though she was a little repelled by the way in which he made everything else seem a joke – every life in South St Louis, including his mother's and father's.

After an hour and two sodas, he still hadn't gotten around to mentioning their relationship ... so she said, 'Len, tell me something, why'd you date me all this time?'

He was tapping the table and staring into his rosy future, a future she felt he'd earned with his studies and would continue to earn with hard work; a future she felt he fully deserved; but still, she wanted her question answered. She loved this boy, and he was going to leave her without a single word about her role in that future.

'What?'

'I asked why'd you date me all this time?'

'Why?' he mumbled ... and then he grinned the grin she'd loved; the clean and innocent grin that had made her kiss him so very many times. They were sitting side by side in a booth, and she wanted to kiss him now ... but he reached down and stroked her thigh. 'You tell *me*, Ellie. I mean, tonight, finally, you *show* me. I've got it all planned ...'

He had the use of his uncle's car, and had reserved a room in a motel far out of the neighbourhood. 'An expensive place, and we'll have steaks and wine.' His hand moved higher. 'Ellie, baby, we've both waited so long. And it's the perfect time for it – our graduation present to each other.'

'I knew the score then, Nickie – and don't look so mad. Any guy would have tried. *You* would have tried. I didn't blame him. It's just that I had to forget love, and change over to sex. Goddam sex! But for once I wanted it as much as the boy did. I wanted that goodbye present, that graduation present. But I said no, I didn't feel it, maybe when he came to visit me. And that's when he blew his stack.'

He jumped up and said, 'You dumb little cunt, why the hell have I wasted all this time on you!' He began to stalk out, then returned to add, 'I figured this might happen. I've got someone else. She's got twice your brains and at *least* your looks, and not cheap looks like Hellie-Ellie! And she's willing; she's damned well willing!' Having said this, his rage dissipated, and he was able to see her face, her chalk-white face. He sat down, tried to speak, lapsed into silence.

She's sure that had he responded in any way but that violent outburst of temper, she'd have eventually gone with him to the motel. Her initial rejection had been, in a way, a test. And, for the first time, Leonard the valedictorian had flunked a test.

After a while, he said, 'I'm sorry. I ... I don't have anyone else. But, Ellie, Christ, you've done it before with the guys at the Jute Joint, and maybe with others since, so why not with me?'

'I've *never* done it.'

He sighed. 'Let's not be stupid about it. I mean, everyone knows about Hellie-Ellie.'

She shook her head. She thought she was going to scream. She couldn't remember anything good about her life; not a single thing. She said, 'Please, Len, go away now. Good luck and write me, but go away now.'

He went away. She sat there, abandoned, lost, and a boy came over and said, 'Hey, Ellie, want to smoke some pot?' and she left, and on the street a young black took her arm and said, 'What a sad, sad chick needs is a *real* man,' and she tore free and ran, ran hard, ran home ... where her mother waited.

'That night,' Ellie said, face grey with the memory. 'That fucking night. She was crazy mad, and that was no surprise. But it seemed worse than it had ever been. I was willing to take a few licks just to get into my bed and close my eyes and forget I was alive. But she was *way* out! First the belt and then the broom and all the time the screaming about my being a filthy whore and damned for all etern-

61

ity and whole such line of shit. She wouldn't stop. She chased me around the apartment and I could hear Liz beginning to cry in her bedroom and I began to feel my head coming apart. I was still holding on, telling myself it would be over in a minute, another minute, hang on, Ellie ... and then she began something new. I had to kneel and pray for an hour, she said. Kneel and pray in the kitchen while she banged me with the broom and belt. For forgiveness for my sins.

'I tried to tell her there'd been no sins, but she was using the belt again. I had to cover my head because she'd turned the belt around, by mistake maybe, I never found out, and the buckle was going to take out my eye or knock out my teeth. And all the time I kept thinking how those sins she was screaming about would have helped me keep Len. All those sins Hellie-Ellie made believe she'd committed. All those sins, those goddam sins, those fucking sins which I *couldn't* commit because this bitch had driven me crazy!

'I felt the belt buckle cut my cheek. I touched my face and there was blood. I grabbed the broom handle from the table and swung at her. I guess I went berserk. I was swinging and swinging, and only when I heard Liz screaming, 'Ellie, *stop*!' did I know what I was doing. I looked and Liz was in the bedroom doorway. When I saw her, I was able to see my mother too. She was on the floor and she was holding her head, but she was also beginning to look up at me, to get that crazy mad expression, and I knew that I had to get out of there. Or else I'd kill my mother. If not that night then another night. Because she wouldn't stop, and the next time *I* wouldn't stop. I went to the door. I hated myself because I was leaving Liz alone with that crazy bitch and Liz was going to get all the grief the two of us had had together; Liz was going to take all the beatings and groundings by herself.

'I couldn't even say goodbye to her, because my mother was looking and Liz would cry and beg me not to go and my mother would remember and say Liz had sided with me. That would mean more grief, more beatings and groundings, so I just ran. Without anything. Just ran and it was night and the neighbourhood wasn't safe at night and I hated men that night, blacks and white both, hated wanting them and being afraid of them and having them want me, always after me ...'

I wanted to ask about that 'blacks and whites both'. She hadn't spoken much about blacks, except for the little boy her mother had chased, and the man who'd grabbed her arm on the street her last night with Len, and yet she'd earlier described her neighbourhood as having *many* blacks. And now this remark. But she was going on with her story, and I thought that perhaps more would emerge later.

She ran until she passed a middle-aged couple, and they stared at her. Then she stopped and tried to compose herself; dabbed at her cheek with a tissue and wiped her tears and went to a pay phone on the corner. She called Gina, who was sharing an apartment with two other girls. Gina said there just wasn't any room for Ellie, not even for the night, because one of the girls (it turned out to be Gina herself) had a man living with her and the place was jam-packed. But she said she would lend Ellie ten dollars to get a room at the Y for a few nights. By then, Gina was sure, the trouble would blow over and Ellie would return home.

'I didn't argue with her, but I knew I'd never go back to that bitch. I waited near the phone booth, and except for two drunks who made me walk away for a while, and a car with some black kids that slowed down and U-turned and came by again and then left when I went into the booth like I was going to call for help, it was okay. Gina and her boyfriend, John, picked me up in his car and she said I should go to a doctor about my cheek or it would scar. Well, I didn't, and I guess you can see the little scar ... I'll get it taken off with a skin-peel, won't I, Nickie?

'They took me to the Y and we all walked in together because I was feeling scared and alone ... and I swear I thought I was going crazy because when Gina was in front of me for a minute, John gave my ass a good feel. I mean, what *was* it with men! Here I was seventeen and alone and shaking and beaten up and he's living with my sister, and he feels my ass! Maybe my mother *wasn't* so crazy. Maybe she had it right, and if I could only forget about men, not feel anything for them, I'd be better off.

'That night I didn't feel anything for men, but I wasn't better off. That night I lay in a little bunk in a room with another girl, Helen, and if she hadn't talked until three in the morning, about her tough life and her boyfriends and her job and a nice apartment she wanted to share with someone like me, I think I'd have gone out the window. Except that the window was only three floors up and I figured with my luck I'd live and be paralysed! But honest, I wanted to die. It hurt too much to live. I remember telling myself to listen to her and not to think of anything, and then I finally fell asleep.

'Two days later, I got a job as a file clerk in an insurance company. Gina had brought me my clothes from home; she'd taken them while Mom was out. And she told me how much she loved John and how much he loved her, and I tried not to think of that

63

either. Helen and I rented this studio apartment she'd found in the Forest Park area, and after South St Louis it looked like heaven.'

So there was no more desire to jump out of windows. But neither was she transformed into a happy teenager. And neither did she take to the boys, and men, who tried to date her at the insurance company, nor to any of the men Helen brought home, and she brought home quite a few, though at first she tried to keep her action away from Ellie.

Ellie had decided that what she wanted now was to *learn*. What school had been unable to do for her, she wanted to do for herself. Or at least to start, by reading. After a few weeks, however, Helen turned their apartment into a noisy way station 'for all sorts of freaky guys. Man, she turned out to be one bad chick, a junkie, a user of any shit she could lay her hands on. And you know junkies – they're always pushing their friends to climp on with them. And not only that, she was a real nympho, or just didn't give a damn how many guys got into her. Really wrong for a roommate, especially for anyone as hung up as I was. But I hated the idea of moving; I wanted to coast a while, not to have to look for a new place and a new roommate. So I spent as much time as I could away from the apartment.

'I used to go to the library, and even though at least one guy a night tried to pick me up, I was able to read and rest and get the feeling there was something else in life beside fucking and drinking and drugs and lies and beatings and everything *my* life had been. And Gina called to say Mom had asked if I was all right and that Liz wanted to see me, so I went over with her. Mom was quiet and I talked to Liz and left after about half an hour. I went back a week later and spent a few hours, and even though Mom started the old crap again, she didn't try to hit me and I was able to take Liz out for a soda. So I began dropping around once in a while. It gave me the feeling I had a home to go back to, though I knew I didn't.

'Things went along like this for about three months, I even dated two guys in my office. Both were quiet and kind of unattractive, and I figured I could handle them. I just wanted company and talk. I was right about one of them. He was good for dinner and movies and lots of talk about books, and he would hold my hand and, after three dates, kissed me. Fine. The other was nice for one date, and tried to make me in a drive-in movie the next date. But still, no real sweat. No muscle or drama or anything like that.' She paused. 'Well, another date or two with some other guys, and I guess I began to want a little more myself, but I wouldn't admit it and so that's the way it went.'

I said she was hiding something behind that 'another date or two with some other guys'. She said no, just a repeat of what she'd already told me, and went on. But her face was troubled. Perhaps it was because of what came next.

'One night I came home late after dinner and a movie with my quiet friend, and there was a party going on. Lots of hippie types and freaky types, and I danced with a bearded guy who was too stoned to care who I was. I turned down acid and pills and lots of other stuff, and finally I shared a joint with Helen ... but then the action got heavier and I was being pulled into the bathroom by two guys ... and I just yelled as loud as I could, 'Everyone the hell *out*! Helen said okay, they'd all leave, except for her new boyfriend. He turned out to be the bearded, stoned character who hadn't cared who he was dancing with ... so I figured it was safe.

'I put up the Chinese screen I'd bought to give myself a little privacy, and Helen and her guy went into her convertible couch and I went into mine. Her lamp didn't go out and I heard them laughing and he didn't sound so stoned any more, so I put on my eyeshades and put in my earplugs and fell asleep. I don't know how long I slept, but suddenly I felt action between my legs and on my breasts. First I thought it was a dream – you know, a sex dream, about some man making love to me. Then I took off the eyeshades and there was Helen and this bearded guy and he was between my legs and kissing my breasts. And *she* was holding his thing and pushing it into me.

'I couldn't believe it, and I was still groggy, so I didn't move for a minute. She pushed him in a little more, and she smiled and said something, and I still didn't do anything except take out my earplugs. They must've thought I was with it. And maybe I *was*, for a few seconds. Helen was saying, 'You'll love it, honey,' and she was feeling my ass with her free hand. She said she wanted me to share her lover and *be* her lover and we would enjoy ourselves every night ... and I jumped up and began screaming my head off. They said to cool it, and moved away from me, and I ran into the bathroom and locked the door. And waited. And, well, I started thinking and ended up by masturbating.

'A real screwed up broad, right? That's what Helen thought, only she was more screwed up than me, with her dope and being AC/DC. She and the guy left for his place. The next day I met Gina for lunch. She'd become pregnant about a month before, and she said she'd married her boyfriend, John Grebes, but later I found out they hadn't bothered with a licence or a minister; just considered themselves married, which is all right if it lasts. I asked her if I could bring my studio couch to their new apartment, and pay a third of the rent. She said she'd speak to John, and that night she told me it was okay. So I moved in . . .'

She continued working at the insurance company, reading a good deal if not very selectively, dating irregularly, and never too long with any one man. 'That's when I met Russ Doon, the football player. He spoke at a company dinner about hiring minority group members, and later we had coffee, and, well, I guess I was flattered that a famous guy would want to date me. And baby, he was one beautiful hunk of man!' She paused. 'And I wasn't going to let those honky bastards stare me out of talking with a man I dug, just because he was black. And did they ever stare, especially when I wrote out my address and phone number in the company lunch room and gave it to him and he held my hand for a minute and we smiled at each other.

'My boss gave me the big-uncle routine the next day, telling me Russ had been brought up on sex offences several times and was a *dangerous* man for a sweet young girl. And while talking he tried to feel my tits, and he was married and had two kids. Well, that's when I decided I *would* date Russ. We went out three times and he was okay, maybe came on a little strong, but then I had to stop seeing him anyway because Gina and John bugged me too much about it.'

When I asked what she meant by 'came on too strong', she shrugged and said, 'Like anyone else, he wanted bedtime.'

When I expressed surprise that she wouldn't resist racist pressure from her sister, she shrugged again. 'Like I said, he was one of those who wanted bed, and I dropped that type, white or black. It wasn't as if he meant anything to me. He was just a friend.' And she went quickly back to her story.

She'd been living with Gina and Grebes about a month when Grebes hit Gina for the first time. 'We were in the kitchen, having dinner, and something didn't taste too good. A stew, I think. Suddenly, Grebes just hauled off and cracked her face. I thought she'd try to kill him, but she was knocked up and under his thumb and she cried and said she was sorry and would do better from then on. I hoped it was a one-time thing, but Gina was a lousy cook and housekeeper and if he wanted reasons to crack her, he had them. And he used them. He was a bank guard, a real cop-type, and not all that goodlooking. I couldn't understand why Gina had ever fallen for him. I mean, coming from a home like ours, you don't go for rough treatment and beatings! But one reason she stuck with him might have been their sex life.'

Despite the beatings, and Gina threatening to run away, Ellie would hear them 'going at it, Gina moaning and groaning, just about every night, almost until Gina's ninth month. I walked in on them one Sunday afternoon, not knowing Grebes was there because it was so quiet. Gina was on her hands and knees, that big belly hanging down almost to the mattress, and Grebes was just putting it into her from the back. I froze for a minute. Grebes looked at me, and then he slammed in right up to the balls. And you know what he did next, the bastard? He threw me a kiss! I ran, but boy, did he change after that! Before, he'd sometimes be around too long when I was trying to dress or undress, and I think he used to peek at me from the bedroom – I thought I heard the door open a few times – but he never tried anything. Afterwards, he started playing big brother-in-law. He'd put his arm around me a lot. He'd pat my ass once in a while. He'd tell me I should be dating rich guys I was so pretty. And as much as he laughed it up, I could tell he was turning on more and more.'

The night Gina gave birth, Ellie and Grebes returned together from the hospital. 'First he had himself three or four bourbons. Then he came at me. No preliminaries. Just grabbed me and kissed me and began wrestling me into the bedroom. He wasn't all that big, smaller than you, Nickie, but he was strong enough. Also, I guess I couldn't believe he'd really force me, so I didn't fight the way I should have. He got me down on the bed, Gina's bed, and plastered kisses all over my face and made a real romantic pitch. "You hot little bitch, I've wanted to get into you from the day we went to the Y!"

'I tried to talk him out of it. I reminded him of Gina and his new son. And while I was talking, he got my pants down and put a finger up my cunt. Then I fought him, using my nails on his face and scratching him up pretty good. He slapped me maybe a dozen times, *hard* slaps, and I went weak and dizzy.'

As with her mother, she reached a point of complete loss of self. She began to scream, twisting her head violently as he tried to cover her mouth; screamed insanely, over and over again. He grew frightened and jumped up and promised he'd let her alone. He pleaded for her to stop. She couldn't stop, and people began banging on the walls and door. Grebes went out the window and down the fire escape. Even after he was gone, she continued to scream ... until the super entered with his pass key. She said she'd had a nightmare, and as he stared at her in disbelief she pushed him out the door. She packed and went to a motel, where she spent the next three nights.

Then she found the apartment she was living in when I met her.

'I needed more money and there wasn't any to be gotten at the insurance company, and anyway I was bored with the place, sick of it, wanted a job where I could have a little more freedom, *be* something...'

But she was still at the same job six months later when she ran into Claire Denniker, a friend from her old neighbourhood. They had lunch together, and Claire said she'd finally begun classes at Missouri University after saving money for almost two years. Claire encouraged her to do the same, and Ellie laughed. 'With *my* scholastic record?' Claire said Ellie could pass the college entrance exams with her eyes closed and 'charm the pants off the registrar. You know, I always wanted to be a member of the gang at the Jute Joint, but I guess I didn't have the looks. I certainly didn't have the guts!' She asked questions about what had gone on there ... and Ellie suddenly realized that Claire *admired* her, even envied her in the way studious girls sometimes admire and envy more adventurous girls.

Ellie wanted to say there was nothing to admire, nothing to envy. Ellie wanted to say she wished she could trade places with Claire and be attending college along with a steady boyfriend, and laugh as much as Claire did, and be as hopeful about the future as Claire was.

They met twice more in the next week, and Claire asked if Ellie would like to come to a party and meet some of her class-mates. Ellie nodded, and then spent three days and nights agonizing over how she would appear to college people.

The party was held in a beautiful ranch home in the prestigious St Louis suburb of Ladue. Harv Cohen's family owned the house; Harv was the host; his date left long before the party ended, moved by anger over Harv's quick and obvious attraction to the little blonde who was afraid to open her mouth for fear of saying 'something dumb, something wrong. So I just sat in a corner and Claire brought me drinks, and Jerry, her boyfriend, brought me Harv. I liked Harv right off. He wasn't really handsome, but he had a warm look, a kind look. And he liked me. And he did most of the talking, so it was all right. He drove me home and asked if he could see me again.'

Harv was twenty-three and Ellie just nineteen. He was completing law school, but hadn't done too well and had no real desire to take his bar exams and enter practice. He was an only son, the co-inheritor, along with his mother, of his father's two large hardware stores. (He had a sister, but she had married against the father's wishes and moved to New Mexico. The father, in a fit of pique, had cut her out of his will, and before he could relent had died of a massive coronary.)

Harv had been working summers and vacations in his father's business and was going to take over active managerial control within the next six months.

'He was a real gentleman. We had a great time together. I began to talk more and more to him. He had plenty of money, and liked to spend it on me, and baby did *that* make things nice! And after our second date he said he was going to stop seeing other girls, and he asked me to stop seeing other men. I played hard-to-get and said we'd wait on that, but I didn't *want* to see anyone else.

'He kissed me goodnight on the first date. We petted a little in his car on our second. By the third he'd taken a motel room and expected we would go to bed. And we did.' She laughed. 'But I stayed dressed and he couldn't believe it. When I fell asleep he *had* to believe it! But he didn't complain, and he didn't push me too much. He introduced me to Charlie Alexis, who'd been a friend of his father's, and talked Charlie into giving me a part-time job in his Lindell store. First I worked only Friday nights and Saturdays. Then I worked five evenings a week, still holding on to the insurance job. Finally, Charlie said I could take over the store when his manager left at the end of the month.' She looked at me. 'And that bring us up to Nick Leib and Hellie-Ellie's new life.' She kissed me.

'Not quite. You've skipped the whole romance with Harv.'

She turned away. 'You want all the bloody details?'

She was sour. She didn't want to go into it. I said it indicated she still had reservations about *us*. She sighed and took cigarettes from her bag. She lit one and inhaled, and then put it out.

'We went together for six months. We petted a lot. We got closer and closer. Then one night he said he had cramps and I asked why and he told me about blue balls. I felt terrible, and pulled him off. It was something I'd never done for him ... or for Len, my other serious romance.'

'Or for anyone else?'

'That's what I said, didn't I?'

But she hadn't. And I felt she was holding back, hiding things from me, things she'd probably hidden from Harv too. I had intimations of painful incidents, sordid incidents, things relating to that rape ... which she absolutely refused to discuss, saying I was 'turned on' by it, and that she wanted to wipe it from her mind.

I said, 'I've no call on your past, honey. As I told you, it all begins now, with us. But about Harv . . .'

'Okay. Maybe you'd like to masturbate while I give the hot details?'

I smiled. She went on, angrily.

'After I pulled him off, we were closer than ever to bed. Holding a man that way, seeing him come . . . it just brought me to the point where I went home and thought about him and wanted him. I was nineteen and it was time I made love.'

'Nineteen and a virgin, right?'

She said, 'Right,' her voice ominous.

There was a long period of silence. Then she sighed. 'Okay, so after six months we went to bed together, and he asked me to marry him. I accepted, and he gave me a diamond ring. But I only wore it a month, because as soon as we were engaged, we began to fight. He said I was playing Charlie in too personal a way, and I said he was on his own all day and I didn't know what *he* was doing, and we broke up. We didn't go out for a while, and then we began again, and about two months later I met you. The end. Maybe of me!'

We had lunch at a roadside tavern. We had a bottle of wine, and because I was driving she drank most of it. When we got back into the car, she began to speak again, rambling a bit, talking more for herself than for me, and therefore getting closer to the truth

She'd begun coming in later and later at the insurance company. She'd begun to feel about her job as she'd felt about school – it was all empty, a lie, useless, a punishment. She'd always had trouble getting up in the mornings; once she began living alone, with no roommate or sister to shove her out of bed, it got worse. And after meeting Harv and staying out late several times a week, it got so bad she was put on notice by her boss.

'Not being able to get up isn't just . . . well, being tired or disliking a job or anything simple. Not with me. It's not *believing* in getting up. Do you know what I mean, Nickie? It's feeling that there's no *point* in getting up, ever.' She was quiet a moment. 'I guess it's not wanting to come alive each day.

'Even after Harv, and after he got me the job with Charlie, I didn't change that much. Sure, I thought I was in love, and I had some dreams about marriage and kids . . . but I didn't really believe in them.' She looked at me. 'I don't know if I believe in them even now, honey, and I've never been so in love in all my life.'

I pulled the car to the side of the road and we kissed and I told her I would change all that. She smiled. 'Don't be angry, Nickie, but Harv said the same thing. And when we were engaged and I did something that really shocked him – I lifted his Diner's Club card from his wallet and used it to buy some things. He thought it was lost and he reported it, so I got picked up in a little clothing store in Ladue. They were going to take me to the police station and I called him. He came down and said it was a mistake and he'd given me the card and forgotten. What would *you* have done, Nickie?'

I said I didn't know. I didn't. 'But I wouldn't have given you up.'

'Neither did he, even though I began to push him to spend more and more on me. I wanted proof that he loved me. At the same time, I wasn't sure I loved *him*. In bed, I wanted to fuck all the time, and he got hung up about it and couldn't deliver as much as he had when I *wasn't* pushing. I put him down, Nickie. I hung him up. And when he made excuses about not seeing me, I called him late at night to check on him, and followed him in my car. I accused him of going out with other girls, even though I was never able to catch him at it.

'One night I bugged him so about not being a real man in bed and going out with frigid Jewish girls who thought he was hot stuff and being too wrapped up in his business and hating me for spending a lousy eighty dollars on his credit card, that he finally lost his temper. He stopped the car and grabbed me by the shoulders and shook me, and then threw me out. But he didn't drive away. I *ran* away. He followed me for blocks, begging me to get back in.

'We had lots of crazy scenes, all my fault. Once we were in a line at a movie house, and I thought he was giving some faggot-looking guy the eye, and it suddenly struck me that maybe *that* was why he didn't want to fuck as much as I did. Later, he went to the men's room and stayed what I felt was a long time, and do you know what I did? I went there and opened the door and yelled in, "Harv, what're you doing with that queer!" He came out of a booth buttoning his pants, his face pale. He said I was crazy.'

I had to laugh. She shook her head and showed her dimple.

'I was always walking away from him, running away from him, making him chase me. I put him through hell ... but I was in love and he wasn't giving me as much as I needed. Not enough words, and not enough sex, and not enough anything. Maybe no one could have given me all I needed, then. Maybe I needed so much, to make up for a whole lifetime of no love, that a dozen men would have failed me.

'Finally, I gave him back his ring. I think he was relieved, but he still wanted to see me. I said no. I began to date around. I met a

71

nice guy at the store, and I met a nice guy through Jerry, Claire's boyfriend, and I had some fun. But no fucking. And I needed fucking. So I began seeing Harv again, because I still cared much for him, and I felt clean with him. We went to bed about once a week, and then about twice a week, and soon he was saying our breakup had been his fault and he loved me and would I take his ring back.

'I was thinking of it. I was getting close to saying yes, when I met you.'

I said, 'I'm glad I got there in time.'

She said, 'Let's stop, Nickie. Let's go to bed.'

We did, and bed was marvellous. We made love for hours, and she cried out that I was the man she'd waited a lifetime for, and I felt she was the girl I'd waited two of her lifetimes for, and we dressed and went walking, holding hands and looking for stars in a cloudy sky.

'I'm still crazy,' she said, as we lay in each other's arms the next morning. 'But maybe you can handle me, Nickie.'

I said I was sure of it. But I wasn't. I was afraid. Because I'd been crazy too, when she'd been away and hadn't called . . .

We arrived at the apartment house at one in the afternoon. We brought Ellie's things up and unpacked and rearranged drawers. I made some lunch and we ate and she returned to the bedroom for more arranging. The phone rang. She was closest and reached for it. I said, 'Wait, if it's my ex-wife, or my mother . . .' She quickly turned away, nodding. But I'd seen her face. And it was a bad face.

But what the hell, it would take time to explain to Louise, and I could *never* explain to dear old Mom, and who wanted to explain in the first place?

It was Harold. 'Something's come up, Nick. You're the one to handle it. A convention in Miama. You like Miami, don't you?'

'I hate Miami and you know it. All those Jews . . .'

'All right with the jokes already. This needs planning. Earn your keep, dammit! October seventh to twelfth. The Fontainebleau. A wholesalers thing, in time to pick up last-minute Christmas items. I'm reserving a booth for us, and I want you there selling.'

'October?' I said. '*October*, and you're screaming *now*?'

'Who knows *when* I can get you. I've been trying for two days . . .'

'Harold, I'm going to hang up. I'll come into the office when I'm ready. You're still making money off my ideas. Please don't forget that I'm still submitting toys and games. And please don't forget the cut I took. And now, Harold, please fuck off.'

72

I hung up. Ellie was nowhere to be seen. I found her in the bathroom, cleaning her skin with an astringent and cotton pads.

'It was my partner.'

'Sure.'

'What do you mean, sure? It *was* my partner. We were arranging the closet and the phone rings and you walk out and act like I *threw* you out.'

She said, 'We were arranging the closet and the phone rings and I reach for it and you get scared. So I'm a secret. So don't push it.'

'You're no secret!' But I felt guilt, and feeling guilt I got angry. 'Just because I want to *gradually* allow a few people, among them my ex-wife . . .'

'You sure you're not banging her once in a while and afraid to lose those goodies?'

I was aghast. I really was. She said, 'Okay, maybe not.'

'And my mother,' I said.

'Your mother's old enough to know you go with girls. Or am I the wrong kind of girl?'

And so we had one hell of an argument, because she was right and I was wrong and I couldn't stop being wrong, not for a while.

We made up in bed, as we always did, and I asked if she would mind saying, 'Mr Leib's wire,' like an answering service, when she answered the phone. 'Just for a while, honey.'

She shrugged. 'I guess it makes sense. How else could I answer the phone and not get into all sorts of bullshit with all sorts of wives and girl friends and relatives? And I'll want to have friends call me from St Louis.'

'You'll want *me* to call you too, when I'm in the city.'

'Jesus *yes*,' she said, mock intense.

I chuckled, but I was upset. 'Listen, honey, it'll only be for a *short* while.'

'Great. But don't start telling people about me until I say okay.'

It was ridiculous, but somehow she'd turned things around and now I was angry at her for *wanting* to remain hidden.

'Let's go out,' I said, trying to escape this buildup to a bad scene. 'Where?'

'A show. I can get tickets for tonight from an agency. Or we can see a movie. Or just drive around Manhattan – I've never really shown it to you.'

She jumped up, her little boobs bouncing 'New York! Wow! C'mon, Nickie!' And she began scurrying for clothing.

Of course, she took about an hour to brush out her hair and put on her eyelashes and change her pantyhose three times – twice for colour and once for a run. And I became irritable and she snapped at me and we didn't go to bed and make up, and I thought. 'How the hell can I *live* with this fool?' and she later told me she'd been thinking 'Christ, how can I ever *satisfy* this character?'

We went out. We had some fun, though she was very quiet and I, in response, became very talky. We saw *Man of LaMancha*. She didn't think much of it. I'd liked it the first time. I agreed with her now. She had a way of cutting through sham and sentimentality; through horseshit. I ended up thinking Cervantes would have hated the musical. She didn't want dinner and we returned home at eleven-thirty.

I was tired and went right to bed. She said she'd be along in a minute. I woke up later, alone, and walked into the living room expecting to see her at the TV. She wasn't there. She wasn't anywhere in the apartment, including the closets. It was two in the morning and she was out alone ... in New York City!

I began to dress, and was almost finished when the doorbell chimed. I let her in. She hurried into the bathroom, dropped her bell bottoms and pantyhose, and peed loudly.

'Ah! Thought I'd bust.'

'Where were you?'

'Walked a little.'

'*This* time of night? It's dangerous.'

'So I found out. This stupid bastard comes up to me ...'

'Look, if you're going to do insane things, spare me the details! You're *not* to go out alone!'

She wiped herself and turned to flush the toilet, presenting me with her bare bottom. 'You're beginning to sound like my mother again.'

When I tried to answer, she pressed the lever and my words were drowned out in the incredible noise our toilet makes ... and keeps making for about thirty seconds. By the time it ended she'd begun using the astringent again. I went to the kitchen and had a beer. She joined me a few minutes later, wearing just the pantyhose and her high-heeled boots. She looked delicious. 'What's to eat?' she asked, and pinched my cheek, *hard*. I yelped. She grinned and that dimple came out. I put down the beer and said, 'You.'

'Me?'

'*You're* to eat.'

'Fine. After food. I'm starving. I get hungry when I'm upset, Nickie. If I get fat, it'll be your fault. And when I get fat, I get

74

blemishes. And then I get miserable. And you'll be miserable too, I promise you.'

I laughed. I helped her find tuna-fish and bread and other food. We laughed together. But she paused to say, 'I'm not kidding.' Still, she ate, and I played with her, and we ended up nude, making it on a chair ... and then into bed to finish with a wildness that had me worrying whether the frame might collapse.

FOUR

I'd known Aaron Hoff for fifteen years, the same amount of time I'd known my partner, Harold, because I found out he was connected with the Mafia, or Mob, or Syndicate, or whatever it was that made it possible for him to have people beaten and killed. Aaron is, or appears to be, a clothing manufacturer, a garment industry cloak-and-suiter, who is big, bald, thirty pounds overweight, rather soft-spoken, and could use a few of his own new suits. Of course, there *is* something about the way he looks at you, something about the way he smiles, something deeply cynical and shark-like. And that's in character for a man in his business, his true business.

It was summer, about five years ago, and for some time I'd been aware that Harold wasn't himself. He'd never been the calmest of men, but what good salesman, what aggressive businessman, is? Still, there was a difference. He seemed to lose weight over a period of about a month, had circles under his eyes, shouted rather more than was necessary, and then asked me to have a drink with him one night after work.

'A drink?' I repeated, staring at him. 'You mean a Pepsi?'

'Don't be funny,' he muttered.

I wasn't being funny. In all the years we'd been together, he'd never drunk anything stronger than Shapiro's Sacramental Wine, and that only at Passover. He ever *looked* the typical teetotaller – tall, thin, with rimless glasses and a perpetually severe expression.

I thought I knew Harold Kraus about as well as anyone could. I'd been going for my Master's in Psychology at Washington Square College when the GI money ran out and I took a part-time job with Gloman Playthings. Harold was an up-and-coming salesman; I was a rubber stamp to back up the seal Mr Gloman liked to affix to his toys: 'Trained psychologists have approved this Gloman Plaything for your child.' I didn't much care for my role in the company, but I was fascinated by the process of toy and game *creation*, and came up with a few ideas of my own. Harold was two years older than me, had a sinus condition which had given him 4-F status during the war and made him, in effect, five years my senior in business, and began taking me to lunch several times a week. He told me I should be fascinated by one other aspect of the toy business – the *profits*. He explained the royalty system which enriched certain inventors who were smart enough to retain rights in their creations, and also the money to be made by manufacturers and salesmen. 'That little checker game you gave to Gloman,' he said over his coffee, 'will make them forty or fifty thousand.'

'That much? It took me fifteen minutes to work it out.'

'Imagine what you could do if you spent a day, or a week, on a game or toy.'

'Well, a week . . . I'll be teaching Psychology shortly.'

'And imagine how much money you'd make if you were not only the inventor, but manufacturer and salesman as well. Or partners with someone who shared those roles with you.'

He then proceeded to tell me how little I'd make as a teacher, or even as a practising psychologist, compared to what I could make in the toy business. And he was a damned good salesman.

We both stayed on at Goman's after I graduated, working several evenings a week on a line of our own. I learned everything about the business, and in two years we formed Kraus & Leib, Inc. Two more years, and we'd put together seven straight sellers and were firmly, and profitably, in business. Nine years later, we were netting close to seventy thousand *each,* and money problems were the furthest thing from my mind the evening Harold and I had our first drink of hard liquor together.

He choked on a martini, but got it down. I sipped mine. He wiped his eyes and looked at his hands and said, 'Listen, I need twenty thousand dollars, fast.'

First I said, 'You're kidding.' Then I asked what he'd been doing with his money. He told me. Solid, dependable businessman, family-man Harold Kraus, who didn't drink, smoked only two cigars a day, went to synagogue on all holidays, honoured his father and mother, spent almost every evening with Harriet and his children, and intensely disapproved of my 'philandering' (his word, not mine), had one little weakness.

He wasn't satisfied with a mere seventy thousand a year. Nor with an eventual hundred thousand. He wanted to be a millionaire, *now*. He had the gambler's dream of quick riches; the stock-market gambler's dream, that it.

'I over-extended myself. I went into highly speculative investments.' He spread his hands. 'A bad break or two, and I had to borrow. I want to pay off before ... the interest becomes too excessive.'

I had an uncle Sol who worked on and off as a waiter, but whose true vocation was playing pinochle in the corner candy store. He too had to borrow. He went to the local loan shark, and then to the family, begging for a way out of the never-ending interest, the constant threats. They helped a few times, and then one night his right arm and leg were broken ... in a fall, he said. Luckily, he died of cancer soon afterward.

So I recognized the signs, but still couldn't quite believe it of Harold, my clever partner. And twenty thousand would either wipe out my savings account, or make me dip into investments at a time when the market was excellent for blue-chips. I asked why he didn't go to the bank.

He'd already borrowed as much as they would give. He was in a deep hole. But he wouldn't sell any portion of the business to me. That he made very clear. When I said he was in a poor bargaining position, he smiled. 'You wouldn't like your new partners, Nick. That I promise you. Ask Aaron tomorrow morning when he comes for his money.'

That's when I learned Aaron's true business. I learned his true nature too, when he came to the office I share with Harold and sat down and looked at me. 'You want Nick to stay?'

Harold nodded.

'I see. He *does* have a stake in this. I hope you got together and raised the money. I warned you, Harold. I don't like doing this to an old friend.'

'I need another six months.'

'The interest will murder you.'

'How much?'

'Five thousand, today. Five thousand more at the end of the six months. And the twenty will still be due.'

Harold looked at me. I was sweating, and I hated him for pressuring me this way. I shook my head. He went pale. The bastard had counted all along on me as his deadline backer. He said, 'Nick ...'

I said, 'You wouldn't have given me part of your million, if you'd made it. Why expect me to absorb your losses, when you didn't make it?'

'I'll pay back in two, three years, at normal bank interest!'

'Meantime I have to take money that belongs to my family ...'

'Your family! You run around with those goddam whores and

leave a fine Jewish wife languishing...' He caught himself then, but it was too late. I'd never been able to think of Harold as a friend; now I stopped thinking of him as a partner. I went to the door.

Aaron stood up. 'If you haven't got it, Harold, I'm sorry. I have to turn in your account to the collection department.'

'Aaron, for God's sake! We went to P.S. Eighty-four together! We played Johnny-on-the-Pony and Ringaleaveo!' I'd paused, and Aaron had paused, and Harold smiled hopefully. 'Ringaleaveo, caught-caught-caught?'

'*Shit*,' Aaron said with cold disgust. 'You insisted on taking the money. I didn't want to lend it. Now you're crying ... the same fucking baby you were as a kid.' He came to the door. I looked at his face. The shark's smile flickered at me. 'They'll be satisfied with his half of the business, Nick. They won't interfere with you. I've told them who has the ideas, who'll make them the money. And if you want to expand...'

Harold said, 'Wait. I'm selling Nick half my equity. He'll give me the twenty thousand...'

'Twenty-five. The new interest began today.'

Harold leaped up. 'You bloodsucking...'

'I don't make the rules. And they're not really rules; just traps for *schmucks* like you. You want out, give me twenty-five thousand, *now*.'

He began to move past me. I said, 'I'll write the cheque. I'll cover it by noon tomorrow.'

Aaron shrugged. He looked disappointed in me. Harold sank back into his chair, sighing. Then he said, 'A *quarter* of my equity is worth over two hundred thousand, Nick. We'll pro-rate...'

I told him it was a loan, and wrote the cheque, and handed it to Aaron. He no longer looked disappointed. He said, 'True friendship,' and laughed. But he added, '*Offen meir gesugt*.' Let it happen to me.

I walked out. Aaron joined me at the elevators. He asked if I was free for lunch. I said, 'I'm meeting one of those goddam whores.'

He laughed. 'Listen, you ever need something done, look me up. You're a *mench*.'

'You mean, if I need money...?'

He laughed again. 'I mean if you want that creep partner of yours killed. We don't do it for everyone. Everyone's not dependable.'

I didn't have time to ask if he was joking. The elevator came. We parted on the street. I had bank accounts to close and stock to sell.

Harold went right back to playing the market ... and recouped all his losses. He paid me off in nine months, with six per cent interest, and then berated me for 'torturing' him the day Aaron came to the office. He said he was considering going full-time into the market and that it would serve me right if he sold his equity to the mob. I almost hit him. And when Aaron called, for about the fifth time, to suggest lunch, I accepted. I asked about the mob.

'No mob, Nick. Just a group of investors with a collection arm to back them. One of the services is disciplining people like Harold, and a spin-off of this discipline...'

'All right. I'm sorry I asked.'

He smiled. 'You know, when Harold and I were playing Johnny-on-the-Pony, I was already working for them. It takes a long time to get in, but it's worth it. I make a lot more money than my garment factory can earn, and something else.' He looked at me. 'Guess the something else.'

'Power.'

'Yes, but make it real.'

'I could beat the shit out of you in any kind of fight, couldn't I, Aaron?'

He nodded, and his smile grew. 'You got the muscle and the *mishigas, boychick.*'

'But I know what you are, and I wouldn't dare.'

'That's it.' He leaned forward. 'It's a beautiful feeling, Nick. When I wanted a divorce from that bitch Rose, I got it, *snap*, like that. And no alimony. Because she knew what I could do.' He lit a cigar. 'You're having trouble getting a divorce, right? Well, our fee of two thousand is peanuts. Your property settlement will run twenty, thirty times that, not to say your alimony...'

I said I had to go. He said of course, and picked up the cheque. Waiting for his change, he said, 'Just so long as it isn't a public figure, you can contact me for any sort of job, any time. A little muscle, that's called doing a quarter. A month in the hospital, that's a half. And a zero...' He spread his hands. '*Yisgadal vi yisga-dash...*' He laughed with such gusto, I found myself smiling.

What's all this got to do with Ellie and me? I wouldn't have thought anything ... except that a part of me had remembered Aaron and that part emerged sometime after we'd settled down together at the end of May.

Settled down is no way to put it. We never settled down. That was the trouble. We had wildness and excitement in bed, and wildness and excitement out of bed. Except that out of bed wildness and excitement wasn't always a good thing.

79

The third day of her stay, Ellie made breakfast; eggs and bacon and toast and coffee. Not bad. We talked and ate and I stroked her hand, and said I had to go to the office. She said, 'Oh.' I said, 'Well, I have to work once in a while,' and laughed. She didn't laugh.

I got dressed and she wandered in and watched me. I said, 'I'll bring you a surprise.'

'How about if I go with you?'

I began to tighten up. 'Well, sure, but what will you do while I spend six hours in the office? You'll be alone...'

'I could shop. I need some clothes...'

'Clothes? You need more clothes!'

'But a lot is out of style, and a lot is from my fat period and doesn't fit me. I hear Saks is the greatest. And Bonwit Teller...'

'Yeah.' I knotted my tie.

She turned and stormed out of the room. The bathroom door slammed.

I knew I should give in. But I also knew she'd want to come up to the office, see the shop, meet Harold and the staff. I wasn't ready for that. Or *she* wasn't ready. She didn't really *speak* well enough; not for a friend of Nick Leib's.

Friend? She was *living* with me. If I introduced her, I couldn't just say, 'A friend of mine, Ellie McBaren.' I'd have to say ... what? My fiancée, I guess.

I could call her Mrs Leib in motels and hotels, but in New York, among the people who knew me? No, not yet.

Maybe never.

Because she might not be here long enough...

I wanted to get out. It was time for a day in the city, on my own. She should clean up the apartment. The breakfast dishes hadn't yet been done. And she'd left some clothing from two nights ago on the bedroom chair. And the place was a lot sloppier than when I'd lived here alone – books out of the case, and magazines and newspapers on the couch and coffee table. I was neat. I never bothered with a cleaning lady; did the job myself and enjoyed the activities, the mindless activity.

I opened the closet to get my jacket, and saw my tennis rackets – the old Wilson and the steel one. Ellie would play with me. And that gave me an idea.

I tried the bathroom door. Locked. I said, 'Ellie?'

'Okay. Goodbye. Have a nice day.'

'Honey, open up. I want a kiss.'

She opened the door. She was using that goddam astringent again, and it didn't seem to be doing the job, because she'd come up with a new crop of blemishes, if little ones, on her forehead and chin. She turned quickly away. 'They run in my family,' she said. 'I told you what happens when I eat too much.'

'You haven't been...'

'I'm up two pounds. You're always pushing me to eat, a goddam Jewish momma.'

'Make that papa.'

'No, *momma*. A goddam clean-it-up old lady.'

'Take it easy.'

She was looking in the medicine chest mirror, her expression as sullen as I'd ever seen it.

'Why don't you take my wooden racket, it's light enough for you, and go down to the tennis courts?' We had four courts in a playground area behind the house.

'And what'll I do, shove the handle up my ass?'

I was getting angry, but I gave her the required laugh. 'Practise serves. Find a game. There's always someone playing this time of the year. Or work out against a handball court.'

She turned. 'You nuts? I never played tennis in my life.'

'Oh, well...'

'You should have found out about these *important* things before you asked me here.'

'Not important at all. I'll teach you myself, starting tomorrow. We'll go down early...'

'Fine. Great. Now go make toys and let me alone.'

'Dammit, stop *bitching*!'

She sneered at me. 'Uh-oh, baby, gonna get a spanking?'

I hated her guts, for one second. Then I took a deep breath and said, 'Put the apartment in shape. Go out on the terrace and sunbathe – the sun hits it about two-thirty, three. Read. When I come back, we'll go out to dinner.'

'And I'll gain two more pounds. Anyway, I'm not a goddam maid.'

'Don't wives keep house?'

'I'm not a wife either. I'm a big secret. Listen, how long do you plan to keep me as your bed warmer? I mean, I should know when I'll have to go home and get another job.'

I turned away. There was no reasoning with her. And she was right. I *should* tell her when she was going home. Soon. We had no way of living together.

I was at the door when she said, 'Nickie,' and came to me and touched my face and whispered, 'I'm sorry. Please give me time to

81

get used to ... well, being alone, except for you.'

My heart melted. I put my arms around her. She nestled against me. We held each other. I kissed her head and said, 'You won't be alone any more, little girl.'

She looked up at me, smiling, that full lower lip pushing out. I kissed it.

'When do I meet Seth?'

I'd spoken to him yesterday and considered putting Ellie on the phone, but Louise had been there and I didn't want to make waves. I had a very good relationship with Louise, just as long as she didn't know about my dates. And if she found out I was *living* with a girl, and such a young girl ... well, she could make it tough for me with Seth. I'd had to give up all visiting rights in order to get the divorce. She'd promised to be 'fair', and I'd trusted her, but she could turn it around, legally, if she wanted to.

Once, when we'd run into each other in the city and I was with Karen Oster, who is a very cool twenty-three-year-old secretary with a Bennington education and a father who has a seat on the stock exchange, well, I wasn't welcome in Teaneck for a good month.

But Seth could keep a secret, and even though he'd never met any of my dates, I felt sure he would like Ellie. She was so much a kid herself! And I couldn't see her not liking him. If the three of us could get away together, go up to the cottage ...

That was something else for Ellie – the cottage. I'd bought it the summer after the divorce, and used it winters too, ice-skating on the lake, bringing various chicks up there, bringing Seth up for occasional weekends. But I hadn't been there since meeting Ellie, now for several months before. I'd been thinking of selling it, but maybe now ...

I said, 'Tomorrow's Friday. Tomorrow you meet Seth. I'll pick him up after school, and if his mother says all right, we'll drive to the cottage for the weekend. It's beautiful in spring ...'

She jumped up and down, just as Seth would have. 'Oh, Nickie, *Nickie*!'

We kissed and she was all over me and I thought I'd end up in bed again, but then she broke away and straightened my tie and smoothed my jacket and said, 'Get going. I'll have a surprise for *you* when you come home.'

I left, and I felt fantastic! So what if we had an occasional quarrel? We'd work them out, once I got her into the Saturday School division of Fairleigh Dickenson. They had a summer session beginning in July. Until then, she could use a grammar work book; maybe one for maths too. And she'd adjust to housework and I'd get back to creating toys and we'd read and see shows and travel and life would be one great big beautiful orgasm!

And yet, I called Ledya, my stacked actress and my heaviest date ... until Ellie had come along. I used the phone in the garage, and she said, 'Well, what's been happening, *Mister* Leib? You sounded so remote on the phone Tuesday.'

Ellie had been in the kitchen and I'd taken the call in the bedroom, and felt guilty.

'Tell you all about it at lunch. Gold Coin, one o'clock okay?'

But I didn't tell her *all* about it. I told her something about it, and the direction of that somthing was a lie. 'I have a girl living with me.' (Not, 'I'm living with a girl.') 'But only for a limited time. You see, she was attacked by a Negro ...' (Ledya had an unhealthy fear of blacks.) 'I know her boss through business contacts and I'd met her while in St Louis and when he called me ... what the hell, so we're serving each other's need for a little while.'

'Are you trying to tell me you're giving therapy to a rape victim?'

I chuckled. 'I'm not denying she's a damned attractive girl, but certainly nothing for the long haul. Marriage is not envisioned by yours truly.'

'I'm sure *she* doesn't know that.'

I chuckled again, but it wasn't going as well as I'd thought it would. 'You know how these things are.'

'No, tell me.'

I took her hand. She tugged it, but not too hard. 'Really, Nick, I'm surprised at you. Either you've met a girl you love, or you're playing a very bad scene.'

'Neither, dear. But let's not go into it right now. Be patient with me. Don't write me off. I'm sure you're not suffering from lack of male attention.'

She smiled. I smiled. We'd had a few sweet evenings and we'd both had others in our lives and she'd had a heavy romance which was only now breaking up. So no sweat. She was dark and sultry and big-chested and doing a daytime serial on CBS and angling for better things in New York and on the West Coast. She liked me. I liked her. We could have become something solid ... except that despite her beauty, despite a good education and a good career and the fact that I could take her anywhere and introduce her to anyone with pride, I just didn't flip out, didn't feel that incredible excitement and pleasure that I did with Ellie.

She asked me to come back to her apartment and look over her new portfolio. 'I took your advice, Nicholas. I've got a few nude shots, for specialized interviews. I'd like your opinion.' Her eyes were promising, and I understood she was competing with the girl in *my* apartment. I could make a damned good thing out of this. I had experience enough in extra-marital affairs to keep Ledya neatly on the side – of Ellie.

'Can't, baby. Haven't worked in so long I'm being read out of the firm.'

'Thought you didn't *have* to work, rich man?'

'Only every so often. Today is every-so-often day.'

I didn't want her. Good deal or not, expert lover or not, I didn't want Ledya Torens. It was as simple as that. There was only one girl I wanted that way – Ellie.

By the time four o'clock rolled around, I was dying to get away from Harold and his production figures and his complaints and his foolish insistence that it took two of us to sit and count the money we were making. It didn't. I was more convinced than ever that I was a free man. Still, I decided to stay on as late as he would, and so I called the apartment to say it would be six or six-thirty before I'd be home. I got a surprise. The line was busy. Someone had probably called me. I hoped it wasn't Mom.

I waited five minutes, long enough for Ellie to take a message, and dialed again. Still busy.

It remained busy for thirty-five minutes. When she finally answered, she said, 'Mr Leib's wire,' and I said, 'What a lovely voice you have, answering-service lady,' and she said, somewhat subdued, 'Hi, Nickie.'

I was upset, and didn't know why, and hid it.

Maybe I did know why. She didn't know anyone in New York. She'd been talking for at least thirty-five minutes and probably longer. If she'd been speaking to St Louis and had done the calling, what a nice fat phone bill I'd get! And *who* was she speaking to?

'What've you been doing?' I asked, keeping it hap-hap-happy.

'It's a surprise. You'll see.'

'Anyone call?'

'Your mother. I made like the answering service and she said to say she'd called. She sounds sweet.'

Sweet was just the word for Mother. But that didn't concern me at the moment. 'Anyone else?'

'No. When're you coming home?'

She wasn't going to tell me. Could it have been the *circuit* that was busy?

'About six-thirty.'

'Got my surprise yet?'

'Not yet.'

'Bet I know what it is.'

'Bet you don't.'

'A credit card. Or a charge plate to Saks.'

'*What*?'

She laughed. 'Just kidding.'

'What about my surprise?' I asked.

'Almost ready. Everything okay about Seth tomorrow?'

I'd forgotten. 'Yes. Have to go now.' I called Teaneck and was lucky. 'He'll be delighted,' Louise said. 'He's missed you. I'm surprised you didn't come over as soon as you returned from your trip.'

We chatted a while, and she told me Denise was going to be home the second week in June, and I wondered how my daughter would take Ellie. Not well, I imagined. Denise didn't approve of my dating anyone under forty. Make that fifty.

I picked up a bouquet of roses, much like the one I'd bought in St Louis, and went home. I wanted to see what her surprise was, and have dinner, and then have a night of love ... before we spent those two nights with Seth. The cottage was just too small for fucking with a kid a room away.

Her surprise was evident as soon as I walked into the apartment, and if it hadn't been for that busy signal, I'd have reacted with lots of gush. As it was, she squealed over the flowers, and I said, 'You forgot the patio doors,' instead of saying the place sparkled, which it did. She stared at me. 'What's wrong?'

'Nothing.' And seeing her face go bleak, I decided to gush after all. 'Hey, the place is really something! How many maids did you hire?'

She smiled a little, holding her roses like a bride. 'You *sure* nothing's wrong?'

'You tell me.'

She turned away. 'Everything's great.'

'Yeah, copasetic.'

'What?'

I had to explain the old jive term for perfect.

'Copasetic,' she said, and giggled. 'Wow.'

She had still another surprise. We weren't going to eat out, or broil a steak, or open a can of tuna, as usual. She'd been cooking half the day. She'd made a chicken and chile dish from a recipe in my *Gourmet Cookbook* ... and it was really great. She watched with delight as I ate more than my share and I poured plenty of wine and we kissed a few times, and then she said, 'Honey, something's wrong, I can feel it, tell me.'

85

She wouldn't push that way if she had a guilty conscience, would she? So that busy signal was either a circuit, or an uncoming call, or a collect call . . .

Why wouldn't she mention an incoming call or a collect call, say to her mother (impossible!) or to Gina (not too probable). But if it were from or to Harv Cohen . . .

'Harold bugged me,' I said. 'Let's forget it.'

We put the dishes in the washer together, and I helped her clean the pots, and we finished the bottle of wine. I began to kiss her, touch her . . . but she said she hadn't been out all day and wanted a breath of air.

We walked toward the East River and it was clear and mild, and even though it grew rapidly dark it was still too early for the drunks and degenerates and muggers to be out in full force. (I had my knife in my pocket anyway.) We held hands and she bumped me with her rear and I looked around and murmured, 'Not on the street.' She said I was too 'organized' and I said it wasn't that, it was fear of attracting sex nuts. She shook her head. 'The way you think!' I reminded her that she'd been raped not too long ago. She changed the subject; asked me why I took so many vitamins after each meal (about twenty-five a day). I went into my lecture about how chemical fertilizers had robbed our foods of much nutritional value and how modern diets lacked balance and I suggested she read *Food Facts and Fallacies* which was in my bookcase. She said, 'You're a nut you know that? A real nut. Are you going to make me a nut too, I hope?' And she turned and grabbed me and we kissed and she squeezed my rear, saying 'Tummy!' I watched the street through slitted eyes, because her dress was mini and she was the most beautiful girl in the world and this was New York where beautiful girls were regularly drawn and quartered.

We went back to the apartment. I relaxed and she sat on my lap and we watched television. A news special came on about the Middle East. I wanted to see it. She said, 'All Jews get uptight about Israel.' I said, 'Is that what Harv told you?' and almost added, 'today'. She said, 'No, he claimed he was cool about it, but he wasn't'. He hated it when I dated Ahmed . . .' She stopped.

'You never told me about Ahmed.'

'Not important. Like the other guys I dated. Once or twice.' And she really turned on the sex. But I was upright again, and insisted on seeing the TV special.

She left the living room. I thought she might be angry. But the show was excellent and I stayed put. She returned in ten minutes, wearing her black boots and pantyhose and nothing else. Her little boobs bounced tautly as she strutted back and forth before the TV set, and her ass – she was right; she *had* gained weight, and just where I liked it – her ass rolled beautifully. And still I tried to resist, even though I was beginning to laugh and beginning to want her. She went to the armchair and kneeled in it head down and ass up, and rolled her hips and said, conversationally, 'Ahmed said most Arabs like ass-fucking. He would beg me to do this, and then he would beg me to let him up my ass ...' I was across the room and had cracked that ass before she could get away. It hurt my hand, so I knew it had hurt her ... but even though she screeched, she turned her head and grinned at me. 'You believe it, don't you?' Later, in bed, she whispered, 'Is it sick, liking it this much? I feel it's all that matters, you and me, doing it. I never felt that way before. I must be turning nympho.'

And I was turning satyr. And it *was* all that mattered.

'I never really fucked before, Nickie. I never knew *how*. Now I know.'

I didn't say it, but the same was true of me.

The next day I gave her a tennis lesson. With the kids at school, and the weather turned cloudy, there were only a few women with baby carriages in the recreation area. She was impatient with handgrips and foot positions, even though I told her I'd paid plenty for a professional to give me just that instruction. She wanted to get right out on the court. So I sizzled the ball past her a dozen times instead of playing lob-it-over-to-baby. She got mad and came around the net and said, 'You mother! You're just getting even because I won't fuck around with the handball court. And I need sneakers and my own racket and an outfit.'

She looked so cute in tight, washed-out Levis and snug white sweater that I wanted to hug her. Instead I said, 'You get sneakers today. You get your own racket and an *outfit* – that's your favourite word, isn't it? – you get them only after you learn the rudiments of forehand, backhand, and service.'

'Rudiments, you bastard, what's that?'

'What are *they*,' I corrected in prissy schoolteacher fashion, and then had to duck as she actually swung the racket at my head. She was white with rage, and I was choking with laughter. After a second swing, at my butt this time, she cracked a little smile, which grew as I danced around her in my white trousers and terry-cloth shirt, doing exaggerated backhands and forehands. Finally, I grabbed her from behind and cupped a breast and began nibbling on her neck. She said, 'If you want to eat me, do it right.' I let her go and she turned to me. Her hair was tied into twin ponytails and her face was glowing and that dimple was showing ... and I said, 'I love you.'

Her smile went away. I said, 'Sometimes.' She nodded and put her hand on my chest. We stood there a while, and across the concrete deck a woman with a child in her arms looked at us and smiled. We went up to the apartment and changed and went out to buy tennis shoes. We had an early lunch at the little German place on Third Avenue. The skies cleared and we walked in the sun and held hands. We looked in shop windows. I didn't have much to say. She talked about clothing and how her sister Gina always shopped for bargains and got junk and how she always shopped for top quality and made out better in the long run. It was all nothing-talk, and yet, so help me, it interested me more than anything I'd heard in years. When she stopped, I asked questions to make her go on.

At a butcher shop, we went in for steaks and wandered around, checking prices. I thought this place, like most east-side Manhattan food stores, was exorbitant, and suggested we wait until we drove upstate. 'There's a supermarket near the cottage...'

She was looking at a display, and in preoccupied fashion said, 'Harv knows quality. I mean, he was *born* knowing it, not like us. He used to make steaks up at my place, or on picnics, and I never once had a bad one with him. He's that way in everything. Man, he would buy ...' She stopped then, having glanced up and, I guess, seen something in my face. She said, 'I'm sorry, honey.' I said, 'What for? Just as long as you're here with me, talking about him, instead of with him, talking about what a great guy *I* used to be.'

She found that 'cute' and hugged my arm.

We returned to the apartment. I wanted to make love, but when she found out we were picking Seth up at five, she grew frantic 'No! It's after three and we have to leave at four-thirty and I need at least that long to get ready!'

Actually she took *two* hours to make herself presentable for Seth, showering, and working on her hair and face, and selecting her clothing. It took half an hour alone to choose what she would wear, and if I hadn't insisted we leave at five-ten, she'd have changed a *fourth* time.

Teaneck is about fifteen minutes from the George Washington Bridge, and the bridge is less than fifteen minutes from my apartment, this timed in non-rush-hour traffic. But five to six o'clock is *the* rush hour on the F.D.R. Drive, and so we inched along and she said, 'Fine thing. First time I meet him and we're late,' and she fussed with her hair in the visor mirror and fumed and muttered, 'Fucking cars!'

I found myself laughing, and she glared at me and asked, 'What's so funny?' I didn't know. Half an hour later, crossing the bridge, I decided I *did* know. Nothing was funny. I was happy ... because she was so excited about meeting my twelve-year-old son; because she considered it so important; which meant *I* was important.

Louis had said she'd be out, so when we parked on the quiet, tree-shaded street I expected Ellie would come in with me. But she shook her head. She looked at the house, a good-sized English Tudor type, and murmured, 'No, I'll wait here. Go on, Nickie.'

I was relieved. This house was the past and full of memories and not all of them were bad. It was my old life, and Ellie was my new ... and I wasn't secure in my new, didn't know whether it was a life, a game, or a long fuck. But I said, 'Why? No one's home but Seth.'

She shook her head. 'It's where you lived with someone else. It makes me feel, well, *funny*.'

I kissed her. She clung to me. She whispered, 'In case I don't get the chance to prove it for a few days, I love you, Nickie.' I kissed her again. 'Sometimes,' she added.

Seth opened the door before I could get there. He's a slender, muscular boy (muscular because of the workouts we did together with weights and the long runs we took together, this from the time he was *six*) with a heavy shock of pale brown hair that goes to blond in summer sun, a lean, wry face that is absolutely beautiful when he grins, and a pair of grey eyes that see everything and enjoy most of what they see. A happy kid, generally, and successful in much he does.

I said, 'Hey, man, you saw me coming, huh?' and kissed him.

He said, 'And I saw you with Ellie in the car,' and laughed.

'Aha, a *voyeur*.'

'That's a peeping-Tom, Dad?' He laughed again, with delight at my surprise.

We went and got his bag. I checked the back door, and when we walked out the front I made sure that too was locked. The good homeowner, except that Louise now owned this home. I'd loved it – the house itself. Until Ellie, I'd missed living in it.

We got to the car, and Ellie leaned over and opened the door. She said, 'Hi! Seth, 'Hi,' very quietly, very shyly ... but his eyes did a fast flicker before dropping, the little skin merchant! Ellie's eyebrows went up and down and her grin was simply marvellous to see. 'Oh wow,' she said, and she looked at me and I knew she really dug my son. I put the bag in back and said, 'You two will have to wait until I'm a lot older, and blinder.' Seth laughed and Ellie said, 'Not *much* older, Seth. Let's see . . . when you're eighteen, I'll only be twenty-six. Right?'

He said, 'Right.' I said, 'Well, that gives me six good years.' Ellie murmured, as if under her breath, but both Seth and I were meant to hear it, 'When he's *fifteen*, I'll only be twenty-three. Why wait longer?'

Seth giggled. I pushed the front seat forward and he climbed in back, still giggling. Ellie said, 'How come *you're* not laughing, Nickie?' I got behind the wheel and said, 'I'm too old to laugh.' She really exploded then, and Seth joined her, and damned if I thought it was that funny. Then she grabbed me and kissed me a dozen times and turned to Seth and said, 'He's great, isn't he?' and Seth – I could see him in the rear-view mirror – was nodding and looking the way he looked when he's having a real good time.

We all had a good time, driving up to the cottage along the Palisades Interstate, stopping at the Rockefeller Lookout for a beautiful view of Manhattan in twilight. Seth is usually quiet with strangers, but he wasn't with Ellie. Back in the car, he answered questions about school ('Well, I can live through it, but *like* it?' and I had to assure her that his grades were quite good), and about friends ('Larry's my best friend, but I've got others and I change best-friends sometimes'), and finally about girl-friends ('I don't really have any, yet, but I guess soon . . .'). He let her hold his hand when we went into the supermarket in Hopewell Junction, and once he said something that made her hug him. She later told me it was, 'I never saw Dad so happy before.' When we got to the cottage, they left me to carry in the luggage and food and raced to the lake-front, two kids, one about three inches taller than the other . . . and Seth beat her by plenty. Two kids, skimming stones over the water and picking the late-May crop of wild flowers.

That was the beginning of the best weekend of my life. I'm tempted to say, the best summer of my life, but the weekend was undiluted by anything negative, and the summer was *full* of negatives.

That first night, Seth and I slept in the big bed and Ellie slept on the convertible couch in the living room. We went running at James Baird State Park the next morning; Seth and I, that is, while Ellie sat on the grass and read a novel she'd taken from the pile of softcover books in my little study. We passed her, coming up the long hill toward the parking lot, and she was studiously avoiding the glances of two young guys who had plumped themselves down a short distance away. I called to her, raising my arm, and Seth waved, and she waved back and threw kisses at us. When we returned, Seth fighting a stitch in his side and I feeling winded after my long layoff while travelling and getting settled with Ellie, the guys were gone.

We fell down beside her and fought for breath and she said, 'Why do you run? I mean, I can see games and swimming and skating and fun things, but what's the fun in running?' Seth said, 'Don't ask me. Ask him.' He was grouchy, as he sometimes is after a run, and I rubbed his head and he pulled away and I shrugged and Ellie said, 'Uh-oh, did I ask the wrong question?' I said, 'Maybe, for Seth. I run because it keeps me in shape better than tennis or swimming or anything else, and I can do it alone.' Seth said, 'Yeah, so why do *I* have to run?' I said, 'You know. To build up your physique. To build your wind. To help you in every other sport, since all depend upon wind, endurance, stamina. Also, as I've explained a hundred times...' He finished it for me, losing some of his irritation, 'Yeah, to give me a varsity sport in high school, in case I don't make it in any of the others. To help me get a college scholarship.'

Ellie then played peacemaker. 'That's good thinking. Track is important in college sports. You'll really have an edge, Seth.' She leaned into me and mock-examined my face. 'As for your father, he isn't quite as broken down as he might be. Running might be why.' Seth laughed. I grabbed her and we rolled around on the grass, and I kissed her. She whispered, 'Nick, Seth's watching!' I let her go. But Seth was smiling, and a few minutes later he got up and wandered away. Ellie said, 'He's giving us some time alone! I could eat him up alive! I feel I've known him all my life, like you.' We kissed, seriously this time, and the hunger rose in me and her hand stroked my neck and her crotch moved into mine. Then she said something I remember, but not with pleasure. 'I know why you run and take vitamins and make love to young chicks. You want to live forever, Mr Leib. And I bet you do.'

We went back to the cottage and made steaks on the hibatchi outside. Ellie was surprised when I gave Seth a beer, and I explained that he loved the stuff and I saw nothing wrong in his drinking a bottle every so often. We ate a lot, and drank a lot, beer and some Burgundy I kept in a closet. Then we dozed for a few hours in beach chairs. When I awoke, Seth was down at the lake, fiddling around with the aluminium rowboat. I got up and Ellie stirred at the noise I made. She was wearing a pair of blue tie-dye shorts and a matching halter. I glanced at Seth and he was looking at the boat, and I bent and put my hands between her legs, stroking ᴜ.ose sunwarmed thighs. She opened her eyes and said, instantly, 'Where's Seth?' I jerked my head and she raised herself up a little and looked, and then grabbed me through my shorts and kissed me with open mouth. God, I wanted her! But I stepped back and walked slowly to the lake, to let myself cool down and *go* down.

'Dad, is my fishing rod still in the furnace room?'

We returned to the cottage and around the back to the little furnace-utility-storage room. His rod and hooks were there, where we'd left them last fall, on the floor near the oars. The boat I left out all year, the solid aluminium basically untouched by two winters.

We all went out on the lake, even though three was a tight fit for the little boat. Seth crouched in the prow, looking out at the lake. I sat with my back to him, rowing. Ellie sat facing me, legs spread wide to allow my knees room between. I looked at her, at her face and her thighs and her crotch. She sang softly, 'Things are looking up, up, up,' and I sighed and nodded and was glad Seth couldn't come around to face *me*.

We toured the lake. We went around the bend to the beach area, not yet open. Seth trailed his line in the water, got two bites and lost both. He said, 'It's better in near shore.' I had an idea. We went back to the natural docking area near the cottage and I helped Ellie out and tied the fifteen-foot anchor line to the clump of white birch at the shore-line. 'Fish for a while,' I said. 'Ellie and I will clean up.'

He was already casting near the lily pads, hoping for one of the big-mouth bass. Ellie and I went to the cottage and looked out the picture window facing the lake. He had drifted to the end of his line, behind the covering screen of shoreline vegation. I grabbed her. We kissed and went to the bedroom. 'But if he comes in,' she whispered as I pulled down her halter and pressed my mouth to her damp breasts.

I went to the screen door and locked it. When I returned, she was lying on her stomach, nude, pretending sleep. She didn't pretend for long. 'Now how did Ahmed like it?' I grunted. She said, '*Ouch!* You've got to use Vaseline!' I had other goals in mind. So did she, and after a while she said, 'Honey, I want to see your face.' She turned over and we pressed together and kissed. She said she loved me and I said I loved her, and we made love, quickly, because Seth might return at any moment.

He didn't come back for more than an hour, and brought four sunfish with him. He showed Ellie how he scraped them and breaded them in corn-meal and fried them in butter. We each had two mouthfuls.

We ate dinner out at the steak house near Poughkeepsie and went to the Fishkill drive-in movie. They were showing *Paint Your Wagon* and Seth conked out in the back seat. Ellie and I held hands and kissed a few times. I was falling very heavily then. I still didn't admit it, but I'd spoken the words twice today, and I'd *felt* even more . . . at least here at the cottage, with only my child as witness.

Seth woke up during the drive back to the cottage. He was quiet when I said, 'Into the sack, right?' and Ellie said, 'That couch is the most comfortable convertible I've ever used,' and I figured he was groggy. But a little while later, when I came into the bathroom to check whether he'd brushed his teeth, he said very low, 'Dad, I want to sleep on the couch.'

'Why?'

'You know.'

'Maybe. But you'll have to tell me.'

'Well, Ellie's not just *visiting* you. And I'll bet she doesn't sleep on any couch at your apartment. And I won't come here any more if I have to sleep with you and she has to sleep on the couch. I mean it. It's *dumb*.'

I touched his head. 'Okay.' I tried to remember how much I'd known at twelve and thirteen, and it seemed just about everything.

I told Ellie as she was taking a nightgown from her bag. She was first embarrassed, and then touched. She went to the living room, where Seth was already in bed. I stood in the doorway as she bent over him and said, 'Goodnight, honey.' He said, 'Goodnight, Ellie.' She kissed him, and he kissed her back without hesitation, which is unusual for him. She said, I like you almost as much as I like your father, and I've only known you one day. Wait until I know you *two* days!' He laughed. She was turning away when he said, 'Me too.' She went out, smiling. I kissed him goodnight and he said, 'She's terrific, Dad. Are you going to marry her?'

'Well, it's too soon . . .'

He waited.

'We'll see.'

I put out all the lights and closed the bedroom door and got into bed. Ellie had discarded the nightgown for her usual sleeping attire – birthday-suit. I took her in my arms and she put her mouth to my chest. When she felt me coming up, she murmured, 'Nickie, I don't want him to hear.' I agreed, but it wouldn't go away and a few minutes later she began touching it and then she went down on me . . . but I wanted to be in her. The beautiful day and the beautiful

93

love – love that included Seth and seemed multiplied by him, geo-metrically and impossibly – made it necessary for me to be in her. I told her, and drew her up, and she said, 'Yes, Nickie, Nickie' ... And then, 'But *quiet*.'

At first I simply put it in her and we both sighed, we both moaned. But then I grew more violent and we took off, still trying to keep it quiet. When it was over, she was angry at me, blamed me for turning her on. Her anger lasted about a minute, after which she hugged me and said, 'Hell, he knows, he's too damned smart to fool, he'll be the world's greatest lover some day' ... She paused, and I knew what she wanted to say because of her evil little grin and her unwillingness to speak when she was usually willing to say just about anything.

'And some day *you* want to make him.'

She nodded. 'Oh, I won't of course ... but I'd *like* to! It would be like having *your* cherry!'

She was getting to me, and I mean exciting me again. Somehow, the more she went for Seth, the more I went for her.

So we had happiness. And there was more of it when we returned home on Sunday night. The good feeling carried over for almost two weeks. Then we quarrelled about the grammar and math workbooks that we'd bought at Brentano's. She just wasn't using them, even though we'd discussed her entering summer session at the Saturday School. Why that particular school? It didn't require any-thing but a high school diploma, no averages considered, and it had classes only Friday night and Saturday, allowing her to escape heavy classroom attendance, which she hated, and do most of her work at home. And even though it was a two-year junior college, it fed directly into Fairleigh Dickenson University, of which it was a part. So Ellie could go to college and eventually get a BA; she could acquire some polish and some knowledge and it was what we both wanted.

Except that she resisted the grammar and maths workbooks, which were necessary preparations to her entering any area of higher education. She really had no idea of grammar at all, and less of maths, and both English Composition and Algebra were given in the freshman year. Without a little headstart, she was bound to flunk out.

I don't know. Maybe I wasn't too convincing about having her matriculate that summer. Maybe the same reason I hadn't been able to answer Seth's question about marriage held true for attacking her reticence with insults and anger rather than being understanding and *leading* her, *gentling* her, into studying. Maybe I didn't really want her to study, to grow, to get to where I could have less reason for not considering her wife material.

Because other things had shown up, for one, a discarded envelope with Harv Cohen's name and address in the waste basket near my desk. She said, 'I *began* to write to him, then figured I had nothing to say.' She wouldn't meet my eyes and I wasn't convinced.

'But why write him at all?'

'Because he's my friend. I don't have any friends here. I don't have anyone but you.'

'And Seth.'

'All right. You and Seth.' She was sullen. 'Still, I miss my friends. I'd like to go home.'

'What do you mean?'

She ran to me then – we were on opposite sides of the living room – and hugged me and said, 'Just for a visit, honey. Please.'

'Okay.'

She squealed.

'I'll go with you.'

She went back to her chair.

'What's wrong? Why can't I go with you?'

She was silent a moment, and by the time she answered I'd begun to suspect her.

'I only want a week to see my family and friends. I want to go around on my own . . .'

'And if we were married?'

'We'll never be married. You'll want me to get a college education and then a masters and then who-knows-what. It'll always be something. I'm not good enough as I am.' She went to the bathroom and shut the door.

I tried to smooth that incident over with a gift; a tennis 'outfit' from Bloomingdale's. It seemed to work, but she still hadn't done more than five pages in the grammar book and only half of the first work-page in the maths, and it led to more irritations and arguments. As for her tennis, it didn't improve much because she did so little work on style, but at least we had some fun on the courts. I couldn't, however, get a real game while fooling around with her.

I had lunch with Ledya, and while she still didn't look nearly as good as Ellie to me, she *sounded* a hell of a lot better. This time I went to her apartment with her and we petted a bit and she got me out of my pants and I began to feel pretty damned hot. But I also began to feel pretty damned uptight, because it was still so much less than what I felt with Ellie, and why bother, and what I wanted from Ledya was some conversation and to continue knowing her so that when, or if, Ellie and I broke up...

Ledya had been doing most of the work, stroking me and rubbing against me, and had she kept it up we'd probably have made it. But she backed off, obviously upset, and when I tried to act ignorant of the cause – my lack of true response – and asked her why, she said she had an appointment and couldn't do the whole bit.

I was glad of the out. I said, 'Some other time, honey,' and kissed her and made myself presentable and hurried to the door. I was already wondering what Ellie was doing. Was she cleaning the apartment as she'd said she would, or was she out shopping, spending too much, or was she merely strolling the streets, swinging her lovely ass around town, being looked at and, perhaps, looking back, checking out alternatives to her grouchy lover?

Or was she phoning Harv Cohen and making arrangements to leave me?

I was opening the door when Ledya said, 'Don't bother to come back, Nick. Not until you really *want* to. You can hardly wait to leave here and get your hands on that mid-Western...'

I'd turned. She laughed sharply. 'If you could only see your face! You were ready to *hit* me if I insulted your ... well, what is she now, Nick? Still the patient being treated for rape-induced hangups? Or is she your one-and-only love?'

I said, 'I honestly don't know,' and left.

I tried calling Ellie from the office, where I was putting in a day on the production of a new hippie-doll series. The line was busy. It stayed busy for more than an hour this time. I went home at four, letting myself into the apartment as quietly as possible. I heard something; and with a shock realized it was Ellie, crying. I came into the bedroom and said, 'Honey?' She started violently and jumped up off the bed, where she'd been lying. 'God, you scared me!' Then she sank back down. 'Grandma McBaren is dying. I called home, just to talk to Liz...'

'Why didn't you do it before, when I was around? I'd like to say hello to her too.'

'Come on. You know how you are about long-distance calls.'

She was right. I felt it was a waste of money, especially when people chattered on about nothing. A quick call to communicate an urgent message, all right. But she'd been talking an hour or more ... and remembering this, I said, 'You were on the phone an *hour* to St Louis?'

'I told you, my grandmother...'

'You can't cure her by talking! You could fly home for the price

96

of that call!'

'You cheap bastard! I gave up my job...'

'Some job. Showing your ass to Alexis so he'd let you get away with murder.'

She leaped up. 'My grandmother's in the hospital, dying! I'm going home! If you don't like it...'

She started past me. I grabbed her. We glared at each other. I then said, 'Take it easy.' She said, 'Why the hell should I?' I said, 'Because we love each other.' The rigidity went out of her, and she dropped her head. I drew her to me. She put her arms around me and cried. I said, 'When do you want to go?' She said, voice muffled, 'There's a six o'clock plane. Can we make it?'

'Do you want me to come with you?'

'Please, Nickie, this also concerns my mother and you know what she is and what she feels about my being with you.'

'Does she know?'

'I didn't advertise it, but she *must* know, after you called her.'

I didn't argue. I didn't really want to go now. I'd relax, see friends...

We made the plane, but barely. We had to run to the gate, carrying her luggage. There was no time for anything but a quick kiss, and then she was gone. But she'd promised to be gone no more than four or five days, and to call me tomorrow night.

I didn't go back to the apartment. I phoned Ron and asked what he was doing. He said, 'At the moment, examining a very old rectum. But I'll be through in half an hour. Want to come over?'

I suggested we dine at the Forum on Route Four. He said, 'What's the matter, lost your taste for home-cooked conversation?' and laughed briefly and said he'd be there.

It wasn't that I disliked his wife Vera. It was just that I couldn't take much of her my-husband-the-doctor talk at the best of times, and this was rapidly becoming the worst of times. I was definitely upset, and I wanted to talk it out.

Ron is a beautiful listener. But that evening his eyes kept going to the pretty blonde hostess, and he finally interrupted me with: 'She moves her bottom like Doris, but Doris had more to move.' He drank his coffee and said, 'Go on, Nick.'

That side of his hadn't been as extraneous as it seemed to be ... because I suddenly wondered if I wouldn't be sitting here someday saying something about *my* lost love, Ellie. Because that was the way it was shaping up as I talked it out to Ron.

Ellie was undereducated.

Ellie was psychologically unstable.

Ellie was, from certain evidence, sexually unfaithful and untrustworthy.

Ellie was a spendthrift, or would be if I loosened the purse-strings.

'If all that is true,' Ron said, 'why the hell don't you send her packing?'

I didn't want to look foolish, and at the same time I didn't want to lie. I was using Ron as a sounding board, trying to see just what Ellie and I had. It didn't add up to much. Still, the answer to his question was, 'Because I can't see living without her ... at the moment.' And so I said it.

He stared at me. 'You mean you're in love?

'Not yet. Perhaps in the process of falling in love.'

'All right. You're falling in love with a girl who hasn't a single redeeming quality?'

'You wouldn't say that if you'd ever been to bed with her.' I laughed it up.

'That isn't enough, Nick, and you know it.'

'No, I don't.'

'You're saying that screwing and *only* screwing is reason enough to live with a woman, perhaps to marry her?'

I knew he expected me to say no. Anyone would expect me to say no. Intellectually, I *wanted* to say no. But I said, 'Yes, at least if it works the way it works with Ellie and me.'

'That's foolish!'

I decided we'd talked enough. Ron, however, went on a bit longer. He lectured me on 'an obviously demeaning and potentially destructive situation'. I couldn't strike back with reminders of Doris. He'd idealized her by now; and besides, he'd been a college graduate, a copy-editor in a softcover publishing firm, and quite verbal ... despite being a psychotic, a shoplifter, a drinker at twenty-three to put most middle-aged alcoholics to shame, and absolutely frigid in terms of achieving orgasm. She was now his lost love, his golden memory.

Ellie was, in fact, without 'redeeming qualities' to present to Ron or to anyone else. Her ability to make me happy was inexplicable, except in sexual terms, and that, to quote Ron and any other logical person, 'wasn't enough'.

Yet walking with her, talking to her, being in a movie or supermarket with her, sharing my son with her – were these sexual in nature? Perhaps; perhaps not; but they made me happy – deliriously happy at times.

I couldn't tell Ron. I could hardly tell myself. I cut the evening short, though he wanted me to come with him to a new club off Route 17 where 'the action is fast and upper class'. I didn't want upper class pickups. I wanted Ellie. And I wanted her even more when I got home and saw her coats in the closet and her shower cap in the bathroom and her pantyhose in the drawer.

I called my mother. I listened to her complaints about her apartment, Brooklyn, the way people treated an old lady, the way she felt, and finally and inevitably, my incidence of visits. I said, as I always did about the last, 'I'm sorry, Mom. You know why.'

'But your father's dead sixteen years and who remembers arguments and we weren't as bad as some, I can tell you. Your fine Aunt Ruthie and Uncle Morris . . .'

I listened until she ran down. I said, again, 'I'm sorry. Do you need money?'

'You send me more than I can spend. A lot more. I couldn't live with a savings account, but I'll die with one.'

I chuckled. She said, 'Are you a little happier, Nickie? You sound a little happier.'

'Yes.'

'Have you found a girl?'

'Maybe.'

'You mean it? Is she rich?'

I began to grow angry. I never spoke to my mother where, at some point, I didn't grow angry. 'She's poorer than we were.'

'All right. As long as she's fine. She's a college graduate?'

'She barely made it through high school.'

'But *fine*, Nickie?'

'Her father's in jail for murder. Her mother beats her children with a belt. She sounds like someone from the *Beverly Hillbillies*, only what she says isn't allowed on television.'

My mother laughed. She laughed a long time. 'Nickie, you devil, you always made jokes. But I'm glad you're a little happier.'

Jokes. I kept my mouth shut.

She said, 'So you won't visit me. So I'll visit you, tomorrow.' Her voice changed, became cautiously pleading, in expectations of my usual, 'I'm busy,' or, 'Going out of town.'

'What if I take the subway in the morning and cook you a nice meal? How long since you had split-pea soup like Momma makes? Or *holiptchas*?'

I had to see her *sometime*. It was expected of me.

Like my dating 'fine' girls.

Like my recognizing 'demeaning and potentially destructive situations'.

I said all right. I'd buy the dry mix she used for the soup, and meat and cabbage for the *holiptchas*, Russian-style sweet-and-sour cabbage rolls. I'd get her a little gift and she'd be happy and I'd have discharged my obligations for another two or three months.

And I'd drive her home by eight, before Ellie's call.

I took a shower. I read a little and went to bed. I closed my eyes and told myself to sleep. But I missed Ellie. She'd been gone about six hours and already the ache was forming in the pit of my stomach, the fantasies of other men tormenting my mind, the physical need for her building in my genitals. That's how it had been from our first night in the Forest Park Hotel – that terrible appetite, that painful longing, one or the other or both. The appetite when I hadn't had her for some hours. The longing when I'd had her and couldn't perform any more and she was free of me for a while, uncoupled from me for a while. Both when she was gone from me, as she was this night.

I finally got up and went to the bathroom. I rummaged around in the hamper, found the panties she'd been wearing earlier today, and took them back to bed with me, trying to laugh at myself. I lay down and held them ... and then sniffed them, found the crotch area, held it to my nose and mouth. And fell asleep.

FIVE

I received my June phone bill while Ellie was still in St Louis, into her second week of that 'three- or-four-day visit'. Her grandmother had died the Tuesday she arrived. I hadn't heard from her since her scheduled call, on Wednesday, when she told me the funeral would be held 'in a few days'. That was nine days ago. I was angry enough, and worried enough, thinking of accidents and rape and Harv Cohen, and not being able to reach her at her mother's or at her sister Gina's – the mother simply said, 'I haven't seen her since Thursday at the funeral,' and Gina tried to be evasive but I finally learned she too had last seen Ellie at the cemetery – and then to cap it all, along comes this incredible phone bill. It totalled three hundred and twenty-five dollars.

Ellie had accounted for more than two-thirds of the cost, having phoned St Louis eight times. The last two were made on the Tuesday she'd left, totaling eighty-six dollars, but they were to the mother and, I assumed, the grandmother's home, and I'd expected it because of that hour-plus busy signal. Four more averaged about twenty dollars each, and burned my ass, but again the mother's number showed up twice and Gina's number once and the last number might have been to her friend Claire Denniker. Anyway, like a man who doesn't notice a skinned knee when his leg is broken in the same accident, I didn't dwell on them ... because of two other calls, one for fifty dollars and the other for thirty-eight. They were both to the same number in Ladue, and I remembered what Ellie had told me about Harv Cohen living in the prestigious suburb.

I called the telephone company business office and said I couldn't account for two calls on my bill. Would they please tell me to whom they were made? The woman said she would check it out and call me back. I made myself a stiff drink and switched on the television, and told myself it would turn out to be something perfectly innocent, if extravagant.

Three hours later, when I was almost calm because of two more drinks and a good Mets ballgame, and also because I'd reasoned that she *couldn't* be so dumb, or so obvious, as to allow another man to show up on my bill, the phone company called. 'A Mister Harvey Cohen,' the woman said. 'Does that solve the problem?'

That solved the problem.

I considered calling Ledya, or maybe Karen Oster, and having dinner and hitting a rock club and then balling ... and telling Ellie to go straight to hell.

But I went to a movie instead, and had a small dinner and lots of wine at the Italian place on Forty-fourth street. And walking home, I began to rationalize. It could still be quite innocent. The fact that she hadn't reversed the charges or tried to hide the calls in any way – even if she hadn't told me straight out, knowing how unreasonable I could be – anyway, letting the calls show so blatantly meant she'd simply chatted with an old friend and felt no real guilt ...

Eighty-eight dollars' worth of chatting?

The drugstore on Second was open and I went in and asked for the strongest over-the-counter sleeping preparation they sold. The pharmacist said they were all more or less alike, and gave me the one his customers reordered most often; a mild hypnotic, but effective if combined with 'a hot bath and relaxing situation'.

I could manage the hot bath.

Ellie called at two a.m. I'd fallen heavily asleep a short time before, but at the first sound of her voice I was wide awake.

'Hi,' she said brightly. 'Whatcha doing?'

'What am I doing,' I said slowly. 'That's a good question. Many things, Ellie. Sweating out your call, for one.'

'Now don't tell me I promised ... ?'

'No, you didn't promise. You simply disappeared for nine days.

And neither your mother nor Gina knew, or perhaps was willing to say, where you were.'

'Oh, well, I got depressed and stayed at a motel and I went to see Claire and just goofed around.'

'Just goofed around.'

'Come on, Nickie.' Her voice was soft, pleading. 'I'm not asking where *you've* been and what *you've* been doing.'

'What the hell has that got to do with it! I've been here and I've been waiting for you to call and to come home!'

'What I mean is ... well, I trust you. Don't you trust me, honey?'

I began to melt. But that telephone bill was on the nightstand near the phone. 'All right, You asked what I've been doing. I didn't finish telling you. I've been eating, drinking, taking pills, and finally falling asleep.'

'Oh, I woke you and you're grouchy. I'll call in the morning.'

'Hold it!' But she'd already hung up.

I stared at the phone. I said, 'Ellie, damn it.' And then screamed, '*Ellie*, you bitch!' and slammed the handset down and jumped up and paced around. And the phone rang again.

'I'm sorry,' she said. 'I was hanging up when I heard you say something.'

I wanted to tell her to fuck off. I wanted to curse her, accuse her, discard her. But I wanted something a little more than that – I wanted her with me.

'Nickie? You're really mad at me, aren't you? That's why I hung up – so you wouldn't say something we'll both be sorry for. But there's no *reason*, honey. You know how I am about time and days and things. I took Liz out and saw a few people...'

'Including Harv.'

'Oh, I had a drink with him. We talked.'

'What the hell could you have to say to each other after all the talking you did a few weeks ago?'

'What?'

'I got my phone bill.'

She laughed a little. 'Big, hugh?'

'Yes, big.'

'What makes you think I called Harv?'

'Ellie, Christ, the Ladue numbers, I checked them with the phone company!'

She sighed. 'Listen, can it wait until I come home?'

I felt a sudden rush of joy, and then was enraged at myself. But joy, and relief, remained. I'd feared she *wasn't* coming home. 'Why can't you explain now?'

'Because I'm at Gina's and it's one in the morning ...'

'It's two here, you oh-so-considerate girl.'

'Okay. We went out. I'll tell you when I see you.'

'I might be too old and senile to understand by then.'

'Six-thirty tomorrow night, American Airlines.'

I wanted to talk, to question, to quarrel, to make her suffer a little of what I'd suffered, but I was also afraid of a sudden change in her attitude. If she grew angry ...

'What's the flight number?'

'I forget. I'll call right before I leave the airport, all right?'

'Yes.'

She was quiet a moment, then murmured softly, 'Still want me?'

'I do. Still want *me*?'

'Yes, Nickie. More than ever. I'm so sure now, honey.'

'What do you mean?'

'I'll tell you tomorrow. I'll tell you everything, I promise, even if you get angry.'

'Will there be anything to make me angry?'

'Maybe. But not if you're smart. And you're the smartest man I know, Mr Leib.' She made a kissing sound and said, 'Ellie wants a big one!' playing little-girl as only she could. I kissed her back. She said, 'Umm! See you tomorrow ... in bed.'

She called me the next night at seven o'clock, six St Louis time, and said she'd missed the flight because of heavy traffic and her 'dumb brother-in-law'.

'The same one who tried to rape you?' I asked, not believing her, heart pounding away, feeling someone lurking behind her, someone who wanted her there for one more night of love.

'He's not that way any more. He's settled down. Anyway, I'm sorry Nickie. I'll take a morning flight. Just a few more hours, honey, and we'll be together.'

'No.'

'What do you mean, no? What else can I do?'

'There's a flight that comes into Newark Airport at about eight. That's New Jersey, and I can drive there in half an hour. It's never full on weekdays. Take it.'

'But how can I get to the airport on time to ...?'

And then she stopped.

'But you're *at* the airport, aren't you?' I asked blandly.

'I ... I went back to Gina's when I missed the plane.'

I said nothing.

'All right,' she said, and the change had taken place; the change I

103

feared. 'So I goofed around too much and knew I'd never make it and because you're so damned grouchy I couldn't tell you the truth. So what?'

'So be here sometime tonight, Ellie.'

'I can't.'

My mouth was dry, and my forehead wet. I knew I could lose her, and feared it like losing my life. And yet, I also *wanted* to lose her. She was bad news. I was getting hooked, and it was get out now or get out never.

'Be here tonight, or don't come at all.' I hung up.

I took more of the sleeping pills, but this time they didn't work. I would ask Ron for something strong the next time we met. I drank, and still I lay awake, suffering for her.

At four-thirty, the phone rang. I waited and told myself not to pick it up, to let her think I'd gone out, to give her a little of her own bitter medicine. But I answered on the sixth ring.

'Nickie?'

'Who is it?'

She laughed.

I said, 'I don't like anonymous callers. I'm going to hang up.'

'Nickie, honey, please. I was with Harv and he begged me and I was going to make the flight, I swear, but he lied about the time and when I got dressed it was too late.'

'When you got dressed.'

'I said I'd tell you the truth, didn't I?'

'I think you're just too stupid to lie convincingly.'

'Then you won't want to pick me up at LaGuardia and I'd better just wait until eight and take a flight back to St. Louis. You can send me my clothes, or keep the fucking rags ...'

'You're in *New York*?'

'You told me to come tonight, or not come at all. Maybe what you really meant was, don't come at all, period.'

'Where are you? What airline?'

She'd not been able to make that last direct flight, into Newark, but she'd taken a flight to Chicago and waited and caught another flight into New York. I was dressed in five minutes, and at the baggage checkout in twenty-five. She was sitting on a bench, as fresh and lovely as ever, her bag at her feet, pointedly ignoring a Navy non-com who was trying to make conversation. When I walked up, she turned to the sailor and said, 'Too bad. He made it.'

The sailor hesitated, and then said, 'Well, if it's too bad, come on anyway.'

I said, 'Fuck off.'

The sailor was about thirty, tall and thin and hard looking. He rose slowly. Ellie jumped up and grabbed my arm. 'Nickie, stop!' To the sailor she said, 'I'm sorry. He's my husband.'

The sailor said, 'Now I know *why* you're sorry,' and began moving away.

It was five-ten a.m. and the only other person around was an elderly baggage porter. No cops. I said, 'You forgot something.' Ellie tried to pull me, but I shoved her off with my left arm and, as the sailor turned, hit him as hard as I could in the neck with my right hand. He sat down on the ground, clutching his throat, and fell on his side and rolled and choked. I picked up Ellie's bag and walked quickly outside. I didn't look back. I kept walking, across the road to the meter-parking lot. When I reached the Porsche, I threw the bag in the back, got behind the wheel, and started up. I was shaking all over.

Ellie was at the passenger's door, pulling on the handle. It was locked. I hesitated just long enough to see panic move into her face; then opened it. We drove through the pre-dawn greyness, over nearly empty roads, and we were silent until the Triboro Bridge tollbooths. Then she said, voice weak, 'That was sick.'

I was still shaking, and holding tight to the wheel to hide it. I was afraid to risk an answer, in case my voice would also shake.

'There was no reason for it, Nickie. I never said a word to him until you came.'

'Then you said some beauts.' My voice was thick, but steady.

'I'm sorry.'

I looked at her for the first time since leaving the airport. She was white, and she was fighting tears.

'You're right,' I said. 'I shouldn't have hit the sailor. It's Harv I should hit. And I will, I promise you.' I suddenly thought of Aaron Hoff, for the first time in years ... then forgot him as she began to cry. She cried heavily, leaning away from me and hiding her face and choking in little high-pitched sobs.

'All right. I'm sorry.'

She continued to cry.

I touched her arm. She quieted. I touched her head, stroked her hair. We turned onto the F.D.R. Drive. She said, 'You scare me. I didn't think you'd ever do such a thing. Hitting him that way, so ... fast.'

'I didn't think I'd ever do such a thing either.'

She turned to me, angry in an instant. 'It wasn't fair! You're bigger and you didn't give him a chance!'

'If you'd like to set up a boxing match ...'

'Don't joke! And what if he'd gotten up and hurt you?'

My pride was touched. 'I'd have killed him.' And then I was touched another way, because she'd worried about me. 'Let's talk about St Louis and why you missed the flight.'

'I was going to, but now I'm afraid you'll hit *me*! I thought you'd understand how important this visit was, in straightening out my head, and in making me see where I really belong ... but now I don't know. You ... you *shocked* me, Nickie. You really shocked me!'

I'd shocked myself. I didn't think I had that much violence left in me. I'd been a bit of a nut as a kid, and in the Air Corps, but it had been years since I'd done more than *wished* I could hit some sonofabitch, and that mainly while driving, which is common enough with most of the men I know.

'It'll never happen again,' I said, and took her hand. 'I swear, Ellie. And I want to know everything and understand everything and then we'll start afresh, being absolutely honest with each other and absolutely faithful to each other. You tell me about Harv and I'll tell you about Ledya and ...'

'You slept with her while I was gone, didn't you?'

'I was *going* to ... I thought of it, but I didn't.'

She was glaring at me, disbelief in her eyes. 'I'll bet!'

'I said we'd both be honest, Ellie. I meant it.'

'And when you went to the office ... don't tell me you didn't see her, or someone else.'

'Lunches ...'

'And a little sack time, sure!' She yanked her hand away.

She was the one who'd run up the phone bills and 'dressed' when with Harv, and now she was giving *me* the hard time! I began to shout ... and then stopped. I said, 'We're almost home. Let's cool it until we have a drink and relax. Please. You say you learned something on this trip. I did too. I learned I can't be happy without you.'

She waited. I wanted to say, 'I learned that I love you,' but there was still her lies, and those unexplained nine days, and yesterday with Harv ... and I wasn't going to make a fool of myself. Not Nick Leib, who'd licked a Brooklyn slum and crazy parents and World War II and the American system and a dead marriage to find money, freedom and, if not love, at least all the prime young cunt he could handle! Not for a girl who might be giving me the shaft, taking me ...

She must have seen a change come over my face, because she quickly said, 'All right,' and leaned across the space between our seats and kissed my cheek. My response – my *inner* response – was so powerful that I wanted to let go of the wheel and hold her and kiss her until the ache was at least eased. It wouldn't be satisfied until I was in her body. It wouldn't be satisfied even then; not until she was mine, absolutely and finally mine. And yet I suspected I would *never* achieve that possession, as I had with Louise, as I could with Ledya and Karen and others; others who were so able to give themselves to a man in that social as well as sexual sense because they could make deals, could succeed at the business of marriage since they had the examples of rational parents, of stable lives, to follow. These were the women who could trade satisfaction of the occasional strong urge, the swift onset of the chemistry, the doubt that any *one* man was natural and right for them, for the psychic and sexual and financial security of the conjugal bed. Not like Ellie.

Not like me?

In the apartment, I made coffee and toast. We sat at the kitchen table. She lit a cigarette and looked at it and then at me. 'Smoke much in St Louis?' I asked, by way of openers.

'I guess so. This is my third ... no, my fourth pack. I bought the first when I got on the plane at LaGuardia. But I've only smoked half of these...' She put out the cigarette and said, quickly, 'Harv asked me to marry him. I said no. It was after we'd spent three nights together ... *without* going to bed. Only the last day, yesterday, he took off from work and I spent it with him. Only yesterday we went to bed.'

My insides knotted up and I smiled and said, 'But you didn't like it, right?'

Her eyes were down. Her voice was down. 'I didn't like it the way I used to like it. I wanted to be with you. I thought of you.'

'So it was a quickie and he fooled you about the time...'

'He didn't fool me about the time. I made that up.' She sipped her coffee. 'It wasn't a quickie. We were in bed from nine in the morning until I called you. He walked out of the room while I called. It was the same motel where we went for our first time. He had music and champagne and he asked me again, as he did the night before, to marry him.' She raised her eyes. An oily film had formed on her face and she looked worried and perhaps frightened, but she said, 'He begged me to *sleep* with him, to let him be with me one whole night, the way it used to be, just one last time.'

'And he melted your little heart.' I could feel perspiration trickling down my sides. 'You just couldn't say no.'

'That's right, Nickie. But I did, when you said I had to come home.'

'Home? Home is where you put your ass!'

'Don't, Nickie. It's not so. Home is where you are. Where you and Seth are.' She leaned over the table and took my hand. 'Don't let's talk any more. Let's go to bed now.'

'And fuck away all our problems.'

I was sick, thinking of her in Harv's arms: her legs opening, her voice saying the sweet-little-obscene-little things she said to me.

'Yes. But first tell me about Ledya and the others.'

I drank my coffee. I shoved toast in my mouth. I knew she expected me to say I'd been faithful. I said, 'Ledya was a centre-fold for *Playboy*, did you know that?'

She shook her head, lips tightening.

'I'll have to show you the picture someday. Her breasts ...' I shook my head in admiration. 'Well, we made it a few times before I met you. Nothing serious. Just good clean fun. But I was upset while you were gone, so...' I paused, enjoying her obvious tension. 'By the way, how many times did you and Harv make it yesterday? Just for the record book. The Fucking Ellie Record Book.'

'I don't know,' she muttered, reaching for her cigarettes.

I laughed. 'It's not something you forget in a few hours. I know, baby.'

Her eyes snapped to mine. 'Five times, *baby,* and I had to run to the bathroom at the end because I was *sore* and he wanted it again!'

It was a game. I was torturing her and she was torturing me. Just a game. But I hadn't fucked anyone, didn't want anyone, and she'd had her old lover and I could see him going into her and I couldn't stand it, suddenly had my hands on her, one on her mouth and the other on her throat...

She said my name; choked my name. I let go and sank back down in my chair. She rubbed her neck and shook her head and went out of the kitchen. I drank coffee. My head throbbed. I felt I was going to cry.

She came back. She sat on my lap and kissed my mouth and said, 'I'm afraid, Nickie, come to bed.'

I was afraid too.

We went to bed. I held her and she shivered and said, 'Is the air-conditioning on?'

It wasn't. I held her closer. I was exhausted, and I slept a little while, and the only reason I awoke when I did was that she was kissing my belly. And murmuring, 'Nickie, I love you, no one but you, no one but you...'

On her, in her, I said I love her, no one but her, and later we swore everything was going to change now, we were going to belong to each other, *only* each other, and we believed it ... for at least three weeks, including another idyllic weekend at the cottage with Seth. Then the phone rang one morning and a girl asked for Ellie. I shook her awake and left the room. I showered and shaved and used my water pic as well as my toothbrush, and she was still on the phone when I came out. At least *I* wasn't paying, this time. I made coffee in the electric percolator and fried an egg and ate it with two slices of whole wheat toast. I took my vitamins. While putting the dishes in the washer, I heard her voice rise in shrill excitement, and wondered what was up, and worried that it might change the idyll.

As I was pouring a second cup of coffee, she came running into the kitchen, nude, and grabbed me and almost lifted my hundred and seventy pounds off the floor.

'If you're going in for weightlifting, you'll need some breakfast. Want eggs ... ?'

'Black coffee, Nickie. From now on, I *starve*!' She looked back at her lovely ass. 'God, I've got middle-aged spread.' She suddenly ran into the bathroom. I followed, and she was examining her face in the mirror. 'And these blemishes ... you've got to take me to a good skin doctor! *Today*, Nickie. Or make the appointment...'

'First you're happy and then you're bitchy. Who was that on the phone?'

She whirled and came at me again and grabbed me again. This time I stopped her by putting a finger up her rectum. She pulled back, giggling. I shuffled toward her, goosing fingers extended like an obscene Bela Lugosi.

'Nickie, stop, wait, I've got to tell you! You're looking at a maid of honour!'

'I love your outfit, especially the bustle.'

'Let me *tell* you! Claire and Jerry are getting married next month. They're putting me up at her parents' house and there'll be showers and parties and then a big wedding. I'm so happy for her. And to think she made *me* maid of honour!'

I didn't get around to the critical question until after we'd had coffee together and she'd complained about her weight and blamed me and rushed to the cheval glass in the bedroom to get a full-length view of her luscious self and screamed in anguish at being 'fat' and began to grow depressed and made me *swear* I wouldn't offer her anything fattening.

'When, exactly,' I asked, 'do we leave?'

We were in the bedroom and she was getting into her tennis

outfit, having decided that daily exercise would be a part of her weight-reducing programme. She waved her hands at me, an oh-silly gesture, and laughed as if it were a big joke. 'Cut it out, Nickie! You don't want to go. It'll just be four or five days...'

'I've heard *that* song before.'

'You're not *serious*? C'mon, let's go down and play tennis. Today I'm going to beat you!'

'I *am* serious.' I sat down at the edge of the bed. I was tightening up inside. 'I should think you'd want me to go. Your mother isn't involved, and your family isn't involved, and we could enjoy it together.'

'But what will you do with all those people you don't know?'

'I'll know you.'

'You'd be bored. Most of them are dumb kids...'

'You mean I'm too old to meet your friends?'

'I never said that!' She clenched her fists. 'You're too *smart* to meet my friends!'

'Including Harv?'

'Harv's as smart as anyone...' And then she shook her head and shouted, 'Why do you always twist the words around in my mouth! These are just old friends and there'll be kids from my high school and it's my past life and I'm *ashamed* of a lot of it, can't you understand?'

'Will Harv be there?'

She left the room. I followed. She went to the kitchen and poured a cup of coffee. I sat down with her. She sipped and didn't look at me. I waited. 'Well,' she muttered, 'he'll probably be there.'

'Didn't Claire mention him?'

'I suppose she did.'

'You suppose.'

'I guess if you were there, it would confuse me.'

'You confuse easily.'

'You can come if you want to.'

'With such an enthusiastic invitation, how can I refuse?'

She got up and went to the bathroom. The door closed; the lock clicked.

She was right, of course. I understood her feelings perfectly ... and hated them *because* I understood. How would I feel taking her to one of *my* friends' weddings? How would I explain my new life to my old? She was justified ... for as long as I didn't tell *everyone* we were living together, were in effect married.

Though by now a lot of people suspected there was a woman living with me. Louise, for one, asked a few times whether I'd brought anyone along when I went to the cottage with Seth. It seems he'd been reacting after our weekends; being rather curt with Louise, making her feel she had competition in the Momma department. I said certainly not ... but she'd gotten that 'Mr-Leib's-wire' from Ellie one day and felt it wasn't at all like me to have an answering service; I'd never had one before; I'd never wasted money that way.

My mother had her suspicions, too, since our little talk about fine, rich, college girls. Ron, of course, knew anw had asked to meet her. And I'd asked Ellie to meet him ... but she'd refused, said she 'wasn't ready' yet, wanted to lose weight and clear up her skin and do some more work in that grammar book.

Ah, yes ... her education. The reason we were getting along as well as we were is that I'd stopped pushing her to crack the grammar and math books (or to do more housekeeping and cooking). She did do considerable reading, mainly novels from my bookcase, but we'd given up the idea of the Saturday School summer session, which had already started, in favour of the fall term. But neither of us believed she would actually register, and in fact I was planning on two weeks in Miami in October, built around that toy manufacturers' convention Harold had mentioned. That would be impossible if she were in school.

At the same time, I knew it was a mistake not pushing her toward school, even if it meant risking fifteen hundred dollars on an aborted first year. It would give her a purpose, an occupation, a way of *achieving*.

It would also present her with male students, and teachers, with social and sexual opportunities ... and I just didn't feel secure enough to risk that. Perhaps the term *after*, I told myself, when we were settled ...

We always made plans, the both of us, and took vows, the both of us, and somehow we let them slide, turned from them, the both of us. And we were in love with each other, I'm sure of it ... though perhaps not often at the same time.

We played tennis that afternoon. She did a little better, having worked on style against the handball wall, and I faked a few missed balls so as to make her happier; her and her audience of teen-aged boys off from high school. Those five or six kids never missed a 'shot' of Ellie bending over to retrieve a ball; and when I mentioned it and suggested she bend from the knees, she laughed and squeezed my butt and said she enjoyed turning them on. Those kids played the most lethargic game of basketball ever seen when she was on the tennis courts!

As we were walking to the elevators, I told her I didn't really want to go to the wedding. She said she would write Claire tomorrow that she couldn't be maid of honour. I said I'd go, if she wanted me to. She nodded glumly. And that's where it stood when we went out that night, first to a movie, then to dinner and for the first time, to a rock club, Le Directoire.

I surprised her. I scored high with her. I'm good at free-form rock. I was good at the Lindy and twist too, but rock is my medium. She's basically a crotch dancer, as I already knew from watching her practise in front of the bedroom mirror; a very good one, with go-go girl's high-steps and arm movements. But I'm better than she is, with more improvisation and more cool (though the gap closed as we danced together several times before she left for the wedding).

That night, she said she hadn't thought I'd be able to dance rock at all. 'You're so ... *dignified,* Nickie! And then you go and *move* like that!'

'Very dignified,' I said. 'As when I slug sailors.'

'Ha, ha.'

'Or choke sweethearts.'

She looked away. The music blasted. I'd had considerable to drink and she was absolutely ravishing in a tan suède mini and red print hippie blouse and suède vest and suède boots and I couldn't stand the thought of anyone touching her but me, ever. I leaned forward and put my lips to her ear and said, 'Or plan to eradicate ex-boyfriends who refuse to remain ex. I swear to you ...'

She gave me an annoyed look. 'I think we should go. You're bombed.'

I closed my hand over her forearm. I squeezed, tighter and tighter, and she finally said, 'That hurts!'

'Did I ever tell you about my old friend who works in the garment industry? Let's call him Mike. He's got friends who kill people for a price. If I ever find out you've slept with Harv again, I'll have him zeroed.'

She stared at me. She ventured a little laugh, which became a near smile, which faded away as she read the absolute, if temporary, murder in my heart ... because I was seeing my beautiful girl in her maid-of-honour dress, on her back, some bastard kissing her and stroking her and taking her. I said, 'Killing is a zero. A bad beating with broken bones and concussions is called a half. A few good shots in the face and gut, a warning of sorts, is called a quarter. Harv will get zeroed, I promise you.'

'Nickie, stop.' She was frightened. I hadn't thought, when I started this, she would even believe me. I hadn't thought *I* would believe me. But she did, and therefore I did too. It suddenly gave me leverage, muscle to use when she was away from me. Before, I simply ranted and sweated and suffered. Now, because of a drunken threat, I had a way to keep her honest.

On the way home, she was quiet. Then, in the garage, she suddenly began touching me, and opened my pants, and said she wanted to blow me right there, 'for a kick'. I resisted, but once she got me with her mouth, I stopped resisting. She blew me, and what with the drinking I'd done I could barely walk to the elevators.

In bed, she snuggled next to me. I was dozing off when she said, 'You were just kidding, weren't you, Nickie?'

I understood immediately. I understood the blow job, and I understood that her fear of me was no temporary thing but strong and real. I was upset ... because she wouldn't fear me that way unless there was a good chance she was going to make it with Harv again, would she? And unless she'd decided that I was capable of doing just what I threatened.

'Sure,' I muttered.'

'You know what I'm talking about, don't you?'

'You're talking about Harv and you're afraid I'll find out you're going to ball him.'

'Nickie!' The bed shook as she jerked upright. 'That's over! I don't want you thinking such things! If you do, maybe I shouldn't come back!'

I rolled over, my back to her. 'You have to. You belong to me.'

'I do not! I belong to *me*! I don't say such things about you, do I? You can't say such things about me!'

'But I do belong to you. I admit it'

'Well, *that* way. But I can't control your whole life, and you can't control mine.'

'Wouldn't dream of it. But no more Harv.'

'Of course not. I told you, didn't I? The last time in St Louis I found out it was you I wanted. Only you.' She lay down again and put her warm arms around me and murmured, 'Honey, turn around.'

She'd perspired a good deal while dancing, and it had broken through her deodorant, and there was an animal, feral smell about her. Normally, it turns me off when a girl has that smell ... but Ellie's odour was somehow softer, somehow exciting. 'Please, Nickie. Turn around.'

'Why?'

She rubbed her little breasts against my back. 'Nickie, come on.'

'Sorry, honey. You blew it, literally.'

I thought that was quite funny. She didn't laugh, and she didn't give up. Her hands worked their magic, and she soon had the old boy performing beautifully. I forgave her everything, forgot everything while in the saddle, and she swore she wouldn't spend any more time with Harv, 'Except at the wedding, Nickie, where I can't avoid him. And to be honest, I don't want to avoid him. I like him, honey, you can understand that, can't you? But he's just a dear friend now, honest.'

She was still sweating over my threat to have killed him. I began to feel like a bastard and said it was just a joke. She displayed a fine bit of insight and said, '*No it wasn't*. But please don't think that way any more, honey. I'd never think that way about you and your friends.'

The following month was a good one, and included two more weekends at the cottage, the last with Seth. My son and my girl were in love. It was incredible how well they got along. Sometimes I was jealous of their relationship; it was so much less complicated than the one *I* had with her.

I worked a day or two a week, on toy design and production, which made Harold a little less difficult. Ellie and I read and watched TV and went to plays and movies and worked a little on her grammar and maths books (very little) and played tennis and I even got her to run with me in the State park one time ... but she stiffened up badly the next day and refused to try it ever again. She was a bitch about her diet – not that she stuck to it as she should have; just bitched about how it was my fault for taking her to good restaurants and making myself tempting meals in the apartment. She didn't lose much weight, and her skin seemed to grow somewhat worse, and on July twenty-fifth, her birthday, she refused to leave the apartment for any sort of celebration. It was also the first day of her period, and while she had mild menses and it never stopped us from making love, this time she had worked herself into a real state of depression.

I tried to get her to dress. She said no, she was going to read. It was a beautiful day and I'd planned a surprise for her at the Gold Coin – a cake and a very special dinner and champagne, and Seth and Denise as guests.

Ellie and Denise hadn't met, because Denise and her boyfriend had departed two days after school ended for a trip to England and Switzerland, using the money they'd saved over the past three years. They'd returned last week, and the meeting was all set, and now Ellie was fouling up the works. Not that Denise was that anxious about it; she'd agreed because of the birthday and because she had enough sibling rivalry left in her not to want Seth to have shared anything with Daddy that she hadn't.

I finally went downstairs and picked up the bouquet of flowers I'd ordered. I also got the delicate pair of gold earrings I'd bought last week and locked in the car's glove compartment so as to assure it would remain a surprise. I came back up and Ellie was in the bathroom. The door was locked. I rattled the knob and said, 'I've got something for you.'

She said she was constipated and would I *please* let her alone.

'But this is your twenty-first birthday! You're of age now, honey. You can even fuck.'

'Very funny.' Flat, flat voice. 'But not who I want.'

I gave it a laugh. 'Sure you can. Me. Right?'

'Are you going to stand there and talk to me all day? Can't I get a little peace even in the john?'

I went to the living room and sat down and waited. About ten interminable minutes later, she came in, wearing my old blue bathrobe, her hair lank and greasy, her face sullen. She saw the flowers, and stopped, and then took a deep breath. 'Thank you, Nickie.' She came to the couch and took them from me. I waited while she put them in a vase and set it on the coffee table; then I drew the little jewellery box from my pocket. 'Happy birthday.' She sat down beside me, trying to look happy and not succeeding. I began to grow tense. She opened the box and said, 'Oh, they're beautiful,' then closed it and said, 'I'll try them on later.'

We sat there. She said, 'I forgot. Claire's mother called while you were downstairs. She wants me there on the fifth, not the seventh. They're having another little party.'

I left the room. I changed for tennis, got my racket and went to the door. She said, 'Nickie?' I said, 'I'll try to find a game. Maybe by the time I return you'll be more human.'

'I'm sorry, honey.'

'Yeah.'

'But please don't ask me to go out tonight. I ... I'm just a little ... tired.'

'From what?'

'Uh-oh. Here we go again."

I began to open the door; then closed it and went to the couch and sat down and held out my arms. She came to me; reluctantly, I felt.

'Why can't we get along, Nickie?'

I didn't answer. I had *many* answers, but they would be in the form of an attack, an argument, and I didn't want that on her birthday.

'It isn't working, Nickie. I ... I feel locked in.'

'Let's not discuss that now.' I was suddenly frightened.

'But it's important.'

'It works for me. Better than it ever worked with any other woman.'

'I mean ... day by day.'

'If you want a job ...'

'What's the point? *You* don't work, not really, and it's not as if we need the money.'

Which reminded me of the gift I'd been saving for the party. It might turn things around right now. I went to the bedroom and found the envelope with the new cheque book. It had Ellie's name, and a balance of one thousand dollars.

She'd spent whatever money she'd had on the three visits to me and on that trip to St Louis. I found out last week when she'd asked if I would pay the dressmaker for her maid-of-honour gown. She'd admitted she didn't have a dime and had been reluctant to ask me for money.

She opened the cheque book, and I waited for her to squeal or laugh or kiss me when she saw the balance. What she did was close the book and shake her head slowly. 'I can't take this.'

The tightness returned to my insides. 'Of course you can. I provide the money in this family, and whatever else you need as long as we're together.'

'And what I was saying before? About it not working? You going to forget that?'

'How could I forget it,' I whispered. She dropped her eyes. I touched her face and said, 'Look at me.'

She did.

'Are you saying you don't love me any more?'

'I ... no, Nickie. But just look at *me*.'

'You look fine. Or you will, once you wash and dress and come down for some tennis. And tonight ...'

'No tennis. I told you I got my period.'

'Okay. But tonight we go out.'

'No. I won't eat ...'

'Then don't eat! But I've made plans ...'

'Please, Nickie.' She was suddenly crying. 'Please, I don't want to fight. I'm all upset. I don't know what I want. I don't know what I am. I'm nothing, I guess. I can't stand it, not being with people ...'

'Tonight you'll be with people. Tonight we're having a party at the Gold Coin.'

She began to say no, and I went on. 'It was supposed to be a surprise. Seth will be there. And Denise. And I'll get Ron . . .'

She jumped up. Her face was set. 'Better call it off right now. I won't go. I'm not meeting Denise when I'm fat and my skin's broken out.'

'For God's sake, you always look lovely and you know it.'

'I don't know it. And I don't want to go out. And it's not just my looks; I want to rest up and I don't want to meet anyone and I *won't*!' Her voice had risen to a scream. 'I won't and you can't make me! I *won't*!'

I stared. She was a ranting, raving little girl. She was insane. And I was insane to want anyone like her.

I got up slowly. 'You can leave for good, after tonight, but I'm not going to change the plans.' I didn't mean it. I knew right then I needed time, a lot of time, to adjust to the idea of life without this crazy bitch, this idiot child who had swallowed my life. 'Make up your mind to that, Ellie. You'll go out tonight if I have *drag* you.'

She ran. I didn't follow. I knew where she was going. The bathroom door slammed shut; the lock clicked.

I went down. Only one of the four courts was taken, but there didn't seem to be anyone looking for a game. Then a woman I'd played with before – last year when life had been somewhat empty but sane, somewhat lacking in excitement but comfortable – came along and said, 'Are you waiting for your friend?'

We chatted a while. She was about thirty-five, married to a lawyer, had taught secondary-school history until the birth of her first child. She now had three, and her figure reflected this. But she wasn't bad looking – a tall, full-bodied matron with a nice face, dark hair, and genial manner. And she could talk easily on any number of subjects. And she could play tennis as well as I could, though I'd always played a bit above my level with her.

Today, she beat me two out of three games. But they were tough games, and when they were over and I came around the net, she said, 'God, I enjoyed that! I wish I could get Garry to play. But he's all golf, and golf bores me.'

'Same here.'

We walked off the courts. No teen-aged boys bothered looking at her . . . and I was aware of it. I missed the excitement of being with Ellie; of knowing that boys, men, just about all of them, everywhere, looked at her with lust and longing, and envied me for being with her. It was part of my feeling for her, my love or my sickness.

Mrs Carlhein, my tennis partner, cautiously sounded me out on Ellie. I said she was 'a close friend'.

'She's a very lovely young lady.'

I smiled and nodded.

'Would the two of you care to come to dinner at our place this Saturday evening? We're having a small gathering ...'

I said I would normally be delighted, but this Saturday we'd be out of town. She said some other time. I said most definitely; and saw Ellie in a gathering of middle-aged professional couple, with which the apartment house abounded ... and I *couldn't* see it.

Mrs Carlhein asked what Ellie did. I said she had managed a clothing store but was now looking for something better. And then we were in the elevator and she got out on the fifth floor and I went up to the apartment. It was empty. I checked the closets, and the terrace, but no games this time.

I found the note on the kitchen table. It read: *'Please call off the party. I won't go. I don't want to meet Denise. Your forcing me wont' work. I've got to think things out before I meet your daughter. Honey, don't be mad. I can't help it I'm such a nut. I'm all mixed up. Be back soon. Love and kisses, Ellie.'*

I called Denise. Louise answered and I had a chat a while. She hadn't been told the real reason I was taking out Seth and Denise tonight. I told her I wasn't feeling well, seemed to have contracted a stomach virus, wouldn't be picking up the kids after all. 'Take care of yourself,' Louise said. 'I wouldn't want to lose that alimony.' We both chuckled. I spoke to Denise and said the same thing. She whispered, 'What about Ellie?'

'She doesn't mind. We'll do it some other time.'

'Fine with me. Fine if we never do it. I don't really understand ...'

'That's enough.'

'Wow, are *you* in good spirits! Want me to put Seth on?'

'No. Just tell him. Goodbye.'

I cancelled the arrangements at the restaurant, and showered, and told myself that when I came out Ellie would be there. She wasn't. She didn't come back for three more hours. Then she walked in, directly to the couch, where I was trying to do a crossword puzzle. She was wearing blue jeans and a yellow blouse and looked fine. 'Hey,' she said brightly, and kissed me. 'I saw a movie. And I got the final fitting on my gown. It looks kinda nice. *You* look kinda nice. Let's go to bed.'

I laughed ... with relief, I guess. She said, 'Here, let me lead you little boy,' and opened my fly, and led me.

Approaching her climax, she panted, 'When you fuck me, Nickie, everything's all right.'

And when I didn't, *nothing* was all right. That was the insight I had while still lying on her, feeling myself shrivel inside her sheath.

I had another insight, later that evening, when she got bitchy again, due probably to not having eaten anything more substantial than toast and coffee for twenty-four hours. Even if we had only one good hour a day together, it was enough for me. That hour was worth a lifetime of civilized, and sterile, living with anyone else.

Her feeling that we weren't working out together and that she should perhaps return to St Louis for good wasn't mentioned again. We had three great days, which ended when I gave into her entreaties to teach her to drive the Porsche.

She'd always driven cars with automatic transmission. The Porsche had a Carrera gear box, a manual shift with *five* forward gears. She said Harv had a Firebird with four-on-the-floor, and she'd tried it a few times, and this couldn't be too different.

It wasn't. She admitted later she'd done badly with the Firebird. She did terribly with the Porsche. She bucked it by releasing the clutch too quickly just about every time in every gear, and she couldn't find fifth about half the time, grinding gears, and my nerves, by jamming the stick in a panic in a dozen different directions. And even though we were on a country road not far from the cottage, there was *some* traffic and she had no time to concentrate on *where* she was going since the clutching and shifting took all her attention. To cut the dismal story short, she almost ran head-on into a station wagon. I grabbed the wheel and swung us back into our own lane.

I did a little shouting. I know it never does any good, but I never claimed to be the most gentle, or stable, of people. And a little shouting is sort of expected, even classic, in such situations. Her response was a sudden, dead stop, right there in the middle of the road, with a car not far behind us, an ear-splitting shriek of, '*Go to Hell!*' and a quick exit. I sat there, open-mouthed, as she ran across the opposite lane to a cornfield. She plunged through the first few rows and was lost to sight.

The car behind sounded its horn, briefly, and I pulled to the shoulder. The driver, a heavy set woman, looked at me and then at the cornfield as she passed by – passed by slowly, as if reluctant to leave such an interesting situation.

I ran across the road and up to the first row of corn. Then I stopped. A cornfield is like a rain-forest, a jungle. I called, 'Ellie? Ellie, this way!'

No answer.

I called again. Still no answer. Perhaps I should return to the car and wait ... but who knew how far that nut would go! And what if she'd become lost? And what if she ran across some randy farm-boy deep in the field ...'

I pushed in between the stalks, which were seven and eight feet high and set only inches apart. I kept pushing, lurching amongst the rows, calling out every so often. It was a hot day, and hot as hell in that field. I'd stopped to wipe my forehead and eyes, when I heard something. I followed the sound, crossing rows to my left, then moving back toward the road ... and quite suddenly I saw her. She was off to my right and a little ahead, squatting on the ground, her arms twined and moving around her head and face. The sound she was making, the sound that had led me to her, was a *whine*, a sort of, 'Oooooohhhhh...' low in the throat. I crashed through the corn to her and said, 'What's the matter? What happened?'

She jumped up and grabbed me and tried to burrow her head into my armpit. 'Get me out, quick, the bugs, they'll crawl up my nose and in my mouth and ears, hurry.'

'The bugs?' I had to laugh. 'But there are just a few little ...'

She pushed into me and said, '*Hurry, Nick*. It happened to me when I was a kid in Bley and I almost went crazy with a bug in my ear and once in my mouth! *Hurry!*' And she was pushing and jerking as if being attacked by a horde of angry bees.

I tried to get her to walk behind me, but she wouldn't raise her head from my chest. So we had to push through that thick cornfield side by side, my arm around her, the stalks crashing against us.

This girl was insane ...

I tried to take her out for another driving lesson the next day, but she refused. She had a better suggestion. 'Why don't you buy me a little second-hand car with automatic?'

I tried to explain the economics of two cars in Manhattan, and how ridiculous it was when we didn't use my *one* car that often. She said she wanted to be able to drive to Westchester, Long Island, New Jersey; to explore and feel free. 'It would help me, Nickie,' she said as we rowed out on the lake. 'It would stop me from getting so down.'

'But in time you'll learn to drive the Porsche ...'

'I *won't*! It's *yours*! You get all uptight when I'm driving it! I won't go through any more fights.' And no matter how much I pleaded, shouted, threatened, joked, she refused to get behind the wheel.

We made love that night. We never missed a night. And it was fantastically good, as always. And sleeping in each other's arms drained away the tensions, as always. And we were both cheerful, driving back to the city the next day ... though I was painfully aware that in five days she'd be leaving for the wedding.

Those last five days were full of calls to and from St Louis. Claire, Claire's mother, Claire's brother, Claire's college roommate, all had last-minute communications for the maid of honour. There was the bridal shower; a change of location. There was another party, this a sudden decision by her college classmates. There were consultations on the gown, on who would pick up who, on who would accompany who ... and I remembered the madness of my own wedding.

I was depressed. I was sullen. Ellie never noticed. She was involved, in something of which I had no part ... and excited and anxious to be off.

I didn't go with her. We both knew I wouldn't, though it hadn't been spelled out. I didn't really care to go. What I wanted was for her to *want* me to go, and she went through the motions that last day, saying, 'Why not, Nickie? I won't be able to stay with you – all the arrangements have been made for me to stay at the Dennekers' – and I guess I won't even see you until the wedding, but if you'd like to stay at a motel nearby ...'

I said no, I'd make Harold happy and do some work, and I'd also spend some time with Denise, and I'd get to see Ron, and I'd make arrangements for our trip to Miami next month, and I'd do some running ...

Oh, I had plenty to do.

We both played roles, and parted at the airport with hugs and kisses. But I knew the truth and she knew the truth and it was another strike against our making it.

She called the next night, at eleven New York time, just as she'd promised. She said, 'God, I miss you, honey!' She described the bridal shower and said that tomorrow night the college friends were throwing their party.

'Only girls?'

She said, 'No, some boys too,' and then, hurriedly, 'Have to get off the phone, Nickie. Family wants to use it. Love you.' She popped kisses.

I said, 'Wait. If I want to call you, what's the number there?'

She gave it without hesitation, and having that number made quite a difference; made me sleep well that night.

I have to admit that I was actually *relieved* to be free of her the first night. And the second, after the call, was okay too. But by the third night, after seeing Denise, and bowling with Ron, and enjoying the lack of drama, I began to miss her. Physically, of course ... but not just physically. The fourth night I was desolate, and wanted to call her, and was afraid to call too early as she'd be out, or too late and wake the family (or, hidden fear, find she wasn't there). The fifth night I called at eleven, ten St Louis time. A man answered, and shouted, 'Ellie, another admirer!'

Another?

She was bubbling. She said, 'Hey, whatcha doing?' I said, 'Pulling on it.' She laughed, and dropped her voice. 'Nickie, not when I'm here. The place is full of people.'

'How was that college party?'

'Okay. I didn't know many of the kids.'

'Was Harv there?'

Did she pause? 'Yes, he had a date.'

'What was she like?'

'Oh, I didn't pay any attention. I had a date too.' And then, laughing, 'Don't get mad. He was the best man. We were sort of paired.'

'Hope you enjoyed yourself.'

'C'mon now, don't get uptight.' She lowered her voice even more, so that I could barely hear it. 'Love you, honey. Miss you. See you in five or six days.'

'Wait a minute! You said you'd be back the morning after the wedding. That's Sunday, the day after tomorrow. *Two* days!'

'Did I say that? But you know how late weddings end. It's an *evening* wedding. Nickie.'

'All right. So you'll take the evening flight on Sunday.'

'There's a post-wedding luncheon or something on Tuesday. They expect the maid of honour to be there.'

'What the hell! Is Claire one of the Four Hundred?'

'Oh, her family did real good since leaving the old neighbourhood.'

'You sure they don't expect the maid of honour to go along on the honeymoon?'

'C'mon, honey. What's another few days? And as long as I'm here, I want to see Liz and Gina and the baby. It makes sense, doesn't it?'

I said that her staying there for good made even more sense. She said not to be 'an old grouch'. I forced a chuckle and a 'Just kidding'. We said goodbye again. Then I murmured, without knowing I would, 'Ellie, please don't make any mistakes.'

She was quiet. I said, 'Ellie?' She said, 'I won't call any more if you're going to be like that.'

'You forget – *I* called.'

'*Goodbye*, Nickie.'

'Remembering what I once told you?'

'I'm hanging up.'

'I'll expect you to call Wednesday morning, before getting on the plane.'

'I think it'll be Friday.' There was laughter in the background. She said something off side, and when she came back on, she too was laughing. It bothered me.

'I'll bet no one there knows anything about me.'

'Claire does.'

'But no one else, huh?'

'As many people know about you in St Louis as know about me in New York. Not counting your children.'

I began to say that meant only one, Ron, but her voice rose and she said, cheerfully, 'Well, got to go now, see you Friday.'

Friday meant she was stretching her original six-day stay into twelve. I wanted to argue the point, but she'd already hung up.

That night I missed her terribly ... and I thought of Harv. I tried to visualize him from Ellie's fragmented descriptions. What I got was a rich, young, kind, gentle, generous muscle-man with a ten-inch dong. It didn't make sleeping any easier.

I dreamed, or perhaps fantasized just before sleep, that he was being shot, cleanly, professionally, and that Ellie had no one to go to, and no one to love, but me.

Ellie didn't call Saturday, the night of the wedding. I suppose it was too much to expect – though *I* would have called. And she hadn't called Sunday by eleven p.m., ten St Louis time. So I called the Dennekers' home. A girl answered; a child by the sound of her voice. I asked for Ellie.

'She's not here.'

'Will you have her call Nick Leib when she comes in?'

'She won't be here any more.'

'But isn't she staying with you?'

'She did, until the wedding.'

'Where is she staying now?'

'I don't know.'

'Can I speak to your mother, or father?'

'They're not here.'

I began to sweat. 'Did you see her at the wedding?'

123

'Yes. She was maid of honour.'

'Was it late when she left?'

'Not too late. It was about ... well, I think it was twelve o'clock. I was still there when she and her boyfriend left.'

Boyfriend. I remember that a pulse began to hammer away in my temples. And that the next day I got my first speeding ticket in two years. And now that I think of it, it was about this time that I began to notice how noisy the people were in the apartment above me ...

I kept my voice oh-so-casual. 'Do you know Harv?'

'He used to come here with Ellie before she went to college in New York.'

'Well, thank you.'

'That's okay.'

I was shaking when I hung up. I tried to calm myself. She wouldn't play around, not after promising specifically not to. She'd simply *left* with Harv ... and why not? He had a car. He'd driven her somewhere; her sister's, probably.

I dialled Gina's number. A man answered. He was as surly as hell, saying, 'It's kinda late, ain't it, fella?' I apologized, though I wanted to tell him to ram himself. This was the pig who had tried to screw Ellie the night Gina had given birth to his son. Besides, a quarter after ten wasn't late by any adult standards I knew.

I asked for Ellie.

'Ellie?' He spoke away from the phone. 'Ellie been here, Gin?' Then, to me, 'She wasn't here. Said she had to get right back to college.'

I dialled her mother's number, though I hated the thought of subjecting myself to that bitch's discourtesies. A voice very much like Ellie's and Gina's, but lighter and younger, answered. I said, 'Liz?'

'Yes.'

'This is Nick Leib.'

'Oh, hello.' She sounded terribly shy.

'Is Ellie there?'

'Uh, no. She called me yesterday. She said she might see me today, but then she called this morning. She couldn't make it.'

'She tell you where she was staying?'

'I think at Claire's. I can give you the number.'

'That's all right, honey. I've got it. I hope to meet you some day. Ellie talks about you all the time. How very pretty you are. How very sweet.'

She giggled, and we said goodbye. Ellie *talked* about her, and Gina, and Gina's baby, all right, but she didn't waste any precious

St Louis moments on them. It was Harv Cohen who got those moments. She'd left the wedding with him, and disappeared.

Of course, it was only one day. And she *might* have gone to see someone else – say her maternal grandmother. If I heard from her tomorrow, and she explained ...

I wished I had thought to hire a private investigator to tail her! I wanted desperately to know exactly where she was. Rather, I wanted desperately to know where she wasn't – anywhere but with Harv.

I'd gotten some sleeping pills from Ron. I took one and washed it down with a beer and tried to read. That required too much concentration, so I turned on the television. Half an hour later I went to bed. I wanted the night to go away, and tomorrow to come, and Ellie's call to come. I knew I was being psycho, and I'd never been this way about any woman before, and still I couldn't reason myself, shame myself, talk myself out of the wild, sick feeling. A feeling of *panic*. What if the night dragged on and I kept thinking, kept seeing her in Harv's embrace ... ?

I heard myself saying, 'I'll kill the bastard! I'll kill him!'

I took another pill. I slept the sleep of the drugged; yet I was up at seven the next morning.

She wouldn't call during the day. She never had; wouldn't expect me to be home, even if she wanted to call. But I couldn't face Harold and the office. I had coffee and two aspirin, and showered and fiddled with my hair and shaved, and didn't look at the time until I dressed. A big hour and a half had passed. How the hell would I get through the rest of the day? And the three days until Friday morning? And what if she didn't call Friday?

I could actually feel screams pushing up in my throat! What the hell was wrong with me? This little bitch was playing me for a sucker ... and she didn't seem to care very much whether or not I knew it.

Except. Except as concerned her fear of zeroing, halving, and quartering. I'd almost forgotten that.

By God. I wouldn't let *her* forget it!

But why not drop her? Why not end it, send her packing, gain the satisfaction of tossing her clothes into the hall and tossing *her* right after them?

No way, as Ellie would say. No way at all. My mind could conceive of such practical and manly solutions. My insides, my guts, could only plan to hold her, some way, any way.

But if I could get interested in another woman?

I phoned Ledya. She kept late hours, my little actress, and answered sleepy-voiced. She sounded cute and sexy, and I asked myself why in hell I couldn't grab her, for the short if not the long haul ... and she would make a beautiful partner for the long haul too.

Of course, I hadn't lost Ellie. No matter what she was doing, she had definitely said she was coming home Friday. Home to me. Whom she missed. Whom she loved. This even if she played around a little. So I'd play around a little too, and we'd be even and this would cool me down, make me what I'd always been with other women – casual, never jealous, able to enjoy just about any situation, including a turn-on from their experiences with other men.

I was whistling in the dark. My insides were still in turmoil.

'It's a beautiful day,' I said. Actually, it was hot and overcast. 'It's a day for the country. How about a drive up along the Hudson? We'll take the Jersey side – the Palisades Interstate – the prettiest road in the East. We'll lunch at the Bear Mountain Inn.'

'Sounds lovely. What will your *patient* say?'

I didn't want to be reminded of Ellie. 'She's off in the boon-docks of St Louis. Who knows if she'll ever be back.' I felt a deep pang.

Ledya wore a hotpants outfit that would have stimulated any male from grammar school to Golden Age Centre. She really should have worn a bra, big breasted as she was, but the heavy jingling was an extra added attraction. I didn't know where to look first – that solid ass straining the hotpants, or those big tits bouncing in the blouse.

You'll just have to take my word for it, but I didn't care to look at *either*.

Of course, that would change once we were at my cottage and in my bed. I had to play it carefully, show her considerable attention, because she was still very sensitive over Ellie and our last meeting. So I talked much and joked much and touched her often, and by the time we'd reached the Bear Mountain Inn she was warm enough to snuggle up to me as we walked from the parking lot. Unlike Mrs Carlhein, my tennis partner, Ledya got plenty of looks from the boys ... as much, in this outfit, as Ellie. Well, perhaps not *quite* as much. Ellie's face, Ellie's walk and manner – so very sexual; so very ... whorey.

Okay. I admitted it to myself. Ledya had looks and sex appeal, but she didn't look that approachable, that available to the men who stared. Ellie somehow did. A man felt if he could just get her alone for ten minutes ...

I'd felt that way on first meeting her. I was wrong ... but by how much? Instead of ten minutes, it had been a few days.

Still, Ledya played the field. All young chicks made it these days.

It was the new approach; it was sexual equality and freedom; it was good.

But not for Ellie! Not for my girl with anyone but me!

I was tightening up again. I overcame it by having two quick Gibsons. With the additional help of a bottle of wine, lunch was lovely. And a café Strega to finish up. Ledya said she didn't remember my drinking that much. 'What happened to the health food and vitamins?'

I said nothing had happened ... but she was right. I'd forgotten the vitamins this week. I'd forgotten about living forever.

We drove to the cottage. A stroll to the lake – and a reasonably successful effort not to think of Ellie here; Ellie and a little kiss, and a little exploration of those hotpants, that full blouse ...

'Not outside, Nick,' Ledya murmured. Her mouth opened hot and wet and her tongue worked my mouth and I knew it was bedtime.

I didn't have a hard on. Of course, I would, once she took her clothes off.

In the bedroom, she took her clothes off. I was dead behind my shorts. She undressed me, and her eyebrows rose. I murmured, 'Overworked, baby.' But I was upset, and ashamed, and afraid. I didn't want her and her big pink tits and her swelling white ass and her light pubic hair. Because Ellie's tits were small, and Ellie's ass was wider, darker, and Ellie's pubic hair was thicker, blacker. And Ellie smelled different. Ellie was altogether different ... and Ellie was the ideal now, the schematic of lust and love imprinted on my brain.

But still, I should have been able to fuck this delectable creature. I *say* 'delectable'. I didn't *think* or *feel* 'delectable'. I knew it with my mind, adding up what I saw, and what the American standard of excellence was, and most of all what I'd experienced with Ledya before I'd met Ellie. Christ, men screwed women without loving them, and while being in love with others. I would too!

In bed, she used her hand and her mouth and up it came. I still didn't want her. I regretted the entire day. But here I was. And there was Ledya greedy to be filled. I filled her. I went on a hell of a long time before making it, and so Ledya hugged me to her afterward and sighed her satisfaction and gratitude and love.

On the way home, she napped and I sped. I cursed other drivers under my breath and wondered if Ellie might possibly call early for a change – say six or seven o'clock. And I hit eighty, and was nailed by a state-trooper.

Ledya awoke as he handed me the ticket through my window. He held onto my licence stub, giving her a long up and down stare. She rubbed her eyes. 'No violations in eighteen months,' the cop said, still examining Ledya. 'You can mail your fine in, Mr Leib.' I said. 'Thank you. Can we go now?' He handed me the stub and stepped back just a little, keeping her legs in view. I wished him the clap. Then I thought of *Ellie* sitting beside me and his checking *her* out that way ... and I was ready to join Weatherman.

I was in the apartment at seven. The phone rang at seven-ten, and I heard myself saying, 'Let it be Ellie, please.'

It was Ron. He wanted me to come over. Vera was out playing Mah Jongg. I said I couldn't. He asked if I'd heard from Ellie. I opened up a little, told him a little of what I was suffering, and he was surprised and then properly sympathetic. But for once, talking to Ron didn't illuminate or ease a situation.

At one a.m., I lost hope and took two pills.

There's no point going into Tuesday, Wednesday, and Thursday. I saw movies, lots of them. I drank liquor, too much of it. I watched television and took pills.

I slept Friday until eight-thirty. I awoke slowly, then snapped erect when I saw the clock. If she called me before her flight, that meant she would call before eight, St Louis time. Or a little before nine, New York time. She would call at any minute!

I waited in that apartment until three. Then I tried calling Gina. No answer. I called her mother. The bitch said Ellie hadn't been there since the grandmother's funeral. She sounded quite happy at being able to tell me that. She was proving what she'd always said – that her daughter was a whore.

I played tennis. I did terribly, even though my opponent was a sixteen-year-old boy whom I'd beaten five out of five times previously. I lost to him twice and was so exhausted I was nauseated.

The phone rang at eleven-thirty. 'Hi, watcha doing?'

My heart leaped. I drew a deep breath. 'Nothing,' I said. I wanted no arguments. I simply wanted her home.

'You sound tired.' Her voice grew arch and cutesy. '*Why* are you tired, Nickie?'

I'd been drinking heavily. 'I'm not tired.'

'Well, I'll be on the TWA flight tomorrow morning. LaGuardia. Will you be happy to see me?'

'Yes.' Then I had to say it. 'But I thought you were coming home today.'

'No. I said I'd *call* today ... didn't I?'

'Maybe. Well, see you tomorrow.' I wanted to sleep now; really sleep for the first time in a week.

'Nickie? What's the matter? You sound ... you all right?'

'Look, I haven't been able to locate you since Sunday night and Claire's sister said you left the wedding with your *boyfriend* ...!' I'd exploded. I hadn't meant to, and I shut myself up as soon as I realized what I was doing. She had to come home.

'Is *that* all?' She laughed, and proceeded to explain away all my suspicions. Or so she thought.

'Claire's sister is twelve. She remembers Harv as my boyfriend from before. She doesn't know we're through. And we are through, honey. I had a fight with my mother on the phone so I couldn't go there, and I changed my mind about visiting Gina when I found out she was talking about me not being in college and making like Grandma Guerney – that's what she told people. So I took a motel room and I rented a car and I kicked around, visiting lots of old friends and Grandma and Mr Alexis and, well, you know. I enjoyed myself and I'm ready to come home to my Nickie love. Because you *are* my love, you know that? Am I yours?'

I'm ashamed to admit it. I was so damned happy I said, 'God, yes!'

And I didn't mention Harv any more. And our talk became the lovely nonsense of lovers, ending with promises of passion, with kisses, with lingering goodbyes.

Not until the next day, or rather the next evening, after we'd made love three times – once before each meal – and she was in the bathroom, the door locked against my intruding on the mysteries of her remaining a blonde, did the rage, the suspicion, locked away inside me break free. I saw her big shoulder purse on the couch and without hesitation dumped its contents on the coffee table. Amidst an incredible jumble of trash (including about a hundred gum wrappers!), I found three pertinent items; pertinent to my loss of sanity, that is. One, her cheque book. She had spent a hundred and eighty-six dollars, and while at first glance that seemed to cover her motel room and car (I'd paid her air fare) an examination of her cheque stubs changed the picture. There were five stubs. One was for seventy-five dollars, and was marked, 'Claire's present'. Three more were marked 'Famous Barr', a St Louis department store. The fifth read 'Liz', and was dated yesterday; obviously for a gift sent to her sister. How then had she paid for the motel room and car!

Second item: An address and telephone number, written on the back of a card, and not in Ellie's handwriting. The front of the card read, 'Russ Doon, Maiglen Investment Fund', and listed a business address and phone number, different from those on the back.

Third item: A little note from Claire to her maid of honour: 'Thanks so much! You were super! Hope you'll be around St Louis when we get back as you said you might. Try to work it out. Jerry says, "Me too," and sends a kiss. No more of that, husband! All our love to Hellie-Ellie and her man, whoever he turns out to be. Love, Claire the Square.'

There was a fourth item, but I didn't find that in her purse. I was sweating as I went past the bathroom door to the bedroom and opened the closet and found her luggage. I went through the supposedly empty bags, looking for anything that would strengthen the case against her. One wasn't quite empty; it held a black plastic writing kit. Tucked away amidst pink flowered paper and envelopes was a used white envelope. It was addressed to Ellie in-care-of Claire Denniker. The back flap was torn. When I put it together, I had Harv Cohen and his Ladue address. I searched for the letter, but didn't find it.

I copied both Cohen's and Doon's addresses into my book and sat in the kitchen, waiting. I was triumphant, and I was sick.

I again thought of letting her go ... and I laughed at myself. I knew the score now. I remembered Maugham's novel and the Leslie Howard, Bette Davis movie, *Of Human Bondage*. But Ellie wasn't that low and calculating, and I wasn't as blameless, as hapless, as Maugham's hero.

Besides, Ellie *lived* with me, and with luck she might never go to St Louis again – alone that is. If I simply *forgot* this trip; if I put away the items I'd taken from her purse and luggage, everything might work out.

I was torn. I was tempted. But when she came out, in new greenprint lounging pyjamas, her hair wrapped turban-style in a towel, calling for a 'great big diet cola', I put the items on the kitchen table.

She blinked, a burlesque of innocence and ignorance.

'From your purse and your luggage.'

She didn't even complain about the flagrant violation of her privacy. 'So? I'm *thirsty*, honey.'

I explained the contradictions of the cheque book. She went to the refrigerator, opened a can, and drank. 'Next,' she sighed.

I pushed forward Russ Doon's card. She said, 'I didn't even know I still had that. You went through my purse so you know how much old junk is there. This was from maybe a year ago, when he wanted to take me out again.'

I pushed forward Claire's letter. She read it through, and snorted derisively. 'Oh, she wanted to hear me say I might be around, so I said it at the rehearsal and made her happy.' She drank again. 'Next.'

She was laughing at me, and it all seemed laughable now. I hesitated with the empty envelope, but then examined the postmark. Dated August of this year. She took it from me and said, 'Now this is *real* evidence,' and pinched my cheek and laughed hard. 'Harv sent me a note saying I looked great at the wedding and telling me he'd be waiting if I got sick of you. And honey, I'm getting sick right now.' But she laughed again and popped her lips at me. 'I threw the letter away, knowing you, but guess I slipped up with the envelope.'

You'll notice I'd allowed her to pass by the cheque book. I guess I *wanted* her to explain away everything, and she had ... everything except the cheque book. I returned to it. 'How'd you pay for your motel and car?'

'Nickie, you had no right to go through my things!'

'*Now* you protest. Now that you can't explain something.'

'I can, but you won't like it, and you won't believe it.'

My heart sank. 'Try me.'

She tried me, sorely.

'Harv paid. I told you he was generous, and I guess he hoped I'd sleep with him as I did the last time. And we did have lunch and dinner a few times and we talked a lot and I told him I was in love with you and I didn't think I'd ever be coming back to St Louis. And we said goodbye.'

I had my answer. I had my choice, too: I could believe her, or not. I chose to believe her.

SIX

The next few months were good and bad, mostly bad. As I said, I'd chosen to believe her story of what she'd done during her twelve-day wedding visit to St Louis. Consciously, that is. But I was short-tempered at times, as was she. And I checked on her when I went to the office, phoning often and getting busy signals occasionally and getting no answer at all much of the time. When I questioned her about the busy signals, she would say she'd phoned a store, or someone had phoned me (and failed to leave a message), or it was a sales pitch, or a wrong number. Once in a while she would say she had phoned Liz or Gina or Claire As for her being out, she'd gone window shopping ... but her windows charged plenty, because she was going through that chequeing account at the rate of about a hundred and fifty a week, and this with me paying all our living expenses.

Ellie bought 'outfits'. We quarrelled bitterly about her spending. She said I lived as if I earned fifteen instead of fifty thousand. I said that having some money didn't mean you had to throw it away. She said, 'Harv doesn't make anywhere *near* fifty thousand and yet *he* isn't tight.'

'*Tight!* You live like a goddam princess!'

'I'll bet that's the way your mother talked about anyone who had a dollar in her pocket, right?'

I had to restrain myself not to slap the sneer off her lips ... and she was quite right. My mother *had* talked that way, minus the goddam. And why not? She'd sweated out every nickel, and this bitch was mocking her, and I just had to tell her the truth, no matter what she did about it. 'You never do a thing around the house any more and you don't even *look* at those workbooks and you don't move your ass out of bed until noon ... and you lecture *me* about how I spend my own money'

'My own money,' she mimicked. '*Everything* here is yours! I'm a goddam guest, your fucking piece of ass ...'

'And not *only* mine! But the others don't pay as much!'

That scene ended with her swinging at me, and me swinging back. We both managed to miss. Then she ran to the bathroom. I tried to kick the door down. She opened up and we glared at each other. She suddenly said, 'I'm calling Harv.'

'Sure. But collect.'

'Cheap sonovabitch!'

'Generous, open-handed soul ... with other people's money!'

She slammed into the bedroom, shut the door, put the button lock on. I went to the kitchen, waited a while, and picked up the phone, covering the mouthpiece with my hand. A deep voice, but obviously young, was speaking: 'I'll accept the charges, operator.'

'Harv?' Ellie said.

'Ellie! How *are* you?'

'Well, not so good.'

I waited for her to spill her guts, to castigate me, to pitch him. And I thought of what I would do to them, the both of them. God, how I hated her for having someone else when I didn't, when I *couldn't!*

'What do you mean?' he asked.

'Oh, I miss everyone.'

'Come on home. I can get you an apartment ...'

'Have to finish summer session. Then I'm going into fall session.'

'*Really?*' (He obviously knew Ellie well!)

'Sure. I told you.'

'What about Nick?'

'What about him?'

'You sure you aren't living together? I mean ... you know.'

'I told you, Harv; he has his room and I have mine. Besides, he still can't do it. That's why he was in St Louis – to see Masters and Johnson, the sex doctors.'

'I can't believe he *never* ...'

'Believe what you want. I'd better go now.'

'Don't be mad, honey. You have to admit it's hard to believe he never even tries.'

'Oh, he tried, all right. And if you have to know, I try to help him. I mean, if he could get it up and be normal, I'd be happy for him. I'd have to move out, of course, but still, he's done a lot for me, Harv, school and all. You yourself said he was good for me.'

'I said if you had to be with any man but me, I was glad it was with one who was so important and that old.'

She giggled. The bitch giggled! I was gripping the phone so hard my hand ached. I longed to be gripping his throat ... no *her* throat!

'You coming to visit again soon, Ellie?'

'I don't know. Exams are coming up. Then I might be going to Florida between semesters. Nick has to be there on business. He needs me to look after him – poor guy's sick so much.'

'Come home and *I'll* take you to Florida, or Las Vegas, or even Europe. You always wanted to go to Europe. I'll be taking some time off in September.'

'That's sweet of you, Harvey.'

His voice, softened, thickened. 'I miss you so much, baby. I miss your ...'

'Have to go now.' She sounded frightened ... and I suddenly realized she was *counting* on my listening in. She'd been directing the conversation, keeping it within limits, keeping it safe – enough to insult and hurt me, but not enough to reveal anything that might have gone on between them during the wedding visit.

'Ellie ... can I visit you in New York?'

'Maybe. I'll let you know.'

'Can I call you?'

'I told you no. He sleeps a lot and if you happen to wake him, he gets very angry. And then he takes it out on me.'

'How does he take it out on you, the old bastard!'

'Oh, he crabs a lot ... listen, he's waking up. I got to go now.

'Bye. Here's a kiss for being so sweet.'

'I ... I still care, Ellie. Remember the last ... ?'

' 'Bye!' She hung up.

I did too, and sat down at the table, and tried to bring order to my confused thoughts and feelings. She'd punished me with the call ... but she still was mine. She's kept Harv on the string, but she'd obviously used him to get at me.

And yet, Oft a true word is spoke in jest.

She walked out of the bedroom, past the kitchen doorway and into the living room, humming. I strolled after her. She was wearing green shorts and a halter and was going out on the patio to catch the late afternoon sun. I followed. She lay down in the lounge; I took the little folding chair.

'What did Harv have to say?'

She shrugged and looked off toward the East River. 'The air here is *filthy*. Don't know why I ever thought New York was such a big deal. At least you can *breathe* in St Louis.'

'I guess you're going back there?'

She shrugged again and hummed to herself, and then closed her eyes and stretched. And spread her legs, showing me she wasn't wearing anything under those shorts. And they didn't fit snugly enough at the crotch.

After a while, I leaned over and kissed her and said, 'You little bitch.' She giggled.

'Of course, it'll do no good spreading your legs that way because I can't get it up.'

She squealed laughter.

'And even Masters and Johnson couldn't help ...'

She sat up, holding her stomach, shaking her head, laughing too hard to speak.

'And so you can use your finger ... or maybe I'll buy you a vibrator.'

She finally managed speech. 'Or maybe the pilot two apartments along can help me.'

'When did you meet *him*?'

'In the elevator last week. He said, "Hey, I didn't think we had anyone like *you* in this house." Man, did he ever check me out! And he wanted me to come to a party. Tall and about thirty-five, right? And built. So if you want me to move out, I'll bet he'd let me move right in. Wouldn't have to carry my things more than a little ways down the hall.'

I began to get up. It wasn't funny any longer. All the jokes were moving in one direction — away from me, toward other men. I knew then what she obviously didn't. It *wasn't* a joke.

She said, 'Nickie, wait a minute. The pilot's out on his terrace, look.'

I turned. McManners, I think his name was. Alex McManners. About ten feet tall and built well, even if his face was big-nosed and lumpy. Rumour had it he was married and the father of three back in Los Angeles, which was the other end of his New York–L.A. run. Here he was a bachelor swinger.

He raised his arm in greeting. I nodded. Ellie waved energetically. He was fooling around with a flower box, but managed to keep turned in our direction so as to ogle Ellie, who was lying with those open legs facing him. The terrace between was empty, and he could see easily enough.

'Close your legs,' I said.

'Louder,' Ellie said, and spread a little more, sighing and moving her bottom.

It ended with me moving my chair to block his view ... and getting so good a view of my own that I finally asked her to come inside.

'Kiss me, Nickie.'

'But he's watching.'

'Kiss me or let me alone.'

I got up, leaned over, and kissed her. She tried to open my fly. I pushed her hand away, glancing hurriedly around. A transistor radio was playing on the terrace one story up and to the north. If anyone looked over the edge ...

I told her that. It seemed to stimulate her more, and led to her getting me out and stroking me while she writhed on the lounge. When I thought I was going to come off in her hand, she said, '*Carry* me inside, Nickie. I want you to pick me up and carry me to the bed and fuck me for an hour!'

I picked her up, keeping my back to McManners, because I was still hanging out, if not loose! As we reached the terrace doors, she said, for too loudly for my ears alone, 'Oh, *Nickie* ... *hurry*!' I glanced at McManners. He was frankly staring at us. Ellie laughed as I stumbled through the doors. 'I think he went more for your prick than for me. Maybe we should call him in for a little party?'

I didn't bother answering. The bitch had managed to turn me on so strongly I couldn't wait for the bedroom. I put her down on the carpet and there we stayed for at least the hour she'd specified. And while it went on, I again knew this was something I had to have, no matter what price I paid.

And when it was over, I again knew the price would be enormous.

That was a relatively good day. There were other days. Days in which she bitched until I couldn't stand it. Days in which she sat staring slack-jawed at the television for six and seven hours. Days in which she disappeared until evening, after saying she was 'going down to the pharmacy for a minute ...' and explained it with, 'I just goofed around the stores.' And the packages would be delivered a few days later – a hundred or two hundred dollars' worth of 'goofing around'. And then she was broke again and bitched about it and asked me to at least *rent* her a car so she could explore the area.

'Let's explore it together,' I said.

'Cheap bastard,' she muttered.

I almost hit her then. I *did* hit her a week later, when she'd called me 'Harv' for the third time. Something new, this, and no game. It simply slipped out of her.

Once she did it in bed, but I wasn't sure and she insisted she'd merely cleared her throat. 'Like *harak, harak,*' she said. I nodded. Harak, yeah.

The next time was when we'd gone to a Buick dealer to look at the Opel GT, a car she liked. I wasn't going to buy another car, but I did enjoy examining new ones. Seated in a yellow model of the sleep little hardtop, she said, 'God, doesn't this *swing*, Harv?' Then she blinked and said, 'And it doesn't cost much, does it, Nick?'

I said, 'No, harak, harak,' and could feel the blood continuing to drain from my face.

She laughed a little. On the way home, she was very quiet, and I said, 'Are you thinking of him?'

She surprised me. She said, 'I guess so,' her eyes and voice down. I felt a sudden rush of pure anguish, followed by slow-building anger.

We went to the Saturday School to register for the fall session. At least that's what we *said* we were going to do when we drove across the George Washington Bridge to Route Four and then to Fairleigh Dickenson University. She was glum, almost sullen. I spoke of how it would give her purpose and pride. Actually, I didn't believe she'd last a month. As we parked near the building she said, 'How'm I going to get here every day?' I said she was forgetting – she only had to be here twice a week; Friday evening and a good part of Saturday. 'You'll learn to handle the Porsche ...'

'I already told you, Nick! I won't drive this car!'

'Then I'll drive you here myself!'

'If you weren't so tight with your money, you'd get me a second-hand car...'

'It's not the price of the car so much as the insurance and garaging!'

'Don't yell! I'm sick of your yelling, Nick!'

She never missed my name throughout the early part of that Friday, which included the ride to the school and our going inside to the admissions office, where she absolutely froze up and I had to do all the talking. The woman behind the desk kept glancing at her, and finally asked her directly if she had any questions. Ellie said, 'No,' in a weak, frightened voice. A heavy-set man with thick grey hair sitting further inside the large office came to the front desk and smiled. 'I can assure you, there's nothing to feel uptight about.' He said the word 'uptight' as if he'd practised long hours in front of a mirror. 'Everything's cool in the Saturday School,' and he chuckled and said it was his 'groovy poem' to make new people feel at home.

Ellie smiled a little. Her eyes finally went to him, and he smiled a lot. He asked her to step to his desk, and she sauntered along in front of him, and he actually rubbed his hands together in anticipation ... of what? I stayed where I was. I hadn't been invited. Besides, I felt she had to go it alone sooner or later. But she was too damned good at going it alone with *men*, and men only.

They sat at his desk and talked. Ellie was answering at length toward the end. Her little laugh sounded frequently. When they finally returned, the man said, 'I'm looking forward to having you in my class, Ellie,' and took her hand and squeezed it. She said, oh-so-sweetly, 'Thank you, Mister Clyder,' or some such name. They batted eyes at each other, and she walked to the door as if I were someone she'd never seen before. I pointedly said, 'Goodbye, and thanks for giving my fiancée so much attention.' His mouth fell open. 'Ah, not at all.'

'Now *why'd* you do that?' Ellie said in the hall. 'I had him just where I wanted him. I'll need all the help I can get...'

'Not *that* kind of help!' I'd made up my mind I wasn't going to waste fifteen hundred dollars so she could play around with Clyder and others!

'Shit! You're worse than my mother! He's the maths instructor and you know I'll never pass maths unless he's on my side!'

'And on your back and on your belly...'

She took off for the front doors. She was moving fast, and her ass shook inside her tight hotpants, and at least five men turned to get a better look.

And all the time it had been *Nick*, because all the time we'd argued rather than spoken pleasantly.

But when we stopped at the Route Four Bloomingdale's to look at the fall fashions, and she saw a suède coat she really liked, she grabbed my arm and said, 'Harv, honey, I'd look so *good* ...' and sighed and smiled and said, 'Harak, harak.'

I slapped her. I don't know if anyone saw me. I did it very quickly and turned and went out to the car, seeing nothing and no one. I sat there cursing, and then I sat there regretting, and finally, when she hadn't shown for more than twenty minutes, I sat there fearing.

I had to go through the entire store before I found her. She was in the shoe department, trying on boots. I came up to her and said, 'Ellie ...' She jerked, as if expecting another slap. I said, 'I'm sorry.' She said, 'The sales lady'll be back in a minute. If you want a *real* fight, stick around. *I mean it!*' Her voice had risen to a shout and people looked at us and I walked away. I waited at the edge of the department, watching her try on one pair of boots after another. Finally, she chose a pair. I wondered where she'd gotten the money. She'd told me she was broke, and I was going to put a few hundred into her chequeing account on Monday.

Then I saw her produce a charge card.

I couldn't understand it ... until I looked in my wallet and saw that mine was missing. I went back to her as she was leaning over the register table to sign the slip. I said, 'Hi, honey.' She said, 'Oh, hi,' and froze a moment, and then signed. She was Ellie Leib.

As soon as we came outside, I asked her for my charge card. She took it from her purse and dropped it on the pavement and kept walking. I wanted to kick her! I picked up the card and reached the Porsche as she did. Before I could ask how she'd gotten the card, she said, 'I took it a week ago. Bought a few little things in New York. So maybe it'll cost you a hundred and fifty. I'll have Harv send you the money. He'll even send you the thousand for my chequeing account, if you want me to ask him.'

I said, 'Why would he do that, with you living here?'

'I'm not living here any more. I'm going home on the first plane I can get. Maybe I spent a little money, but I never *hit!*' She turned to me as she said this. 'I told you, Nick. *Say* what you want, but never hit me!'

I tried to explain what her calling me Harv had done. 'Three times ...'

'I talked. You *hit*. I'm through.'

I apologized over and over as we drove toward Manhattan. I swore I'd never hit her again. She said, 'That's right, you won't, because I won't be here for you to hit.'

'Please,' I said, 'hit me back.'

Before I could repeat the plea, she did. She smashed my face with as hard a slap as I've ever gotten, and then punched my shoulder three times, really slugging away. The Porsche swerved and I choked back curses. (I had bruises for a week, and I rarely bruise.)

'Okay,' I said. 'We're even. You won't call me Harv and you won't flirt with teachers and you won't steal my credit cards. And I'll never raise my hand to you again.'

She didn't answer. She didn't talk all the way back home. As I was backing into my spot in the garage, she jumped out of the car and ran away. I finished parking, locked up, and followed. I was sure I'd catch her at the elevators, but she wasn't there. Nor was she in the apartment.

She didn't come home until two the next morning. I was waiting in the living room. I said nothing. I'd hit her and I had no right to censure her for anything, *this* time.

She went right to bed. I joined her. She turned her back on me. I touched her shoulder. She jerked away. I said, 'Ellie, please, can't we at least say goodnight?'

'Goodnight.'

'Honey, I'm sorry. Where did you go?'

'I visited a friend.'

'What friend?'

'Now you're not so sorry any more! Just listen to your voice. *What* friend!'

'But you don't know anyone...'

'That's what *you* think.'

'Well then, fine. I'm glad you made a friend. Maybe we can all go out together some night.'

She laughed. 'Oh, he'd like that!'

He. I knew I was playing the fool. I told myself to shut up. But I couldn't. I kept questioning her. Finally, she turned and said, 'It was Alex, the pilot. He was in the lobby when I came in. He said he was going out for a drink and would I like to join him. So we had a drink.'

'From four-thirty until two a.m.? Nine and a half hours?'

'We had a *few* drinks.'

'You're not high...'

'And dinner and went to his apartment and talked.'

'Talked.'

'Oh, he kissed me a few times and felt me up a little and wanted more...' She turned then, because I was sitting up; because I wasn't apologetic any more; because I was going to do something.

'I went to a movie, goofy,' she said, and put her arms around me and kissed my side. 'Then I ate at the German place, alone. You can ask Griff.' He was our waiter. 'Then I went to another movie. You can find the stubs in my bag. Want to ask me what movies I saw?'

She told me the names and gave me a crazy plot summary of each – 'and then this horny old man takes this hot old girl into the bedroom and we're supposed to believe they planned a prison break for their nephew, but wow, when they come out, you can see from their faces and how tired they are...'

We kissed and she hadn't been drinking, not at all.

We made love. She played a little game, saying the pilot was watching and then joining us. She used his name, and since it was him and not Harv Cohen I enjoyed it.

I had nightmares that night. I was so goddam insecure with this girl, increasingly more jealous of whoever she might know. Yet she was jealous too, especially of my phone calls. Ledya called several times. The last time, Ellie was in the kitchen, and I began setting up a luncheon, and then Ellie walked in. I tried to end the conversation, but Ledya had launched into a discussion of agents and how she was planning to change hers. And Ellie must have picked up something from my expression, my clipped responses, because she came over and sat down at the edge of the bed beside me ... and zipped open my fly. I tried to wave her away, with a smile. She stroked me erect, and went down on me. I said, 'Hey, someone at the door,' but Ledya talked right on over my words, and Ellie sucked on my cock. And despite tension, and a deep resentment of being *attacked* this way, I began to approach orgasm. When I covered the mouthpiece with one hand and pressed down on her head with the other, she withdrew abruptly and left the room. I got off the phone and went after her. She was on the terrace, reading and would *not* come in. I had my first case of blue-balls in years.

Another time, Harold called me in the morning. Ellie was in bed beside me, sleeping. She came awake after a while and turned and listened as I argued against this decision to stay with our old Flip-Chip game instead of redesigning it along the lines of professional hockey, with a goalie target, hockey-stick lever, and chips marked Ranger, Hawks, Canadians, and so on. As I talked, I felt her hand creeping along my thigh. I got out of bed, hooked my foot around the black chair and drew it over. As I sat down, she went to the closet and got her black boots. She put them on, and her gold choker, and dabbed a little chanel on her sex. And came to me and presented that sex to my mouth. I kept moving my head, kept arguing with Harold, finally covered the mouthpiece and said, 'C'mon, Ellie, not now!' She stopped. I spoke to Harold again. She sat down on my lap and kissed my mouth.

Harold said, 'What?'

'I didn't say anything.'

She whispered, 'Fuck me.'

'What the hell are you playing at, Nick!'

I said someone had come in and I'd get back to him. As soon as I hung up, she tried to get away. But this time I caught her. After we finished, I called him back. He was angry, saying I was 'whoring around' while he was trying to talk important business. When we'd finally resumed our discussion, Ellie returned to grab at my penis. Somehow, it wasn't funny, wasn't loving, *was* a physical attack.

She took to going out almost every day about two, and I followed her once and saw her enter the phone booth on the corner of Third. When I walked up and tapped on the glass, she surprised me. Without hesitation, she opened the door and motioned me inside. I began to come in, but the odour in that enclosed space was overpoweringly rotten, and I backed hurriedly out again. She said, 'Got to go now, 'bye,' and hung up. She came out, laughing at me. 'My stomach's upset. Ate a can of beans at lunch.' She swung away. I caught up with her and grabbed her arm. She laughed, 'Bombs away!' and farted loudly. I glanced around, and she laughed again and said, 'Guess I know how to handle you now, Nickie. I'm going to buy a *case* of those beans!'

I finally got to ask who she'd called. She said, 'Gina,' I asked why she hadn't called from the apartment. She said, 'I talk half an hour for a buck and a quarter, then cut out on the extra charges.' I asked if she did it every day at two p.m. She said, 'No, not *every* day, but a lot.'

'Well, why didn't you tell me about it? I'd have approved.'

She said, 'Why make a cheap bastard happy?' And skipped quickly away as I considered kicking her.

The next time she went down to the phone, I searched through her luggage, closets and drawers ... and found a letter stuck away under a pile of blouses. Yes, from Harv Cohen. He didn't say much, just filled her in on some friends of theirs I knew nothing about. Said he missed her. Said he couldn't forget 'Room 54 of the Glenroe Motel and the beautiful time we had there after the wedding.' The envelope wasn't addressed to her at the apartment, but to a Grand Central Station Post Office box number.

I paced up and back, talking to myself. I shook and perspired and told myself to hold tight, not to blow up and throw everything away. But what the hell did I *have*! I tossed down two Scotches and paced some more. She came in a few minutes later, having been gone less than an hour, when for once I could have used half a day to cool off.

As soon as the door closed, I went to her. And handed her the letter. As she said, 'You searched my things again and I told you never ...' I raised both arms above my head and clenched my fists and brought them down on her head. She sank to the floor. I bent over her and I was going to smash her until she couldn't hurt me any more and she was moaning, 'Nickie, please, *please*!' I stopped. I said, 'You whore, you liar, you filth, run, run ...' and my arms rose again. She scrambled away, then ran. I sat down on the couch. I clasped my hands together and rocked back and forth and tried not to see her and Harv in that motel room. I fought for control, and heard her weeping wildly in the bathroom.

Perhaps half an hour passed; perhaps more. She came out and went to the bedroom. Closet doors and drawers opened and shut. I knew she was going to leave me, and I knew I should welcome it, and of course I couldn't *conceive* of it.

When I came in, she was packing. I took the suitcase off the bed and dumped the contents on the floor. I put the case in the closet and said, 'You can leave when you pay what you owe me. I'll figure it out later. Several thousand ...'

She laughed, a screeching, raging sound.

I went to the bathroom and washed my face. I thought of Aaron ... then put the thought away. I heard her moving around. I went back to the bedroom, expecting to find her packing again, not knowing what I would do to stop her.

She was hanging clothing in the closet. I said, 'Listen, we have a find a way ... have to be honest, loyal ...'

'Sing the Star Spangled Banner, why don't you! But beat the shit out of me first!'

I went back to the living room and the couch. I lay down. My head was splitting. I sat up when I heard her. She was opening the hall door. 'Don't,' I said.

She closed the door and looked at me. 'Want to tie me to the bed?' But her chin was trembling, her eyes filling.

'Ellie, why ... you promised ...'

'I had to.' Tears began to run down her cheeks. 'I just had to. He kept begging me to marry him and begging me to let him and I didn't know how to say no. But I told him it was the last time. The

142

very last time. I swear on Liz's life.'

I asked her to get me some aspirin. She did, and I took two, and said, 'All right, if it's the very last time.'

'That's what I said, didn't I? You want me on my knees, holding a Bible?'

I was numb. I was afraid of pushing her any further. And I was beginning to hate her.

I lay down. She cleaned the apartment, glassy-eyed and white of face. I felt ... guilty. I'd hit her again. Did *anything* justify hitting her?

Later she made lunch and we split a bottle of rosé, and I said, 'I'm sick about ... striking you.'

'Yeah, sure.'

I touched her hand. She didn't move it away, but her face was sullen again, her attitude bitchy again. We were back where we'd started.

I asked her about that post office box.

'I've got to have *some* privacy, right? I mean, I'll go crazy...'

'All right.'

'I'd have told you, maybe next week. That letter – you were at the office the day I got it and so I brought it home to read like a human being instead of always reading in that post office with the winos staring at me. And I forgot and put it away. He writes a nice letter, doesn't he?'

'A very nice letter,' I said in Jewish dialect.

She flared. 'No grammar mistakes, are there?'

As a matter of fact, there had been a mispelling and a misuse of the past tense. But who knows or cares how to write letters any more? It's a lost art.

I said no, there'd been no errors.

Two days later we were to meet Ron and a date – not his wife, who wouldn't have dug Ellie at all, and who would have talked about her to Louise, but a girl of twenty-three he'd met at the new cocktail lounge. We were going out to dinner and a show.

I had to call it off. Ellie got 'sick' that morning.

Saturday evening, we were taking Denise and Seth to the Gold Coin. Sunday afternoon, Ellie twisted her ankle playing tennis. While there was no inflammation or swelling, I had to practically carry her off the court and up to bed. I took the kids to dinner, alone. When I came back, she was on the couch, reading. 'Managed to hobble here on your own?' I murmured. She nodded, and went back to the book. Later, she 'limped' to bed. The next day, she was fully recovered. When I suggested we have Denise over that night, she said, 'Will you stop pushing your daughter at me! I mean, Seth is a kid and okay. Denise is only three years younger than me. She won't like me being alone with her father. So *let me alone*!'

'Yeah, Seth is a kid, and male. Denise is eighteen, and female.'

'Brilliant *mans*,' she said in baby talk. She went to the kitchen and made herself something to eat. She didn't ask if I wanted anything.

I received my phone bill. There were *twelve* calls to St Louis, but all were identifiable – Gina and Claire and the mother and one she said was Claire's new apartment. And one to Charlie Alexis, 'just to shoot the breeze a little and find out about my old friends'. A hundred and twelve dollars total. I wanted to ask her to phone evenings and take advantage of the night rates, but I didn't. She'd call me cheap. A hundred and twelve bucks, but okay. Just as long as Harv's number didn't show up. Though I had no illusions about her not speaking to him. She either used the booth on Third, or called him collect.

September passed. We quarrelled more often. We laughed less often. We went out less often. I went to the office two and three times a week, just to separate myself from her and avoid the arguments. Then I would wonder what she was doing, and with whom. We made love every night, and while it was always good we rarely used the *word* love any more. I knew it wasn't working, not in any rational, sensible way. We were isolated from everyone but Seth. She was more isolated than I was, obviously, as this was my town containing my friends and job and family. Also, I would sneak a lunch with Ledya every week or two, though I'd dropped Karen and the others.

In order to date Ledya, I had to pay my dues – go to bed with her occasionally. But I never really wanted to; would have preferred not to; and if I were to try and grade the degree of pleasure I felt, it would be about one tenth of what I felt with Ellie. So I didn't consider it a betrayal, such as Ellie being with Harv, because I was simply making payment for cheerful, intelligent, highly-verbal female companionship.

Well, perhaps it wasn't *that* simple. Perhaps I was trying to loosen the bonds, to reject my total dependence on Ellie, to deny I could be so much in love with someone I didn't *choose*, on all levels, to be in love with. Because, dammit, if it were a matter of choice, I'd have opted *out*!

But it wasn't a matter of choice. I was still crazy about her. I still had to have her, and felt I would always have to have her. I just didn't know how to change the ugly tenor of our day-by-day existence. That she was suffering too became apparent when I found the jar of pills under her pillow.

She generally made up the bed. This morning she was in the bathroom a long time and *I* made the bed. When she came to the kitchen for her prune juice cocktail, I held out the jar.

'God,' she muttered, 'I forgot. Needed them last night...' She made a grab for the bottle. I eluded her, and read the label aloud. Gina Grebes was the patient. V. S. Vereux was the doctor. And the pharmacy was a discount place in St Louis.

'You shouldn't take your sister's medication. What is it?'

'Tranquillizers. A standard kind, you know, so it's okay.'

They didn't *look* like tranquillizers, and I decided to test her. 'No they're not.'

'Now give them to me, Nickie! I don't have to explain...'

'I'm going to have Ron check them out.'

'All right, dammit! They're *Ups*, dexies! You got to know everything, so know that if I didn't have them I'd lose my mind here!'

I was shocked. Staring at her, I realized she *was* looking ragged – a darkness under her eyes and a tightness to her jaw muscles. And her weight was up again, after going down for the wedding, and I'd learned to dread that, because of what it did to her emotional balance.

'Have you been taking them long?' When she began to answer with renewed anger, I quickly added, 'I'm not prying. I'm *worried*, honey. Dexedrine can be dangerous. All amphetamines can be addictive, and if you take enough they'll give you hallucinations and delusions.'

She snorted. 'Jesus, they're practically *nothing*. If you knew what I used to take...' She got the prune juice and mixed it with apple and grape, as I'd taught her. I waited. She stood near the refrigerator, sipping. Finally. she looked at me. 'Aw, is baby all shook up?'

'You're kidding me,' I said, and felt a chill as she smiled and looked away. She sipped again. 'Ellie,' I said, 'please tell me.'

'Sure, why not?' She sat down at the table. She was in as bitchy a mood as she'd been in all week, and that's saying quite a bit. 'These pills are shit. Gina's chicken, though she needs a little help living with that pig, Grebes. Dr Vereux was *my* doctor before I came here.' She laughed. 'Some doctor. Your friend Ron's probably the same.'

'If you're implying Ron's a pill doctor, making money by indiscriminate prescriptions...'

'Okay, okay, so your friend is God almighty. Like all doctors, right?'

That was another thing about Ellie – her near hatred of doctors.

Cops and doctors. Not that I'm too fond of the medical profession and its exorbitant fees ... but Ron is the only doctor I deal with, and Ron is my friend.

'Virgil,' Ellie said, 'would give me any damned prescription I asked for. That's the V in V. S. Vereux. Good old Virge.' She laughed, and tossed down the rest of her juice as if recalling stronger brews. 'What he had in mind, see, was to get me on his examination table, which he never used for exams. I used to string him along. He was about your age, but sort of beat up ... from taking too many of his own pills, I guess. When I'd reach for my purse, he'd give me a father – *hal* – hug and he'd say something like, "No, no, my dear, we'll discuss your problems when you come back ... say later tonight?" I'd always say maybe and he'd move his hands around a little, or try to, because I was very fast in those days with old men.' She fixed me with a vicious eye. 'I've slowed a lot, haven't I?'

'You know where the door is, junkie.'

'Sure, but what do you want to bet you won't let me use it?'

We looked at each other. I could feel the rage building, because she was right, she had me pegged, she was achieving the upper hand. She must have read my face. She laughed and patted my arm and said, 'Hey, let's go down and practise backhands.'

Her laugh had been phony, and so had her pat. She was still looking to hurt me ... and was still looking to learn more about the girl I loved.

'You *were* a junkie, weren't you? Or are you still?'

'Anyone who smokes a single joint is a junkie to people like you, right?'

I'd smoked pot when I'd smoked cigarettes, as far back as when I'd been a G.I. and gone across the border into Mexico. But I wasn't going to explain myself to her. She would only mock me from her unassailable position of age twenty-one and history of varied drug use. What I did say was, 'People like me? I'm some sort of stranger now? Some sort of enemy?'

'Enemy, that's for sure.' But she wouldn't meet my eyes, and when I remained silent she became fidgety. She finally said, 'Listen, I was real uptight for a while, I guess I've always been uptight – my mother and father and everything, that's a natural start for the uptight life, right?

'So before I met Virge I'd pick up a joint at a party, or from a boy, or from Helen, that turned on roommate I told you about, and from her I also got some pills, ups and downs and who-knows-whats. Then I met Harv and for a while I was cool, and straight.

But it didn't last long.' Her voice grew quiet, and sad. 'Like with you, Nickie. Nothing seems to last. For a while with you I didn't think I'd even take *aspirin*, but ... I guess it's *in* me. Though, honest, I haven't been taking much lately. And I wouldn't go to Virge and let him start pawing. I just used Gina's prescription, the first time when I went home for Grandma's funeral, and again when I went back for the wedding.'

I nodded. I couldn't speak. Not because of the pills, though it upset me terribly, that and her past association with drugs. It was her explanation of *why* she needed the dexies. 'Nothing lasts long,' she'd said. 'Like with you, Nickie.'

What she was saying, in effect, was that it was over. She was saying things like that more and more often. And if I'd been rational about her, I'd have agreed and taken her to St Louis and helped her get settled and returned home feeling relieved, if a little sad.

But there was never anything rational about my feelings for Ellie. There's nothing rational about the obsession we call love. So I ignored everything but the pill information, and questioned her about other drugs.

'Oh, I had a good source for pot, but when I stopped seeing the guy I didn't smoke so much any more.'

'What guy?'

She shrugged. 'Hell, it was Russ. Russ Doon, the football player. When he got bounced off his team for another sex rap and the league froze him out, he turned on more and more. That was the time I was seeing him. He turned me on to a lot of shit. All kinds of pills. Once I tripped out on acid, but never again! She shook her head. 'Oh baby, *bad*. I'm just too shook up a type for acid. But I was fine on hash and I was fine on the pills and even had a little snort. You know?'

'Cocaine ...' I said, cold all over. 'How old were you when Doon gave you this stuff?'

'About eighteen, I think. Close to nineteen.'

'The bastard,' I whispered, knowing that all those drugs and all those trips hadn't been taken in a sexual vacuum. She'd lied to me; Doon had been her first man, not Harv. And she understood, instantly, what I was thinking, and fought it with a sneer.

'You mean *black* bastard, don't you, Nickie? Liberal Nickie. Jewish liberal Nickie. Russ always said it was a load of shit about Jews wanting to help blacks because they went through the same thing ...'

'Russ and I *have* gone through the same thing.'

'Bull!'

'We've gone through *you*.'

She said, 'I want to play tennis.'

'So now you've told me about drugs. When are you going to tell me about men? And not that crap about Harv and me being the only ones.'

'I said there were *two* beside you, didn't I?'

'Yes, and Harv was the first and the other was practically rape, right?'

She ignored the part about Harv being first. She said, 'Yes, practically rape.'

'And just that one time, right?'

'I didn't say that.' Her voice was low and level. 'If you keep pushing me, I'll tell you about it. You'll probably turn on like most honkeys with their dirty stories and pictures...' Her face suddenly twisted and she was crying.

I rose and drew her up and into my arms. I held her, rocked her. She didn't cry very long. 'What's the use of talking this way, Nick? So it was Russ who was really the first one. And I saw him for some time. Only I ... I can't explain what it was like. Not love, Nickie.' She pulled back to look at me. 'Christ, so far from love for the both of us ... though he has, I mean he had, a thing for me, a pretty strong thing.'

I didn't want to hear any more. That slip in tense – 'has, I mean *had*, a thing for me' – was too much. I couldn't face the thought of Harv being part of her life, and now Doon...

'But you *do* hate blacks, don't you, Nickie? I mean, all that talk about giving to the N.A.A.C.P. and CORE, that was in the old days, wasn't it, when you could think you were giving to women and the men were mostly good ole Toms. Now when the men got balls, black balls, you hate them, just like the honkeys in St Louis. Right?'

I was struggling to find words to explain how I felt. Yes, I'd wanted to say *black* bastard. And yes, I hated him for having balls ... with her.

'C'mon, Nickie. Admit it. Be honest and admit you're afraid they got big cocks and can make it better than you and that once a white girl tries them...' She half-closed her eyes and wriggled her bottom and said, 'Mmmm! I'm just remembering. Maybe all that honkey shit's true. You think so, Nickie?'

I wanted to kill her! She *wanted* me to want to kill her. She stepped back, cowering a little, but she was also smiling. 'Oh, yeah, you're like all the rest.'

'I hate every black,' I said, 'who's fucking my girl. I hate them

148

almost as much as I hate Harv Cohen. If Russ Doon were fucking Gina, I'd be perfectly cool about it. If he were fucking Ledya, I'd compliment him on his taste and her on shaking a crippling prejudice. But if he's fucking you ...'

'All right,' she said. 'I'm sorry I pushed you so hard, Nickie. Let's drop it. Keep the pills. Throw them away. I want to try and drop them anyway. All right? Can we kiss? Can we make up now, honey? Ah'm *tahred* of fighting.' She was putting on her little hillbilly act again, and coming in against me, and I was tired of fighting too. And why the hell did the black man in her life have to be a freaked-out muscle bastard like Doon? Why couldn't he have been someone like Cole Patterson, who dated one of the secretaries in the office, and who was able to charm even a sexually frightened square like Harold?

Of course, if Cole were to pitch *Ellie* ...

I had a headache. I was way down. I actually considered taking one of those dexies when Ellie left the room. I settled for a jigger of brandy in my coffee.

That night, we went to a movie. When we returned, the phone was ringing. I ran to get it. Ellie followed and I was just saying hello to Ledya when she came in. I tried to avoid sounding personal or affectionate, but after all ...

Ellie began stripping, began her sexual attack ... then suddenly said, 'Shit!' and stormed out, slamming the door.

And both Karen Oster and my orally-inclined married friend, Ruth, called before ten the next morning. Both wanted to know what had become of me. Both were told I'd been travelling, and I was on my way out now, and could I get back to them. Ellie, who'd tried to remain asleep during Karen's call, finally jumped out of bed when I said, 'Ruth, hey, good to hear your voice ...'

At breakfast, she shouted, 'Just don't ever give me any more crap about letters or calls from Harv! Just don't bug me about Russ or anyone else – and baby, there's going to be *plenty* of them!'.

I explained that I hadn't seen the two women in months, didn't care to see them, cared for no one but her ... and she yelled, 'And what about that actress-whore, Ledya!' and ran to the bathroom. I began to follow; then sat back down. Actually, I didn't feel that badly about it. She'd been gouging my insides for weeks. She was *able* to gouge because I cared. Her reaction this morning made me hopeful that she too cared, and that I'd been wrong, perhaps, about her loss of feeling.

We went on this way, which was mostly bad, until October and time to go to Florida for the toy manufacturers' convention. The night before we flew to Miami, I took her to dinner at the Plaza's Oak Room, a first for her. She was charmed with the place. We sat in those marvellous black-leather armchairs at a table for two and drank Chambertin and ate steaks and finished with *crepes a la Grand Marnier*. She said, 'This is one time I don't mind gaining a few pounds!'

I began to talk about Miami. I said tomorrow would mark a new start for us. She grew morose, 'I hope so, Nickie.'

'It will, honey. We'll have a ball. I'll rent a convertible and while I'm working you can go wherever you want. We'll have a suite and cabana at the Fontainebleau and go out every night. After the convention, we'll drive to the Keys and then the Gulf Coast and Sanibel Island and I'll show you some land I own, perfect for a winter cottage. And then we'll drive home, sightseeing all the way, returning the car in New York. Or, if you'd like, we'll drive to St Louis and I'll let you kick around on your own, see your family and friends . . . just as long as you come back to me each night.'

'Honest, Nickie? But what'll you do all day?'

'I'll go to the Masters and Johnson clinic. . . .'

I hadn't heard her laugh that hard in weeks.

But right from the beginning, the land of the outstretched palm was a disaster. First of all, it was terribly, humidly hot all during our stay. And it rained every second day. And she wore a bikini so tiny it embarrassed me. On top, all right, since she was small, but on bottom . . . well, I walked directly behind her that first day going to the pool.

Our cabana boy was young and blond and big on muscle, and *very* attentive to both of us. I knew he'd be even more attentive when I'd be working the convention and Ellie would be alone. And guess what his name was, if you can believe it. 'Call me Studsy, suh,' he said, heavy on the Southern accent.

Just what I needed – Studsy!

He explained it, laughing, as a 'nickname, kind of, cause mah real name's Sturdivant and man, no one likes to be called Sturdivant!'

Ellie thought that very cute, and giggled, and rolled over on her stomach, presenting him with that nearly-naked bottom. He looked, and then looked away as *I* looked. He said, 'Say, you ever hear the one . . .'

'Yes,' I said.

He said, 'Oh, sure, you want to rest now,' and swaggered off, but not before he'd taken a second, longer look at her bottom. It was slack season now – the slackest of all, post Labour Day – and old Studsy would have plenty of time to lavish on his few customers, right up until November and the beginning of the winter season. And I had a feeling that even in February, he'd find time for customers like Ellie.

I asked why in the world she had to wear so small a bikini.

She murmured she wanted to get as much sun on as much of her body as possible.

I said that we would buy her another, more suitable swimsuit in the hotel shop.

'Are you starting already? What you'd like to do is wrap me in a blanket with just my nose sticking out!'

'It's not your *nose* that's sticking out now!'

She raised herself on an elbow and stared at me. She shook her head slowly. 'The trouble is you don't trust me. A man who trusts his woman, he doesn't care if she's absolutely naked. He knows no matter what the men who see her want, she won't give.'

I laughed. 'Of course, I've no reason . . .' I choked myself off. We were starting again. 'You're right,' I said, and leaned over the space between our lounges and kissed her shoulder. 'Peace?'

'Yeah, peace,' she muttered.

She slept. I lay there, looking around the half-empty sun deck, catching male eyes directed at Ellie every so often. I *would* have liked to wrap her in a blanket! I finally got up, wandered over to the pool, and tested the water temperature with my toes. It wasn't too cold and I decided to use the high dive board.

On the way to the ladder, I got a bit of eye-action from two more-than-passable chicks in their late twenties.

One said, 'You going into that *freezing* water?' I said, 'My hot blood'll warm things up.' She and her friend laughed a lot.

I posed a bit on the way up the ladder and on the board. I'm still hard enough and lean enough to bulge a bicep and pectoral . . . but I screwed up my dive. I hit the water belly first, making a hell of a splash. The chicks knew from nothing about diving and applauded and yelled, '*Yay!*' I grinned. Studsy, however, came over and said, 'You want a little instruction on diving, suh, I'm available after five o'clock. We could work out say half an hour . . .'

I said I'd see, and went back to the cabana. Ellie was awake.

'Oh, wow, and you complain that *I'm pitching*!'

'Can I help it if my magnificent body . . .'

'*Sheeit!*'

'I haven't heard it pronounced quite that way since I left the army and stump-jumpers from ole Miss.'

We didn't talk much at dinner. I asked if she wanted to go dancing. She said the flight and 'all our happy talk' had knocked her out. We went to bed at ten. Yes, we made love, and yes it was great . . . but the bitch threw a dagger into me at the end by sighing, 'Oh, you're fantastic, Studsy . . . I mean, Harak, harak.'

I laughed; it was so patent a gag. But oft a true word . . .

Had she been playing the old-bored-marrieds game of substitution?

The next day I checked out the booth allotted to Kraus & Leib in the main convention hall. I met several people I knew from other Manhattan toy outfits, and also a few from out of town, and what with the necessity to talk a little shop and have a few drinks, it was two-thirty before I managed to get back to our tenth-floor suite. I changed into swimming shorts and went down to the cabana. Ellie's robe, sunglasses, and novel were there, but not Ellie.

I wandered around. No Studsy either. And then I saw them coming down the stairs from the upper deck of the two-deck cabana building. He was ushering her with a hand in the small of her back. She was swinging her ass and flashing her teeth. And what the hell was on that second floor that wasn't on this more desirable ground floor . . . except, of course, empty cabanas to which the cabana boy had the keys. Cabanas that could be entered, then shut against intruders. And a padded lounge would do as well as a bed for a quickie.

He saw me, and his hand dropped away. She saw me, and her smile became less convincing. She said, 'Hey, how'd it go?' I said, 'Fine. What were you doing up there?' Studsy said, 'Excuse me, Ellie, suh, getting a signal,' and muscled himself away. Ellie said, 'Oh, we were goofing around, he was showing me the view and stuff.'

'And how *was* his stuff?'

She laughed; then she absorbed my look and stopped laughing. 'Nickie, why don't I just go back to New York and wait for you?'

I sat down and rubbed my face. What the hell was happening to me? Why was I always raging? Why couldn't I trust her?

The answer was simple. I mistrusted her not because Studsy was competition, but because *Harv* was. If there was *one* man she could love beside myself, then *all* men became suspect.

I said, 'Forget it.'

'I'm sorry, Nick, I can't. I don't ever want to hear . . .'

'Shut up.'

'Don't talk to me that way!'

'*Shut the hell up!*'

'You're going to hit me again?' Her hands were on her hips; she was glaring and grinning at the same time. 'Right here Maybe

Studsy won't like it? Maybe he'll protect...'

It was the wrong thing to say. I was on my feet and had her by the arms before she could finish. I dragged her into the cabana and shoved the doors closed. In the semi-darkness, I put my face to hers and said, 'Don't play with me. I once joked with you about having Harv killed. I'm not joking now. If I ever find you with another man, *any* man, that man is dead. I swear it ... on Seth's life. I don't care about anything but you. Not my work and not my life ... nothing but you.'

'Nickie...' She was trying to come up against me, but I shoved her away and went to the sink and ran the cold water. She opened the door. I washed my face and neck.

'What ... what made you say all that, honey? You don't believe I'd do anything with a poolboy?'

I went out and looked around. Studsy was near the pool, talking to a pot-bellied man. I called to him. He nodded, spoke a moment longer, and came over. 'I'd like a bottle of Scotch and some ice,' I said.

'Sure thing. How about a snack?'

'No.'

'How about you, Ellie?'

She was in the cabana doorway. 'No.'

He said, 'Johnny Walker Red okay?'

I nodded.

He looked at me and looked at her and said, 'Yeah, well, coming right up.'

We sat there. The waiter brought the tray and I signed the tab and began drinking. Ellie had a few too, but I went through half that fifth in half an hour. When I felt I was going to have trouble walking, I got up and went to the room. She must have followed almost immediately, because she arrived as I was closing the door. I went to the bed and lay down.

'Nickie, let's talk.'

I said, 'Go away,' the room beginning to swim. I heard her move toward the door. 'But not too far away.'

Then I fell asleep.

We ordered dinner from room service. We didn't talk much. We ate and watched television. She said she wanted to go down for some air. I said the purpose of an ocean-front suite with a terrace was to allow the guests to take the air without leaving their rooms. She went out on the terrace. I thought I heard crying, but I didn't check on it. She came in and went to the bathroom. The shower ran; then she reappeared in her lounging pyjamas, her hair wrapped in a towel, her face shiny clean. She hesitated. 'Nickie . . . ?' I didn't answer. She came to my chair and sat down on the floor at my feet. I continued to watch television, but I could smell the bath-clean smell of her hair, her body. She leaned against my legs.

How it happened, I don't know. A sob ripped from my throat. I put my head down and, for the first time since I was a child in Brooklyn, I cried. I hadn't even cried at my father's funeral! I began to get up, but she pulled me down. 'What is it? Nickie, tell me!' And she began to cry with me.

So there we sat, crying together. And if she had to ask me why, then how could I tell her?

We eventually went to bed. We eventually made love. It was a silent thing, I'm tempted to say a *deadly* thing, because toward the end I squeezed her buttocks beyond passion's demand, making her cry out, and she was already raking my back, and not in the controlled way she always had before. We punished each other in the one area that had previously been free of anger, of punishment. Still, I felt her physical satisfaction, and knew my own. I also knew that there was no longer *any* place where we were safe from each other.

We did much in the following week, trying to bring ourselves back from the abyss, and at the same time fighting and hating each other. Miami steamed in one of its worst heat waves in years, and we steamed with it. Instead of staying in the air-conditioned comfort of the Fontainebleau, we drove everywhere, seeing and trying everything . . . because we were afraid to stop moving, afraid to sit and think and talk.

I got to know Miami in a way I never had before. There was the glaring sun that bleached everything during the day, and the blue-black heaviness that stained everything at night. There were all those clubs and bars, more to the square foot than New York ever saw. There were the hippies and druggies making their play now that the tourists, the squares, were mostly gone. There were the roads leading to keys and coasts and crackers. And there were the damned generation gaps, so concentrated and obvious here – so many old people and so many young people and so few inbetweens like Nick Leib. And because of Ellie, because of the people looking at us, I was aware of this gap, of the chasms and conflicts between the generations. And I wondered if it was possible for Ellie and I to bridge such a chasm. It didn't seem likely, and we were both afraid.

There was the night we drove through a tropic downpour to a huge hotel rivalling any on the strip. I'd had a nothing morning pitching our teeny-TV, complete with *Sesame Street*-type slides a child could operate himself. It was a well-built toy, an educational toy ... and obviously going nowhere. Not that I gave a damn, but Harold was expecting results and I felt I had to satisfy him.

We had dinner in the hotel's show room, and left both food and entertainment unfinished. We strolled around an ornate lobby. I'd been to Miami seven times in the past ten years. I'd never liked it, but the family had and after all, the sun is the sun. I'd explored every hotel on Collins Avenue and knew them from the most garish to the least tasteful, which is about all the spread you can hope for in Miami Beach. Now I decided to show Ellie the incredible mezzanine floor in this *shlack* palace.

It's a hallway lined with doors to offices and private meeting rooms, but that's not its distinction. It's also lined with a clutter of statuary, paintings, and antiques. Ellie stared and said, 'Isn't it kind of *much*?'

'Much *too* much.'

We moved up the hallway and examined Louis Quinze chairs and Grecian statuary and pseudo-impressionist paintings, all cheek by jowl, something new every two or three feet. I was walking a little ahead of her. I don't know exactly when she stopped, and I don't know exactly when that bellhop appeared on the scene, but I missed her and looked back. She was stooping to examine a vase, and he was standing to the side, hands behind his back, as if on guard duty, examining her. She straightened and glanced his way, and they exchanged a smile.

He was a dark, good-looking boy of perhaps twenty-two, twenty-three. He stepped closer and said something in a low voice. She laughed and shook her head and came to me.

'What did he say that was so amusing?'

She asked me about a painting. I told her it was a poor imitation of a Dufy water colour, and repeated my question.

'It was nothing.'

'Then tell me the nothing.'

'C'mon, Nickie, are we going to get uptight because some kid made a joke?'

'Not if we tell that joke.'

She was growing red in the face. I was growing sick in the stomach. But I couldn't stop. This was the *modus operandi* of all our quarrels. She would be devious with me, because most of what she experienced with other men, even the briefest of associations, was sexual in nature.

'I want to know!'

'He asked if I could ditch my father and come back later.' She walked away. I turned and stared at the bellhop. He smiled vaguely, then made a sudden decision: he went back inside the office.

I caught up with her. 'You thought that was funny, did you?'

'It *was* funny,' she said, chewing her lip. 'Can we get out of here? I'd like to go dancing.'

The club we went to was in the old part of Miami Beach, down near the Algiers and other passé hotels. It was almost empty, but those present were recent graduates of the teeny-bopper class. Also, the music was painfully loud, even for rock. We danced twice, and neither of us turned on, and we left.

The next day, I didn't do much selling behind my booth. Instead, I wrote out a sales approach based on something that was growing very real to me. I worked with a pencil and pad, and by three-thirty, despite increasing action with the buyers, I had something I felt would fit our motorcycle and car line very well.

At five, I went to the room. No Ellie, though she'd promised to meet me there. I went down to the cabana. Ellie was lying on her stomach reading. Studsy was on a lounge drawn up close to hers, the one meant for me, talking ... right at that half-naked ass, it appeared. I went over and said, 'It's damned hard to read when someone's making noise.' He sat up slowly. She glanced up and murmured, 'Doesn't bother me,' and went back to her book.

I looked at him. He said, 'Man, hey, no sweat,' and rose and walked away.

'Oh that was nice,' Ellie said, still behind her book. 'Big man's had another bad day, so he takes it out on the hired help. Safe, too, because hired help can't fight back. Like me ... I'm hired help.'

I went to the room. I showered and by the time I came out she was there. We dressed for dinner and drove to Hollywood Beach and a French restaurant. She ate very little, but drank almost a full bottle of wine. I ate a lot, and drank gin and tonics. We ended up at a drive-in movie, staring bleary-eyed at technicolour images. I felt empty and frightened. During the intermission, I reached across the seat of our rented Chevy convertible and drew her gently toward me. She said, 'Christ, wait until we get to bed. You don't have to prove anything any more.'

I shoved her away. She said, 'Sorry. Wish I had those dexies.'

The next day, I tried my sales spiel on a group of four buyers. It hid its punch at first, opening to the true point slowly.

'... we play to the subconscious desires of young parents to achieve freedom of mobility as represented by these hippie dolls and their motorcycle, so that they buy for themselves as well as their children.

One of the men handling the dolls, cycles, and cars was the younger of the two Closter brothers, buyers for their own chain of five-and-dime type stores throughout middle-America. A sale to them of any one item would be a major triumph. And these items were priced low enough for their three dollar maximum.

I interruped myself to say hello, and to allow him to examine a model chopper, and to remind him of the success of hippie motor-cycle movies like *Easy Rider, Little Faus and Big Halsey,* and others. They should, I said, help us sell this particular item. The older brother, a bland marshmallow type in comparison with the younger Closter's athletically intense style and manner, was looking off to the right rather than at my toys. I glanced there too. It was Ellie finally come to see me at work, probably because it was storming outside. She was wearing her sexiest mini-dress, a yellow with brown-and-red print flowers she'd picked up at Saks in New York. It hugged every curve and crevice, turning me on when we were alone, and making me sweat when we were in public.

What also made me sweat was her little smile as she listened to my spiel. A supercilious little smile. A smile that seemed to say – as she already had during the course of an argument back in New York – that I was a huckster, a slick salesman who had prostituted his education, his degree in psychology, for the almighty buck.

So I really turned it on, to show her just how good I was!

I pitched the Closters, and the group of others that had grown to eight, on a line of hippie items for children that was in the works ... and the marshmallow Closter finally began giving me, along with Ellie, a little attention. I demonstrated the Demo-Derby car – 'based on the demolition races that are so popular with Americans in the mass if not intellectuals in the particular'. A few chuckles from the middle-American Closters. 'Cars that swipe each other, crash each other, destroy each other ... but of course the child can place the fenders, bumpers, and hoods back on the frame for the next demolition race. And there's nothing psychologically harmful about any of these items, including the new Karate Pillow. Quite the contrary. We could get any number of child psychologists to attest to the tension-releasing qualities ...'

I watched Ellie from the corner of my eye. I watched her little smile drift away as I got to the nitty-gritty, to the part so deeply rooted in all that was happening to me.

'What to the uninformed, and misinformed, may appear a de-structive type of play with items triggering such negative play, is in reality something quite different, and quite positive. Children share the pressures and tensions of modern society. They can achieve, as

157

we can, a sense of oppression lifted, an accommodation with grown-up reality, and, through the simple expedient of speed toys, demolition toys, that much maligned term, violence ... and while I don't condone these realities, as long as they exist our children as well as ourselves have to learn to deal with them. Also, let me state that according to *African Genesis, On Aggression, Territorial Imperative,* and other scholarly works, it's a terrible mistake to deny our million-year heritage of energy and violence, *especially* when dealing with such a basic honest mechanism as the child.'

Ellie was looking down now, but still listening. I told my audience that a booklet embodying the points I'd just made could be produced to accompany the toys, but the younger Closter said he thought that would be a mistake. '*We* can appreciate your arguments, Mr Leib, but no need to bring up spectres of brutality and violence to parents who cheerfully buy all sorts of weapon toys for their children anyway. It's no problem, believe me, though that booklet might be useful in answering certain *professional* critics.'

I went on to display some yard games, tether-ball, embodying elements of football and soccer, and to state that here again there would be satisfaction gained by a definite winner. Watching Ellie, I knew she hated what I was saying, knew I was frightening her. And it may me feel good.

'... the surge of pure joy when we've defeated an opponent, humbled even a close companion ... denying these instinctual responses is denying our inner selves.

'Not all areas of satisfaction are, or should be, motivated by love. Some must necessarily be based on ego, territorial drive, and aggression ... to again borrow from learned investigators like Ardrey. Whatever games or playthings cater to these badly maligned personality requirements serve society as surely and beneficially as the much overused and often hopelessly inadequate cerebral and love-oriented games and playthings.'

Ellie was turning away. I raised my voice, and she paused, and we both knew I'd been speaking directly to her these last few minutes.

'As modern researchers from Krafft-Ebing on have revealed, sex is often quite unloving and even degrading to one of the partners. Children, whom we must recognize as sexual beings in light of current research, reflect this truth, this reality...'

She finally walked away. I threw my words after her, drawing in more and more buyers with my pitch.

'Let me tell you, gentlemen, that any human being, and children are human, though some of our critics would have you believe otherwise ... any human being who cannot obtain satisfaction from the basic drives built into these toys, is in deep trouble. Quite bluntly, he or she is mentally ill, unresponsive to the challenges and rewards or society offers ... and I'm sure you know what *that* indicates. As a trained psychologist, I don't hesitate in labelling it, Lack of Will To Survive! And whoever ignores this, ignores impending doom.'

Ellie was gone. So was my need to speak, and I muttered, 'Thank you for your kind attention,' fearing I'd gone emotionally overboard ... for a sales pitch. But the Closters led the group in a spattering of applause.

'*Damndest* way to sell toys I ever heard?' the younger brother said, and he proceeded to take stock numbers on three items. So did some of the others, who watched and followed the shrewd Closters.

The next night Harold called to say he'd heard 'fantastic things' about my presentation and expected a solid order from the Closters. He used this as a basis for arguing my return to a full-time role in the business and gaining back my fifty per cent.

I didn't dispute the point, but not because I agreed. I wanted to get off the phone, quickly. Ellie was marching to the closet in high heels, pantyhose, and a purple blouse. Her hair was freshly brushed to her shoulders. Her ass, tanned almost solid, rolled enticingly. And I remembered that bit in my sales pitch about sex, about if often being quite unloving and even degrading to one of the partners. I now had a terrible lust and an equally terrible need to degrade her. As soon as I was able to get off the phone, I went to the closet, where she was about to step into a skirt.

She was cold. 'You said the Americana had a good show. You want to be late?'

I threw the skirt away. She said, 'C'mon now!' I grabbed her around the waist and gripped her buttocks and squeezed. She yelled. 'Nickie! That hurt!' I hauled off and smacked her bottom, twice. She tried to slap me. I grabbed her wrists and dragged her to the bed and threw her down. When she tried to sit up, I pushed her down. I did it three times, and then she said, voice trembling with anger, 'Go ahead. If I don't want you to get it, you won't!'

I went ahead. I stripped, and she laughed and shook her head and said, 'No way, baby!' I got on the bed and tore off her blouse – literally ripped it down the front – and then her brassiere. 'You bastard!' she shouted. 'What're you trying to prove!' I kissed her so hard she yelped, and my own lips were bruised from contact with her teeth. I peeled down her pantyhose. I got her legs apart, but she kept swivelling her hips from side to side, opposite to my thrust, and I couldn't get in. I paused, and she clamped her legs closed and made raging, laughing sounds at me.

It was my first experience with a rape-type situation, and I realized certain things immediately. In order for rape to be effective, you must either have an enormous advantage in strength (more than mine over Ellie's); or have the woman tied, drugged, or otherwise rendered physically immobile; or she must become willing at some point and, consciously or otherwise, begin to help you; or you have to terrify her, say with a weapon, threaten her life or the life of someone very important to her.

I thought, briefly, of tying her up with belts ... but then understood that I didn't really care about entry. I had something else in mind.

I rubbed my body against hers and played at trying to get in. I used my fingers and almost *did* jam my penis inside her ... but at the last minute she pulled away, despite the fingers, and, I assume, some cost in pain. She fought hard to turn over on her stomach, and while I could have stopped her, I finally allowed her to do it. She made a sound of triumph, but it was short-lived. I worked my penis against her ass, and got my fingers into her from behind. I used those fingers vigorously, and heard the way her breath mounted, the way she began to grunt. I realized I might yet get in ... if I wanted to.

I turned her back over without too much trouble. She definitely wasn't fighting as hard as before. The wrists I'd had to hold clamped together in my right hand were no longer jerking and occasionally, pulling free to slap and punch at me. They were stretching out over her head. Her entire body was stretching out sensually, and her thighs were no longer clamped tightly together. She sighed deeply, a hot, wet flower opening under me, a prize of flesh I'd won in combat. It stimulated me to the point where, with all the wrestling, all the rubbing, I was almost ready to come. I rubbed once, twice, three times more on her pubic bulge.

She said, 'All right you sonovabitch,' her gasping voice and spreading legs belying the tough words.

I lunged up over her chest on my knees and said, 'Little whore, little love!' I stroked myself faster and harder and she was looking up at me, right at my cock, and it felt so wild, so good, seeing her, *aiming* at her. I came all over her face.

She didn't cry out, or show disgust, or even try to get out of the way. She simply closed her eyes. When my ecstasy ended, I realized her body was squirming, heaving. I looked back and saw her

160

masturbating; then bent my head between her legs to watch, and to help.

Fun and games. But I'm not sure just how much fun was involved. We barely spoke two words to each other the rest of the evening. Like an old, embittered, married couple, everything said and done and finished between us, we ate, drank, and danced without words, without smiles. And yet, I couldn't wait until we returned to the suite, and bed.

We spent nine days at the Fontainebleau – the six of the convention and three more. Then we packed and drove to Key West. The very act of travelling made things better. The narrow roadway seemed to skim the blue-green waters, built as it was on old railroad pilings. From key to key we drove, and stopped to eat and swim and walk, and once to rent a motorboat. We grew soft with each other, because we were alone with each other. Alone with Ellie, I managed to forget Harv and deceit and the certain knowledge that she cared less for me than she had at the beginning, and that I hadn't heard her say, 'I love you,' in weeks, and that I was losing her. And that even if I could keep her, as I was determined to, I still didn't know what to do with her, beside fuck her.

We took the open-bus tour of Key West, and it began to storm, and we sat huddled as close to the centre of the little canopied bus as possible, laughing as we slowly but surely were drenched by windswept rain.

That was the high point; that and the night of softness and fire that followed. We swam the next morning, ate lunch in a marvellous seafood house, and drove back along the narrow highway. We intended to spend the night in Miami, then head for St Louis ... but something changed our plans.

SEVEN

In the ballads of my youth, we heard the lover rejected bewailing his fate, or being cute and clever about it, or at worse lachrymose and moony. But in rock, the lover rejected becomes the lover avenged.

Ever hear Bing Crosby, Sinatra, Como, or Dorris Day threaten to murder their sweethearts? Jerome Kern, for example, has nothing to parallel a song on one of my favourite tapes, Led Zeppelin *Three*, in which the singer asserts, 'Gave my baby a twenny-dollar bill if that don't get that woman then my shot-shot-shotgun surely will.' And the early Beatles song, '... catch you with another man that's the *end*, little girl!' And Hendrix asking Joe where's he's going with that gun in his hand, and Joe replying he'd caught his lady in *flagrante delicto*, shot her, and is heading for Mexico. And so many others.

Music that hath charms to soothe the savage breast is music as we knew it *then*. Now, I think, it has the opposite effect. It got inside my head the night Ellie and I drove back from Key West. We listened to rock in the car, and then in a club ... and I wondered if what happened could ever have happened with a Sinatra or Doris Day on the stage instead of a Soft Machine.

We crossed the City of Miami line at about eight-thirty of a heavy, overcast night. We'd had an early lunch, and decided to try an Italian restaurant on Key Biscayne that had been touted to me by a fellow toy salesman. As we turned off the main road and onto the MacArthur Causeway it began to rain; but nothing could dampen our spirits. We sang along with the rock songs and tapped out the beat and looked at each other.

We left the restaurant at ten, and drove back along the dark road through what was now a downpour to a place that had caught our attention earlier. *Club 7-Keys*, the blue neon sign proclaimed, and out front a spotlit billboard showed a group of shaggy musicians and stated that the same Soft Machine would be playing each night from nine 'till real, real late'. I suggested we continue our romance with rock onto the *7-Keys* dance floor. Ellie said fine with her, but where would we spend the night since we hadn't made any reservations? I explained that this was Miami in off-season and there were a hundred motels with a thousand vacancies, so no sweat.

The sweat came about two hours later ... although right from the beginning the vibes, as Ellie would say, were bad. I was parking and she called me Harv as she asked if she could drive the car tomorrow. She didn't realize it, and I told myself it meant nothing beyond the fact that she was a scatterbrain. But the good feeling ended right then.

There were twenty or more cars in the blacktopped lot beside the low building, with bay water gleaming like ink in the background, and we threaded our way through them as we made for the front doors. She was wearing a cute hotpants outfit of thin green suède, and I was watching *her* rather than where I was going. I hit a patch of water, and the blacktop was slick, and down I went, twisting my left ankle. Ellie heard me grunt, and looked back and laughed as I sat there. Then she came over, said, 'I'm sorry, honey,' and asked if I was all right. I got up, refusing her helping hand, wincing a bit as I put weight on that ankle. But it couldn't possibly be sprained and I felt sure it would hold up for a few dances. I said, 'Fine, let's go.' What I should have done, of course, was admit I'd hurt myself and then headed for a motel, a hot bath, and a night's rest. But her laugh, her cruel young laugh, had made me want to ignore any possibility that I'd been injured ... a laugh she repeated as she said, 'You should have seen yourself, Nickie? Flat on the old tush!'

I nodded, chuckling, and we resumed our course toward the doors. Only now I moved far more carefully, and slowly. And I could feel that ankle radiating pain.

We could hear the music even before we entered. The heat was hard, acidy, wild, and woolly. Ellie paused under the overhang and looked at me. 'You sure you still want to do this? You've had a long day of driving, and that fall ... you were moving kind of slow just now.'

If I'd been sure of *her*, I could have admitted to being unsure of this course of action. But I was fighting for my girl, for her total admiration. Childish, yes, but that's how I'd always felt, all along.

We entered directly into a small bar with beamed ceiling and dark-wood panelling, and a dim lighting provided by old-English lanterns. The bartender was wearing a Scotch costume complete with kilts and ruffled lace shirt. A cute, red-headed waitress, picking up a tray of drinks, wore a mini-kilt, with knee-high tartan stockings and a plaid pullover. She was worth a second glance, and I gave it her. Several men, mostly in their thirties, were sitting at the bar. The music came from an adjoining room, and sounded less raucous indoors than out.

It certainly looked like a nice, respectable place, an expensive place that would discourage single male action, that bane of rock joints in Manhattan.

When I finished my examination and turned to Ellie, I saw her eyes flicker away from the far end of the bar and a small smile touch her lips. She took my arm and said, 'Hey, this is gonna be fun!' I nodded, and looked to the end of the bar. A man, no more than twenty-five, sporting very long, blond-streaked hair with a red Indian band around the forehead, a bright print shirt, love beads, and a hoody instead of hippy look, was readjusting himself in a booth, his eyes still fixed on Ellie. He'd obviously just risen for a better look. I gave him *my* best look, the one that usually turned eyes away, or at least made them act disinterested. I had a different breed of man here. He smiled at me, said something to another heavy type sitting across from him, then looked at me again and smiled again. And returning to examining Ellie.

163

Nothing I could do. Looking was legal. But that was *all* he would do.

A kilted waitress, the cute red-head I'd checked out before, ushered us into the adjoining room with many smiles, where the *Soft Machine* were leaving the stage for a break in their long sessions.

More bad vibrations. Ellie had two martinis in about ten minutes. 'Why so heavy on the booze?' I asked.

'I don't know. I just feel like getting high. Wish we had some pot.'

So did I, before an hour had passed. I had two Gibsons; she had four martinis. A joint or two could never have made her as high as all that liquor. And the higher she got, the more unpleasant she got. She grew moody, introspective, sullen, then silent ... except for complaining that I'd only danced with her twice. The ankle was killing me. I was considering admitting it to her instead of simply repeating, 'the music doesn't *move* me, honey,' when I noticed the hoody guy standing in the bar doorway. How long he'd been there, I don't know. Ellie was facing that doorway; I was sitting with my side to it. I'd turned to look for the waitress and that's when I'd seen him. He was again giving Ellie his best leer. She didn't seem perturbed.

'Your friend is smiling at you,' I said ... and the vibrations were *very* bad now.

'What friend?' But she glanced at him and she could have been smiling. She certainly wasn't frowning.

'Are you giving him a come-on?'

She laughed. 'I'll give anyone a come-on who'll dance with me.'

I got up and went onto the dance floor.

The longhair in the doorway watched. My ankle kept me from moving properly. Suddenly Ellie said, 'Jesus, you're dancing like the thousand-year-old man,' and returned to the table.

I joined her. I'd begun to explain about my ankle, when I realized she was looking past me and smiling and dropping her eyes. I said, 'But I *am* the thousand-year-old man, you know that.'

Her eyes snapped to me. 'I thought we were having fun tonight! And don't tell me you weren't playing eye-games with our cutesy, cutesy waitress ...'

'After the way you just acted, that doesn't deserve a reply.'

'Then let's get out of here!'

I turned again, not only to locate the waitress, but to check out my leering competitor. He was no longer in the doorway. He was almost at our table. Ellie said quickly, 'Now take it easy, Nickie.

Other girls have been leaving dates for a dance or two . . .'

The voice was smooth and pleasant, but it wasn't directed at me. Neither were the pale blue eyes. He was about six-one, strong looking, very definitely unaffected by my hard stare. The vibrations hit Red for Danger.

'Hey,' he said. 'Got time for the generation?'

Ellie glanced at me. I sipped my drink. Encouraged by this sign of sanity, she smiled and replied, 'What generation?'

'Ours,' he said, and put his hand on her arm and drew her up out of the chair.

'You didn't ask *me*,' I said. I put down my drink.

He laughed. 'Come *on* now, man.'

Ellie said, 'One dance, Nickie,' as she assessed what she thought was this man's mastery of the situation, and my helplessness in the face of all those customers and hired help. I felt she was testing me, loosening the bonds, preparing for an eventual flight from our nest.

I stood up. They were already stepping toward the dance floor. I moved forward on my good ankle, shoved Ellie aside with my left arm, spun him around with my right. He said, 'What's *with* you . . . ?' his fists beginning to clench, a rather *pleased* look on his face. But the pleasure didn't last, because I wasn't going to box him, just as I hadn't the sailor, just as I never had from the time I'd been a kid in Brooklyn and realized that the way to keep your teeth and perhaps your life was to hit first and hard and get the hell out.

I did just that. I caught him on his open mouth with a good left and on the ear with a very hard right, and as he began to fall I caught him again in the mouth with the left. I couldn't go for the end-of-the-fight shot to the Adam's Apple, or a rabbit chop to the back of the neck, or even a few good kidney shots. I had an audience, and I wondered whether his friend from the booth would make the scene. But down he went anyway, and the blood on his mouth was simply beautiful, and the way he rolled onto his side and moved his arms and legs and couldn't get up was even more beautiful. I took Ellie's arm and moved her toward the door. She seemed dazed. Our waitress appeared, saying, 'But sir . . .' I was already reaching for my wallet. I got out a twenty and said, 'This should cover it, goodnight, and tell your manager he should protect couples from dirty thugs.' Then we were in the bar, and I glanced back. He was being helped up by several men, but his head lolled and he didn't look as if he'd pose a threat for quite a while. And none of the helpers seemed inclined to make a judgement in his favour. His booth was empty, his table friend nowhere in sight.

We got outside. It had stopped raining. I was still holding Ellie's arm, only now I was leaning on it to cover my limp. She didn't notice; wouldn't have noticed if I'd whipped out a crutch and used it. She was staring straight ahead, her face white. Then she tore free and ran headlong at the car. She tugged at the door, but it was locked. I said, 'Honey, I'm sorry . . .'

She whirled on me as I came toward her. 'Oh that was cool! That was big man stuff! You're so good at big man stuff, you should've been a goddam *cop*! Then you could beat up people *legally*!'

'You saw the way he . . .'

'Big man! Fighting over a girl! Just like on the old Late Show movies!'

I reached her, tried to touch her. She jerked away and screamed, 'Listen, John Wayne, either take me some place where I can sleep and forget the big man, or I'll go back inside and get someone else to do it!'

For a moment, I was so filled with hopelessness, with fury, my fists rose and I couldn't stop them and I thought I was going to smash her.

She shrank away, but whispered, 'Big *man*.' My hands fell to my sides. I unlocked the door.

The road back toward Miami proper was deserted, glistening-wet, spattered by occasional gusts of rain. We didn't talk. I felt no regret about hitting the punk, but I was too upset by the things she'd said and done to want to talk to her. She'd really hammered home the generation gap with that old-Late-Show-Movies and John Wayne crap. And she'd encouraged the punk; at least, she'd failed to *dis*courage him.

We hadn't travelled a third of the way back toward the Mac-Arthur Causeway when I saw headlights in my rear-view mirror, small enough to be at least two or three miles behind me.

Normally I'd have forgotten them, since normally they'd have stayed behind me for quite a while. But I kept watching these lights because they grew larger at an incredible rate. I mean, they were catching up to overtake as if the Chevy were standing still instead of doing a respectable fifty-five miles per hour. The damned fool must have been doing at least a hundred, and on a night like this . . .

I watched him coming, and pulled far to the right to give him plenty of room. We were still on Key Biscayne, so there were sandy shoulders sloping directly onto sections of beach and strips of palm trees. If that idiot came too close, I'd simply pull off the road. No use taking chances.

It had begun raining harder, and I slowed as a Camaro Z-28 with custom above-hood supercharger came alongside . . . and stayed alongside. I glanced to my left, getting a glimpse of the driver as he leaned down to look at me.

A young guy with long hair and a red headband.

I braked, just as he cut in sharply to drive me off the road. Ellie said, 'What's wrong with *him*?' and then peering ahead, 'Is he the one from the club?'

'Yes.'

The Camaro was slowing on front of me. I slowed along with it. 'You started it,' Ellie said. 'Let's see you finish it.'

I looked at her. She was smiling, and hooking up her seat belt.

'This is cool, is it?' I asked, and slowed to a crawl behind the Camaro. If he wanted to get out and fight, fine. But something – about the situation – worried me. He wouldn't be this anxious to renew a fight that had already put him on his ass. He'd want an edge . . .

Ellie said, 'Pull alongside him. He's going to race you.'

'And if he wins, you change cars?'

'I couldn't do worse than you. But he'll just scare you a little . . .'

I stamped on the gas and swung out around the Camaro. This Chevy wasn't made for racing, but then again, I wasn't in a race. Ellie was a naive fool. The punk was intent on *killing* me, not putting me down.

I wished I were in my Porsche. The Chevy had a big enough engine, but it also had an automatic transmission and soft passenger-car suspension, and manoeuvring at high speeds would be hairy. And it was a convertible, a death trap if we turned over. And that made me wish another wish; that there was some way to let this grinning idiot-child beside me out of the car so she wouldn't run the risk of dying at age twenty-one.

And yet, I couldn't be sure. The punk in the Camaro *might* have some romantic notion about beating me in a race. *Ellie* bought the idea, and they *were* of the same generation . . .

I was passing him; he suddenly accelerated like a bullet and, from my right, swung in front of me, trying to force me into the opposite lanes and a car approaching head-on. Ellie said, 'Jesus that's dumb!'

I braked hard, swung to the right, stepped on the gas, and got by him. He straightened and came up behind me. I was doing ninety-five, but he went ahead, on my left, and again cut in.

'God!' Ellie moaned, beginning to get the message.

I could probably have slipped by, cutting left and shooting

around. But I didn't. I did cut left, but not quite enough to miss him completely. I hit his rear-right fender, crumpling it and spinning him around, and was in the clear and doing ninety a second later.

I was beginning to feel something; something beside the dryness in my throat and the ache in my gut. Something that sang with the blood in my ears and told me the punk wasn't good enough; that I could take him; that I could kill him.

Ellie said, 'He's coming again! Nick, we'll be at the causeway and the toll booths soon! There are police there...'

'To the death, baby," I said. 'For the fair damsel! Besides, we *hate* the pigs.'

'*Please* don't scare me!'

'But this is what you wanted, isn't it?'

'He's got a hot car and you can't...'

He was roaring up on the left again, that supercharger shrieking. I began to play block-'em, swinging left when he went left, right when he went right. Ellie was moaning, 'Nick, please, please,' and I *loved* it, and laughed, and decided to see what the punk would do if I allowed him to pass again. I had enough room on the four lanes of empty road to counter just about any manoeuvre he might make.

It was a mistake. I didn't figure on the 'manoeuvre' he had in mind. He came alongside, and I concentrated on the road, and Ellie screamed, 'A gun ... Nick!' I glanced left, and he was trying to steer with his left hand and aim across the seat and through his open window with his right. He had a revolver that looked as big as a cannon. I braked and ducked. A shot sounded, but the Camaro was already past us. *He* braked, tyres skidding on the wet pavement. I accelerated and went by him on the right.

Ellie screamed, 'Go back to the club!' She was white with fear.

As for me, how to explain what I felt? I was scared shitless, but I was also tremendously excited. The excitement didn't allow the fear to take over, and it had elements of hatred in it ... for the bastard in the Camaro; for Ellie; perhaps for myself for being whatever it was that had brought me here.

That's about as close as I can get. Ellie later told me my face was frozen into 'a crazy smile'.

I think I also felt good ... because I'd been given the chance to show her something she would never forget.

The Camaro was screaming up behind me. I again played block-'em. No letting him pull alongside. Not here. Maybe somewhere with trees alongside the road ...

Ellie was lying on the seat, her eyes just above the level of the dashboard. 'I see lights. The toll booths!' she laughed. 'He'll have to turn back!'

I didn't want him to turn back. He'd gone for my life. I wanted his.

He was trying the right side again, probably his last move before giving up.

I pulled far left and slammed on the brakes. We skidded a bit, but the Chevy holds the road beautifully on stops. Ellie lurched against her seat belt. I moved too ... and swung all the way left, U-turned over the divider, bouncing and swerving and heading away from Miami and back into Key Biscayne, away from the toll booths and police and back into darkness.

Ellie was staring at me. 'God, *why*?'

'Because I have to win the hand of the fair damsel.'

She lay face down on the seat then and covered her head with her arms and began to sob.

I wanted to comfort hert. But there was no time. I used the moment or two it took the Camaro to turn and come after me to examine the road and off-road area. We were somewhere before the Seaquarium, and there were frequent stretches of trees ...

The Camaro was behind me. Again he began trying to pass on the left. Again I played block-'em, and thought that if I were he I'd smack into the Chevy from behind, try to knock it out of control, at least get it to swerving so I could come alongside and use that gun.

The thought only reinforced my feeling that I had it over the punk. It gave me the confidence to carry out the simple plan I'd formed a few moments before.

I blocked him on the right, and on the left. As he swung back to the right, I deliberately failed to accelerate, failed to match his sudden burst of speed. I could imagine his exultant grin. He must have felt he had finally used his superior horse-power, and brain-power to outclass me. He came tearing up on the right. I shouted, 'Hold on, Ellie!' and swerved into him. I was going about ninety. He must have been up over a hundred when we hit.

The sound of metal on metal was lighter than I expected, but the Chevy bounced left, skipping and shrieking and serving. I had all I could do to hang onto the wheel and keep us from turning over. I'd expected just that, was prepared for it ... which was my edge over the bastard – make that the *poor* bastard – in the Camaro. He *wasn't* prepared for it. And even if he had been, instead of swerving around on pavement, he'd have been knocked onto sandy soil studded with palms and pines. The action was considerably wilder there.

I didn't see the whole thing, but when I had my car under

control, I turned for a quick look backward. He was just colliding with a palm tree, buckled metal seeming to explode like shattered glass. There was a flash of flame. Playing Ellie's baby-talk game, I sing-songed, '*All* finished! *I* win!'

She raised her head dazedly. I U-turned and drove slowly by so as to get a good look. The Camaro was blazing merrily. Ellie put a hand to her mouth and said, 'Maybe you should stop ... call an ambulance...'

'Tell the police I killed him ... get ten to twenty years.'

I picked up speed. There was still no one around. 'Perfect,' I said. 'Now to see what's happened to our car.'

I stopped about a mile further, and got out with the torch. The right side was scraped and crumpled, but not as badly as I'd thought. Still, I didn't want the officers at the toll booth to see it. If I remembered correctly, there was a lit booth on the far right, and the officer would see only our left side, the undamaged side.

That's how it happened. And by the time we'd driven across the Julia Tuttle Causeway into Miami Beach, I'd worked out how to handle the repairs. I'd drive to Fort Lauderdale tomorrow and bring the car into a body shop I'd seen on Highway A1A. I'd explain the damage had been done overnight in a motel parking lot, I had no collision insurance, I wanted to beat the high cost of repairs charged by the car rental agencies, and I was willing to pay a little sweetener to get it done quickly. I'd rent another car and use it as long as we had to wait for the Chevy; then we'd drive the Chevy east and turn it in there, far from the scene of the accident.

The way that Camaro had been burning, there didn't seem to be any chance that paint-scrapings would remain to identify the colour of the other car. Not that there was any reason for the police to believe there *had* been another car – the fool had simply run off the highway and into a tree.

So I was reasonably calm; actually quite pleased with myself. This apparently horrified Ellie. Forgetting her own role in the affair, she said, 'Don't you feel ... *anything*? You *killed* him!'

I would have expected that from Louise and Ledya and Karen and most of the women I knew, the standardized, middle-class women I knew. But Hellie-Ellie? I was disappointed in her.

I said, 'I feel fine. I know I killed him. I could explain feeling fine by saying he tried to kill me, with a gun as well as a car, but that's crap. I'd feel just as fine if I'd killed him while we were racing.'

She stared at me, I said, 'Honey, don't give me the big look of horror. You don't feel a thing for that bum. What you're feeling is something for *someone* else.'

I'd scored because she quickly said, 'I'm too tired to talk. And just remember, I can pick up the phone and call the cops any time I want.'

I laughed. I put my hand on her thigh and rubbed up and back and said, 'Before I went to trial, I'd pay you my respect.'

'Christ! Always so fucking heavy! I was just kidding, you know that!'

I did. At least, I *thought* I did.

I asked her to come close to me. 'Baby needs comfort,' I said.

She slid across the seat. I put my arm around her. I fondled her breasts. She looked at me. 'Don't tell me you can think of that after a night like this?'

'All right, I won't tell you.'

It was almost one when we drove into Bayshore, the eastmost section of Miami Beach and full of motels. I examined only those on the ocean side of Collins, and finally chose one about a block from the Americana Hotel called the Casa D'Oro. It was small and just short of shabby. What recommended it to me was the parking lot; there were only four cars there. I wanted to spend these few extra days in the sun with Ellie, and *only* with Ellie.

We had to knock at the manager's door, which was located behind the desk in the small, dim lobby. The woman was sleepy, but most anxious to land another paying customer. We took a room on the second floor of the two-storey building; then carried up most of our baggage.

It was a far cry from the Fontainebleau, but it would do – big room with twin beds, a kitchen unit behind an accordian screen, functional air conditioning and a tiled bathroom.

I went down for the remaining luggage. When I returned, Ellie was in the bed furthest from the door, her back to me, breathing heavily.

I put down the bags, went to the bathroom, and turned on the shower. I came back to the bedroom, pulled the sheet off Ellie, and examined my nude little girl. 'Mmm,' I said, unbuckling my belt. 'Hate to have you miss the fun by being asleep.'

She stirred and muttered. I didn't believe it. 'Want to shower before or after? I suggest before, smelly.'

She mumbled again. I finished undressing and said, 'Well, so it'll have to be after.' I lay down beside her, worked my fingers between her legs ... and she shouted, 'Goddam it, not tonight!'

I don't know why, but it was the funniest thing I'd ever heard. I laughed and laughed, rolling around and holding my sides, and after a while she giggled. I held out my arms. She said, 'You *must* feel something, Nickie. I don't blame you – I was just so shook up and all before – but, well, *killing* someone . . .'

I kissed her. 'Maybe I'll feel something tomorrow. Maybe I'm just numb.'

'Numb, hell,' she said, as I pressed her hand to my rigid penis.

We made love. We used the shower that had been running the twenty minutes it took us to make love. We returned to bed. I went down on her, and she kept saying she was tired, and then she stopped saying it. I loved her; was full of love . . . and hadn't I proved it in time-honoured fashion? Hadn't I killed a rival for my lady's affections?

At eight the next morning, I left her sleeping and drove up the highway to the auto repair shop. It all went smoothly, a twenty-dollar tip getting the Chevy in the works for the next morning. I could pick it up in three days. And the owner gave me a lift to a Budget Rent-A-Car, where I got a little Pinto with three-speed floor shift. I was back at the Casa D'Oro by eleven. I thought Ellie would still be asleep, certainly not yet dressed and out, but the room was empty.

I changed into swim trunks and went down the single flight of stairs and turned left, walking through a court with doors opening onto it, toward the pool, and beyond the pool toward the beach and the sea. It was a clear, hot morning; a beautiful morning. All it needed to be perfect was Ellie.

An elderly couple was sunning and reading at the poolside. The man was pot-bellied and thin-shouldered, the woman a mass of blubber and facial wrinkles. They looked up and smiled and said good morning. I mumbled a reply and hurried past them, shuddering inside.

I approached a flight of wooden stairs leading down to the sand. The beach was empty. On my right was a high bamboo fence separating the Casa D'Oro from an adjoining motel; on my left a sun-deck. I turned to the sun-deck, which ran about thirty feet before ending in another fence. It had a boardwalk railing on the beach side, and the motel on the inside. There was a blue-and-white striped tent at the far end, against the fence, and several wooden lounges scattered about. But no Ellie.

Then I heard her giggle. From the tent. 'Oh God,' I said to myself, 'here we go again.' I walked slowly, trying to keep my sandals from slapping against the concrete. I was beginning to tremble.

I opened the flap. Ellie was seated on a high pile of lounge mats, wearing her tiny bikini instead of the one I'd bought her at the Fontainbleau, swinging bare feet and smiling down at another Studsy. This one was a little older, a little taller, a little slimmer ... but still, another golden muscle-boy. He was sanding down a badly-flaked lounge frame. It wasn't very exciting work, but the way he bulged inside his brief, tight swim-trunks, *something* was exciting him.

No matter. I was so relieved at not finding them playing around that I laughed and said, 'Hey, are you two hiding from the sun?'

She slid off the pile of mats, said, 'See you, Oran,' and went by me and out the flap.

I wanted her to join me, certainly ... but the way she'd done it made me seem more like a brutal father than a lover.

I smiled at Oran to counteract that impression. 'Think you could fix us with a couple of lounges?'

He nodded, looking at me as if to discover what had made Ellie jump that way. He was about thirty, maybe a year younger, and better looking than Studsy, his face leaner, finer. 'That'll be a dollar a lounge by the day, or five each by the week.'

'We won't be staying more than three days.'

'Oh?' He seemed surprised.

'Did Ellie say we would?'

'She said she might.'

I was speaking of 'we', and he was speaking of 'she'. She evidently hand't mentioned there was a man with her. And while travelling, we were Mr and Mrs Leib and she wore the gold wedding ring I'd bought her at Bloomingdale's ...

Now that I thought of it, I hadn't seen the ring the past few days.

Oran said, 'You, uh, together?'

I said, 'Yes,' and turned to the deck. Ellie was leaning against the railing looking out at the sea. I came up beside her and kissed her shoulder and took her left hand. 'Where's your ring?'

'In my jewellery box.'

'Why don't you wear it?'

'What, for swimming and sunbathing?'

Oran came out with two mats and began setting up the lounges. When I glanced at him, he glanced away from Ellie's ass. I was tired of blocking men's looks. I was tired of Miami, of any place where strange men could look at Ellie, approach Ellie ... where I couldn't control the situation. It would be worse in St Louis.

'I called Harold,' I said. 'There's an office crisis and he needs me.

We'll have to go directly home, soon as the car is ready.'

'Home is where I put my ass, you once said.'

Her eyes were fixed on the sea. The laughter that had sounded for Oran had given place to deep gloom for me.

Oran said, 'Lounges all set, sir.'

I gave him two dollars and he went back inside the tent. We lay down. I said, 'You make friends easily.'

'Uh-oh, you gonna kill him too?'

'Be *quiet*!'

She laughed. 'Take it easy. I was only kidding. But Jesus, isn't it something to know what you did?'

Knowing what I'd done didn't bother me. The punk had first tried to take my girl, and then tried to kill me. It was unlikely I would ever run across another like him the rest of my life.

But if my life were spent with Ellie?

Then it wasn't *that* unlikely!

I rolled over on my stomach. Ellie said, 'I'm sorry I talked that way, honey. I'm a real grouch this morning.'

'Only with me, not with Oran.'

'Shit! And listen, you said we were going to St Louis. I told Liz, and Gina and Claire...'

'Then tell them it'll have to wait.'

'Why can't I visit on my own; fly down there? One week...'

'Which will stretch into three weeks with two weeks of disappearance. No thank you.'

'What if I decide to go anyway? What if I just take off?'

I rolled over and looked at her. She said, 'You want to kill me too, Nickie?'

I kept looking at her. She said, 'It doesn't scare me. Do you think it scares me?'

'No one wants to die.'

She met my eyes. 'I wouldn't mind.'

'Last night you were so frightened...'

'Did it ever strike you I might be frightened for *you* as much as for me?'

I shook my head slowly. 'Not lately. You know how you've been.'

'*Me*? What about you?'

'Ellie, I've come more and more to need you. While you...' I was afraid to say it. I was afraid of another discussion, ending in the logic of: If she wanted to leave me, she should be allowed to.

'Well?' she asked.

'You finish it.'

She looked at me, and her face began to change; began to come apart. She got up, kneeled by my lounge, put her arms around me. She said, 'Nickie, love me, be easy with me, go along with me, don't frighten me, I won't leave you, I want to be with you, I love you, I swear I do, but don't choke me, don't scare me, love me . . .'

She was shaking and crying and kissing me and I couldn't stop her and I was too stunned to absorb it all. She finally quieted and we held each other. Oran came out of the tent and looked at us and she didn't pay him any attention.

She said, speaking in my ear, 'I don't care about that jerk last night. I thought maybe *you* would, but I don't. Not at all. Does it shock you?'

I said no, it was a vindication of what I'd thought she'd feel. 'We're alike.'

'No we're not, because I'm afraid of violence. If he hadn't gone for us with the car, with the gun . . . but he did, so better him than us.'

I nodded.

'But you . . . you might get crazy with someone else, someone who doesn't deserve it.'

'Not as long as you tell me you love me.' I was beginning to absorb what she'd said, and I wanted to *shout* I was so happy! I'd never thought to hear those beautiful words again. I kissed her, looked around, saw we were alone, ran my hands over her thighs and bottom, 'Oh, God, Ellie . . .' Someone gave a long loud whistle. I jerked my hand away, and sat up. Out on the beach, two boys, about thirteen or fourteen, were walking by, looking at us. They were too far away to have seen more than the clinch.

Ellie laughed, then dragged me down and kissed me and grabbed me by the crotch. The kids whistled again, and Ellie and I were helpless with laughter . . . and I was helpless with passion as well. 'Let's go to the room,' I said.

'All right.' She hugged me.

'But give me a minute. Go back to your lounge so I can walk . . .'

'I like to see you bulging that way. C'mon. No one's around. The kids are gone.'

'Oran and an old couple are just around the corner at the pool. What if they stroll out here?'

'Oran can pull off, and the old couple might get young again.'

I shook my head. She began to drag me up from the lounge, that crazy grin lighting her face, that deep dimple showing. I stopped caring who might surprise us and came at her and crushed her against me.

175

She whispered, 'Do it to me *now*.'

'What?'

'I love you, Nickie. I want you, *now*.'

It was insane. I said so. She pulled me down on top of her on the lounge.

'Do it fast. I'm ready to come right this minute! We'll be finished before anyone can catch us.'

As she spoke she drew my penis from under my trunks, spread her legs, and slid aside the crotch of her bikini. And I was in her.

I thought I heard voices from the pool, from the beach. I wanted to stop, but she was humping under me, and I moved, and I came. I tried to pull out, but she said, 'A few more good ones. Harder . . . Nickie, *Nickie* . . .' I slammed in several times and she groaned and threw her legs up around me. I didn't want that because it was so obvious and my back was to the beach and what if the kids had returned . . .

She sighed and relaxed. I tried to pull out. She held me, laughing, until we heard feet slapping on concrete. I jumped up, turning my back, adjusting my trunks.

Oran came around the corner. 'Want anything to drink?'

I faced him. Ellie was lying with knees up, legs crossed. She said, 'What about you, Nickie?'

I said a Coke would taste good. She said make it two.

We swam in the pool and walked along the beach and she hugged me and played with me and teased me in her old loving way. She told me she loved me and asked if I loved her, and I did, God I did. But I had to ask how and why it had all happened today.

She grew silent. Her arm remained around my waist, but she looked at the motels and the sea and not at me. I said, 'I don't want to push, honey . . .'

'Then let's not talk about it. Isn't it enough that it's *happening*?'

I said, 'I guess so.'

A little later, she said, 'Sometimes arguments and other people and the past become unimportant when something else happens, something *really* important.'

I didn't understand. We were passing a group of three women and one was a knockout – good figure and a beautiful, fair-skinned face. We looked at each other. Ellie said, 'I bet you'd *grab* her if I wasn't here!' and gave me a shot on the shoulder. I laughed and said I might *look* but I couldn't even handle what I had.

'And what if we couldn't fuck for a while, say a month or two?'

I shrugged. 'As long as it was a good reason – not a rejection, not another St Louis trip, but a medical reason – I'd never . . .' And then I stopped walking and looked at her. 'Are you trying to tell me something?'

She made with the big laugh and said I was the most suspicious man in the world and ran into the ocean. I chased her and we splashed and ducked each other, and now I wanted to stay in Miami for a month. But, at the same time, I watched her, and she seemed different, worried, and I began to worry too.

Back in the room, she told me.

I was towelling after we'd showered together. She was lying on the bed, nude, looking down at herself. 'Nickie, c'mere a minute.'

I went to her, sat down beside her, bent and kissed first one breast, then the other. She said, 'I'm about two weeks late.'

I straightened. 'You're kidding! The pill ...'

'You know me. I forgot to take it a few times.'

And that explained our beautiful day. I stood up. 'You love me, huh?'

She sat up. 'Honest, Nickie! It came to me today that we have a chance now, *if* we want it. I'm not saying we shouldn't talk about whether we should have the baby ...'

'And how do you know it's mine?'

She paled before my eyes. '*How?* But ... who else, you bastard! There's been no one else and you know it!'

'Harv, during your last trip to St Louis.'

'But that was ...' She shook her head. 'Let me think! That was months ago! And if I'm only two weeks late ...'

'The wedding was in August. You were there until the eighteenth. If you skipped *last* month ...' I watched her carefully.

'I *didn't*. I ...' She looked away. 'I stained a little. You can't stain if you're pregnant, can you?'

'Did you forget some pills in August too?'

'I always forget some pills,' she screamed. 'I'm a fucking idiot, you know that, and now you're telling me I'm a fucking whore! I'm sorry I said I loved you and sorry I thought something good could happen to us and ... get out of here! Get out! Get out!' She was screaming and sobbing. I went into the bathroom and closed the door.

She continued to weep. I began combing my hair; then stood looking in the mirror, and shook. If it was Harv's ...

We had to return to New York. I had to call Ron and set up a pregnancy test. I had to find out just how far gone she was. And because there was a chance another man had impregnated her, I burned, burned ... and I wanted to go in there and hurt her, making her feel the same agony I felt.

At the same time, part of me wanted to believe she was carrying my child and loved me and would marry me and be with me forever.

But now I was unable to block the image of another man's body lying with hers.

I shaved, I powdered, and deodorized. I came out and she was under the covers, her back to me. I went to the closet, glancing at her. Her eyes were closed, and she kept them closed as I dressed. I went out, banging the door; then paused outside. If she had called me, I'd have gone back in. Because, truth to tell, I didn't know where to go. Miami was full of bars and clubs and restaurants and theatres, but what good were they without Ellie?

I had to stop thinking that way! This woman was poison in my blood! It wasn't love; it was *sickness*! She lied to me, and betrayed me with Harv, and called me by his name, and tried to leave me ... then feared pregnancy and picked me as the winner. Love, she said. Love, when she needed a father for her child. And who was to know whether she hadn't fucked for others since returning from St Louis? Her attitude had been far from love ... and what did I really know about her ... and how could I let her have a child, especially if it was mine, she being what she was and me being what I was with her?

By the time I'd driven around and had a few drinks and picked at a dinner, I'd worked myself into a state of absolute panic, absolute despair. I had to free myself of Ellie; and the only way to do that was to let her go back to St Louis and her own kind. I'd become a madman because of her. It could get worse. The answer was to have an abortion, no matter who might be the father, and then part.

Once she was gone, I could become involved with Ledya, or Karen, or a new woman. There were so many young, beautiful, intelligent women around; why was I sinking into the muck with this ... tramp?

It was ten when I left the restaurant. I wanted to see girls, sexy girls, girls who would excite me and prepare me for New York and a return to sanity. I hadn't enjoyed a woman since meeting Ellie. I would tonight!

I went to a club near Havlover Beach Park, part of a huge motel complex. Despite it being the off-season, and despite almost every other place being more than half empty, I could barely find room to stand at the bar, and most of the tables were also taken. This was due, in no small part, to its famous pickup action. It was also due to a hot Dixieland band alternating with a hot rock group, and a gang of go-go girls in mini-costumes who did stints dancing on the tables.

I drank steadily, not paying too much attention to women who came and went, some looking my way. I drank seriously, putting distance between me and my brain. I drowned the early urges to return to the Casa D'Oro and Ellie; to see if she was still in the room. I drowned the thought that she might be with Oran, or another man. Let her. I had to get used to the idea; had to get used to not caring.

Later I turned, drink in hand, and began to look around. I was pretty well bombed. But I could see, and I could hear, and I heard two men beside me discussing something in a newspaper folded on the bar. Damned if it wasn't an accident on Key Biscayne.

'He was usually high on hash and booze,' one man said. 'And you know how he was with women.'

'Don't I ever. The bastard pitched my wife.'

'Says here he was clobbered by some guy over a girl, and tore out of the Seven Keys like a maniac. Must've been high again.'

'When's the funeral?'

'I gotta call his mother.'

'It's his sister runs that family.'

'You coming?'

'Not me. I wouldn't lose an hour's work for Jeff Markson, dead or alive.'

I laughed. They looked at me. I looked at them. They drank up and walked away. The one going to the funeral looked back at me, loweringly.

Well, fuck you too, buddy. It's women I want, not drinking companions. Never did need men; nor women either, for that matter. Not the women I grew up with. Not the woman I dated as a youth. Not the woman I married. Needed *cunt*. Like Ellie. Like these go-go girls.

I turned for another drink. The newspaper was still on the bar. I drew it over, looked at a picture of the bastard in the Camaro. Without the headband; hair not as long. Taken some time ago. Survived by the two brothers, a sister, and a grieving mother. Obviously speeding and lost control of his vehicle. Had been drinking. Had an arrest record for sale and possession of marijuana. Brawler and womanizer.

Well, so he had brothers and a sister and a mother. So I felt a little twinge, and ordered another Gibson. When I paid, I realized I didn't have too much cash. Should have brought along some traveller's checks. But I had more than enough for this place, and if I went somewhere else I had my credit cards.

179

As it turned out, I wasn't quite right.

I looked at the newspaper, and tried to read beyond the headlines and titles, and couldn't focus my eyes. And didn't care. Funny, I hadn't even thought to buy a newspaper this morning and check on my victim. Neither had Ellie. What the hell sort of people *were* we? '*Baaaaaaaad*, Nickie,' as Ellie would say in baby talk. But forget her, and babies . . .

The go-go girls came on again, a line of about eight or ten, dressed bunny-style, prancing to the rock music. I leaned my back against the bar and tapped my foot to the music and watched as they broke up and scattered around the club. One went up on the stage with the musicians, and the others climbed onto tables, helped by gallant, grinning, gash-hungry men. They began to dance.

I spotted one on a table to my left, not far from the dance floor, and stopped paying attention to the others. I almost stopped breathing. She was so beautiful, she was barely believable – long black hair and perfect cameo features and a magnificent body, big where it should be big, but somehow petit in general. The kind of girl one sees every so often in a show, a club, a dive.

I had sudden memories of myself as a kid at the Brooklyn Star Burlesque, sitting with a hard on and aching, *dying* for Sherry Britton, Margie Hart, other pink, fleshy, gorgeous strippers. Of surreptitiously rubbing my cock in the Supreme Theatre, not for any of the big stars like Bette Davis or Merle Oberon or even the packaged sexiness of Bettle Grable, but for some walk-on Hollywood cunt, busting out of her dress during the minute she was on screen. And for Honey, the bad girl whose mother owned a candy store on the fringes of our neighbourhood, where it wasn't too safe to go since the micks and wops hung around there too. Honey wore tight sweaters and would rub her titties up against a guy, a fifteen-year-old guy who didn't know enough about himself to go after her; who drifted by once in a while when tormented by fantasies, but who spent most of his time on Alabama Avenue with the nice Jewish girls, who, if they were sort of crazy about you, might give you blue-balls.

But this go-go girl was all the great girls of the world rolled into one . . . or so it seemed to me that drunken night. The strippers and walk-on actresses and Honey and Ellie too – this girl had them all beat. If I could get her, I'd achieve the millennium! Lay her and I'd lay them all, all the girls I'd wanted from the age of fifteen on. Lay this girl and I'd lay the ghosts to rest.

They were finishing their stint. In go-go fashion, they stepped down from tables and stage, formed a line near the dance floor, and began prancing, like cute little ponies, past the bar and toward the door from which they'd emerged, a door I imagined led to a sort of cunt heaven.

Without planning to, I stepped out and blocked my dark-haired beauty's passage. I guess the girls behind her simply went around us, but I can't be sure because I was staring directly into her face. It was a fragile face, a delicate face despite the professional damp-lipped smile. Then she stepped back a little and I saw a massive, pink-jacketed, Mafia-type bouncer moving up in that smoothly-oiled manner that promised a quick end to my evening, and my state of health. I quickly said, 'It's not Ellie I want. It's not anyone but you, the most beautiful girl in the world. I've *always* wanted you. If I could ...'

The bouncer had arrived, and a hand was descending onto my shoulder. The girl, however, had been reached. She said, her voice as girlie as the rest of her, 'It's all right, Vinnie. We're old friends.'

The bouncer moved away. She began to step around me, saying, ''Bye now.' Again I blocked her path, and began to speak ... and I became aware that men at the bar were watching, and trying to hear.

Music came to my rescue; thunderous rock, blasting out anew. It isolated us; at least our conversation. I moved closer. 'Forgive me if I'm wrong ... but what does it take to have you?'

She was staring at me. I said, 'I'm sorry. I'll go.'

She put her hand on my arm, and murmured, 'Fifty for an hour. A hundred and fifty for the night. But only when I get off at two.'

I remembered my shortage of cash, and sighed and shook my head. 'A bargain, definitely, but I've got about twenty-five. Would you take a credit card?'

She laughed then, her head going back, her throat rippling. I waited out the laughter, smiling. She said, 'Listen, I've got a twenty-minute break now. Stay right here.' She left for cunt heaven.

I moved to the bar on a direct line with where we'd been talking. I had to squeeze between two men, one large and one small ... and one of them didn't like it. 'Have to stay right here,' I mumbled. Luckily, the one who didn't like it was small. The one who didn't mind leaned close and said, 'How'd you do? I hear those girls can be had.' I said, 'Are you speaking of my estranged wife?' He blinked and said, 'Sorry, fella. I never thought...' I interrupted to tell him the story of our shattered marriage; how her great beauty put temptation into her path, brought a constant flow of theatrical agents, actors, and just plain makeout artists; how she'd finally run off from our home in St Louis to Miami ...

She appeared in the open doorway, crooking her finger at me. I said, 'Reconciliation awaits.' He said, 'Good luck!' And off I went, though none too steadily. The long night of boozing was beginning to catch up with me. I hoped I'd be able to perform.

She was wearing a short raincoat and the same mesh stockings and black high-heeled shoes she'd worn while dancing. She took my hand and said, 'Hi, I'm Andra,' and led me at a quick pace through what began to seem an endless progression of dimly-lit passages and twisting half-flights of stairs. Finally, we were in a room and she was locking the door.

I stood watching as she took off the raincoat, to reveal a good sized pair of boobs, quite bare. She stripped off her mesh pantyhose and a pair of black bikini briefs, and she was naked. Very naked. She was still the most beautiful girl in the world ... but I knew right then that I was no longer the boy lusting in the burlesque and movie house and candy store. We'd come together some twenty years too late.

'C'mon, honey, we only got about fifteen minutes now. Though I heard the average isn't more than seven minutes, start to finish.' She laughed and came over to me, swinging her hips and shaking her boobs ... and I began to want her. And I began to remember what it was like wanting the strippers and actresses and Honey. And I told myself I was going to lay the ghosts to rest, and that included Ellie.

Mistake thinking of Ellie. Pang in chest. Where was she now? Revenging herself, solacing herself, because of my absence? First time I'd ever run out on her, given her the *right* to take another man. Of course, she'd done it with Harv, by right or not.

Mistake, mistake ... but Andra rectified the mistake by undressing me and kneeling as she drew down my shorts and pressing kisses to that rool of evil.

When she straightened we came up against each other. I was certain then that all thought was ending; that the big erotic dream was beginning. This girl's kiss was soft and sweet and she was a truly turned-on creature, professional or not, and when we got to the bed I played with her and she was sopping wet.

I stopped to look at her. I said, 'Don't disappear now. You always did before, when I was pulling off.'

She moaned, stroking me, and said, 'Do you really want me more than this Ellie, more than *anyone*?'

'Yes, because you're the most beautiful girl in the world.' And the liquor was so strong in me that the room swirled and the girl swirled and I didn't know whether I still had a hard on. But I must have, because she was putting me in, and as she did I felt it again.

She was reaching for the bedside lamp. I said. 'No, please, let me watch.'

She laughed. 'I was putting it *on* ... *more* light.'

So it was dim in the room and I didn't know it. So I was fucking the most beautiful girl in the world and I didn't know it. I made the right movements and looked at her face and looked at the joining of our bodies and she was really going wild and I said, 'Wait a minute, I can't see. I want to see it all, the dream ... *all*.' But maybe I didn't actually say it, maybe I only thought it, because she didn't stop, she kept going, faster, faster...

I simply came, squeezing her bottom and hearing her say, 'Just a little more, don't stop for Chrissake, just a minute more.'

I gave her the minute or however long it was that she needed. Then she pounded my shoulders with her fists and said 'Rotten goddam pig stops my car and rapes me and oh, Christ, don't hurt me, officer, don't use your gun, please, I'll do whatever you say, don't, baby, don't, *ah* ...'

Well, even a whore is allowed her fantasies. This one was still young enough to joy it all. I felt sorry I couldn't enjoy it with her.

I was sitting on a chair with my pants over my knees, counting out all the money in my wallet. She said, 'Hold it, that's three more than you owe,' but I finished and dug into my pants pockets and came out with change and poured it into her cupped hands and said, 'Gold and silver pieces for the most beautiful girl in the world.' She laughed and said, 'I gotta go. Get dressed now. Same deal tomorrow?' I said I'd try and she was gone and I was looking across the room into a mirror. The Nick Leib in the glass said, 'It was nothing.'

He scared me.

Everything was nothing, except Ellie.

And if it changed to *include* Ellie.

Then *I'd* be nothing, and dead.

That half-sobered me and I dressed and found my way out to the back of the club and the parking lot.

I drove very carefully. I hoped Ellie would be in the room. If she was, I'd apologize ...

But she wasn't.

And it was after midnight. And where could my little love be, and with whom? I almost preferred that she be with Oran, a decent

183

enough guy, than in some bar, alone, letting the men look at her and approach her. Some hard guy, some bad guy, taking her in his car and parking and she wanting to go home and he frightening her, forcing her, hurting her, raping her ... and she liking it.

I was standing in the bedroom with my fists clenched and my eyes squeezed shut, saying, 'Ellie, come *come*!' I went to the bathroom and washed my face with cold water. She'd gone out to a movie. She'd simply gone for a walk on the beach ...

And met someone and was in his bed now.

I had no right to think this way. It was *I* who'd been in someone's bed.

And yet it made no difference, because again and always, I wanted no one but her and enjoyed no one but her.

I went down to the lobby. It closed at ten, and so there was no one to talk to, to question about Mrs Leib's whereabouts.

I went out to the pool. No one. I went around to the deck, and opened the flap of the tent. And then took a mat and spread it on a lounge frame and lay down to think things out ... and went to sleep.

I awoke to voices. Ellie's voice. Oran's voice.

A dream?

I opened my eyes and saw them. My lounge was up against the building, in the shadows. They were out at the railing, in the moonlight, about twenty feet to my right. Oran had one hand loosely around her shoulders. I wanted to hurl myself at him and tear that arm from its socket! But this was a God-given opportunity to watch Ellie when she thought she was unwatched. Besides, they weren't doing anything – just standing and talking and smoking.

The wind wafted a little of that smoke to me. Sweet, different. Oran raised the cigarette to his lips and I saw the scroungy tube, the handrolled butt and realized they were joints.

Ellie was saying, '... he had a pound of it back there.'

Oran laughed. 'Bet he'll be waiting until morning for you to show up.' He hugged her. 'You're something else. Getting a *waiter* to give you pot!'

She dragged deeply, looked at the roach, dragged again; then flipped it over the railing.

'You shouldn't have done that. We could save the roaches and use them in my pipe.'

'I've got two more.'

'For tomorrow night?'

'Maybe.'

'You think your ... uh, husband ... ?'

'My friend.'

'You think he'll be away tomorrow too?'

'Maybe.'

He dragged and blew smoke in her face. She smiled a little and looked out at the sea. She was wearing her sexy print mini from Saks, the one that turned me on indoors and made me sweat outdoors. It made Oran sweat too. As she examined the sea, he examined her. He said, 'Ellie, you're the cutest chick ever.'

She didn't answer. He dragged on his joint, then stabbed it out against the railing, examined it, and put it in his shirt pocket. And put both arms around her and turned her to face him. 'Hey,' he said softly, 'don't I get a kiss for being a gentleman like you asked me to be?'

She smiled. 'Then you won't be a gentleman any more.'

'Sure, if you *give* it to me.'

'Sorry. I never give kisses.'

'Can I buy one?'

'Now that's different. A dime.'

They laughed, and suddenly he clutched her to him and his mouth went down on her and his hands began to move.

I stayed put. I was dying, but I stayed there in the shadows. I wanted to see just when she would stop him.

One hand was on her ass, sliding the short dress up and ducking under to stroke the panties. She moved her head aside. 'Oran, that's enough.'

He said, 'Aw, Ellie, c'mon, what's the harm?' and kissed her again.

She began to push at him, to struggle ... but only a little. She seemed undecided. He held the kiss. She moved her head aside. He took her chin in his hand and kissed her again. She made a sound of protest. Her hands were on his biceps, pushing ... but still not hard. His hand on her ass was now inside her pants. She got her mouth away. 'Look maybe tomorrow ...'

He kissed her. She struggled violently for an instant, and I felt exultation mixed in with my pain and rage, and began to rise. Then she stopped struggling. Then he turned her with her back to the railing and began grinding against her, socking it to her. Then he took his mouth from her mouth and kissed her neck and worked a hand between them to her breasts. Her body began to move in that unmistakable manner. I heard her breath panting, panting ... though she did say, 'Oran, I don't want to ... not now ... maybe tomorrow ...'

He had her. Her dress was coming up and her pants down. She

gasped, 'Please, please ...'

An explosion was building somewhere in my head. I got up, yawning. Ellie gave a little shriek. I said, 'Hey, what's going on?' and stood rubbing my eyes.

She'd adjusted her clothing. He was looking back at me, and moving his hands in front. Allowing just a fraction of my true feelings to show, I said, 'What've you been doing with her?'

'Man, nothing ...' And then, facing me, 'Nothing she didn't want.'

And so it was here again, and I moved toward him, prepared to talk a bit and set myself and take him out with something quick.

Ellie saw it coming. She said, 'Oran, if you don't leave now, I'll scream my head off and tell everyone you were forcing me. And in a way you were, so do as I say!'

I paused, giving him a chance to go. He didn't want to. His blood was up, along with his pecker. Ellie shoved him. He moved slowly toward the pool. I began to move after him, the need to hurt him building, the need to get the pressure off my heart and brain, the need to pay him back for playing with my little girl, my little love, my Ellie.

She ran to me, held me, said, 'We didn't do anything. What you saw was the whole thing. I'd never have let him ...'

I laughed. Then I felt her shaking. She was trying to press against me and hold my arms and look at me at the same time. She expected to be hit.

I said, 'Take it easy.'

She relaxed, her head on my chest.

Oran went around the corner.

I said, 'Where did you go?'

'Can we sit down?'

We sat on my lounge. I realized I was trickling sweat. She said she'd waited for me until nine; then gone down to the lobby. Oran had been there, 'goofing around' with the switchboard girl, a cute French Canadian chick. He'd talked to Ellie, and invited her for a ride on his motorcycle. 'Big Honda ... we went around Miami and off some side streets. I told him he had to be a gentleman, and he was.'

'So I saw.'

'I mean, until we got back and smoked and he turned on a little too much.'

'But you didn't turn on, right?'

She took my hand. 'A little. Because I checked the room when we came back and I didn't know you were down here and I figured you were shacked up with someone. And where *were* you?'

'Let's finish with you first. After riding around on his Honda – and in that goddam mini ...'

'I watched myself.'

'I'll bet everyone did!'

She sighed. 'Anyway, we went to a little rock club where lots of pool boys and kids go. We danced. Then we went to a restaurant and then we came here.'

'How'd you get the pot?'

'He knew a guy ...'

'I heard him say *you* got it.'

'Oh.' Another sigh. 'Well, this waiter turned on for me and when I was going to the ladies' room he followed me behind a sort of rack where they have wine bottles and he tried to get me to ditch Oran and come back later. He said he had pot and we could have a party. I told him to give me a little on account, and he did.'

'Four joints, just on the promise you'd return? Come on now!'

'All right! So he put his hands on me, and I gave him a kiss. I tell you, after being left alone and after the things you said and the way you acted, and knowing that I was nothing but shit to you, I'd have fucked him or anyone else for a few joints! I needed them tonight! And where were *you*, running out at four or five and not coming back ...'

'Don't shout. You'll wake people up.'

'Fuck people! I don't give a shit about people! And come to think of it, why should I be worried about *you* any more? It's over, isn't it? An abortion and ship the bloody cunt back to St Louis, right?' She was standing, and she suddenly slapped me in the head and tried to do it again. I caught her wrist. She tried the other hand. I caught that wrist too.

'You weren't worried about me,' I said. 'You were worried about Oran, about my hurting him. And you were about to get fucked right up against that railing when I interrupted.'

'I'd never ...'

'Let's call that points one and two. Point three, you slept with someone besides me in August – Harv Cohen. He's the one you *admit* to, which leads to point four – you might have slept with more.' She choked in fury, but I raised my voice and went on. 'And you might have slept with someone in September, but even if you didn't, I have a strong suspicion we'll find you're *six* weeks late, not two weeks, because you didn't have a regular menstrual period last month. That's point five. Point six is that you haven't said a loving thing to me in months, but today, suddenly, you said you loved me ... and then said you suspected you were pregnant.'

187

Her wrists now lay limp in my hands. I let her go. She went to the railing. I didn't follow.

'Do you really expect me to play the traditional expectant father, leaping with joy, telling you not to lift heavy things, kneeling at your feet and thanking you for the gift of a child, under *these* circumstances?'

She didn't answer for a while. Then she said, 'You're smarter than me, Nickie. We both know that. And I've done some dumb things, but only with Harv. And tonight with Oran was the closest with anyone else ... but still, it's because at first you didn't care enough and then, later, too many arguments, too many putdowns. And even now you're ashamed of me.'

I began to protest. She said, voice level but overriding mine (perhaps because she was right), 'Maybe you love me, I don't know, but you're still ashamed of me. If we were all alone somewhere, you'd be everything I want. If we were always moving around with strangers – well, *maybe* I could forget your being ashamed, which I can't now. But living normally, it's no good. Harv isn't ashamed of me. That's why I've been thinking of him. That's why ... it happened when I was with him.

'Anyway, everything was going bad with us. And then I decided maybe I was pregnant. That was last night, sometime, when I went to the bathroom and suddenly *felt* pregnant. A hunch, you could say. As soon as it happened, I knew who I wanted to be with when the baby came, knew who I wanted to marry, knew that only with him would I even *think* of having the baby. And it was you Nickie, and so it just came out of me, saying I loved you.'

My chest ached. My eyes burned. Nothing had been changed regarding my doubts as to who was the actual father, but if she was telling me the truth, if I was the one she really wanted ...

'That was this morning, Nickie. Now I don't feel that way. Now I don't want the baby, if I'm pregnant, and I don't even feel pregnant any more.'

'*Alevia*,' I said, and didn't bother explaining it was Yiddish for Let-it-be-so. We went to the room. I wanted to shower, but was too exhausted. We lay down in our separate beds. I began to drift off. She slipped in beside me and I felt her lips on my face, tasted her tears, heard her choked voice. 'Nickie, I'm so scared. You always make love to me at night. Don't change that. I need it, Nickie.'

We kissed. Her hand worked on me. Always before I'd come up no matter what. But tonight I'd drunk too much, and I'd had another woman, and I didn't come up. I said, 'Booze ... wait till morning.' She said, 'Ellie'll make better,' and ran her lips down my chest and belly, and licked my belly button and then my penis. I came up instantly, but she jerked away and sat up and stared at me. 'You pig,' she said, not shouting, just stating a fact. 'You fucking pig.' She went back to her own bed.

It took me a moment to understand; then I flushed hotly. But she couldn't see it in the darkness, and I said, 'What's the matter with you? Was it the smell? Because male genitals, unwashed, smell rather like female genitals.'

She said, 'You fucked someone tonight,' but she wasn't sure any more.

I asked if pot always made her psychotic. I said I'd been drinking; so much so that I couldn't have fucked if I'd wanted to. Then I went to the bathroom and used a soapy washcloth and called myself an idiot. Because I'd simply forgotten to wash after having Andra.

When I came out, she was lying on her back, hands under her head, staring up at the ceiling. I suggested we smoke the two remaining joints. She said, 'I'm beat!'—I said, 'You mean, Ahm *tahred*, don't you?' sitting down at the edge of her bed and stroking her hair. She didn't pick up on the game. I got into bed with her and kissed her. She turned her back on me, but put her ass in my crotch in her favourite sleeping position, and murmured, 'Cuddle me.' I did, and said I would wake her before the night was over.

I began drifting off as soon as I closed my eyes. I believe I heard her crying sometime later, but I just couldn't wake up, and I never did remember to ask her about it. Nor did I wake at any other time during the night to make love to her. When I finally did get up, driven by an urgent need to relieve myself of some of the liquid I'd ingested the night before, she wasn't there. It was a few minutes after ten, and that was early for Ellie, but still, I didn't worry . . . not until I entered the bathroom. There I saw an ashtray holding two roaches, and inhaled the sweet odour of pot.

Two joints before breakfast!

I didn't bother with washing, shaving, brushing teeth. I got into bathing trunks and ran downstairs. She wasn't in the lobby, or at the pool. On the sundeck, Oran leaned against the railing, looking out at the beach and sea. He glanced at me as I turned to leave. I hoped she hadn't taken the car . . .

'You looking for Ellie?'

I said I was.

He pointed over the railing. I went there, looked at the beach, saw several women but none of them was Ellie. 'The ocean,' he said. I raised my eyes, and still didn't see her. 'Way out,' he said. I raised my eyes further, then further still ... and saw a pale yellow dot that looked half a mile out. Ellie owned a daisy-decorated bathing cap.

'That's not her, is it?' I asked, my insides begnning to churn. 'She isn't a very good swimmer.'

'Even the best shouldn't be out *that* far.'

I began to run toward the steps. 'Then why the hell didn't you stop her!'

'*Me*?' he called pugnaciously. 'She wouldn't even stop for my good morning.'

I'd reached the beach and was kicking off my sandals. 'Oran, c'mon!'

I ran down to the water, and before plunging in glanced back. He was walking across the sand, a sullen look on his face. 'You're the guard here!' I shouted. 'And she's going to drown if you don't ...'

But I had no more time. I was diving under a wave and swimming as hard as I could. Too hard, in fact; I began to blow and struggle for air. I settled into a rhythmic pace, trying not to raise my head and look for her until I'd come out a ways.

I kept telling myself I could look after another ten strokes. And then I'd add seven more. And five more. And so I kept going quite a while.

Finally, I looked. It took a moment to find her. She was about fifty yards further out. God, with two joints in her! And with that inefficient, head-up, splashing swimming style! 'Ellie ... turn back!'

She looked around. I saw her face for a moment, awash in rolling grey immensity, mouth open and gasping for air. She seemed about to go under, yet she turned from me and began splashing further out.

I swam harder. I didn't care if I lost my breath now. I just didn't want to look up and *not* see that yellow cap.

I lifted my head and saw her and changed direction slightly. I called, 'Ellie!' but didn't get much power into it because I had to keep going. I swam another ten strokes and was able to see her with just a snap upward of my head. Ten, twelve feet away. I gasped 'Ellie ... here ... turn. ...' She turned and looked at me and went under.

I know I screamed. I lunged forward and stroked insanely, and she came up. 'Kick!' I gasped. 'Paddle!'

She moved her mouth, gulping air, and said, 'No.' I didn't hear the voice, but the lip-movement was unmistakable. She began to go under again.

I reached out and clutched that yellow cap. It tore off her head, but I was able to grab a handful of hair with my other hand. Then we both went under, and it took a while to draw her up so that I could grab her body. I kicked and we rose, and rose, and when the hell were we going to break the surface? I began to panic, but somehow, I didn't let go of her. I remember that, whenever I doubt the love I felt for Ellie. I remember that, because I held onto her as I held onto my own will to live.

We broke the surface. She was fighting instinctively now. She was climbing up me, away from the water, clutching at my arms and face and hair. She was stopping me from swimming, from taking her and myself back toward shore. I knew I had to do something; get her under the chin and escape those clawing, climbing arms and legs ... but my Red Cross life-saving course lay twenty years in the past and she was pulling me under.

Perhaps I'd have hit her, tried to break free, even have left her if it had continued. I don't know. I'm trying to be honest. But I don't think so. How could I have left her to die there?

We didn't go under because Oran swam around behind her and hooked his left arm under her chin and said something about my grabbing her legs. I don't know whether this method is approved of by any authorities, but between the two of us we immobilized her and began working our way in toward shore.

It took forever, and at a certain point she stopped struggling. She was facing me, as I held her ankles with one arm and stroked with the other. Oran's arm under her chin pulled her head far back, but her eyes seemed to strain downward to fix on me. I managed to say, 'Soon, honey,' and wondered when the hell we'd reach shore and wondered if I could keep going another second ... and Oran was standing and walking and then I was too.

Some people had gathered and were watching when we staggered up on the beach. Oran was about five steps in front of me, supporting Ellie with an arm around her waist. Her bikini bottom had slipped down and seemed about to come off. I said, 'Oran,' and when he stopped and looked back, I tried to reach them. But I simply sank to the sand. 'Her bikini,' I said. He saw what I meant and tugged it back. She was sagging against him, head down. When he let her go, she dropped to her hands and knees. He waited, and she got into a sitting position, and he went on toward the motel. She breathed heavily, and leaned over, and began vomiting.

A broad, hairy man came over, squatted beside her, and said, oh-so-solicitously, 'You need some help, honey?' He put his hand on her shoulder. 'Want me to take you to your place?'

She looked at him, and vomited again. He moved back a little, still squatting, and waited. I wanted to go to her, but just couldn't catch up on my breathing. I saw Oran reach the steps, sink to the first one, and begin his own fight for breath, out of reach of prying eyes.

The hairy guy was moving back near Ellie. She said, voice surprisingly strong, 'You're what I remember from home. Go away ... you stink.'

She coughed heavily.

He said. 'What the hell's wrong with *her*?' standing up and looking around. An elderly woman said, 'She wants to be left alone. Some girls can't even drown in peace.'

Ellie stopped coughing to laugh a little. She looked at me and said, 'Like your momma, I bet.'

I was strong enough to crawl over to her. We sat there, and she vomited a third time, and nothing came out except a little bile. I rubbed her back and said, 'If you can walk, we'll go to the room. I think you should have a doctor.'

'Fuck you *and* your doctors.'

The elderly woman must have heard that, because she turned abruptly and walked off. Like my momma, I thought.

I got up, helped Ellie up, and we went slowly toward the motel. Oran saw us coming, and walked up the steps. 'He saved you,' I said.

'Big *mans*,' she said.

I was suddenly enraged, and shoved her, and she fell to the sand. 'You don't respect anything!' I said. She nodded, looking up at me. 'That's right. Why should I?' I started away; then went back and helped her up. 'He could have drowned,' I said. 'I could have drowned. Just because you got stoned and went swimming.'

'Is that how it was?' Sullen, bitchy voice; sullen, bitchy face.

'Then how was it?'

'You should've asked me when I was going under.'

'I did, in a way. You didn't want to be saved.'

'That's right, so why should I thank ...' She cut herself short with a muttered, 'Shit!'

'So you were trying to kill yourself?' I made myself laugh.

She shrugged, and began to walk.

I stopped her and turned her to face me. 'Ellie, no ... why?'

'Why not?'

She went on toward the stairs. I followed. Oran was sitting on a lounge near the pool, talking to a tall, brown girl in a red bikini. The girl came toward Ellie and said, 'You all right? Can I get you something?'

Ellie shook her head and went right by. The girl, who operated the switchboard, said, 'You all right, Mr Leib?'

I said, 'Yes,' and went over to Oran. 'Thank you.'

He nodded, examining a scrape on his foot.

I hesitated, then went after Ellie.

She couldn't have made it to the room before I did by more than a minute, yet she was in her bed, fast asleep, when I entered.

She stayed asleep until nine that night. Then we went out to dinner, and drove along A1A, and talked. Or, I talked and she looked out the window. I wanted to know if she'd made a deliberate try at suicide; if she'd gone into the water *knowing* she was going to swim far out. And if so, what were her reasons.

She finally said, 'Listen, when I first came down I was going to the pool. I was stoned and I had this idea I wanted to lie in the water. Then Oran came over and said hello or good morning, and I don't know ... I just walked away and went to the ocean. I was going to lie in the water there. But I began to swim. Little by little, floating and swimming, I went out so far I couldn't see the shore. *Then* I began to go for broke.'

'What do you mean?'

'I mean I decided to swim until I couldn't swim any more.'

'But that means you would die.'

'I guess so.'

'You *guess* so!'

'I just didn't think it through. I can't understand it myself. I just wanted to ... well, end all the crap.'

We were in Hollywood Beach. I pulled to the curb and took her in my arms. She was very still, very unresponsive. I kissed her. Her lips were passive under mine. Then she patted my cheek and said, 'Let's see a movie.'

We went to a drive-in, not because I thought the picture was good, but because I wanted to have the opportunity to talk to her. The picture turned out to be *very* good, and she was soon engrossed, and laughing, and murmuring to me that a particular scene was great and a particular line 'true as dirt'. And this morning she had tried to die!

On the way out, I said that as I saw it, suicide required either a tremendous amount of physical or mental pain, or a total lack of hope. 'Would you say you have tremendous mental pain?'

'Not tremendous, no. Maybe not even pain. I mean, sure I was uptight last night' ... she shook her head. 'I don't want to talk about it. I just felt *down*.'

'All right, so that brings us to a total lack of hope. But you must have *some* hope. If not in me, then . . .' I had to fight to get it out, 'then in Harv.'

She nodded. 'I guess I have. But I *didn't* this morning. I don't *always* have. I mean, if I don't have hope in myself, then I don't have hope in anyone, right?'

I nodded slowly.

'This morning I didn't have hope in myself. Now let's drop it Nickie. I'm not really sure I wanted to kill myself. Hell, I was so scared when I thought I was *going* to drown . . . anyway, I'd find an easier way than that!'

I picked up the Chevy the next morning, returned the Pinto, and was back at the motel at eleven. Ellie said she couldn't tell there had ever been any damage to the right side. We took our luggage down, and while Ellie went out to the car I paid the bill. I left five dollars for the maid, and fifty dollars for Oran.

In the car, I surprised myself by suggesting she go to the pool and say goodbye to Oran.

She smiled her cynical smile. 'What for? And you don't have to tell me; I know. Say thanks for saving my life, right?'

'It's up to you.'

'*You* saved my life as much as he did, and I haven't said thanks to you. And I never will.'

I began to back the car out.

'Listen, if it'll make you happy, okay. But the only kind of thanks he wants from me is the kind where I'm flat on my back.'

'Forget it.'

'If you want to wait fifteen, twenty minutes, it is all right with me. After all, what's a fuck compared with my precious life, right?'

I managed the laugh, but I drove out of there without further discussion. A moment ago I'd wanted to shake the man's hand, and have Ellie say something nice to him . . . and then she'd said that filthy thing!

That true thing.

I'd suddenly seen them as they'd been last night against the deck railing. And I visualized them as they would be if Ellie 'thanked' him as he did, indeed, wish to be thanked. And I wanted to be back out there in the ocean with him so I could drown him!

My hate was so strong it shocked me. I was a nice enough guy, it seemed . . . except when it came to Ellie. Then I was a madman.

It took us two and a half days to drive home. We didn't talk about the near-drowning, or the possible pregnancy. We played it for relaxation and laughs, and it was fine. Until we drove across the

George Washington Bridge into Manhattan, and I said we still had time to set up a pregnancy test today, and she said, 'Yeah, great, and why not do the abortion tonight?'

EIGHT

So now we come to it; the single biggest mistake I made with Ellie, and she with me. The abortion.

I know all about the population explosion and the desirability of zero population growth. I'd signed petitions and made donations to help pass the liberal abortion laws we now have in New York. And I already had two children. Besides which, Ellie and I were about the worst prospects for parenthood you could find; we'd have driven a kid *insane* with our happy home life!

But I can never think about it without terrible pains, terrible regret, despite my still believing there was nothing else to be done, considering the circumstances. Nothing but having the child and taking our chances. Nothing but giving love – stupid, illogical, irrational love – a chance to change things, slim though the chance might be. Nothing but surrendering to the feeling that life born of such intense desire and passion should be allowed to emerge.

All sentimental nonsense, obviously, and all in the second-guessing and Monday-quarterback department. But how much better, how much less nonsensical, than what it led to.

I arranged for a pregnancy test on Monday, the same day that we returned from Miami. Ellie treated it as further indication of my unseemly haste to put her under the knife. But she didn't fight it, except with cold smiles and bitter glances. Ron called a lab in Fort Lee after I called him, and at four p.m. Ellie and I drove back over the bridge to New Jersey. Ellie gave a urine specimen for the Ortho Chemical Pregnancy Test to a sour little woman in a neat little waiting room, and we drove around, looking at Mediterranean Towers and Horizon House and other monstrous apartment-house complexes, unwilling to go home and face what was happening to us. We even ate in Fort Lee, at a delicatessen, stuffing ourselves with corned beef and pastrami and Dr Brown's celery tonic. But eventually there was nothing left to do but return to Manhattan.

That evening she began a process that was to last for eight days. Quite simply, she wrecked any organization that was left to our home and our lives. Clothing, books, magazines, newspapers, dishes, tissues, food-packages, *anything*, was thrown around more quickly than I could pick it up; and when I attempted to pick it up, I got the mockery, the laughter, the accusation that I was a little-old-lady. Because of what awaited her, I didn't want to respond, to argue, so I let it go. The apartment became a shit box almost overnight, and this hardened me in my attitudes, and she hardened in reaction to *my* hardening, and so we trundled merrily along to the day of the scalpel.

Ron called the next morning at ten, with Ellie and I still in bed. She remained with her back to me, seemingly asleep, as I grabbed the phone on the first ring.

The results were positive.

'There's no chance of error?' I asked, heart pounding.

'In the frog and rabbit tests, yes. Not this. She's pregnant, all right.'

'*How* pregnant?'

'What difference does it make? I'll arrange the abortion as soon as I hang up. Or have I misjudged your attitude?'

I said, 'No, go ahead,' but you have to understand that I was still thinking we would have some miraculous coming together at the last moment, some marvellous resolution of the vast differences between us, of the lies and suspicions and mutual rages, and then cancel out the operation.

Ron said, 'Fine. It's the only sensible way to go, considering what you've told me about her. I have a friend in Manhattan, Sheb Danorian, an excellent gynaecologist, and an experienced abortionist. He was one of the few surgeons at Flower Fifth to be assigned legal abortions by the authorities at a time when they were almost all *il*legal. Now, of course, he can operate with the patient's consent. I assume we won't have any problems there?'

'I don't think so.'

'He'll make it easier for both of you by doing it in his office. No dragging around hospitals and wasting two, three days and running up all sorts of unnecessary bills.'

'Thanks,' I muttered, wanting to lie down and close my eyes and sleep and forget everything. I glanced at Ellie. She hadn't changed position. 'When do you think it will be?'

'Call you back in about fifteen minutes with your appointment. And I'll make sure he keeps the price under three hundred.'

'About finding out how many weeks' pregnant . . .'

'There's some doubt that you're the father, is that it?'

I suddenly disliked him, with his brisk, helpful attitude and quick mind and totally logical ways. 'That's it.'

'Ask Sheb. He might be able to make an educated guess, after he gets inside her. Otherwise, there's no way of telling.'

'Won't he have to see her, to make sure she's physically able to *have* an abortion?' (Because if she wasn't, then the decision would be made for us and we'd be *forced* to have the child and we'd be *forced* to marry...)

'He'll do that the day of the operation. Just don't worry, Nick. It's a simple matter. A scraping of the uterus.' He paused. 'In the early stages of pregnancy, that is. Any chance she might be into her fourth month? Because then it'll be a far more serious situation.'

'No chance at all.' I remembered her menstrual period in July and how we'd ruined two good bedsheets up at the cottage. 'It's a matter of, say, three weeks, or seven.'

'Well, even eight weeks isn't bad. Call you back.'

We hung up. I lay down. Ellie said, 'I'm knocked up, huh?'

'Yes.'

'All set for the abortion?'

'Not yet. He'll call again.'

Her back was still to me. We were both quiet. Then she turned and came into my arms. We kissed and she buried her head in my chest. I wondered if she could hear my heart hammering. I waited for her to say something, and felt she was waiting for me. Neither of us said anything. We began to stroke and pet each other; she took my penis in her hand. 'How can it be hard, Nickie? I mean, *now*?' I stroked her thighs, and then her cunt. I slid a finger in and she was wet. I didn't ask the parallel question, because her mouth had come to mine and we kissed and kissed. And made love, wildly, satisfyingly, as always. After it was over, she went to the bathroom and the water ran for a long time and I wondered if I heard weeping.

I went to the door. It was open. She was brushing out her hair. Her eyes were red. I said, 'Honey, what do you think?'

'I said everything I think in Miami.'

'Would it make sense to...?'

The phone rang. I tried to finish my question. She said, 'Get that goddam thing, will you?'

It was Ron. 'Sheb's going out of town for a few days. I'll have the Ortho-test results sent to him, and he wants Ellie to take a few blood tests. I'll call the lab with full instructions, so just drive over and in a few minutes you'll be through ... until next Wednesday. That's when he'll do the job, seven a.m., sharp. Please be there on time, Nick. He's really doing this for me...' He went on about having had to pressure good old Sheb, who was up to his eyes in scheduled operations, and I mumbled thank-you's. We said goodbye and I went back to Ellie, who was now in the kitchen. She was

197

throwing things around again – a paper bag went on the floor, egg shells on the counter, she left out everything she'd taken from the refrigerator.

When I tried to get back to the subject of us and of the abortion, she said, 'Look, once you think of a thing like that, it's *done*. I mean, how could I want your baby now, when I know you're thinking of killing it?'

Her tone was venomous. I put milk and butter and eggs back in the refrigerator, and said, 'Let's not forget that there's some question of whether it *is* my baby. And a lot of other questions too.'

'Right. So fuck it. So let's get it done. And then I'll go home and you can forget all the questions and get back to Ledya and your other brilliant cunts.'

I didn't argue the going-home part, but I didn't believe it. Something would happen.

What happened were those eight days of incredible sloth on her part, touching off a sinking into apathy on my part, leading to us both dragging around the apartment and seeing and speaking to no one and going out only late at night.

We drove out the cottage at two one morning, and walked to the lake, and despite chill air and damp grass she pulled me to the ground and rolled around with me and got me out of my pants and drew down her jeans and straddled me and fucked me there, in bright moon and starlight, fucked me for half an hour, not letting me out of her. I stayed hard and approached orgasm a second time, and she gasped, 'Fuck me, *fuck* me! That's all there is anyway!' Always before it had been, 'Fuck me, Nickie. When you fuck me, everything's all right.' Now nothing was all right. I looked at her. She tried to move on me, but my cock was shrinking inside her. She rolled and looked up at the sky. I said, 'Honey . . .'

'Don't say anything, Nickie. It'll be bullshit, whether or not you know it.'

I got up and brushed leaves and grass off my clothing.

She said, 'Men and women. Cock and cunt. That's the story. The *whole* story.'

'That's not so.'

'With *you* it is.'

'And with Harv?'

'I'll have to find out, when I get home.'

'Home,' I muttered.

'Yeah, I'll be putting my ass down in St Louis from now on.'

Again I didn't argue it, and again I was sure something would stop her from leaving.

Tuesday night, the night before the abortion, we went for a drive toward Long Island, and stopped at a fair with sideshows and rides, and walked and looked and ate all sorts of junk. On the ferris wheel, she took my hand and put her head on my shoulder. 'El-lie...'

'No, don't say anything. Please. No more bullshit.'

It was *then* I had to say, 'The abortion is off.' It was *then* I had to tell her I loved her, wanted the baby, wanted it despite a chance that it might be Harv's, wanted *her,* forever.

But I *couldn't* say it. We were just too mismatched!

And yet, that night, holding her, pretending to sleep, suspecting she too was pretending, I also knew how *matched* we were. In bed—matched perfectly! God, were we matched—in the crazy imperfect love we had for each other!

I almost shook her, almost spoke to her ... but then I thought, '*Had* for each other.' It was past tense, our love. And it had never made sense; civilized sense; husband–wife and mother–father sense. Never.

We were up and dressed at six a.m. She sipped a little black coffee, and I spent a long time in the bathroom. My bowels were loose, my stomach queasy. We went down at six-thirty and drove uptown along Park Avenue until the Eighties, were I began searching for a parking space. I found one on Eighty-seventh near Madison, and we walked back to Park and the big old apartment house and Dr Sheb Danorian's private entrance marked by a tarnished brass plate.

We'd barely said a word since getting up. I now said, 'Feeling all right?'

She nodded, not looking at me. I pressed the bell button. We heard the ring, but no one answered. I checked my watch. 'Ten to seven. Guess we're early.'

She took my hand. 'Let's walk a little.'

We walked. Our fingers entwined. My stomach ached. I thought of all the people I knew who'd had, or helped their women to have, abortions. I was acting like a fool. You didn't bring a child into a situation like this. You didn't use a child as an excuse for marriage. Two adult human beings chose each other first, decided they could live together, and *then* had children.

And so on.

And we walked and said nothing.

And returned to the office, where a heavy little man with untidy grey hair was just opening the door. A young black girl in nurse's white was standing behind him.

We all entered together. Dr Sheb Danorian shook hands with me, smiled at Ellie, said, 'Oh, what sad faces! It'll be over in an hour, and that long only because it takes time for the anaesthetic to work. You won't feel a thing, darling, just leave it all to Shebsie.'

Shebsie? My stomach did a barrel-roll.

The nurse took Ellie away. Danorian watched them leave, then turned to me, smiling. 'A pretty child. Why can't we teach them to take their pills regularly?'

I think I managed a smile. I didn't want to antagonize the man, before the operation.

He said, 'How's Ron? Haven't seen him in three months.'

I said Ron was fine.

'Come into the office. My nurse handles the injection of anaesthetic. We have a few minutes to chat.'

We went to his office. Through an open door on the left, I saw Ellie being helped into one of those short hospital gowns that tie at the back. She looked good even in that. Sheb Danorian waved gaily at her. She raised her hand, as if hypnotized, then let it fall. He sat down, motioned me to a chair, and launched into an explanation, with full medical terminology, of what he was going to do. He suggested I stay here in his office, and said he might call me into the operating room, which was simply his examination room, 'to assure the patient that all is well, that she hasn't been abandoned'.

I nodded. I must have nodded a hundred times. And I nodded when he suggested I write the cheque for three hundred dollars now, so as to save time later, 'when the patient will want to return to familiar surroundings'.

'Right after you finish?'

'Immediately, if not sooner,' Sheb said, and grinned and slapped my arm. 'All this nonsense about days in bed. She'll be ready to dance tomorrow.'

I began writing the cheque; then looked up as Ellie passed through the office. The nurse hadn't tied the robe properly at the back. It flapped wide as she went past us. followed by the nurse's pointed finger to an open bathroom door. Her tanned buttocks with the narrow white area rolled at me ... and at Sheb Danorian, who watched intently. '*Lovely* child,' he murmured. I returned to my cheque, hating him and Ron and every doctor who'd ever lived.

Of course, it was myself I hated, but I wasn't ready to admit it.

Sheb decided we should have breakfast while the anaesthetic took effect. We walked one block west to a cafeteria, where he had eggs and bacon and a corn muffin and two cups of coffee. I had coffee and tried to eat a slice of toast. He talked about Ron and medical school. He talked about abortions, of how easy they were in the early stages. Which reminded me.

'Could you tell me how far gone she is, Doctor?'

'I can guess, later. No way of being sure, except for allowing the pregnancy to continue to stages where the foetus takes on recognizable, and gradable, form.' He smiled. 'I don't believe you want to go quite that far, do you?'

I didn't know what I wanted. We returned to the office. I sat near the desk and he patted my shoulder and changed into a white coat and went into the operating room. He left the door open. I heard him instructing Ellie to put her feet into the stirrups. 'That's a good girl,' he said, as if she were five. 'Now move your knees...' His voice changed, grew crisp. 'Put her knees apart.' The nurse must have been slow, because he added, 'Please.'

Ellie said something, sounding drunk. He chuckled. 'Of course he's here. You want to see him?' He raised his voice. 'Mr Leib.'

I went through the door. Ellie was on the table, feet in the stirrups, knees up and spread wide. There was a forceps-type instrument hanging from her cunt, pulling the lips apart, revealing redness...

I looked away. She was being defiled, and I had brought her here.

The doctor said, 'Give her a kiss for luck and then wait outside. Don't look so *unhappy*, Mr Leib! I'll call you back again to see how easy it is, how happy our patient is.'

The man was an idiot! But I obeyed and went to the table and looked down at her. Sombre little face. Sad little mouth. I bent, and she said, 'Nickie,' and reached up and touched my cheek. *God, God!*

'You see?' the doctor chortled. 'Better than any of the hallucinogens these children take. She's *high*, and happy. And she won't feel a thing.'

I kissed her. I murmured, 'Ellie, I love you.'

She smiled. Her eyes closed.

I returned to the office. Time passed. I heard the doctor's voice, the nurse's voice, several times Ellie's voice, responding to the doctor's questions. Then he called me again.

I froze at the door of the room. He was removing a bloody piece of *something* from her vagina. He dropped it into a pan at his feet, which held other bloody somethings, and said, 'See how clean? Practically nothing. I'd say she wasn't pregnant more than five or six weeks. You won't even have to come back ... though I suggest an examination in a month. And no sexual intercourse for that month. And no internal washing. No douches. No baths. Showers only.'

Ellie said something at that point. I said, 'What, honey?' moving to her, seeing the nurse, who'd been wiping her face with a damp cloth, change expression, register some sort of emotion.

Ellie said, 'Nickie,' her voice low, drawn-out, sleepy. 'Honey, did we have a boy?'

The doctor said, 'See? Doesn't even realize why she's here. A dream. A sweet dream.'

I went back to the office. The doctor joined me a while later, saying it had gone perfectly. He wrote out a prescription, noted that she would need sanitary napkins for her 'staining', repeated the no-sex-for-a-month and no-interior-bathing-of-the-vagina.

Ellie stayed on the table, dozing. The doctor shook my hand, sent his best to Ron, and left for the hospital. The nurse sat in the waiting room, reading a magazine. I stayed in the office, nursing a headache and a growing sense of wrong-doing, of error, of disaster. Half an hour later, the nurse returned to help Ellie dress; then brought her out to me. Ellie walked in a dream. She smiled and murmured, 'No pain, honey.' I nodded, and couldn't meet the nurse's eyes.

The nurse said, 'I suggest you call the doctor for birth control information. Abortion cases often repeat...'

The doctor wanted to give Ellie a coil, or a shot that would last from three to five months. I nodded, and went to get the car. When I pulled up in front of the office, the nurse had the door open. I ran to where she was leading Ellie out. We got her in the car, and the nurse said, 'She'll sleep quite a while. When she wakes, she can eat anything she wants ... but make sure she has her medication by this evening. It's an antibiotic to prevent infection, and *very* important.'

I drove home. Ellie leaned back against the seat and slept. I parked in front of the apartment house, and told the doorman Mrs Leib had received a strong injection at the dentist and had to be taken upstairs. He allowed me to leave the car outside 'for just a few minutes' after I slipped a dollar into his waiting hand. He watched us, as did several people in the lobby, as we walked slowly inside. Ellie holding to my arm, leaning heavily against me, and smiling dreamily.

I got her undressed and into bed. She wore what looked like a king-size sanitary napkin, only slightly stained on the outside, and turned onto her side and went to sleep immediately. I went down, parked the car in the garage, and walked to the Second Avenue drugstore. I bought Kotex napkins, large-size as per instructions, and waited to have the prescription filled. I examined a rack of paperback books. Dr Spock turned up in three separate slots, and I looked at deodorants and perfumes instead.

Ellie awoke at four, having slept more than five hours. I was just using a dust-mop under the dresser, and turned at a throat-clearing sound. She was looking at me. I quickly layed the mop down, but she said, 'Little old lady cleaned the house?' I went to the bed and sat down and touched her hair. She said, 'Don't,' her voice terribly cold. Well, today would be bad. Tomorrow would be better. And by the weekend she'd ber ready for the cottage and perhaps a trip to Vermont...

'I'm leaving tomorrow,' she said, and sat up and put her feet over the edge of the bed. Her napkin was heavily stained now, but the blood was dried and brown. She looked down at herself. 'I'd like to change this.'

I said there was Kotex in the bathroom. She got up and staggered a little. I grabbed her elbow. She took a few deep breaths, said, 'I'm all right now,' and walked slowly out of the bedroom. I followed her. She shut and locked the bathroom door. I said, 'You shouldn't lock yourself in. What if you feel dizzy...?'

The water came on, drowning me out. Yes, today would be bad. But she wasn't serious about leaving tomorrow. She couldn't be. She wouldn't be able to travel for at least a few days. And by then we'd have made our peace, and she would realize we'd done the only sensible thing.

I put the broom and polishing cloths and Windex away and ran out with two large bags of garbage, dumping them in the incinerator. When I returned, she was just lowering herself onto the couch, dressed in my old blue bathrobe. 'Nice job,' she said. 'The place looks almost as good as before I came here.'

'I'll have a maid in once a week...'

'What for? I won't be here to shit it up, and you're neat as a fucking pin.'

I laughed. 'That's me, all right.' I didn't know what else to say, and tried, 'This will give you a chance to go over your workbooks, and read a few good novels, and by the time you're ready to do some shopping and play tennis...'

'I'm going to watch television.'

'Forever?' I laughed, and came to her and began to sit down.

'Get away,' she said, looking right at me.

It was the anaesthetic wearing off, I told myself. And a certain natural resentment.

I turned on the television and asked if she was hungry. She nodded. I went to the kitchen, put on the oven, and slid in the pan holding the steak I'd seasoned earlier. I made a salad with her favourite dressing, Caesar. I was just slicing in tomatoes when I sensed a presence and turned. She was standing in the doorway, watching me. 'I'm sorry I was so rough, Nickie.'

I dropped the tomato and reached for her. She came into my arms. I tried to speak and couldn't. She said, 'It'll be better when I'm gone, for both of us.'

I turned back to the salad. 'We'll talk about it in a week or so.'

She ate in the living room, watching a movie. She finished everything and got up and went to the bedroom. I cleared away the dishes, and went to join her. The bedroom door was locked. She was speaking on the phone.

I wanted to lift the kitchen extension, but didn't.

I didn't have to. She came out in about five minutes and said, 'I called Harv. He'll meet me at the airport in St Louis. I'm taking a seven-fifteen American Airlines flight out of LaGuardia tomorrow night.'

'You *can't*! You need rest...'

'I heard the doctor tell you I'd be ready to dance tomorrow, so I can certainly sit on a plane.'

'He was just trying to reassure me.'

She'd already turned, and was going back to the bedroom. I followed. She opened the closet and reached for her suitcase. I stopped her. She said, 'I'll go with *nothing*, if I have to. I'll take a cab...'

'Ellie, Christ!' I drew her to me. She didn't resist. She just stood there. 'Wait a week. All right, two days.'

'No, I can't.'

'Why?'

'I don't know. I just can't.'

'Honey, that's a natural reaction after an abortion.'

'Don't *say* that word!'

She reached for her suitcase again.

'You'll have all day tomorrow to pack! At least rest tonight!'

'Promise you won't stop me?'

'But if you feel differently...?'

'Then I'll tell you. But promise you won't stop me if I want to go?'

'Well, of course...'

She went back to the living room. I closed the closet door. She'd feel differently tomorrow. If only I could take her in my arms, kiss her...

Fuck her. *That* was what I couldn't do. Always before, we'd fucked away the problems, the anger, the desire to leave each other.

Now we couldn't. She wouldn't be able to fuck for a full month.

Realizing that, I also realized something else. Say she insisted on going back to St Louis. She'd spend some time with her family, and with her friends, and with Harv. But she wouldn't be able to fuck. I could finally trust her in St Louis!

And before the month was up, she'd return to me, and we'd start again, fresh.

If she decided to leave tomorrow ... which I halfway hoped for now!

I joined her in the living room. We watched television. I made some comments on the shows. She nodded twice and shrugged once. I took her hand. I threaded my fingers with her. She looked at me, and laughed. 'How romantic,' she said.

I felt my face going white. 'We did the adult thing,' I said, and it sounded ugly and stupid.

'Did you ever happen to think you might have killed your own baby?'

I held tightly to my temper, and my reason. 'Emotional nonsense. Doesn't make any difference *whose* baby. Besides, we'll never know now.'

She carefully removed her hand from mine. She leaned back and watched the screen a while, and then her eyes closed and she began to doze. I moved closer, put my arm around her shoulders, drew her head to me, kissed her lightly on the lips. She said, 'Jesus, can't I even *sleep*?' She got up and went to the bathroom. I went to the kitchen and poured a big Scotch.

I heard her going to bed shortly afterwards. I had another, smaller Scotch, and showered, and joined her. She was really out. I snuggled up to her, careful not to wake her. I put my crotch in her ass and one hand on her breast and sighed, and felt my cock hardening. I rubbed it lightly against her, and she murmured and pushed back at me, as if remembering passion in her sleep. I stroked her hip, her ass ... and felt the napkin truss. I felt sad, and felt glad, because let that bastard Harv try for it now!

She was up before me the next morning. In fact, I couldn't seem to awaken, and even though I heard her moving around, I held to my sleep, kept my mind closed against the new day. And I was right to do so, though I only blocked it out until eleven. A lousy day. It started with luggage all over the place and closets open and drawers half-empty. I left her to her work and went to the kitchen and made coffee. I came back to ask if she wanted some. She said, 'Yes, in a minute,' voice so very cool, so very remote.

I set out two cups and some cheese and crackers and sat down.

She joined me, still wearing my old blue robe. She looked pale and wan. I asked if she felt all right. She sipped her coffee. 'I bled a little this morning, but it's okay. I guess he did a good job.'

I nodded.

She finished her coffee and returned to the bedroom.

She packed, or tried to decide *what* to pack, most of the day, and asked if she could borrow my large flight bag. I said of course. She filled three suitcases, and said she'd have to leave most of her clothing here.

'So what? You'll be coming back.'

'Maybe,' she said, not looking at me.

I knew I should play it cool, but I went to her and turned her and said, 'I want a kiss.'

'Give me some time, Nickie.' So very cool. So very different, my little girl, my sweet Ellie. My insides had been hurting since yesterday. The hurt increased.

'Where will you stay?'

She returned to her packing. 'My mother's. Maybe Gina's. At least at first.'

'At first? You'll be back in a few weeks, won't you?'

'I don't know.'

Don't push it. She *would* be back. I had most of her clothing, and I'd give her only enough money to buy necessities, and when I'd write and phone I'd beg her and she'd return to me and we'd begin our new life.

At six, we were in the car, driving along the East Side Highway toward the Triborough Bridge. I said, 'Honey, remind me to write you a cheque when we get to LaGuardia.'

She nodded.

'You didn't even ask me . . . and you'll need money.'

She nodded again. She didn't even seem concerned about what should have been a vital matter.

Was that because she knew Harv would be waiting with open arms and cheque book; Harv who was always so 'generous'?

After the bags were checked and her ticket purchased, we had half an hour to kill. We sat in a coffee shop and she asked me to get her a pack of cigarettes. I used a machine near the door. When I came back, she said, 'You were going to give me a cheque.'

I smiled and nodded. I'd *wanted* her to ask. It weakened the thought of Harv having offered her money on the phone. I wrote a cheque for two hundred dollars. She examined it; her mouth twisted slightly; she said, 'Thanks,' and dropped it into her purse as if it were a chewing-gum wrapper.

I began to burn. 'You'll be living with your mother or sister and you'll be back in a few weeks. You won't need more.'

She lit a cigarette and inhaled deeply and looked away. I took her free hand. 'Ellie, honey, don't go.' I hadn't thought I would say that, but suddenly I was afraid. 'Let's go back to the apartment.'

'You weren't anxious for me to stay this morning.'

'Of course I was! But you were so set, and you made me promise...'

'You haven't tried to talk me out of it since last night.' Her eyes dug into mine; a thin smile touched her lips. 'I can't fuck for a month, can I, Nickie, and so you're kind of glad to be rid of me. After a month, I'll come running back, ready for action, right? And meantime, no one can touch me.'

'Then why am I asking you to change your mind now?'

'Maybe you're not so sure any more that I *will* come back. Maybe I'm walking away from you for good. Right, Nickie? Admit it! C'mon, be honest for once in your goddam cheating life and admit it!'

She was almost shouting. People looked at us. '*My* cheating life?' I regained control. I stood up. 'I'll get your luggage. We're going home.'

'Home is where I put my ass, and tonight my ass will be in St Louis. You can keep my luggage, but I'm going to St Louis. You can have your cheque back, your *big* two hundred, but I'm going to St Louis. No matter what you do, I'm going to St Louis. And baby, I'm not promising I'll *ever* be back.'

I sat down. I felt dizzy; felt myself trembling. Then she was leaning across the table and holding my hand and whispering, 'Nickie, kiss me, honey, now, kiss me, please.'

I kissed her. I didn't care about people watching. I stroked her head and kissed her and said, 'Please don't go, Ellie.' I was almost crying.

'I'll be back, honey. Don't worry. I'll be back in a month, maybe less.'

'Promise?'

'Yes.'

We kissed again, and it was time to go, and we walked to Gate 25, the last on the long corridor. She got her seat number and we moved to the loading ramp and she turned to me. She was terribly pale; her eyes were wide, unblinking, fixed on mine. She whispered, 'Nickie...' I kissed her. She came up against me, her mouth opened, her tongue searched my mouth, and it was all done desperately, tremblingly. I sensed a death, an end, an irretrievable loss.

The ache in the stomach, the fear in the heart, reached a peak.

'Ellie, let's talk, take a later flight, don't go.'

'I'll be back. I have to ... my clothes.'

'You're weak. You're sick. You shouldn't ...'

She waved, and was gone.

I had a drink in the airport bar and the ache, the fear, diminished. I even began to feel a small sense of relief, of oppression lifted. And refused to remember that I'd felt that before, whenever Ellie had left me ... and that it hadn't lasted more than a day or two.

I walked to the meter parking lot. It was a beautiful fall evening. I'd have many beautiful fall days and nights to enjoy.

I got in the Porsche. I remembered how she'd tried to drive it. I wondered what would have happened had I thrown economic sense to the wind and bought her a car with automatic shift. Would it have changed things?

Foolishness. I drove out of the lot toward home, and decided I would put in some work on three toy ideas that had been germinating for over a month. And I'd see the kids. And date ... yes, damn it, date *heavily* and perhaps break the hold Ellie had on me.

And since she couldn't fuck for a month, I had that month as grace. And when it ended, I could get her back ... if I still wanted her back, and this time I was going to try, really try, *not* to want her back!

I spent the evening with Seth. Denise was coming in for the weekend, without the boyfriend for a change, and I arranged to see her on Saturday afternoon. I worked on Friday, and thought of calling Ellie at her mother's or sister's ... but told myself it was too soon and she hadn't called me and so on. (And inside, in Truesville, I feared she wouldn't be at either relative's home, and unable-to-fuck or not I didn't want to risk that.) But I made several other calls, setting up lunch on Monday with Karen Oster, my cute Bennington grad, and a late afternoon snack at my apartment with Ruth Golon, my married blow-artist, and Wednesday night (with a hold on next Saturday night) with my Great White-titted Hope, Ledya.

Everything going along beautifully, right? And with tennis and running and workouts scheduled, everything moving into the groove physically too. Soon I'd be back to my old self; cool and calm and healthy. Soon the insanity of Ellie would dissolve; the obsession be forgotten.

Except that after a two-hour workout with the bar bells, and a long hot bath, and a soothing hour of Brahms tapes and Krishna

Merti, I just couldn't fall alseep Friday night. The damned bed seemed enormous. I kept rolling around, trying to fill it.

Of course, I'd retired rather early, ten-forty, so getting up at eleven-thirty wasn't really a defeat, a giving-in to insomnia. After all, I wasn't actually *missing* Ellie, just allowing her a few random thoughts. I felt, well, *guilty*. As normal a post-abortion reaction for the male as her hatred (temporary, certainly) of me was for the woman.

Jesus, my stomach *ached*! Was I developing an ulcer?

I went to the bathroom and found the sleeping pills; not in line with my movement back toward health and exercise, but just to get me through the few rough nights I had to expect.

Right. I took one. And then decided to look through Ellie's drawers and closets and see what she'd left. And was comforted by the vast amount of clothing ... though that comfort was cancelled when I realized that she'd taken just about everything she valued, including her red maxi coat she'd said was a gift from Harv. Then I saw her black plastic writing case, and looked through it, and on a sheet of stationary was a list of names surrounded by doodled flowers, pierced hearts initialled E.M./N.L., smiling idiot-cartoon faces, and a rather elaborate and surprisingly-good sketch of an old-fashioned rocker cradle. The list:

> Nick Leib, Jr.
> David Leib
> Roy Leib
> David Roy Leib
> David H. Leib
> Nicholas David Leib
> Ross Leib
> Ross David Leib
> David Ross Leib

This last was underlined several times. Obviously, David was her choice going away ... for our baby's name. And even that David H. Leib – H for Harry, almost certainly – didn't bother me. *Nothing* bothered me, I insisted, as I took the sheet of paper to bed with me, and tucked it under my pillow, and wondered what she'd have done if it had been a girl ... and then fought to close my eyes and mind against all the lachrymose, saccharine, nonsensical, and absolutely futile regrets.

I wanted to speak to her. It was only ten to twelve; ten to eleven in St Louis. But her mother might react badly. And Gina's husband ...

Too soon to call. Mustn't press her. That natural reaction after the abortion.

The phone rang later, and I came awake and grabbed it and looked at the clock as I said hello. Three-fifteen; too late for anyone but my little nut to call.

There was no answer. I said, 'Ellie?' The line clicked. A gag? New York was full of such clever gagsters. A wrong number? Ellie, unable to make herself speak to the man who had killed, helped kill, killed along with her, our child?

Shit! This wasn't Nick Leib! I was a big boy, dammit!

I closed my eyes and turned my back on the phone ... and it rang again.

This time she answered my hello. 'Hi, Nickie. Watcha doing?'

'Sleeping.'

'Alone?' Little laugh. 'Don't answer that.'

'Jesus, Ellie, of course!' (But why such outrage, when the plans were laid, the women soon to be?)

'All right. Then say, "Fuck Ledya!" Say it *loud*.'

'Really ...'

'Go back to your fun. Just wanted to tell you I'm okay. Of course, if it wasn't for Harv, I'd go crazy.'

'Fuck Ledya! Fuck everyone but my love, Ellie!'

She laughed a little.

'Did you call a minute ago?'

'Yes, bad connection.'

I let that go. 'Are you all right? How's the bleeding?'

'Oh, more than I thought, but nothing scary. I think I'll see a doctor here.'

'Your old gynaecologist?'

'I never had one. Harv's mother said ...'

'You *told* them?'

She was quiet.

'Ellie, you *didn't*.'

'What's the matter? You ashamed of that *adult* thing?'

'No, but still ...'

'I told Harv. He said you're a dirty sonovabitch.'

I suddenly knew it would be smart to end this conversation quickly. And yet, I wanted to hear her voice, wanted to talk to her. But not this way.

'Look,' I said, 'why don't you take Laura out, and buy some presents for Gina's baby, and have yourself a good week. And come home.'

'*Why*, Nickie? I can't fuck. And that's all you want.' I tried to speak, but she shouted me down. 'Let me say something! You're always cutting me off, putting me down, lying to yourself about what you feel! I'll come back, to visit, at the end of a month. I'll give you what you want, the *only* thing you want, and get my clothes, and come back to St Louis.'

'But how long ... ?'

'I'm going to *live* here, Nickie! I'm going to find an apartment and get a job and make a life for myself! You'll get me once in a while, don't worry, because I have to pay off, don't I? Now good-night!'

'Wait! Where are you? Where can I reach ... ?'

'I'm sorry,' she said, voice changing, softening, growing tired. 'I'm just upset. All that bleeding. Harv wanted to take me to the hospital, but I said no and then it stopped. Would you stay with me two days, all day and all night, with a bleeding closed-up cunt, and take me places and talk to me and hold my hand and *feel* for me ... ?'

'And pay for you?'

'If I'd let him, yes. But I won't let him. Why should he pay for *your* fun?'

'Ellie, I'm so sorry. I don't know what to say.'

'Oh baby, you *always* know what to say. You're saying it now, by saying you don't know what to say! Psychology, right? You always have Mr Leib in mind, don't you!'

'That's not fair! You did more damage to our relationship ...'

'Relationship? Ha! It was a master–slave bit! It was a customer–whore thing! And when the whore got knocked up, cut the bitch apart!'

Natural reaction, I kept telling myself. Natural resentment. And my inability to answer intelligently was also natural – part and parcel of male guilt. But I was sweating over that phone and I wanted to see her and touch her and tell her this was her Nickie, the man she loved, the man who loved her.

But *did* she love me?

And *did* I love her?

'I'm sorry,' I said again. 'If you stay longer, I'll send more money.'

'Sure. Because you're afraid Harv ...'

'Because you can't work for a while and I'm responsible and I'll pay!'

'Don't shout! Not any more! Not at me, you bastard!'

'You're being your usual insane self!' I took a deep breath. 'Honey, please, let's talk rationally.'

'Good*bye*, Nickie!'

'Wait a minute. You haven't told me where you're staying. A phone number. An address.'

The line clicked.

Okay. No tantrums. No pain and no shouting into the empty darkness. Hang up nicely, quietly. There. Now go to sleep. She'll probably call again in five minutes.

She didn't. Still no sweat. I'd call *her* tomorrow, at her mother's or sisters. So to bed, to bed, you sleepy head, as Mom used to sing, with a north of the Dnieper accent. I remember how fast I used to fall asleep, and rocked myself.

I was still awake at four-thirty, and took another pill.

The next day, having lunch in Teaneck with the kids, eating Louise's great lasagna that she'd left in the oven before taking off for some family gathering or other, I suddenly felt ill. That gut ache again. Denise stared at me with those cool grey eyes and announced that I looked *dead*.

'Not so. He sees. He speaks. He breathes.' I managed a smile as the pain eased.

'Man, he's breathing *mighty* low,' she retorted.

I laughed. I put on records and made her rock with me. I tried to teach Seth, but he was still at the age when he felt awkward, though he wasn't. And then I went upstairs and closed the bedroom door and in the room where I had suffered the death of a thousand lustless nights, I phoned Ellie's mother.

Again I was lucky; Liz answered.

'Is Ellie there?'

'Ellie? No, she's in New York.'

I called Gina. Again luck; *she* answered. 'I didn't know she was coming to St Louis, Nick. Everything all right?'

A little inane, elusive talk on my part, and I was off the phone.

Nothing to shake about, though I shook. (Had my body ever trembled this way before Ellie?) She was hiding out for a while. Quite natural after an abortion. (The word now sounded obscene to *me*.) And Harv was probably playing Big Brother. That was *all* he could play ... now. But could he score points, get himself in good with my little love, and then, after a month ...

She'd called me last night. Rough or not, she'd wanted to talk to me.

Or had she wanted to check on me; to see if I was with another woman?

Still to the good. She was jealous.

Or had she simply wanted to torture me?

Again, good sign, as any psychologist can tell you. She cared enough to want to hurt me.

And she *had*.

I was sorry I hadn't made a date for tonight ... but still, the weights and television and some sleep, which I badly needed. And tomorrow the cottage and some country air and a few miles of running and then back to the apartment for my Monday lunch date with Karen of the cute, dark face and classic ass and fine legs. *Mmmmm*, I'd start living again!

Mmmmm, I was full of shit. It was *Ellie's* ass and legs I wanted. Ellie's cute face. Ellie, period.

From there on, life fell apart more quickly than I care to remember.

Lunch with Karen. She was as cute as ever. She had a new boyfriend, ... 'but a date or two, Nick ... well, what's this I heard about your living with someone?'

We were on for next Friday night.

Ruth Golon at my apartment Tuesday afternoon; tall and curved, with those big round thighs. We talked. She wept a bit about our 'long separation'. I put my arms around her in the living room and she came nicely to the bedroom. A little lip-work on her pear-shaped tits and a little finger-work on her fine, roomy cunt and a little verbal appreciation of all she had to suffer from husband Alvin (a goof-ball, as Seth would say), and her mouth came sweetly to my cock. Except that it took a hell of a long time before she got any juice. And my orgasm was so weak it hardly qualified as such.

She had to run immediately afterward, which was lucky, as I was all shook-up and couldn't have given her the flowery talk she required. She said she'd see me next week. I said I'd be looking forward to it ... and told myself the next orgasm would be better.

Ledya, Wednesday night, at the theatre, and then dinner, and then her apartment. Lady Bountiful's body was *almost* a match for whatever was draining desire from mine; almost but not quite. I mean, we made it and I faked a great explosion to cover a teeny one, and she whispered, 'Nick, we could be a team, you and I,' and I said she was right, and I *knew* she was right ... and I felt as if I were still married and fucking by rote.

I was afraid that night. Not just because I was beginning to miss Ellie as I had on all her other trips to St Louis, miss her so strongly that fear was natural, but also because I felt I was losing my manhood! It was as if I wanted Ellie so much, there was nothing left for anyone else. I could fuck Ellie for hours, and no one else for even a moment ... with true pleasure, that is.

So there it was. Wanting Ellie was fine. But being able to want *only* Ellie, not so fine. Terrifying, in fact. And I'd had indications and symptoms of this malaise since we'd first bedded at the Forest Park Hotel.

I drove to the cottage and worked on a new toy and ran at the state park and along a country road in LaGrange. The weather was turning cold, and invigorated me. I ate sparsely and worked out with grippers and weights and didn't think too much about Ellie and Seth here, except at bedtime. And on Wednesday morning I awoke from a nightmare of trailing a trickle of blood across a concrete plain and hearing Ellie's voice and finally finding her with Harv Cohen, fucking in blood and crying out, 'Fuck me, fuck me, Harvey, when you fuck me everything's all right!' He looked at me and laughed and I couldn't move. I was tied hand and foot and had to watch her fuck him and suck him and his cock was enormous and she pointed at me and mine was shrivelled to nothing and she said, '*Nick?* He's so sick and old he could never make a baby. It was *yours*, honey.'

I drank wine for breakfast that day. I did no running, no exercising. I finished half a bottle of chablis before I felt I could survive.

I drove back to town by three, for my four o'clock date with Ruth. She turned up looking Orbach-matronly, cut-rate stylish, and packed full of suburban lust ... which meant she wanted a quickie as she had to get back to Larchmont and the kiddies by six, including a stop at Bloomingdale's to get her mother-in-law a purse for her birthday. 'The bitch,' she added, to show her contempt for middle-class values in general and her marriage in particular.

She was on her knees, sucking my cock in five minutes. We both watched in the cheval glass. She blew and blew, and then looked up and said, 'What's wrong?'

'Just greedy,' I said. 'Stopped myself from coming three times; now I don't know if I can.'

She went back to work, fondling my balls ... but the fondling was a little impatient. She had schedules to meet and purses to buy and miles to go before she rested in Westchester county.

I closed my eyes and thought of Ellie. And came.

As soon as she left, I phoned Louise. 'Would it be an imposition to invite myself over for dinner? I'll bring the works from the Gold Coin, or if you're not in the mood for Chinese ...'

She said Chinese was fine, and I thanked her and meant it. I needed to be with Seth, with someone I *loved*, because my other love was in St Louis. And because lust, which had always filled the void, was deserting me ... and I didn't know what was happening and I missed Ellie and I didn't want to think of her. And before going to the Gold Coin, I phoned her mother's home. The woman said, 'Yes, she was here today, but I don't know where she's staying.' I thanked her. She was quite gracious, replying, 'That's quite all right, Mr Leib.'

Was that graciousness, or *satisfaction*? Was she pleased because Ellie had left me, had made definite arrangements to stay on in St Louis?

I phoned Gina. No answer.

I wanted to speak with Ellie!

No, not 'wanted'. Too weak a word. *Needed.* Still too weak, Hungered, thirsted, *had to!*

We ate together, Seth and Louise and I. We talked and watched the little counter-set TV just as in the old days. Then Louise went on a date, and Seth said he had a lot of homework. I found myself holding him back. 'Hey, didn't we have some fun up at the cottage, you and Ellie and I?'

He nodded. 'Where is she?'

'Visiting St Louis, as before.'

'Is she coming back?'

Now why the hell had he asked that? What had he read in my face, my voice? 'Of course. Doesn't she always?'

He went upstairs to do his work. I watched television, and at seven-thirty tried Gina again. Grebes answered. I said, 'Is Ellie there?' He said, 'Ellie! For you!'

My breath stopped. I got it going again to make my voice calm, steady.

'Yes?' the sweet baby-voice said.

'Hi, how's it going?'

'Fine.' Giggle. 'Who is this?'

Rage. Pure red rage took over. No logical reason. No reason at all, except that she was open to a world of men ... she spoke to a world of men.

I reminded myself that *all* she could do was speak.

Of course, she could use her hand. Her mouth. Rub that sweet ass ...

'C'mon now, who *is* this?'

'It's Nick.'

'Oh, hi, I've been thinking of you.'

Just like that, the rage was gone, the pain eased. 'In what way?'

'Just wondering what you were doing. If you were playing tennis. How Seth was.'

'He asked about you. I'm at my old house in Teaneck right now,

215

He's doing his homework.'

'Can I say hello?'

'Of course!' I ran to get him. He spoke his usual brand of telephone short-hand: 'Yeah ... well, sometimes ... no, he was here...'
Then a laugh and, 'Ten. Yeah ... 'bye.' He handed me back the
phone, grinning.

I kissed him and he left. I was beginning to feel *alive* again. I
said, 'Now what did you two say?'

'I asked how many girls you'd brought to the cottage this week.
He said ten.' She laughed. 'That's covering for the old man.'

'Ellie ... I ...'

'No mushy-ushy-yushy.'

'*That's* new.'

'Yeah. A friend says it.'

'Harv?'

'How'd you guess?' She laughed. 'Only kidding. It's Liz.'

'Are you feeling all right?'

'Still staining a little, but getting there, baby. Got sexy last night.
Thought of all sorts of things ... yours included.' Again she
laughed. I felt less happy.

'That's a good sign. When are you coming home?'

Silence.

'Ellie?'

'I'm home, Nickie. I'll visit when I said I would.'

I breathed heavily, away from the phone. I'd get her here, and
keep her here! 'That's in about two weeks. Why not set a date?'

'We'll speak before then.'

'How can you be sure? I don't have a number...'

'Write this down.' I got out my pen and address book. I'd
crossed out Ellie's old St Louis number ... and felt my stomach
turning as I copied down the new one. The address was in Ballwin,
a suburb of St Louis.

'That's near Ladue, isn't it?'

'Not too near. How've you been? How's Ledya?'

'She's fine. Everyone's fine. Except me. I want you here, honey.'

'Good.'

I tried to think of something bright, something cool ... and
blurted. 'You just can't forget everything we had!'

'I can know it's finished.'

That gut pain was growing. Stop now, I told myself. And said,
'How could you possibly cut out a love affair so quickly? I mean ...'
I laughed to cover my anguish. 'Tell me, because I'd like to do it
too.'

'Try having an abortion, Nickie. That'll do it every time.'

'Listen, you bitch! It was as much your decision as mine! Point out one occasion that you actually argued against it! Go on . . .'

The line clicked. I dialled quickly. She answered, and I said, 'Don't you ever hang up on me again! If you do, I'll come to St Louis and I don't care what happens to either of us and I'll finish that fucking Cohen bastard, finish your fucking sister and family . . .'

I was almost screaming, and remembered Seth. I said, 'Hold on a minute, hear me?' and went to the door and closed it. When I came back, she said, 'Nickie, let's not fight. I . . . I'm sorry. I guess I'm pushing you too hard.'

Again I folded. 'It's not only that, honey. I *miss* you terribly. Don't you miss me?'

A bad scene, crawling, begging. But I needed something, some *words* if not her presence.

'Yes, a little.'

'And . . . I love you.'

Silence.

'Don't you . . . can't you tell me . . . ?'

'Please, Nickie. It's still too soon. Wait until I visit.'

'In about two weeks, right?'

'Yes. Will you take me to Dr Danorian? I should be examined.'

'I'll make an appointment as soon as I know when you're coming.'

'I've got to get off the phone now. My sweet brother-in-law has important business. Probably his bookie.'

I finally asked what had been on my mind from the moment she gave me the phone number and address. 'Do you have a place of your own?'

'You'd like it, Nickie. Big bedroom, big living room, a small kitchen with a dinette area. It's a garden apartment, ground floor, with a pool for summer, and tennis courts and lots of grass and some trees.'

'Sounds great. But . . . why commit yourself so soon? You might change your mind.'

'I won't. But say I did, what's a month's rent anyway? You'd pay that for me, wouldn't you, Nickie?'

'Yes.' Ping-pong. Hit Nick's emotions from sad side of the net to glad side; back and forth, back and forth; the score kept by that stomach ache. 'I'll pay it right now . . .'

'Let's wait, Nickie. Let's see. I . . . I *do* miss you, honey.'

'Ellie . . .' My voice was thick . . . and then I wondered whether she missed me, or *feared* me, me and my threats of zeroes, halves, and quarters.

'A little, sometimes, when I'm alone,' she added.

'Jesus!'

She giggled. 'Just kidding. 'Bye now, honey.'

'Listen, how did you pay your rent and a month's security?'

'I've got my old job back. Mr Alexis advanced me some money.'

Or Harv had given it to her. But either way, I was going to wipe that out. 'I'm sending you a cheque for five hundred.'

'You don't have to do that.'

'I want to. I want you to pay back that advance.'

'All right.' The voice was softer now, more like the old Ellie. And then she spoiled it. 'That's very generous of you, Nickie.'

'That's not generosity! That's love!'

Silence. And in that silence I thought of St Louis and its suburbs and the near lack of public transportation.

'How do you get to the store from your apartment?'

'Oh, I only started yesterday, and I'll get rides in other people's cars until I find a good second-hand car of my own.'

'Harv's car?'

'Well, he *has* helped me ... I told you ... and nothing you say will change ...'

'I'm not going to say anything.' But what I *felt*! 'I just want you to let me know when you find a car. I want to buy it for you.'

Silence.

'Ellie, even if you come back home – here, I mean – you can use it in New York.'

Little laugh. 'Whatever happened to the *economics* of a second car in New York?'

'It went out the window, when you went out the door.'

'*Clever*. My clever Nickie. Always good with words. But what do you *feel*, honey?' Her voice was changing, growing bitchy again. 'Guilt? Sorry you killed the hot cunt's baby? *Your* baby? Think you can buy her back again, and get more good fucking, and then dump her when the fucking gets better somewhere else? Ledya not working out? Karen married or something? The other cunts not tight enough? Got used to mine? Well, don't worry, you'll break in a new one ...'

'Shut up!'

'That's more like the Nicky I know. Shut the bitch up. Keep her cunt open and her mouth closed. Right? Well it's not going to *be* that way! Because Harv likes to hear me talk. He's not ashamed of

218

me. And others, there are plenty waiting . . .'

'I told you what I'd do,' I interrupted quietly. 'I meant it.' *Did I?*

'Sure.' But she immediately added, 'We always talk too long, Nickie. I'm sorry. You should be sorry too. We both said bad things. Look, I'll see you in two weeks and *then* we'll talk. Okay?'

I said okay, and she hung up.

So the ping-pong ball had *stuck* in the net, halfway between sad and glad.

Let's get the next three weeks out of the way, because that's how long it took for Ellie to come to New York. I was able to get her on the phone only twice in that time, though I must have called every second night. She never called me. That last time I got her in, I asked where she'd been. She said, 'I can't sit around, Nickie. I've been shopping for second-hand furniture and bought some, and for a car, and bought that too. A mustang convertible. You should see it.'

'But how . . . ?'

'Harv signed my auto loan. It's twelve hundred dollars. You don't have to pay.'

'The cheque goes in the mail tonight.'

'Well . . . if you really want to.'

'I want to.'

'Thank you, honey. And for the five hundred too.'

'How did you pay for the furniture, *and* pay back the advances on your salary, out of only five hundred dollars?'

'It just covered it, and Charlie said I didn't have to pay it *all* back, and I also got a raise. He hadn't replaced me, imagine! He'd been using part time help. He said he felt I'd be coming back.' She giggled. 'He said I'd *matured* . . . I'd become a real woman.'

I said nothing.

'And guess what, Nickie. Today is just one month from the . . . the operation. I took a bath last night. I washed it out and it felt as good as new.' Long giggle.

'Let's not announce it to the world.'

Lots of laughter.

'Are you . . . seeing much of Harv?'

Silence . . . and then, 'I see him.'

I waited.

'Not too much. And, of course, nothing . . . well, no sex.'

'I don't believe you.'

'That's *your* hangup.'

'You can't tell me you've been spending all that time with him and never kissed or petted or handled his goddamn cock!'

'I'm a big girl. I can play with boys.'

'The hell you can! You can play with me and no one else!'

She sighed. 'Will you please stop being such a dumbshit?'

'A *what*?'

She laughed. 'Okay, I'm coming to New York...'

'What was that you called me?'

'Dumbshit? Just a joke.'

'Mushy-ushy-yushy and dumbshit. My, your vocabulary's growing by leaps and bounds. You didn't find *that* in your grammar book.'

'I threw the fucking grammar book, *and* the maths book, in the garbage the day I unpacked my bags!'

'And *where* did you unpack your bags? Because you weren't at your mother's.'

'At a motel, where Harv put me up without expecting anything in return! Not like you, baby! You'll collect on my visit, won't you? And keep collecting until you get your goddamn money's worth! And I don't need your cheque for the car because I can pay it myself and Harv will help...'

I took the phone from my ear. She was getting tight with Harv again. Okay, I'd known it would happen. It was time to do exactly as she said I was doing – fuck her on visits and fuck others and look to those others for the important woman in my life.

Except that I *couldn't* fuck anyone else. Didn't *want* anyone else. Needed mushy-ushy-yushy with Hellie-Ellie, dumbshit that I was.

I put the phone back to my ear. 'Shut up.'

'Sure. The cunt always shuts up.'

'Give me the date, flight number, and time of arrival. And then go back for Harv and Charlie and anyone else who'll pay for the privilege.'

She tried to answer ... but she couldn't. She was crying. It shocked me. My enemy was crying. 'Say you love me, Hellie-Ellie. Say you still care, and it will all change and I'll come to you and do whatever you want.' I felt tears of my own. 'Give me back what we had.'

'I ... I can't.'

'Well,' I looked around the room as if to find an answer in my past. 'Is it Harv?'

Silence.

'Be truthful. Maybe then I'll be able to accept it.' Oh liar, looking to trap his enemy, his love.

'I don't know. He's ... becoming important, but there are others. I mean, I've been dating, and even without real sex ... and it's a way of telling if a man really likes you and isn't just after your cunt.'

'Oh sure. And you never heard of *patience*?'

'Just because that's all *you* can think of ...'

'I think of that, yes, and of you, and of the mistake we made at Shebsie's office ...'

'Don't you tell me that! It's too late to change the *mistake* and you're too fucking good at words, words, all the goddam words!'

'And Harv is the strong silent type? Or just too stupid to speak?'

'He can speak all right! You should have heard him *speak* last night! Speak *and* ...' She stopped. Last night had been the end of the month of no-fucking no-washing. Last night she'd bathed her cunt. Last night Harv had been rewarded for his patience.

'Oh,' I said ... meaning, 'Oh, you whore, you fool, you killer.'

'That's nice,' I said ... meaning, 'That's the end of him.'

But, as always, she changed. Because of fear? Because of residual love? No matter. She changed, and I forgot hate (but not as *completely* as the time before). She changed, and I grew hopeful again.

'Honey, you're still the most important man in my life.'

'And you're the only woman in mine.'

'You ... you really want me back, Nickie?'

'God yes, Ellie! We can take trips. We'll see more plays, operas. You'll meet more people ...'

'Wait. Show me on my visit. Make ... believe.'

'All right.'

She gave me a date, an airline, a time of arrival. I ran to Lincoln Centre for opera, and to Broadway for a play ... and then I went to the Plaza on impulse. We'd have a suite. We'd escape the bad memories in the apartment. We'd eat in the Oak Room again, as we had before leaving for Miami. We'd dance at Le Directoire. We'd ball, and become one again. I'd forget Harv and what she might do this week of her revived sexual capacity. I wouldn't think of anything but her visit, a long, beautiful week ...

She hadn't told me how long she was staying. And her job ...

But it didn't matter. She wasn't going back to her job, or to her apartment, or to Harv. I'd put on the biggest selling campaign of my life. And ... I'd marry her.

Once the decision was made, I thought I'd relax. After all, I'd settled everything.

If she accepted my proposal.

Of course she would! It would *prove* my love, and all her talk of lies and bullshit would go out the window.

Though I refused to think out the actual details. Though I put off facing the fact that we'd be as rough together as we ever were.

The point was, I was fast learning I couldn't live without her. I didn't want any more lessons, such as the ones I was getting day by day ... or, rather, night by night. Late night by late night. When I would reach for the phone and then be afraid to call. When I would wonder if she was in Harv's arms, in someone else's arms, *right now*. In her own apartment, or a motel, Harv's place, or someone else's place, her body pulsing ...

The night before she was to fly to New York, a Thursday, I tried to reach her. I tried her home at midnight, playing it safe. Well, only eleven in St Louis, so it wasn't unexpected that she wouldn't answer. But then I called her every half-hour until four-thirty in the morning. And then two pills brought sleep; that and the thought that my proposal of marriage would change everything.

But where, I asked before drifting into drugland, *was* the bitch? She would say her sister, her mother. But why *sleep* there when she had her own apartment in the same city?

She was with Harv.

She was fucking for Harv.

God, if I didn't settle this soon I'd have to kill him with my own hands *slowly* so as to wipe away the image of his body crushing hers, his tool in her cunt, his kisses on her face and lips, his love making her cry out the words that belonged to me!

She was with Harv. She was telling him she'd be back in a week and that he shouldn't worry because the sick-old-man couldn't fuck, and then she'd give him that marvellous ass movement ...

When I met her at LaGuardia, she said, 'You look terrible, Nickie. Been sick?'

She looked absolutely ravishing in an open coat – new, black, maxi – and a new dress – deep red, midi, with russet suède boots and matching purse. Her face glowed and her hair shone and she was the most beautiful girl in the world. And I wanted to hit her. She saw it, and said, 'Is *this* the way we're starting our visit? Maybe I should go home?'

I nodded. 'In a box,' I said. 'Where were you last night?'

'At home, why?'

Two bearded musician-types coming off the plane looked at her, and one turned to look again, and an airport porter looked at her, and she was the most beautiful liar in the world, and I said, 'Ellie, please let's get back on the track.' I had to know. 'I called all night. Until three-thirty your time.'

'Was that you?' Shake of head and lovely dimple-grin. 'Gee I'm sorry. I had some nut calls earlier, you know, and I was tired, worked late at the store, and maybe I'm still not as strong as I used to be ... well, I turned down the ring and forgot it. Honest. Honey, come on now.' She touched my arm, and I touched her face, and we kissed. It didn't feel right, her kiss, but I couldn't possibly have gotten what I wanted in that airport, so I took her hand- and we went to get her luggage.

She was delighted that we were staying at the Plaza. 'Wow! My mother once said hotels were for rich people. It was in St Louis, when I was a kid. I don't remember the hotel, but she wouldn't take me in because she said I'd better not get rich *appetites*. If she could see *this*!'

'It's all ours, for seven full days.'

She was looking out our Central-Park-view window, and turned quickly. 'Not a *week*, Nickie.'

'It's all right. I can afford it.' I took her in my arms for the kiss that would make all-better, and she *still* didn't feel right. She was, somehow, standing *back* from me, when what I wanted was to get into that big double bed with her and fuck for a full day.

'I don't mean that. I told you, I only have three days. I have to be at work Monday afternoon.'

I stared at her.

'Didn't I tell you?'

I shook my head, and let her go. 'We have the opera tomorrow night, but there's a play for Tuesday and I figured Seth ...' I went to the phone. 'I'd better call Dr Danorian and try to get an appointment for today or tomorrow.'

I didn't really have to call at that moment. The nurse had assured me Ellie could come in any day except Sunday between the hours of ten and two. But my voice was shaking; *I* was shaking; I'd become a wreck and had to do something to cover it.

I spoke to the nurse and arranged to come to the office in an hour. When I hung up, Ellie said, 'I'm sorry, honey. I *thought* I told you. Charlie wouldn't give me a week's vacation *this* soon, would he?'

Charlie would give her anything, if she sweet-talked him. We both knew it, but I nodded in agreement with her.

'Maybe after I put in a few months on the job, but not before. You can't blame him, can you?'

'No,' the dumbshit replied.

We went to Dr Sheb Danorian's office instead of making love. Once again I was invited to sit in the office and 'peek in if you want' while he put her into the stirrups and opened her cunt with that forceps-thing and expressed his absolute delight with the view.

In the office, he said, 'The best, I mean the very *best* job, I've ever done.' He waited for my congratulations. I smiled and nodded. He then launched into a description of the advantages of the three-month birth control shot he administered over others which I'd heard were somewhat dangerous. And he leaned close and murmured, 'She's not the type for a coil, Mr Leib. You'll have problems. Pain, bleeding ... she's a little too *youthful* to accept ...'

I smiled and nodded. He invited me back to the examination room, where Ellie was now fully dressed. 'This won't take a minute,' he said, and told her to bend over the table. She looked at me. I said, 'The doctor wants to give you a three-month birth control injection.'

'Exactly,' Shebsie murmured, having already hauled up the midi and pulled down the pantyhose, and with such a flair that I suspected as much practice in fornication as in medication. The nurse handed him the hypodermic; a little squirt in the air after a little alcohol on the ass, and he slapped it in. He rubbed, gave a jovial pat, said, '*Lovely* child,' and I was back in the office paying him twenty-five dollars. 'Every three months, to be safe, Mr Leib. But if it goes to five, no real worry.' He smiled. 'I have a patient who went *nine* months on one injection, but perhaps her husband, *and* paramour, were not quite as *potent* as we are!'

Smile and nod, and slight case of nausea. Ellie came out. He leaped up and escorted her to the waiting room with an arm around her waist. I had formed a very definite dislike of old Shebsie. He sent his best to Ron, shook my hand, smiled long and longingly at Ellie, and we were on Park Avenue.

'I think Shebsie would like to examine me alone some day,' Ellie said, making a face.

'Yes, and so would I.' I wanted to get back to the suite for some love, a bottle of champagne, some love, a room-service dinner, and some love. Ellie wanted to go to the San Marino, which I'd raved about at one time or another. So we ate *laguistine a la marinara* instead of making love. And then we went to Saks to look at the winter fashions, and to buy a maroon jumpsuit, instead of making love. And when we finally entered the suite, she said she was 'all pooped out' and that the shot must have had something to do with it, and she stripped off her coat, fell face down on the bed, and went to sleep.

I looked at her. I couldn't possibly disturb her (the *bitch*!). I'd let her sleep a few hours (and resist pulling up her dress and pulling on my cock). I'd unpack both our bags (and *not* look through her purse for pictures, letters, incriminating evidence). And I'd propose right after we'd had our first, glorious fuck, and before our second.

Two hours later, I returned from the sitting room and the colour TV, and she hadn't moved an inch. Well, I'd given her enough rest. I'd waited five and a half weeks for this moment, and 'waited' didn't get close to describing what I'd experienced. I wanted her ... and 'wanted' didn't get close either.

I was well into my tremors as I stripped and lay down beside her. I took off her boots, blessing the zipper sides. I drew up her dress, with considerably more difficulty than Shebsie'd had, because now she was lying down. I drew down the pantyhose more easily since I didn't give a damn if it tore or not. She moved and murmured something, but I was looking at Ellie's ass. My concentration was absolute. Only my cock moved, and when it was up even *it* seemed to freeze.

I'm making with the big laughs. Anything else would be funny; for example: My throat choked, my eyes burned, I lusted and longed with every part of my trembling body. Though that's exactly what I felt.

I began kissing her feet. The make-out king didn't have an audience; his lover was unconscious; which means I *wanted* to kiss her feet. They were rather chubby. They tasted good. I then kissed her calves. A little bristly; she needed a shave; but the good taste continued. Her thighs were heaven; I couldn't get enough of them, and continued up to the cool buttocks, the hot cleft, burrowing deep, trying to get down and into that slit, that haven.

I wanted IN!

I used my fingers, digging into her from the rear, kissing her bottom, tonguing whatever I could reach. I feasted, satisfying a five-week hunger ... and she began to move, began to rotate her ass, began to breathe heavily. The moisture came; her cunt grew wet; I turned her over as gently as I could, murmuring, 'Oh God but I'm crazy about you.' Her eyes were still closed, but she helped me when I stripped her dress up over her head. Her eyes stayed closed as I got the brassiere off.

I kissed her lips, just briefly, and so didn't allow myself discomfort over their seeming lack of mobility. I kissed her sweet little boobs. I kissed her belly and her nest, and began tonguing her cunt. But I couldn't be that sophisticated this first time around; I needed the total Ellie. I went wild over her flesh, her aroma. And then I was between her legs. 'Put me in, baby. Bring me back home, little love.'

She moved her head. She sighed. She took me and held me.

I couldn't wait. I grabbed it myself; plunged into her. We began to fuck. It felt like heaven. It felt better than ever before. I came very quickly, but wanted more, and kept going. I waited for the signs of her approaching orgasm – the quickening movements, the way she had of throwing her left leg up and turning slightly toward the right, the mounting of her breath. She moved a little faster, but the leg didn't go up, and the breath ... I wasn't sure.

I began to work for her. I began to use technique and style, *consciously,* something I'd never before done with Ellie, never before had to do with Ellie. I began to fuck for effect, to score points, to make my little love come. I was working, and it wasn't the loving we'd had before. And then her head tossed and she cried out, 'Oh Christ, Nickie, it's no good, no good, we lost our chance, it's no good!'

I got up immediately and went into the bathroom. I was shaking again, badly. *No good, no good.* I couldn't arouse my girl, couldn't make the woman I loved hot, couldn't give her an orgasm. Harv could. Others could. But not Nickie.

Oh God oh God oh God ...

I got in the shower. I let it run hot and hard.

When I came out, she was in the sitting room. She wore a new lounging robe – long, white, fur-fringed. I said, 'You've got a lot of new clothing.'

She watched television.

I could have screamed. I could have struck her.

I went to the phone and ordered champagne and caviar from room service. I was learning, I thought. The art of self-control had been lost with Ellie, and now it was returning ... I thought.

Later, when we'd finished the champagne, she said it was the first sex she'd had since the abortion, and that Dr Danorian had triggered too many memories, too many bad thoughts.

'I'm sorry, Nickie. Maybe I'll change.'

I was grateful for even such small favours, and came to her and sat on the carpet at her feet and kissed her hand and rested my head against the fur fringe of the robe that Harv Cohen had almost certainly bought.

I wanted her. I loved her. That crazy red feeling was a simple physical reaction to tension and nervousness. I would propose to her before the three days were up. I'd stretch the three days into a lifetime. I *wouldn't* think that she was lost to me, logical though the thought was; and that men gave up women they loved when the love wasn't returned and soon stopped loving them; and that the best medication for unrequited love was to find a love that *would* requite. And that there was Ledya and Karen and women I hadn't yet met – my old boastful, comforting litany that no longer comforted.

And I'd kill Harv Cohen if this visit didn't work out! Or perhaps I'd wait one more visit – my visit to St Louis, say, in a few weeks. I'd kill him, have him killed, eliminate him, and she would have no one to turn to and I'd be there...

It wouldn't be necessary. I'd propose and we'd marry, so it wouldn't be necessary. But God, how *satisfying* it would be to know he was shot, stabbed, smashed, burned, finished, destroyed, cold dead, my enemy, the man who had once possessed my girl and who had certainly played with her this past month and who had made himself 'important' to her; the man who certainly would put his cock into my Ellie, my little girl, my little love, if she went back to St Louis.

'What's the matter?' she asked, stroking my head.

'Stomach ache.'

'Your face ... Nickie, don't *do* that!'

'What?'

'Look like that. Dr Jekyll and Mr Hyde. You looked like Dr Jekyll.'

Poor baby. Sweet dumbshit. I explained that horror movies about mad doctors notwithstanding, Dr Jekyll had been the good guy, Mr Hyde the madman.

'All right.' She was irritated. 'So don't look like Mr Hyde!' She got up and went to the bedroom.

The shower ran. I ordered another bottle of champagne. When she came out, in that fucking fur-edged robe again, Cordon Rouge was waiting in a silver bucket. She said, 'I was going to roll us some joints.'

She took a plastic bag of greenish-brown grass from a suitcase pocket. It looked like damned near a pound! I said we could share a joint anyway, with the champagne. She said she sometimes 'flipped out' mixing pot with alcohol. I said champagne hardly qualified as alcohol, and asked where she'd gotten the stuff.

'Oh, Harv has a contact...'

A new dimension to mine enemy. He smoked pot; if indeed it was he who'd given it to her, and not someone else. She said he didn't drink, didn't smoke, 'just a joint once in a while. He said you could keep this.'

'Thank him for me, from the bottom of my heart.'

She looked up from the coffee table, where she was rolling the joint. 'Why do you have to *mock* when he's nice enough to ... oh, hell, that's the way you are.'

'And what did you say to make him give a pound of pot to the man he called a dirty sonovabitch? That I'd need it when you told me the two of you were engaged again?'

She shook her head. The dumbshit was annoying her.

We smoked and drank. I got a lovely high. She became loose and limp, her legs sticking straight out from the couch. I parted the robe and played with her legs, and with that black-thatched cunt. And she responded. She wriggled and spread her legs wider, wider, opening up shamelessly. She said, 'Fuck me here, *now*! I want it *now*!'

We ended up on the floor, and God was it good ... but she never once said my name. It was, 'Oh, fuck me, *fuck* me!' And, 'Rip my ass off! I want you ... rip ... fuck!' She had, I believe, three orgasms ... with her nameless wonder, her anonymous stud.

We went to bed. She didn't manoeuvre her body into mine, as she'd always done before. I did the manoeuvring. She looked back at me and smiled and went to sleep. I slept too. I had vague horrors all night, but I slept.

We had a good morning. We fucked for half an hour, and she began crying out, 'Nickie, Nickie, Nickie ... !' toward the end. Just my name. No love words. But patience, patience, a little at a time.

We had a good afternoon too, lunching long and visiting art galleries. And for the evening we had tickets at the Met.

The opera was *Carmen*. The Met was its usual glittering self, and Ellie fitted right in with the thick red plush, the star-burst chandeliers that withdrew into the sky-high ceiling, the entire posh production of tier upon tier of balconies and boxes filled with well-dressed escapees from the world of movies and TV. She had a very beautiful and expensive gown for our evening out, did Hellie-Ellie. It reflected the changing styles, harking back to the thirties. It was of a purple, silk-like material with a heavy gold-leaf pattern. It was practically non-existent on top – just two straps over the shoulders broadening out a little to enclose her boobs – and tight at the waist and full-skirted down and over her black suède pumps. She wore no brassiere, and because she was small didn't seem to need any. But when we sat down in our tenth row orchestra seats, the straps sagged a little, and those boobs peeked out and threatened to fall out. I felt she was the most beautiful, the most exciting, the most desirable woman in the entire place.

I'd seen *Carmen* once, years ago. I didn't remember a thing about the story, beyond the broad basics of a beautiful gypsy thief who seduced a Spanish officer and betrayed him with a toreador, this leading to her death. I doubt if I'd known more the first time

I'd seen it. But Ellie had been reading a book of librettos, and when I muttered something about wondering where the first act took place, she leaned close to me and began to explain. At first there was enough noise on stage, with squabbling women and strutting soldiers, to drown out anything short of a bullhorn, but then there was an instant of relative silence preceding Carmen's entrance, and I saw the man to Ellie's left glance at her with irritation. She straightened at that moment to concentrate on the stage, and his look of irritation changed to something else. An instant later, I realized that her left boob was completely free of the gown.

I reached out and tried to tug the cloth over it. She looked down, said, 'Oops,' and simply pushed the breast back into place. Then she glanced to her left, at the man, who was still looking at her. She glanced quickly away, flushing a bit, but her dimple was beginning to show as she smiled slightly.

I glared at her. She looked at me, mocked an answering glare, and returned her gaze to the stage. A little later, she leaned over again and did further explaining 'Don José's girlfriend comes from their home town to tell him about his mother . . .'

I watched as the man to her left glanced our way, or rather *her* way. He was no longer irritated. He was now an admirer, and not only of her breasts . . . though it was evident he was waiting for her to straighten again and give that sweet little boob a chance to slip free. He was looking her over, checking her out completely, and I knew she was aware of it.

He was a big man with thick grey hair, of the type called 'distinguished' in old novels. I'd have called him *horny*.

She finished her explanation, and began to straighten, and I glared at the man as he leaned slightly forward for a better angle of vision. Ellie very casually cupped her breast and kept it in place. It seemed to please her admirer.

I continued to glare. He didn't notice. Ellie had placed her arm on the rest to her left, and I wondered if her admirer had his arm there too. She seemed closer to him than to me.

I watched them from the corner of my eye. He no longer looked her way, and she was seemingly absorbed in the action on stage, but I had a feeling . . . the way they were sitting . . . I began to sweat.

When the curtain came down, she said, 'It's not as good as *Butterfly*, Nick.' Her voice was just a trifle loud, as if meant to reach ears other than mine. And I was *Nick*, not Nickie, and her diction was very correct. 'The soprano isn't very strong, is she? Don José is fine . . .'

I said, 'Let's get a drink.'

She rose with me, and smoothed out her gown, and looked around, everywhere but at her admirer, who was ignoring a rather handsome woman and gazing up – and down – at Ellie. I took her arm and pulled rather than led her into the aisle.

'Nickie! Not so fast!'

'What the hell's going on with that man in the next seat! Do you think I'm an idiot? You've been playing elbows with him...'

She laughed. She took my arm and swayed up the aisle, gazing into my face. She said, 'He got a good look, didn't he? I mean, when my tit fell out. So we're sort of ... *intimate* now, right?'

I managed the laugh.

She kissed my cheek. I looked at her, murmuring, 'You're so beautiful tonight,' and refused to wonder who had bought her that expensive gown. 'I want you so much. I love you so much.'

Her smile dimmed. 'Nickie, please, let's just have fun.'

It killed me. No way past the remoteness. And she looked at men. And men looked at her.

Yet I couldn't help feeling proud of how *many* men looked at her; men with attractive women of their own. That dimpled smile; that pouting lower lip; that body moving with so much promise. Men looked at her as we went up the curved staircase to the bar. Men looked at her as we stood sipping champagne near the enormous windows overlooking the fountain. Men looked at her as we returned to our seats, especially her admirer, who began to smile as we waited in the aisle for the people in the first two seats to rise and let us pass. His smile died as *I* entered first, to sit beside him, leaving Ellie to share an armrest with a sweet lady of sixty-odd years. After that, I was able to concentrate on the opera.

We went out to stroll the staircases and lobbies during both of the remaining intermissions. Having her on my arm was a particular kind of heaven, and hell. Hell because she was no longer my own. I tried to talk about visiting her, but she changed the subject, laughing and saying. 'That man next to me ... know why I sort of warmed to him? He looks just like a teacher I had in senior year high school, Mr Garrison. Of course, Garrison didn't have this man's c'othes ... but I met him again, not too long ago, at my Grandma's funeral. He wasn't there for *her*. The funeral parlour had another funeral in another room, and as we walked out he came up to me and said, "It's Ellie McBaren!" Boy, did his eyes *sparkle*! I mean, I knew he'd have tried to get me alone, ask for my number or something, if he'd had the chance.'

I was sweating again. 'And you'd have given it to him.'

'I don't know. Maybe. He looked ... better than I remembered him, and he was always nice to me.' She gave it more thought as I felt my stomach beginning to ache. 'I wonder what it would be like, with a teacher I had in high school! And he really looked *young* . . .'

I said I was going to the bar for a drink. Did she want one? She said no, she'd wait near the windows. I got myself a Scotch, and when I turned from the bar a young guy with much black hair and a big moustache was speaking to her. She was smiling, nodding, and as I walked up, said, 'I could live without *Carmen*. Not so *Madame Butterfly*.'

She got a great deal of mileage out of her two operas, my little love. I belted down my drink as she turned to me. The guy with hair and moustache seemed undecided what to do. Not so Nickie. He put his glass on a ledge and took his girl away. She looked back and called, ' 'Bye now.'

'What *is* it with you?' I asked, feeling my underwear turning sodden. I'd perspired enough tonight for a six-mile run! 'Why all the flirting? What are you proving?'

'Nickie, your voice. *Shhh!*'

'Then answer me!'

We were coming down the aisle. She was quiet until we'd almost reached our row. Then she said, 'I'm not proving anything. Men always talk to me. Most times I don't pay any attention. But here, I mean the Metropolitan Opera House, well, they're nicer, safer, if you know what I mean.'

I didn't ask any more questions. I was fighting off waves of rage and pain. She was either unaware of what I was feeling – and this was hard to believe, considering how I'd been when we'd lived together, how I'd reacted to other men in New York and Miami – or she was torturing me (perhaps not consciously).

Either way, she was doing a great job. But it was a mistake; a terrible mistake. It brought me closer to that point of no return, that edge of violence.

Back at the hotel, she asked what I'd thought of the opera. I said that if she'd allowed me to relax a little, I'd have enjoyed it thoroughly. The performers were excellent, and the music beautiful if a little *shmaltzy*. She said, 'I don't know. It disappointed me. I mean it. I enjoyed *Butterfly* much more.'

So had I, but not because of content and artists. We'd been in love then, the both of us. Now one lover was missing.

Not that you could tell it from *our* performance that night. We fucked for more than an hour. She was coming all over the place, and my name received prominent billing in her *kvitchers*. When it was over, she patted me cheek. 'One thing I'll say for you, Mr Leib ... can you fuck!'

I thanked her. It wasn't exactly a declaration of love, but perhaps tomorrow ...

Sunday started badly. She was withdrawn and sullen. She wouldn't fuck in the morning, saying she felt sick. I tried to gentle her into a better humour at breakfast, and then took her to the Metropolitan Museum, and by lunch she'd smiled a few times. But when I leaned across the table of the little French restaurant and asked for a kiss, she snapped, 'Don't you ever get off that goddamn subject? Don't you think of *anything* but kissing, fucking, sex, sex, fucking goddam sex all the time!'

I nodded. I said, my head hammering, 'Yes, on rare occasions ... and I wasn't aware that this particular kiss was particularly sexual in nature.'

'*Sheeit!*'

'As I was saying, I sometimes think of other things. Like where you got all your clothing, you filthy whore, and what I'm going to do to the mother-fucker who bought it for you.'

It never failed to work. She sighed and leaned across the table and kissed me and said, 'Bad *boy*,' trying to play her old baby-talk game but not quite making it. And having her change didn't please me much, not this time. This time I couldn't help thinking she was going to bat – with smile, kiss, and baby-talk – for Harvey Cohen.

I watched her as we ate. With coffee, I said, 'Ellie, I want to ask you two things. First, will you marry me? Second, what does Harvey mean to you?'

She laughed. She shook her head and drank coffee. She said, 'You kill our baby and then ...' Again she shook her head. Again she drank coffee. 'Let's go back to the hotel.'

'Are you tired?'

'No, I want to fuck.'

'Ah, yes, the one thing I'm good at.'

'The thing you're *champ* at!'

That pleased me. 'Better than Harv?'

'Oh, well, it was a while ago ... and he's not as experienced ...'

My face was flashing signals again. The smart signal-reader said, 'But anyway, yes, you're better.'

'Thank you.'

She smoked a cigarette. I ordered a Sambuca, and set it aflame when the waiter failed to. She sipped some after it cooled, and liked the liquorice liqueur. I ordered one for her. We each had another, and took a cab to the Plaza, and went right to bed.

Great fucking. My cock was crazy about it.

I was pretty happy about it too. But not the way Nick Leib should have been with his Ellie.

Then again, this wasn't *my* Ellie.

Still, it was better than no Ellie, and no fucking at all. Because without Ellie, there didn't seem to be any fucking.

A good enough basis for marriage, wouldn't you say?

'Honey, I wasn't fooling in the restaurant. I want you to stay with me, and to consider marrying me. Or marry me immediately, and forgot about considering it.'

She got out of bed and shook her ass over to the closet. She'd lost weight. She looked good, my little girl, though I liked her ass a bit larger.

'You're crazy,' she murmured. 'I mean, how can you ask me ... can't you tell ... it's different, Nickie.'

Hurt. The supplicant rejected. Wounds opening up all over my body. Stomach aching. Ass-hole ruptured and bleeding. Make funnies, Nicholas. As my mother would say, 'At least you're laughing.'

It *was* different. She barely liked me any more. My cock, yes. Me, no.

But she'd liked both of us even less Friday night. We'd made progress.

'My second question in the restaurant,' I said, ignoring the ruptured ass-hole. 'What does Harv mean to you?'

'He's my *friend*! The best friend I have! Now let me off the fucking witness stand, will you?'

I said, 'Yes. Witness excused.'

She looked at me, suddenly worried. 'You act ... different, Nickie.'

'That's because, as you said, it's different, Nickie.' I rolled over onto my face. I was going to shout. I was going to tear this fucking bitch apart with my hands. I was going to cry. I settled for my spastic attack.

I felt her sit down beside me; her hands touch my head. 'What's wrong? Don't shake that way! You scare me! When did you start doing that, Nickie? Have you seen a doctor?'

Dumbshit said, 'I started doing it the night after the day after you left me. I've seen Ron and he assures me it'll go away when I solve whatever problem is causing it.'

I felt her get up. I got under the covers. It was eight or nine, who knew or cared, but I had to sleep. I said, 'Come to bed, Ellie. Snuggle with me, little girl.' I didn't look at her. I didn't want to see her expression. Dumbshit was begging.

She said she was going to shower first.

She showered. And she stayed in that enormous Plaza bathroom a very long time. When she came out, she walked softly, wearing her fur-trimmed whore's robe. She shut the lights and went to the sitting room. I heard the television.

I waited. Days passed. She came tiptoeing back so as not to wake the dumbshit. She got into bed as far from me as she could. I said, 'Snuggle me, honey.'

'Oh, I thought ... all right.'

She snuggled me like a lamb snuggling a tiger. I grabbed her and shook her and she screamed in fright and I shouted, 'Stop it! I love you and I can't stand another minute ...'

She was weeping hysterically, and through the hysteria I heard, '... time ... give me ... time ... Nickie ... please ... can't help.'

So justification fled and guilt came and I was not only the dumbshit, I was the abortionist monster and somehow I'd lost all clear sense of what we'd *really* done five weeks ago and I was weeping and saying, 'Forgive me, I want ... I didn't think you wanted ... if we could try again ...'

She was no longer hysterical; she was silent.

Even a dumbshit has *some* pride. I hied myself to the great Plaza bathroom and washed my face and sat down on the john and did deep breathing and deep control exercises. Then I went back, to find a supposedly sleeping Ellie.

I said, 'One thing, will you visit again?'

'Of course, Nickie.' She was awake at the first sound of sweet reason in my voice. 'You know I will, honey.' Her arms opened.

I was enfolded in Ellie. I kissed her, and she kissed me back ... and no, I did *not* grade the intensity of those kisses; they were simply tender make-up kisses, though never before had she kissed me with anything except vacuum-cleaner strength and intensity. And no tongue. All gone, tongue.

'When?' I asked.

'I can't say right now. But another three-day weekend, maybe in a month.'

'If I come to St Louis in two weeks?'

'We'll talk on the phone, Nickie. But it might not be too good an idea. I *do* need some time, honey.'

And that's where it rested.

She snuggled. It's hard to tell a real snuggle from a false snuggle. And maybe this *was* a real snuggle, because her goodnight kiss had something going for it.

Was it the fact that it *was* goodnight and close-the-door on this last day of awful visit?

I was getting persecution-complex edgy. I was still bleeding from the asshole. But hold on, patience, Nickie, you *will* visit in two weeks. You'll check out St Louis, and she'll come to New York two weeks after that, and then you'll be back in the groove again and repeat the proposal and she'll accept...

I didn't believe it any more.

It was time to give up.

Well, perhaps not yet. She was in bed with me, wasn't she? We'd fucked half a dozen times and they'd all been great, except the first, right? She was still on that natural-reaction-to-abortion kick, right? She'd wept she needed time. Given the girl time to come back to you. Give her time to make your life whole again, or make her hole Harv's again...

Cool it, Nickie, because the trembling is starting and that gut-ache...

We went to the apartment in the morning and she packed almost all her remaining clothing. A bell tolled.

At the airport, I couldn't seem to find a word to say. And since this was a first, it bothered her and she found many words to say. She kept assuring me she'd visit again.

'No more, Ellie,' I said as we approached the gate. 'Please, honey, no more talk.'

Her lines. She stared at me. We kissed, I said, 'I love you.'

'Nickie ... you mustn't ...'

'But I do. Try to think ...'

'I've got to go now.'

'Yes.'

She kissed me again, slitted her eyes regarding me worriedly. Then to the gate to turn and wave, and she was gone.

At the apartment, I found she'd left my flight bag ... with two pairs of panties in a side pocket. The panties were raunchy; gift of the gods; enough to carry me for two or three weeks.

I also found I was exhausted; couldn't keep my eyes open. I went to bed and slept until eight that night, when stomach cramps awakened me. I thought I was starving, but except for a beer and some peanuts, nothing appealed to me. And my eyelids began closing even as I finished the beer. Could I be sick?

Yet even as I stumbled back to bed and felt myself drifting off, I knew what it was. I didn't want to be awake, to think, to begin reacting to our three-day weekend.

She called at twelve-thirty. 'Thank you for the most wonderful time. I'm sorry I was such a bitch Sunday. Try to understand, honey.'

'Yes. I . . .'

'What?'

'Nothing. Just more mushy-ushy-yushy.'

Silence.

'Goodbye, Ellie.'

'Nickie, wait, I want . . . us to be friends.'

'Friends.'

'I mean, we were never really friends and I want that. I think . . . much of you, honey. Even if we can't be what we were, we can like each other, can't we?'

'But we *can* be what we were.'

'I don't really want to talk about it.'

'I said goodbye once, didn't I?'

'Don't be angry. Why can't we just *like* each other?'

'I like you.'

'You're putting me down again! You're making shit out of what . . .'

A male voice spoke in the background. I felt myself go cold; deep-freeze cold. Ellie tried to go on. I said, 'Harv doesn't want you upsetting yourself, is that it?'

'Don't be silly!' There was no steam behind her supposed anger. 'You're always suspicious.' And her argument went nowhere else.

'He's there,' I said, and the certainty came that he was going to be there from now on. 'He's your lover, isn't he?'

'I don't have any lovers! My mother was right and I'm never going to get involved again and whoever gets into my bed will be a *friend*, nothing more!'

'Don't let anyone become your friend then.'

'What?'

'Because no one is going to get into your bed, or your cunt, but me. Because I'm going to come to St Louis, and I won't tell you when . . .'

'You stop that! You have no more right to me than anyone else! *Less,* you dirty bastard! You had your chance and blew it and it's over!'

I went on as if she hadn't spoken. 'I won't tell you when I'm coming and I'll find you and if you're with anyone else, that anyone is dead.'

'You're insane! No one can threaten . . .'

There was a scramble of sound, and then a deep male voice said, 'Leave her alone! Don't bother her again! If I have to, I'll personally see that the police . . .'

Another scramble, and she was back on the line. 'Nickie? He . . .

I'm sorry. I'll make sure he never does anything like that again.'

'No,' I said, looking down at myself, at my wildly trembling self, hearing my voice, my deep-frozen dead-and-buried voice. 'No, little girl, *I'll* make sure he never does anything like that again.'

I hung up and sat there. I hurt so much tears burned my eyes. I began telling myself I'd made my threats and they'd both sweat about it and that was enough. Time now to drive up to the cottage and resume work on the three toy ideas and begin a really heavy exercise schedule. And then, perhaps, a trip to Los Angeles with Ledya, if we could put our schedules together. She wanted to check out the studios and see her West Coast agent . . . and we could get really close on the trip out. Christmas in L.A., with Ledya. New Year's in San Francisco, with Ledya. I had to give her a chance. I had to give myself a chance.

Ellie with Harv, in his arms, her mouth open under his, her body open under his.

I got up and began to dress. The phone rang. I wanted to let it ring, but I also wanted to hear her voice. *Christmas and New Year's with Ellie . . . for Harv.*

'Please don't hang up, Nickie. We have to talk. We have to be sensible.'

'Come back to me.'

'How can I? I don't feel . . .'

I hung up. I dressed. The phone rang a while and then stopped. I packed a small bag. The phone rang again. I answered it.

'Nickie . . .'

'Spend Christmas and New Year's Eve with me; then I'll try to be sensible.'

'New's I already *promised* someone! He made arrangements. I just can't . . .'

'Harv?'

'Yes, because after all he was so nice . . .'

'Christmas.'

'It's only two weeks away, Nickie! Liz expects me to take her to Gina's. We're *all* going. It's a family thing, so how can I cancel out?'

'You're *my* family,' I said. 'You and Seth and Denise are my world.'

When this was greeted with silence, it became syrupy and stupid. Dumbshit was begging again.

She finally said, 'Just give me a little more time, Nickie. Just promise me you won't . . . think crazy. I'll call you, honey. I'll write you. We'll talk on Christmas and New Year's . . . and then maybe I'll be able to come to New York for another three-day weekend. Okay? *Please* say okay, Nickie!'

'Okay.'

'Really?'

'Yes.' I was beginning to hope again. 'I'm going up to the cottage now. The lake should be frozen over. Maybe I'll iceskate. If you visit this winter, we can skate together – you and Seth and I – though I'm lousy at it.'

'I never skated.'

'Seth'll teach us both.'

She laughed a little. 'Well, I'd better go now. Beauty sleep, you know.'

'Harv's going to be beautiful too, I guess.'

'Don't be silly.' Her voice seemed to drop. 'He got upset when I called back, and went home. Anyway, I wouldn't have called with him around if we were *doing* anything, would I?'

I wanted to say yes, she would, in order to placate the dumbshit abortionist-monster. I said, 'Guess not.'

'Here's a kiss,' she said, practically whispering.

I kissed her back, and tried to end it that way, on an upward note, and couldn't. 'Remember what you once made me say on the phone? You thought Ledya was here and I had to shout, "Fuck Ledya!" Want to bet you won't shout, "Fuck Harv"?'

'That's silly.'

'Do it.'

'C'mon, Nickie.' She laughed. 'You're acting like a baby.'

'I'm acting like *you*.'

'*I* was being a baby. I was ashamed of myself afterward.'

'Say it, and I'll be ashamed afterward too.'

'Oh, shit! Fuck Harv.'

'*I* could barely hear it. How could anyone else in your place? *Shout* it!'

'Don't be a fool! Goodbye now, Nickie! I'll call you; I'll write; I promise.' The line clicked.

I got the car and drove to the West Side Highway. It was cloudy and cold in the city and snowing lightly in northern Westchester, at about the Mohansic State Park exit. I had another thirty miles to go ... and the further north I drove, the heavier the snowfall. By the time I reached Arthursburg Road, I was passing stalled, stuck cars. The Porsche, along with other rear-engine cars, was just about unstoppable, but I had to slow to a crawl. I got to the cottage and parked right off the road instead of at the front door. I crunched up the driveway through two or three inches of snow, turned up the furnace, unpacked my bag, made myself a Scotch and water ... and gagged. I barely reached the bathroom, the vomit came so fast.

I was sick for about an hour, vomiting until there was nothing left inside me. Then I washed and prepared for bed. There was a flowered shower cap in the bathroom, hairpins on the nightstand, a new pair of pantyhose in the drawer where I kept my pyjamas. I lay in that big bed – the makeout king had king-sized beds where he put his ass – and hugged a pillow and cursed myself for forgetting to bring a pair of her panties. And despised myself for settling for panties when I should find some way of getting the woman herself, or forget her. And then I was back to Harv; back to that voice telling me to let her alone. And the voice was deep and manly and the man was with her now, *at this very moment*, and they were making love, or had made love and were sleeping in each others' arms.

All right. *I'd* had her, and now *he* had her. The oldest story in the world. It had never bothered me before. I'd had girls and other men had taken over, either before I was ready to let go, or after. No difference. No sweat. Sometimes a little chagrin.

So go to sleep.

In his arms, this moment! My Ellie, my little girl, my little love, in *his* arms! His genitals nuzzling her ass ... or penetrating her cunt, if they'd awakened for another go, and she'd said he could go five or six times ...

Sleep!

But I'd slept too much. Now I was awake.

I went to the study and my portable typewriter. I wrote her a letter. I told her I loved her and had to have her or I would die. 'And if this is so, then fighting for you is in effect fighting for my life. And it's only a projection of the right of self-defence, the instinct for survival, that I get rid of whoever stands between us, because whoever keeps you from me keeps me from living. I'll die soon, little love, if I don't have you. I can feel it happening ...'

I tore it up and made hot chocolate with Droste's and lots of condensed milk and got a book and sipped and tried to read. I glanced out at the lake. The snow had stopped and the sky had cleared and everything was glistening white; the world was a shiny white-tile room. I said, 'Ellie, look ...'

NINE

The next two weeks, right up to Christmas Eve, I spent more or less alone, in both the cottage and the apartment. I did see Seth twice, for a few hours each time, and he asked me if I was all right. I said sure and found myself talking about Ellie, and acting as if she would be returning for good in a short time. I also saw Ron, and he gave me a new supply of sleeping pills, and a prescription for Librium 25, a strong tranquillizer. He invited me to his annual New Year's Eve party, and when I hesitated he added that I could accept right up to the night itself. 'There'll be some female or other to keep you company.' I must have winced. He said, 'You simply have to exercise some control, Nick! You have to rid yourself of that girl!'

The girl had rid herself of me, but I didn't tell him that.

Harold called several times, and he was back to his miserable pressuring self. I managed to send one game idea into the office, by parcel post, and I didn't bother checking on what he thought of it. I didn't care one way or the other. I was in hell. Ellie didn't write, and she didn't call when I was at the apartment, and I wasn't able to get her on the phone. I'd allow the phone to ring on and on, but never an answer. She had a turn-off switch, obviously, as even a soft ring would drive her batty if it went on a *hundred* times, as I once allowed it to do!

I sent her a telegram, saying: 'Will be waiting for your call Monday night at midnight my time, eleven your time. Important. Nick.'

She didn't call.

So those two weeks became something very special; a turning point. She was telling me to buzz off. A normal, sensible man – even one in love – would say fuck you and forget her. I kept *trying* to do just that, and couldn't. I called Ledya, and said I was stuck with a deadline on a toy development project, and wouldn't be able to see her for a while. She was cool. She'd obviously expected a New Year's Eve invitation. She'd thought we'd do *something* during the Christmas season. But I couldn't make myself plan for pleasure.

All pleasure fled my life.

Real heavy statement, right?

Here's something heavier.

With pleasure gone, what was left was hard to describe – like a day-by-day listing of prisoner activities in Auschwitz. And if you think I've got one hell of a nerve making that comparison, you haven't lived through true loss and longing. It was more painful, for example, than what I'd felt after my father died. And it got progressively worse, with an assist from my mother.

I spent Christmas Eve with Seth. We ate out in a Steak & Stein, and I kept slipping him beer. Then we went to my apartment and watched television and he complained about all the 'crappy Christmas stuff'. I agreed with him, and gave him some champagne, and he fell asleep on the couch. I undressed him and covered him and went into the bedroom. I called Ellie. I heard the phone ringing. It was only eleven-ten in St Louis, and she was probably at her sister's for their tree and party, and Harv was with her, and no chance of her answering. But I'd made a bell ring in the right place where she lived. It was a contact of a sort; something to keep my head from exploding.

I lay in bed. Hours. I called again at three. The phone rang and rang ... and then was lifted. I said, 'Ellie?' my heart hammering; and hope, goddam hope came that whatever I was heading for could somehow be averted. But the line clicked even before I'd completed that one word, that brief, 'Ellie.' Someone had lifted the phone and put it back down, to cut off the ring.

I got up, staring at the phone still in my hand. Until this moment, no attack had been made upon me; no act of violence directed at me. This changed it. The cruelty of what she, or he, had done was an attack of *great* violence.

I put the phone back in the cradle and went to the closet and looked for my gun ... and then realized it wasn't here. I'd brought it in a few times to show to people, but this was New York City and the Sullivan Law prohibited hand weapons on any but very special licences, and my Colt .38 Trooper was secured on a hunting and target-shooting licence in Dutchess County, where the cottage was located. My revolver, and my Remington rifle, both unused for almost two years, since I'd given up the rifle ranges and playing at marksman, were at the cottage, in the big storage closet. But even if they *had* been here, what would I have done with them? Why had I wanted the pistol? I wasn't going to put it in my pocket and go to St Louis and shoot anyone. Was I?

And still, I wanted the Colt in my hand.

I'd get it this week. Not to use ... just to oil and clear and hold.

And what would I do about Ellie?

Break free of her with others, in time. Just let time pass. Suffer, if you must, dumbshit, but let time pass and the pain and rage will also pass. So it has been and so it will be, time out of mind ...

Poetry. Edna St Vincent Millay. I went to the living room book-case, moving quietly so as not to waken Seth, who wouldn't norm-ally waken if a cannon were fired off in his ear. But, of course, he wakened now and breathed quickly and whimpered and said he'd had a nightmare. I sat down with him. I asked what sort of nightmare. He shook his head, and looked at me strangely.

'Was I in it?'

'Yes ... but it was goofy.' He was recovering his sense of reality.

'If you speak it out, you won't have it again.' It was I who was having a nightmare, *living* a nightmare, and wanted conversation so as to forget it.

'Well, we were in the Porsche. I was in back and you were in front with Ellie and she was crying and you said you were going to do something to her ... you know, punish her, like if she did something bad. She turned around and asked me to make you change your mind. I tried, but you yelled at us, you yelled loud, angry, and then you ...' He stopped and said, 'See, it's goofy.'

I was interested. If I hadn't been planning my next call to St Louis, I'd have been fascinated. The boy had picked up vibrations. 'What happened?'

'Oh, you turned the wheel and I could see we were going to smash into something, a big truck, and then I woke up.'

He shivered. I hugged him, and we shared a Coke, and he said, 'You want to see Ellie again, don't you, Dad?'

'Yes.'

'And she won't come back?'

'In time.'

'What happened? You have a fight? I didn't think you'd fight with Ellie.'

'Oh, grownups fight no matter how much they like each other.'

'Yeah, but Ellie isn't exactly ... well, like a grownup.' He laughed a little. 'Is she?'

I was hurting. I was remembering games at the cottage. 'No, not exactly. Hey, you'd better get some sleep.'

He went back to the couch and I tucked him in and he said, 'You really like her, don't you, Dad?'

'I do. Very much.'

'Gee, I hope she comes back. Denise says you're *suffering*. She hates Ellie. She says Ellie *took* you, and then went away. That's not right, is it?'

I shook my head. Now I wished he would go to sleep. Now I wanted to be alone with the phone and my growing madness. He was reminding me that I was a father, a big strong man and important to him and Denise, and not just a dumbshit abortionist-monster with the tremors and a need to do something, anything, to get back his little love. He was threatening my obsession, and I couldn't lose it, because if I did, if I accepted things as they were, I'd lose Ellie.

I returned to the bedroom with a collection of American poems. I didn't read a single one. I dialled Ellie's number. Busy signal. I undressed and went to bed. Dozed. Wakened. Dialled Ellie. Busy signal. Dozed. Dreamt. Awoke shaking. Dialled Ellie. Busy signal. Dialled the operator. Asked her to try the number. She did, and checked with the Ballwin operator, and we were told the number was 'out of order'. I asked if that could include having the phone off the hook. The Ballwin operator admitted it could. I went to the living room and sat on the floor and put my head next to Seth's.

I kissed his cheek. I remembered his birth, and how happy I'd been. I remembered Denise's birth, and how happy I'd been. This in spite of never being happy with Louise.

I could be happy with *someone*, couldn't I? Someone besides Ellie?

If it wasn't too late, I'd take Ledya out for New Year's Eve.

But, of course, I knew it was too late. A girl like that, free for a week before the biggest date-night of the year? No chance.

And I didn't care. I was only offering myself placebos. No real medicine existed for what I felt ... except a bullet in Harvey Cohen's head. *That,* I knew, would make *all*-better.

It was dawn. I dialled Ellie's number. Busy.

I dozed. I awoke when I heard voices, music. Seth playing the TV. I closed the bedroom door and dialled Ellie's number. I hunched over, waiting. She wouldn't answer, or she would hang up. I hoped she wouldn't answer. Hanging up a second time would be too much.

It rang perhaps twenty times, and then she said, 'Hello?' voice sleepy and thick.

'Ellie, it's Nick.'

'Oh, hi, what time is it?'

I turned and looked at the alarm clock. 'Nine-thirty.'

'Oh, wow, and I was up so late . . .'

'You hung up on me. I called and called ... and why didn't you call or write as you said you would? And why didn't you respond to my telegram. *Why, dammit, when I've been waiting ...!*' I was screaming. Seth might hear. I shut myself up.

'Here we go again,' she said with deep disgust. Dumbshit was annoying her.

'Why didn't you?' It was all I could do to limit myself to those few words. There was so much bottled up inside me, so much built up during the past two weeks, that it was *too* much. I knew I wouldn't be coherent.

'Listen,' she sighed. 'I've been working late, you know, pre-Christmas. And, well, I was thinking, trying to get my head together about us, and well, I *did* write you, a few days ago. Didn't you get it?'

'No.'

'You will, today or tomorrow.'

'Today's Christmas Day. No delivery.'

'Yeah, forgot. Then tomorrow. Or the day after. We'll talk after you read it.'

'*How* will we talk when you never answer and hang up on me . . .'

'I *don't* hang up! But last night the phone kept ringing and I was dead and how'm I supposed to know it's you? Too damned many creeps keep calling . . .'

'Ellie, stop it. I've been . . . sick about you. I need to see you.'

'I'll visit in a few weeks. I told you that, Nickie. We can go to the opera again and that rock club and maybe this time I'll get *four* days.'

My heart leaped. But then I thought of how long 'a few' more weeks would be. A few more weeks with no phone calls and no letters . . .

'What did you write in your letter?'

'If I told you, you won't have anything to read.'

'Anything that will make me . . . feel badly?'

She yawned. 'It's too early for talk, Nickie. I'll call you back.'

'When?'

'When I get up.'

'Give me an exact time.'

'Christ! One o'clock!'

'Your time or mine?'

'Yours!' She hung up.

I thought of St Louis. I thought of her apartment. I thought of her bed. I thought of Harv with her now, complaining that I was disturbing his rest, and then saying, 'As long as we're up,' and the both of them laughing and then sighing and then groaning.

I had breakfast with Seth and we played rummy and the morning crawled by. I kept looking at my watch, and he kept looking at me. One o'clock came and went. He wanted to go down. I said I had to stick around. Two o'clock came. I tried not to go to the

244

phone, but Seth was picking up vibrations and wanted to go home and this wasn't fair to him.

I closed the bedroom door and dialled. She answered on the third ring.

'It's Nick. What happened?'

'Hey! You should taste my coffee! I get whole beans and grind them myself ...'

'You were going to call at one o'clock, my time. I've been waiting.'

'Did I say that? I was half asleep.'

'Goddam you I've been sitting here with Seth and sweating and he feels it and you don't even remember and you never, you never, I'm going to ...'

'Nickie, you sound crazy!'

'Oh God, Come back. Please. I can't take it. Give me another month, another few weeks, then maybe I can work myself out of this insanity and let you go. But not now. Now I need you, honey. Now I can't live another day without you. Please, Ellie. *Please!*' I'd have cried, grateful for the release, if she hadn't been listening.

She was silent a while. I waited it out. She said, quietly, 'I can't come back. No way, Nickie. But I'll visit in two weeks. I promise.' Pause. 'Aren't you dating? You should get out and have some fun.'

'And fuck?'

'Well, if you want to ...' little laugh ... 'and I guess you always want to. Just don't tell me about it.'

I gave her a laugh. I tried to recapture the feeling of Nick Leib, world traveller and make-out king. I asked how she was getting on at the store. She gushed about an unexpected Christmas bonus and a raise and increased sales.

'Meet any handsome new men?'

'Oh, sure, they're all over the place.' End of response.

'Harvy still ... important?'

'Yes, but nothing special. I mean *no one's* going to be special, just as I told you.'

It made me feel better, as long as I believed her, which was about two seconds.

'Did you say Seth's with you?' she asked. 'Can I speak to him?'

I got Seth and he spoke in the kitchen. He was a little reserved with her this time. It took her a while to warm him up, to get him giggling, to bring that happy sound to his short-hand conversation. When he said goodbye, I was back at the phone in the bedroom. But she'd hung up.

I called her and said, 'What happened?'

'I thought we'd finished. I told you I was coming in two weeks, so what's to talk about?'

Dumbshit didn't know; simply wanted to hear the sweet voice, to hold to the faint hope of love a little while longer.

She said, 'Did you tell Seth anything about ... well, about me, or us?'

'No, why?'

'He didn't sound right at first. Not friendly.' She giggled. 'But I changed that.'

'Yes, you've got the hoodoo sign on the Leibs.'

'The *what*? Hoodoo sign?' She laughed. 'That from when you were a kid, Nickie? Like zapasetic?'

'Copasetic.'

'Yeah. Everything's copasetic! Wow!'

'I seem to be getting older by the second.'

'Not where it counts, baby. As Ledya and half the cunts in New York probably know.'

'No one knows but you. It's all yours ...'

'Sure. You're true to little Ellie forever and ever. You know what you're true to? Your goddam pride. You can't believe I could walk away, even after you cut my cunt apart.'

'Enough, please, you've cut my *guts* apart.'

'Words, Nickie.' Very cold, that voice. 'No blood came out of your guts. Blood came out of my cunt ... and so did our baby, in pieces. That's the *truth*, and you give me *words*. So don't complain. I didn't owe you a thing.'

'Except the five hundred and the eleven hundred.'

'I was waiting for that. Did I *ask* for it?'

'No, but you accepted it.'

'Didn't I try to stop you?'

'Not very hard.'

'Want it back?'

'You couldn't manage it.'

'I can have it in the mail in a week. Want it?'

Harv. He was the only one with that much money. I said, 'No,' and then, 'Can I call to wish you a happy New Year?'

'You mean on the first?'

'New Year's Eve. Just to give you a kiss. Just to tell you I love you.'

'Nickie ... please.' She sighed. 'Well, I don't know where I'll be. We're going to a few parties ... his friends', Gina's, and then Charlie wants us to drop by.'

'Wants the happy young couple to drop by.'

246

'I think we've talked enough, Nickie. Merry Christmas.'

I'd sent her a card. I asked if she'd received it.

'Oh, yes, thank you, honey. I loved it.' Pause. 'Nickie, I never send Christmas cards. Never. I didn't even send one to...' She stopped.

'But Harv has *you*. He doesn't need cards.'

'I was going to say Liz,' she muttered. Neither of us believed it. 'Look, if you'll be at the apartment at midnight – I mean one o'clock New York time – I'll call and we'll have our New Year's kiss.' Her voice grew soft. 'Okay, honey?'

I said, 'Yes,' grateful ... for the right to wait at home New Year's Eve.

She said goodbye. I asked for a kiss. She gave me the lip-popping sound. I returned three, and she laughed briefly and hung up.

I felt all right until I took Seth home and returned to the apartment and packed a bag and began the drive upstate. Then I began to feel abased. Then I began to feel reduced. Then I began to feel alone.

Most of the houses along the lake had trees out front. Even some of the summer people had come up for the holiday weekend, because it was beautful and mild. But there was still snow on the ground from the last fall, and the lake was full of skaters, and everyone was with someone. The air was crisp, sweet, and full of laughter.

I'd brought the pot along with me. I smoked and drank myself to sleep.

Let's get to it. She didn't call New Year's Eve. I tried calling her all night, and towards morning the phone was raised and left off the hook. I called again at ten. She answered, her voice sleepy. I said, 'It's Nick, remember?'

'Oh, Christ, I'm sorry. I was sick, Nickie. Harv took me out and I began to feel nauseous, not from drinking or anything but because I was thinking, about us. He was worried and upset and I made him take me home and made him leave and then I threw up.'

'You *forgot* about promising to call?'

'I ... I'm not sure. Maybe I remembered, but maybe I wanted ... to hurt you.'

She couldn't know how much I preferred that to her simply forgetting. Or *could* she?

'Happy New Year, little girl.'

'Happy New Year, Nickie.'

'What were you thinking about last night?' Dumbshit asked, wanting anything but to be forgotten.

'How we met. How good it was sometimes.' Pause. 'That I'd be getting a belly by now, if we hadn't...'

'You can get a belly again, in a few months.'

Sharp laugh.

'When are you coming to visit? Next week?'

'Well, I asked Charlie, and he needs me for a season's-end sale the next two weeks – I mean on Friday and Saturday, our big days and nights. So it'll have to wait.'

'Let me come to St Louis.'

Long silence, and then: 'I can't see you in St Louis. It ... it would confuse things. I'll visit in three or four weeks.'

'Or three or four months.'

'You're lucky I'm willing to come at all!'

'Oh yes, so very lucky.'

'Then why not let me alone? Why not forget me? Let's just call it quits. And before you mention the money, I'll have a cheque for sixteen hundred sent to you. And before you add some expenses, I'll make it two thousand. Two thousand goes in the mail soon, and that's the end, all right?'

I wanted to say yes. But I couldn't. No way. And I remembered that two thousand dollars was the price Aaron Hoff had quoted for a killing.

I decided to go to St Louis, *without* telling her.

The decision brought me instant peace. A course of action! A way out of the insanity of thought and sleepless nights and loneliness. I'd go to St Louis, and when I was there I'd think of what to do.

'Nickie? I'll mail the cheque tomorrow, all right? And we'll be friends?'

'You can mail the cheque, but we'll never be friends. Lovers. Husband and wife. But never friends.'

'Look, Liz is here. She's waiting for me to take her to Forest Park Zoo.'

'Give her my love.'

'I will. She asks about you. She says you sound so nice on the phone.'

'Can I speak to her?'

'Well ... not this time. She's waiting *outside*.'

It was Harv who was waiting. I said, 'I still didn't get that letter.'

'Forgot to tell you. I found it in my purse. You know how I am. I mailed it a few days ago, with a note. You'll probably correct my grammar. Anyway, here's a kiss.'

A kiss. Forget about me, Nickie, but here's a kiss.

I returned it. 'Will you call?'

'If you want. But what's to say?'

And she wouldn't call. So I was packing and going to St Louis.

'Nothing, I guess.'

We said goodbye, and she hung up. I never hung up first. I always waited for something.

I remembered I hadn't checked my mail today and I'd been up at the cottage two days and her letter might be waiting.

It was. She'd written one page in pencil. The note accompanying it said. 'Sorry I forgot to mail this. Love, Ellie.'

The letter said: 'Dearest Nickie. Well, I said I'd write and so I'm writing. Because youl expect it and be mad if I don't. I'm working hard and seeing Liz and Gina a lot. Hope your feeling better. I mean not so *uptight*! Honey you've got to understand we're different people now. I was a little girl. You still call me that but I'm not any more. I'm a *big* girl now and I don't fall in love as easy as before. You think I can feel the same. I can't. Your pride is hurt that I can't. That's all it is. You *don't* love me!!! How could you let me go through the operation if you do? No, your just upset because you can't get me again. Sorry, it's over. We can't be the way we were. But I'll see you, honey, if you want. You'll get your money's worth, right? Give Seth my love. Ellie.'

I packed. I'd brought the Colt from the cottage, and a box of fifty rounds, and began to pack them too. But I couldn't take them on a plane. It was a Federal offence. All right, I'd drive. That way I could take the gun, maybe to scare someone.

But if I wanted to follow Ellie, she'd recognize the Porsche. I'd have to rent a car anyway...

As I mentioned, my mother helped complicate matters. She did it right then ... or I learned about it right then.

The phone rang. It was a neighbour of Mom's and she'd taken my phone number some time ago when she and Mom decided each should know the other's next-of-kin in case of emergencies. The emergency had come. My mother had collapsed and been taken to Jewish Hospital. The neighbour had tried calling and first gotten a busy signal (Ellie) and then no answer (me checking the mail). I thanked her. I said I'd get right to the hospital. Then I sat still a while and tried to assess what I felt.

Harv was right. I *was* a sonofabitch, a bastard, a bad guy all the way. I felt terrible ... that I couldn't leave for St Louis.

On the way to Brooklyn, I began to feel other things. But still, I was more involved with Ellie than with my mother. I felt I would be more involved with Ellie than with *myself*, if it were *I* being

249

rushed to the hospital. But, of course, that was words, thoughts, bullshit, as Ellie had pointed out, and didn't save me from being the sonofabitch bad guy.

Mrs Kate Leib, Dr Aberfein informed me some two hours later, had suffered a cerebral vascular accident, an occlusion of blood vessels on the right side of her brain, which had resulted in hemiparcsis . . .

I interrupted to ask for plainer language. He said she'd had a stroke, and since the right side of her brain had been damaged, the left side of her body was paralysed. At the moment, she couldn't speak and couldn't move her left arm or leg. She was in the intensive care unit, and her condition was listed as serious.

I nodded. I tried to absorb it. 'Is she conscious?'

'She was, briefly, but lapsed back into unconsciousness. Not too uncommon in these cases.'

'Will she live?'

'There's no way of being certain, at this stage.'

'What are you doing for her?'

'Several things. Feeding her intravenously so as to prevent a weakening of the total physical condition. Treating her with Reserpine so as to prevent further rise in blood pressure. But mainly allowing time to pass. Time is the healer in stroke cases. We just sit on the sidelines and root.'

He then patted my arm as we stood in the hall, a nice middle-aged Jewish doctor comforting what he thought was a nice middle-aged Jewish son. He looked rather like a thin Shebsie, and I wondered how good *his* technique would be in baring Ellie's ass for needle or penis. And that brought Harv back to mind; and I could almost *see* Harv's technique . . . 'Back your ass against the wall, here I come, balls and all.' Oh, yes, a very strong and satisfying technique indeed!

The doctor was looking at me, and said, 'Try to relax, Mr Leib. Tensing up this way won't help your mother, and you'll need all your strength for the weeks to come.' He paused. 'I shouldn't say this, but my experience in these matters, my instinct in such cases, leads me to believe she *will* survive, though to what extent she'll recover her faculties . . .'

I asked *when* we'd know about survival and extent of recovery, thinking perhaps I could leave for St Louis at the end of the week.

He spread his hands, palms upward, and hurried off to dispense uncertainties to other patients' relatives.

I waited around until six that evening, spending most of my time in the coffee shop, and then drove to my mother's apartment off

Eastern Parkway. Brooklyn, in general, depresses me, because that's where I had my delightful beginnings. Her place, in particular, depressed me, because despite it being reasonably cheerful and well-furnished, it was, to her, a place of exile. She'd lived in Teaneck with Louise and me and the children, until a week before the divorce. She'd felt it a 'sin against your children and God too', as she said just before I left the apartment. And I'd heard her weeping as I stood outside the door, and then walked away.

The super let me in. He shook his head, an old man, almost as old as my mother, and he tried to say something and then he shook his head again and went away. I was glad. I felt no grief, not even true shock, and would have hated to answer expressions of sympathy with lying platitudes. I checked her things, and found her Blue Cross and Blue Shield cards, and in the process found her collection of photographs, most of them of me. Little Nickie on a pony a street photographer used to sucker his poverty-ridden clients. Little Nickie in knickers, smiling his false smile for the world ... because it *had* been false so much of the time, and always false in photographs. Nickie in high school, thin and pinched-of-face, the smile barely believable. Nickie the war hero, in heavy furlined leather flying suit, posed before his P.T. 19 at the primary flight field in Bennington, South Carolina. Nickie in college cap and gown. Nickie with Louise at the lodge in Vermont where we'd honeymooned ... and where I'd begun looking at other girls, especially a chubby waitress who was turned on by the idea that a boy who was fucking his bride three and four times a day would stare at *her* ass that way. Then pictures of Denise and Seth. One lone picture of my father, at my wedding, stiff in tux, a potato or other edible (I think he said it was a potato) bulging his cheek, a silly smile plastered on his face for the photographer intent upon getting candid shots. He'd died nine months later.

No pictures of Ellie here, and yet she dominated Nickie's life and thoughts. No pictures of the little blonde *shiksa*, the cunt fucking away in St Louis ...

I called the hospital. No change in Mrs Leib's condition. I called Louise, and she was shocked and promised to visit the very next day. I went home, and without expecting an answer called Ellie. She answered. I said, 'Remember my funny Jewish mother? She had a stroke.'

'Oh, Nickie, I'm sorry. Is she ... ?'

'She's alive. For the moment.'

'Are *you* all right?'

'Yes. Just wanted to ...' What had I wanted to do? To get her sympathy? Yes, for *me*. To make her sorry for Nickie. To bring her closer somehow. 'Just wanted to let you know.'

'I'm glad you did, honey.'

'Would you let me know if anything happened to someone *you* cared for?'

'I don't know.'

'You wouldn't.'

'You're upset, Nickie. You shouldn't talk any more now.'

Nothing more to say anyway. All words were finished. And these words hadn't helped, hadn't brought her closer. 'I love you, Ellie. I'm thinking of you now, and I'll think of you always. No way out, little love. You're stuck. No way out, so try to care.'

'I *do* care. I want her to be well.'

'Care for *me*, I mean.'

'Why do you think I care about your mother when I've never met her?'

'Care meaning *love*.'

'I . . . I do love you, Nickie, in a way.'

Exhaustion was overtaking me, and I was beginning to remember my mother, even as I talked to my love, and so her words almost went by me. I expected so little from Ellie now that I didn't quite grasp what she'd said. 'Well,' I said, 'take care, honey. I'll be calling . . .' And then it hit me. 'In a way? As much as . . . anyone else in your life?'

Her voice was low and shaky. 'More, Nickie. Always more. Even if I never see you again. Because I came to you so much in love and so trusting and I wanted you to love me so much and I never felt that way about anyone, not Harv and not anyone, and I don't think I'll ever feel that way again.'

'Feel that way again about *me*! I feel that way about you, Ellie!'

She sighed. 'Not tonight, Nickie.'

'All right,' I muttered, too tired to fight. She loved me more than she loved him. I would remember that, build on that, when I came to St Louis. 'I'll call again.'

'Yes, let me know what happens.'

She sent me a kiss and I sent her several and she hung up. I lay down, slipped off my shoes, and wonder of wonders I was asleep.

Hospitals are all alike. I spent months in an army hospital, and it wasn't much different than that Jewish Hospital in Brooklyn.

I met Louise there the next afternoon. She squeezed my hand.

I met aunts Lila, Rose, Eva, and others whose names I barely remembered, it had been so long. Later, uncles came, and I fled.

She regained consciousness at eleven that night, and considerable ability to speak before morning. She also began moving her arm, if not her leg. This was told to me by an exultant Dr Aberfein in the hall outside the intensive care unit. 'Incredible strength, that woman has! It won't be too long before she'll be leaving us!'

I smiled, planning a quick trip to St Louis.

A cautionary note entered the doctor's voice. 'But don't misunderstand, Mr Leib. She'll never be as she was. What I'm saying is, she'll live, and her recovery should be fairly rapid from now on, but it won't bring her back to the fully ambulatory and self-sufficient person she was before. The leg in particular worries me. You'll have to make some decisions about how and where she'll live . . .'

Cancel that quick trip.

I'd be allowed to see her in about fifteen minutes, after the conclusion of certain tests. I went down to the hospital flower shop and bought a mixed bouquet.

When I entered her room, she was just being brought into a semi-sitting position by a nurse using an electric control that raised the back of the bed. The nurse took the flowers from me. I said, 'How are you, Mom?'

She nodded, face waxlike. She cleared her throat and said, 'Me? I'm fine.' I almost laughed and then realized why. It sounded as if my mother were drunk . . . and my mother *never* drank.

The nurse returned with the flowers in a vase. She set them on a bedside table and said, 'Don't tire her. About five minutes this time, please.'

I approached the bed. My mother was shrunken. But then again, she'd been small and thin for some years now; since entering her seventies, as I remembered. Before, she'd been medium-height and lean. When younger, she'd been less lean, with a figure that set the men to whistling outside the New Lots Bar and Grill.

She smiled as I sat down beside her. Despite a slight imbalance – the left side of her mouth went further up than the right – her smile was just about the same; the smile I remembered from childhood on; quick, sharp, seemingly sweet but actually bitter. It generally preceded a gem of Jewish-Momma observation and wisdom, such as the time she'd met me as I was walking a college classmate home along Livonia Avenue, having taken the subway from Washington Square College. This classmate was female, and Negro, a lovely deep-black girl with a stunning smile and mind to match. I'd dated her a few times and was much taken with her. She'd spent three nights in my bed and was much taken with me. We'd considered tilting a few windmills together, but decided we were both too poor, and too ambitious, to consider adding an interracial marriage to our struggle. My mother greeted me, and I introduced her to the girl. My mother nodded, and then smiled, and I couldn't stop whatever was coming and hoped it wouldn't be too bad. 'He was always Emma's favourite,' my mother said, patting my arm. 'Emma was our cleaning girl, and a finer woman you *never* met.'

Now she was smiling again. I wondered what was coming. She didn't disappoint me, stroke or not, slow, drunken speech or not. '*Oy*, Wallace, how long you took to come.'

Wallace was my brother, born two years before me, and dead seven weeks after birth. Wallace was a name my mother hadn't used since I was a child, when she used it as a bludgeon; *i.e.*: 'If Wallace had lived, he'd have made A's in all his subjects, the doctor said he had such an *intelligence* in him.'

I said, 'It's Nickie, Mom.'

'Nickie?'

The doctor had warned me her mind would be 'fuzzy' for a while.

'Nicholas Leib, your son,' I said, trying to kid her.

'*Nicholas?*' She stared at me, no longer smiling. Then she closed her eyes; her voice grew weak. 'What sort of name is Nicholas? For a Jew?'

She'd actually forgotten she'd named me after the family's only *goy*, Uncle Nick, who'd paid the hospital expenses for the destitute Leibs when I'd been born. 'Okay,' I said. 'I'll change it to *Moishe*.'

No answer. I said, 'Mom?' She breathed regularly. I stood up. She slept. I left the room and went to the waiting room and told the assembled relatives they could probably see her tomorrow. Then I left, outdistancing uncles and aunts and cousins who wanted to eat or drink or chat with me.

I couldn't face going home so early. I went to the movies, and then to a restaurant, and then home to a hot bath and two sleeping pills and a drugged nap. I awakened at eleven and called Ellie. No answer, which was lucky, because I'd only have played dumbshit again. And which was unlucky because *where the hell was she?*

Why at work, of course!

Big realization, right? I'd known she was working for Alexis again; she'd told me. But I'd 'forgotten'. Not until this moment had I thought of calling her at work. I *think*. Because, of course, I couldn't really forget such an important part of my little girl's life. I'd simply been unwilling to reach her where Charlie Alexis and her past associations with Harv resided. I'd lost her and they'd regained her and it hurt. Also, I'd been holding back on what was essentially a process of harassment.

She'd given me her home number. She'd pointedly *not* given me her business number. There could be no ignoring the phone at work, no hanging up or leaving it off the hook.

Now I told myself I'd somehow forgotten she could be reached at work. Now I called St Louis Information, and asked for the number of Alexis Fashions for Men, Lindell branch. I got it, and dialled, and a man answered; not Alexis, as I recalled his voice. This one was slightly accented – French, perhaps.

But an answer. There'd *always* be an answer! And when I asked for Ellie, he said, 'Hold on,' which meant she was there.

She came on laughing. 'Hi! Watcha doing?'

I knew, instantly, she thought she was speaking to someone else. I hadn't given my name ... and it killed me that she sounded so *happy*, when she never sounded happy with me any more.

I deepened my voice. 'Nothing.'

'That's good! Better keep it that way, Harvey-boo, long as I'm not around!' She laughed again. 'You coming here, or meeting me at home?'

'Love to come there, but it's a long trip. Can you wait until tomorrow, Ellie-boo?'

She knew then. She laughed again, but it was a false laugh. I was sweating and well into my tremors.

'Oh, hi. Ahmed said ...'

'Ahmed?' The Arab ass-fucker! All the men from her past were back in her life! I had to choke down obscenities, shouts, accusations.

'Oh, not the same one.' Another laugh. 'How's your mother?'

'How many Ahmeds can you know?' I was proud of my self-control.

'Oh, well ...' More phoney laughter. 'Actually, it's the same one but I never ... I mean, I made all that stuff up, you know, as a gag.'

'You also made up Harvey-boo as a gag?'

Silence.

'What's Ahmed doing there?'

'He's our accountant. Comes to each store once a week to do the books.'

'Convenient. Don't bend over too far.'

Laughter, a little less phoney.

'Whose home are you meeting Harvey-boo at – his, yours, or the one you now share?'

'Mine. Is your mother better?'

'A little.'

255

'You see her every day?'

'Yes.'

'How's Seth?'

'Fine. And Denise. And everyone ... except me. I'm sick.'

'What's wrong?'

'I miss someone. I love someone. Someone who said she cares more for me than for any other man, and then meets her Harvey-boo at home, and comes on laughing after her Ahmed ...'

'I can't talk now. A customer just walked in. You at home? I'll call you back.'

'Sure you will.'

'I will. Have to go ...'

'Don't hang up! I don't give a shit about your customers! Don't hang up ... not until I'm ready!'

She hung up. I dialled again. Ahmed answered. I asked for her. He said, 'Ellie, for you.' Then the mouthpiece must have been covered. And then he said, 'She's busy now. Your name, please?'

'Harvey-boo,' I said, and hung up.

I washed and made coffee. I was on my third cup when the phone rang. I took it in the kitchen. It was Harold. He began to berate me. I told him about my mother, said I was leaving for the hospital, and hung up. The phone had to remain free.

It rang as I was beginning to pace. Ellie said, 'Hi. Sorry, but you can't just call me here ...'

'Oh, but I will. All the time. And in different voices.'

Silence.

'Have a good ass-fuck?'

Silence.

'And has Harvey-boo been good and strong?'

'Nickie, there are people coming in.'

'Yes, I remember, a veritable Saks, that store, thousands rushing for clothing. And all when I call.'

'There *are* customers.'

'Don't hang up or I'll call all day!'

'I'm not hanging up! I'm asking you to please let me go!'

'Now or forever?'

Silence.

She was telling me, over and over, that we were through. She was trying to free herself. I had no right to do what I was doing.

Fine. I'd stated the obvious. It made no difference.

'Well, you can go now.'

'Did you get the cheque?'

'What cheque?' But I knew, I knew, and it was another bell

256

tolling.

'The two thousand to cover what you gave me. It'll come soon. Please accept it, and then let's be friends. We'll see each other once in a while...'

I said, 'Goodbye, Ellie-boo,' and hung up.

I went down for the mail, and there it was. A cheque on the account of Ellie McBaren, for two thousand dollars. Harv was *really* important now. I went directly to my bank, trying to walk off the anguish, telling myself I'd cash the cheque and bring the money to Aaron Hoff. But then I tore it into little pieces, and drove to Brooklyn and the hospital.

My mother had made progress. She was taking food. She was seeing relatives, and recognizing most of them. She was speaking clearly. She called me Nickie today, and asked how much this private room in Intensive Care was costing. I said she shouldn't worry.

The doctor said she would be moved to a semi-private room tomorrow. He suggested I examine a list of nursing homes I could get at the desk, and when I asked why, spread his hands. 'She's not going to be fully ambulatory, Mr Leib. You couldn't notice it since she's in bed, and since her face and, to a considerable degree, her arm have regained mobility. But the leg...' He shook his head. 'She can't walk.'

I examined the list of nursing homes. I left the hospital and drove to Teaneck and spoke to Louise. I made her an offer – handle my mother's incarceration, and I'd pay for the services. She acted shocked, but she was always one for a deal. She said she realized I was busy, that I had to 'support my children', that I'd never been able to deal with my mother ... and on *'those bases only'* would she consider choosing a nursing home and handling the details of closing out Mom's apartment and so on. Then she said there was a sale at Korvette's on colour TV, and a new Entertainment Centre Console, including hi-fi, tape, record-player, and recording devices, was going for twenty-percent off ... a mere eleven-hundred dollars.

Would she visit the hospital each day, speak to the doctor, handle the details of Blue Cross and additional bills, which I would then settle with her? Would she bring Seth and Denise to see my mother, when it was advisable, and generally handle the visitors?

She sighed, but a gleam came into her eyes. She was so damned *good* at such things. 'If you insist.'

I insisted, and drove directly to Korvette's to place the order for the Entertainment Centre.

And then I was free ... to do what?

I decided on heavy running, to work off my energy, my tension, that sickness eating at me. I tried Central Park, along the edges of the road, and was choked by gas fumes. I tried the river path along the F.D.R. Drive, and the carbon monoxide was even heavier there. Running in Manhattan was worse than no exercise at all. I had to drive up to the cottage ...

It was five days before I was able to do so. By then, my mother was ready to leave for a nursing home. Her recovery was 'quite remarkable', according to the doctor ... whose bill was also quite remarkable; a resounding four hundred and eighty dollars, just for hospital visits. When I checked it out with Ron, he said it was 'average for specialists'.

Fucking doctors, as Ellie would say.

I didn't call Ellie. I was proud of myself for not calling Ellie. But then again, what was left to say?

After driving to the cottage, I ran in James Baird State Park in the morning, and along La Grangeville road lined with winter fields toward sunset. In between, I worked on the second of my three toy ideas. At night, I went to bed, telling myself I was physically exhausted, healthily worn out with exercise and work ... and remained awake until three a.m., when I washed a sleeping pill down with a beer.

Two days of this, and I realized the cottage was no longer an answer for anything. I had to go to St Louis.

I phoned Louise from Hopewell junction. She had chosen a small nursing home near Peekskill in Northern Westchester. My mother was to be taken there tomorrow by private ambulance ... unless I wanted to save the eight dollars and drive her myself? I said no, and thanks. She asked me to meet her at the home at noon. There were papers to sign and deposits to give. 'And,' she added, 'there's something I have to discuss with you.'

The nursing home was a rambling old place on spacious grounds between the towns of Peekskill and Putnam Valley. Louise was waiting at the desk. My mother was being settled in her room. 'She seems to like it,' Louise said.

I nodded. I touched her hand. I liked *her*. She knew a good deal about Nick Leib – at least the old Nick Leib.

I saw my mother. She was in a fuzzy mood again. She kept falling asleep as I talked to her. She called me Wallace when I said goodbye. The nurse assured me she would soon improve 'under our ideal conditions'.

Louise and I had lunch in a local roadhouse. She fiddled with her salad. 'Are the kids all right?' I asked.

She looked up. 'Oh ... it's not the children.' Another moment of fiddling, and out it came. 'Nick, I'm going to be married. Not right away, because Seth doesn't really know Philip yet. But I've said yes ...' She gave the details.

I nodded. So many things happening at once. 'Much luck, Louise. You deserve it.'

Small smiles on both sides. I drove her home, mostly in silence. Once she said I was driving recklessly, and I slowed down.

At the house, I asked if I could take Seth to dinner.

'I'm sorry, Nick. Tonight we're having Phil and his son over. Phil is a widower. Chris is the cutest nine-year-old ...'

So Seth not only had to learn to love a new father, but to live with a new brother. I hoped the kid wasn't a goof-ball.

Louise said, 'Perhaps tomorrow night?'

'I'm going out of town.'

'See? You've got your own life, Nick. Seth needs a full-time father.'

I guess she couldn't help twisting the knife a little. She'd been hurt by the divorce; never really forgiving me for it.

I did sixty on the F.D.R. Drive, cutting in and out of moderate traffic ... and I was nailed by a motorcycle cop. He lectured me. I said, 'Write the ticket and let me get about my business.' He gave me a hard look. I returned it, waiting. He decided against a confrontation, and wrote the ticket. I did something I'd never done before, something indicative of my feelings about the future. I tore it up and flushed it down the toilet. Then I packed, phoned for airline and motel reservations, and drank myself beddy-bye.

I arrived in St Louis at nine-thirty a.m. Central Time, and was at the Parkway House Motel via cab at five-to-ten. Strange feeling; unreal feeling. I was finally here.

An hour later, I had a rental Ford. I called Ellie at the store, mouth dry, heart banging away. The man I spoke to sounded like Charlie Alexis. He said Ellie was off today, Thursday, and tomorrow too. She'd be back at work on Saturday. 'Who should I say called?'

'Nick Leib.'

There was an instant of silence, and when he next spoke his voice was decidedly cold. 'All right.' He hung up.

Had she been talking to her turned-on boss? Had she been baring her little heart to him, or her not-so-little ass? Or did he simply hate me for taking her away in the first place?

I drove up Lindbergh Avenue, the four-lane highway on which the motel was located, to a gas station, and asked directions to Ellie's address. I also got a map.

The directions were simple; the roads few and easily located; I was at the garden apartment development a few minutes to noon. I parked in a black-top area with lined spaces, and walked onto a sidewalk and along a row of fully attached two-storey brick buildings. She was right; it *was* a pleasant setting, and even though the trees were all saplings and bare this time of year, there were many of them and all seemed to be doing well. There were large grassy areas, still green despite it being January. and the weather wasn't all that cold, Under other circumstances – say visiting Ellie on invitation, to stay with her at her apartment – I'd have felt happy with where I was as well as with whom I was going to see.

No happiness in me now. Nothing but sick tension, sick excitement. Because I'd found number 912 and had entered and was facing the first door on the right, the door bearing the name-plate, 'E. McBaren'.

I hesitated. Stay or run? Knock or lurk? Reveal myself, or tail her?

I was nowhere near a decision when the door opened. I froze. The woman who emerged was small and round and black. I said, 'Is Miss McBaren in?'

'No one's in.' She shut the door behind her; then turned and looked at me.

'When do you think she'll be home?'

'Don't know. I work for Mr Cohen's family. He sends me here once a week.'

I nodded. She continued to wait. I had a sudden hunch, and said, 'I'll try them tonight. Thank you.' I left. I went back to the Ford and got in.

She came along a moment later, and drove off in an Oldsmobile sedan. I returned to number 912 and lifted the doormat. Nothing. I stepped back to the little foyer and checked the mailboxes, peering through the slot into Ellie's. No key that I could see. Back to the door, and two kids came down the stairs, and I fumbled in my pockets until they were gone. Then I reached above the door, feeling along the narrow ledge ... and there it was.

I used the key and opened the door and stepped inside. For a moment I couldn't seem to see; couldn't seem to think. My eyes were clouded; my brain was clouded. I was overcome by a sense of unreality, born of not wanting to face this special reality. Before exams, as a kid in high school, I'd had that same feeling, fearing the test. I feared this test too.

I closed the door. I was here. I'd come to Ellie's home. Harv

Cohen hired a cleaning lady for Ellie's home. Harv Cohen didn't want a mess where he fucked. Or did he *live* here?

The pain, the rage, the hate, awakened me, and I began to look around. I stood between a living room running lengthwise to my right, and a small dinette on my left. Beyond the dinette was a kitchen. Straight ahead of me was a short hallway with a door at the end, a door on the left, a door on the right.

The living room was furnished well – gold couch and two brown bouclé chairs and a desk before the picture window. Tan figured wall-to-wall carpeting. Drapes drawn back from the windows. Bookcases with stereo tape-player and speakers, TV, stacked eight-track tapes, and some books. Prints on the walls ... and nothing looked second-hand.

The dinette had a wrought-iron, glass-topped table, small and round, and three wrought-iron chairs. There were *chatchkas* hanging and setting – spice-shelf and spices in dark wood on the wall; tall glass vase and good bouquet of coloured wheat and ceramic flowers, on the table; cornucopia of fruits and vegetables of painted pottery on the wall; a mobile of birds and bees hanging from the ceiling. Rather much ... but still, nothing cheap or second-hand that I could see.

The kitchen was fully stocked with silverware, glasses, china, and copper pots and pans, the copperware displayed on wall hooks over the stove. The refrigerator held much food and drink, including five cans of beer. Ellie didn't drink beer.

I walked down the small hallway to the door at the end. A linen closet, fully stocked; more than I had at home. The door on the left was a bathroom, modern, a glass shelf full of Ellie's makeup and perfumes. The medicine chest held not only the standard unisex drugs and toiletries, but two prescription jars, one with green and white capsules, the other with small white tablets. The pharmacy was on Lindell. The doctor was a Walter Roesch. The patient was Miss E. McBaren. The directions on both labels were the same ...'1 before meals for stomach disorder.' That could be a cover used by a pill doctor to feed Ellie her dexies, her ups and downs, whatever drugs she needed. There was also a complete set of expensive Danish men's shaving material – foam, after-shave lotion, talc, skin gell, hair cream and hair spray, plus an adjustable Gillette razor. There were two tooth-brushes in a glass on the sink.

I entered the bedroom, and the case against Harvey Cohen was complete. Item: His photograph on the dresser, next to the one of Ellie I'd never seen. Item: His clothing – suits, slacks, coats, *et al.* – in one half of the closet. (As with me, Ellie's clothing took up the lion's share of the storage space; a closet and a half.) Item: Pipes in a wooden rack on a nightstand, and tobacco in the drawer. Also, underwear and shirts and ties and everything that made the man, in drawers.

The furniture was again good and obviously not second-hand – a Mediterranean style in light oak, with king-sized bed, chest of drawers, long dresser and black mirror. A lady's vanity with lighted oval mirror stood catacorner near the big window. A tan princess phone was on the vanity. The ring control underneath had a click-off position not found on any I'd ever owned.

I checked it out, calling the operator and saying I thought my phone wasn't ringing. Would she call me? She said she would.

I waited five minutes without hearing a ring, then moved the control back toward loud. A moment later, the phone rang. The operator said she'd been trying to get me for five minutes. I said sorry, I'd been called to the door. I hung up, and wanted to tear the damned thing out of the wall. It had tormented me for months!

I went to the dresser and examined Harv's photo. How did I know it was his? The heavy scrawl across the bottom had hit me as soon as I'd entered the bedroom. 'To Ellie, with love, from her Harvey-boo.'

I wanted to smash it against the wall. Instead, I examined the youthful smile, the forward-combed shock of dark hair, the medium-long sideburns. Not a good-looking face; rather heavy and apelike. But then again, I was prejudiced. Phone and photo remained un-harmed; Ellie and Harvey-boo would remain unwarned.

I returned to the kitchen. I took a beer from the refrigerator and drank it from the can. I was terribly dry of mouth, and sweating a bit, but I didn't have the usual stomach ache or trembling. I wondered why, because of all times *this* seemed the time to be most shook up. Perhaps because I was numb. Perhaps because all this added up to so much more *serious* an involvement on Harv's part than I'd expected (though I'd expected *some* involvement), that I was unable to react. Harv was paying for too much to be the casual lover. Harv was paying like a husband; a doting husband. Harv was living here, and probably expected to soon *become* a husband.

Or had he already? Was my little Ellie now Mrs Harvey Cohen?
And if so, what would I do about it? Go home, sensibly, and make sure my son didn't forget me? Find myself a lovely contender for the position of Mrs Nicholas Leib, say Ledya, and concentrate on creating a real life instead of the erotic fantasy I'd lived with Ellie, the hellish fantasy I'd lived alone, and the violent fantasy I'd begun

to live recently?

My Ellie, living with, married to, another man?

The ache moved into my gut; the trembling began; I gulped the rest of the beer and wanted something stronger.

My Ellie!

I wondered what would happen if she or he or both walked in on me. I wasn't quite ready to do what had to be done. If I did it myself there'd be immediate satisfaction, and a probable end to my life. No point in satisfaction without the ability to capitalize on it; the ability to get Ellie back.

It had to be done through Aaron.

I wondered if Harv had taken out insurance, and if Ellie were his wife and therefore his beneficiary. I hoped not. If she got twenty or thirty or fifty thousand dollars, she would be that much more independent of me, that much more difficult to handle.

Again I fought the madness, the need to destroy anyone possessing my little love. Again I told myself to go home; to resume normal living...

I ran to the bathroom, feeling I was going to throw up. I gagged a little, felt better, began to leave, and saw the clothes hamper. A big one, not the bachelor size I owned. It held much dirty linen. One of the sheets was spotted. It was sperm, had to be sperm, or a mixture of sperm and my little Ellie's love juice. And there were panties and men's shorts, and the mixture of spotted sheets and panties and shorts was too much, was the clincher, made everything as sharp and clear to me as if I'd stood at the foot of that bed and watched them fucking. The vomit rose so quickly I didn't have time to reach the toilet. It spurted from my mouth, and I bent to the sink and retched for a good five minutes. Then I used a wash-cloth from the shower to clean up some that had landed on the tile floor, and rinsed the sink out thoroughly, and used cleaning fluid from a cabinet to deodorize sink and floor and cloth. I hung the cloth back over the shower's curtain rail, took the beer can with me, and left. I drove back to the main road, and then remembered the key in my pocket.

I wanted a key of my own. But not this one. They might change the lock if a key were missing. A copy. I'd passed a five and dime in a shopping centre on the way here.

It was at the next intersection. I went in. They had a key machine at the hardware counter, and I had a copy made. By the time I returned to the garden apartments, I'd calmed a bit and was able to look for a Mustang convertible, or a Pontiac Firebird, Harv's car. Neither was there, and so I went to 912 and put the original key back over the door and returned to my car and then on to my motel.

I drank about a pint of Scotch before three, and slept, and awoke at nine with my hands clenching and unclenching, dreaming of spotted sheets, trying to rip them apart.

I showered and went down to the dining room and had a hamburger and a beer. I could barely finish it, though I wasn't that hung over. I went back to the room and called Ellie's apartment. And she answered.

'Hi,' I said, and I was calmer than I'd been with her in months. Everything was decided, settled, waiting to be accomplished. 'It's Nick.'

'I've been worried about you! Where've you been?'

It was almost a shout; definitely angry.

I laughed. 'You mean you called me?'

'Of course! Don't you realize it's been close to two weeks since I heard from you? You never went this long before.'

I laughed again.

She said, 'If it's so fucking funny, then to hell with it!' and hung up.

I dialled her number, smiling, wondering what she was, how she functioned, what went on in that head, how I could love her as I did.

She answered. I said, 'Guess Harv isn't around. You were shouting.'

'What makes you think Harv's always around?'

Oh little love, don't.

I said nothing.

'How's your mother? I thought maybe ... she's all right, isn't she?'

'She's in a nursing home. She's alive, and she'll improve, they tell me.'

'Did you get the cheque?'

'Yes. Thank you. And now we're friends, right?'

Small voice. 'I hope so, Nickie.'

'I tore it up. I'll soon tear Harv up.'

It had come out of me so quickly, so quietly, it fooled both of us. She said, 'Oh,' and then, 'Nickie, you didn't?'

'You mean, Nickie, you *wouldn't*. But I will, Ellie. Because he's with you all the time.'

'You're threatening again!'

'No. I've given up making fists like a little boy. How's Liz? I wish I could meet her. I wish you and Liz and Seth and I could go out tomorrow for a ride around town and lunch and a movie and then dinner. I wish we could put the kids to sleep at nine or ten and then you and I could walk around and hold hands and kiss and later make love ...'

'Nickie, stop.' Sad voice; shaky voice. 'Please, honey, no more.'

I visualized her at her vanity, that picture of Harv on the dresser and his pipes on the nightstand and his clothes in the closet and his shorts in the hamper along with her panties and the spotted sheet.

'If you were married,' I said, 'would you tell me?'

She laughed.

'I have a feeling, Ellie. I know you're living with Harv.'

'I ... I'm seeing a lot of him, but I'm not living with him. I see other men too.'

'Tell me the truth. Please.'

'Nickie, I want to wash my hair!' It was a babyish wail for relief from interrogation, and I had to laugh a little.

'Goodnight then,' I said. 'Here's a kiss.' She returned it and said goodbye. I waited for her to hang up. She always hung up first. Now she didn't. I said, 'Ellie?' She said, 'Yes ... Nickie ... I miss you.'

I *wouldn't* allow that ping-pong game to start again. But I couldn't help saying, 'Do you, little love? Do you really? Even with Harvey-boo? Can you mean it?'

'Yes. I don't want to mean it ... but when I don't hear from you ... when the phone doesn't keep ringing...'

'When you don't have to cut it off.'

'Yes, that too. Then I worry about you, miss you ... I must be insane! I want us to go our separate ways, Nickie, I really do ... but sometimes I think of you with Ledya and I go crazy. Nickie, are you making love to other girls?' Before I could say anything, she laughed. 'I know the answer. A man like you, so goddam sexy...'

She stopped. I heard ... nothing. A hand-over-phone nothing. Had someone joined her?

'I'm not making love to other girls. I'm sexy only with you. Please, baby, *please* let me visit you ... tomorrow.'

'We went through that, Nickie.' Different voice; hurried, worried voice. 'I've got to wash my hair.' She said goodbye, and I thought I heard a voice in the background, and she hung up quickly.

There was no point in sticking around St Louis. I couldn't do anything more here.

But she said she went out with other men. *Who?*

I wanted to see her, watch her, know everything she did.

I drove back to the garden apartment and parked at the end of the lot, which was now almost full. I walked past cars in the darkness, and saw a Mustang convertible, three years old, and then a Firebird hardtop, about two years old. Peering inside, I could see that the Firebird had a stickshift. Harv's car ... she said she'd driven his stickshift Firebird and not done well.

I walked to number 912 and went inside. I went right to her door and put my ear to it and heard voices – a deep voice, Ellie's voice. She laughed.

I left before I went insane, thinking of her alone with that man – with *any* man – and the night stretching ahead.

The next morning at seven-thirty, I was back at the garden apartment. I didn't park in the blacktop area. I parked on the road. Later, people began coming out and getting into cars and driving out and past me. At eight-twenty, a young man in a grey tweed coat came out and went to the red Firebird. Harv Cohen. About two inches shorter than me and somewhat stoop-shouldered. He drove past me. He was tinkering with his radio and never even glanced my way.

I waited until nine; then drove to the shopping centre and a phone booth. I called her. The phone rang and rang. I hung up. I tried something. I dialled and let it ring *twice* and hung up. Too many people used the one-dial signal. Ellie was devious. She'd try a switch. Maybe two, maybe three, maybe more.

I dialled again. She answered almost immediately. 'Hi! What's the scoop?'

'It's Nickie.'

'Oh, Nickie. You just call me?'

'Yes. It disconnected after two or three rings.'

'Oh.'

'Just wanted to say I'm going up to the cottage to work. I'll probably stay there a week, maybe more.' I chuckled. 'So you won't be all shook up if I don't call.'

'Well, have a good time.' She was anxious to get me off the phone. She expected her Harvey-boo to call.

But that wasn't like Ellie. Her Harvey-boo had just left. She didn't talk much, when she was *with* a man.

I was probably wrong, but the idea stuck. I said goodbye. She gave me a kiss without my asking for it.

Back to the road beside the parking lot. Back to watching cars leave ... and later, some cars enter. I couldn't see all the way to Ellie's building from here. I drove into the lot and parked where I could see. Her car was four stalls away. If she came out, I'd just duck down ... or perhaps I'd call out and she'd freeze in shock and I'd say, 'Hi,' and we'd go somewhere for lunch and then to my motel and I'd make love to her, show her I was still the right man ...

An old Volkswagen came in and parked near the sidewalk. A dark man of about thirty got out. Very dark; very Semitic looking. Could be an Arab. He walked quickly, the stride of an athlete, with bounce and vigour, until he reached 912. Then he disappeared.

Ahmed?

I laughed at myself. I got out and went to 912 and up to Ellie's door. A woman came down the stairs, and I took out my wallet as if checking something. She stayed in the foyer, reading her mail, for what seemed like an hour. When she finally left, I put my ear to the door. Ellie's voice. A man's voice, very soft.

Oh God! Don't jump to conclusions. Perhaps innocent visit. Friends. Business. Checking the books.

Checking her cunt.

I went outside. Both her windows faced the walk. The living-room drapes were open. I stepped over a bush and looked in. They were on the couch and the bitch was on his lap and his hand was parting her robe, that fur-fringed robe, and I saw white flesh and black hair and that hand ...

I went back to the car and said, 'Harvey-boo, you're getting the business,' and shook and wanted to die and wondered had she done the same to me with the pilot, with someone she'd met on the streets, with Studsy in the upper cabanas at the Fontainebeau? Would she have done more, if I'd left her alone, trusted her alone, the way Harv did? And how many men would I have to kill to get her back?

But this man, Ahmed, if it was him, was unimportant.

Maybe she wouldn't even fuck him? Just play a little. After all, she'd *told* me she was seeing other men.

I went back. A couple walked toward me. I walked slowly. I looked around and I was alone and I stepped back over the bush. Room empty. I went to the next window; the bedroom window. Drapes drawn.

I went into the building and up to her door and pressed the bell button, in and out, in and out, three times. I wanted to stay, but then I'd end up in jail and I couldn't let that happen. I ran to the back, down a flight of steps to a basement area with a laundry room at the end of the corridor. And heard Ellie's voice, sharp, upset, calling, 'Hey! Who is it?'

The door closed. I waited. I went back upstairs and pressed the bell button twice and ran back down. Again the door opened. This time it slammed quickly. This time I went back up and out to my car. I waited. I wished I had a bug in her bedroom. Was she frightened? Did she think that Harv had something to do with the doorbell?

Ahmed came out to the parking lot a few minutes later. He hurried. He didn't look around but got right into his beat-up Volks and took off.

I followed. No time for Aaron with this one. I'd *seen* this one; his hand on her white flesh, beginning to finger her black patch. *I'd seen it!*

I didn't know where we were going, until we got off the highway at Kingshighway Road. Then I recognized the Forest Park area, near Alexis's Lindell store. But the Volks didn't go there. It went toward Washington University, turned into a side street of brown stone houses, and pulled to a stop. He got out. I was at the corner, and when he walked down to a basement entrance, I drove up closer. I waited. About five minutes later, I got out and went to the basement entrance and hesitated with my hand on the iron railing; and then walked down to an apartment door and a window beside it.

Question: Why do so few Arabs commit suicide?

Answer: Because it's hard to kill yourself jumping out of a basement window.

We'd let the Poles off the hook this time around ... unless Ellie had a Polish boyfriend.

The nameplate beside the bell button read, 'Ahmed Dahnoran'.

The ass-fucker. Had he had time to make it before he'd left?

Oh God, oh God, oh God ...

When I had stopped shaking, I went back up to the street and drove to a gas station a block from the Forest Park Hotel and asked if they had a gasoline can I could use to help a friend who was stuck on the highway. They said yes, a two-gallon can, but I'd have to leave a three-dollar deposit.

Done, and I filled it with high test. Then I went to a supermarket and bought three bottles of soft drink; I didn't notice what kind, because I was looking for thin glass, unlike the thick Coke bottles, and sixteen-ounce size.

I returned to the car. I had a handkerchief, and some rags in the trunk, for wicks. I had the ingredients for Molotov cocktails. I wanted to make them in the car, and throw them, all three of them, through that basement window and fry that Arab ass-fucker. *Now!*

I actually began to empty a soft-drink bottle, when I realized I was insane. Not for wanting to fry Ahmed. Oh Christ how I wanted to fry Ahmed! But because I'd be caught. I was on the street in broad daylight and I'd never get out of St Louis and Ellie would still have Harv and I'd rot in jail...

I drove back to the parkway. I got lost three times, and asked directions four times, and made it to my motel, with a stopover at a supermarket for liquor. I drank enough to feel better, but not enough to forget that ass-fucker with Ellie. I called her, using the two-ring signal. She answered, sounding worried. I made my voice a crazy growl and said, 'Al Fatah will not triumph,' and hung up.

Let her sweat a little tonight. Let her feel a little of what I was feeling; though I doubted that was possible.

I went to the coffee shop and had a sandwich and a cup of tomato soup and left at least half of each. My pants were loose at the waist. I wondered how much weight I'd lost in the past few months.

I went upstairs and drank more Scotch and lay down. I think I slept. Either I slept and had nightmares, or I was awake and my fantasies betrayed me. Or I was somewhere in between. I awoke or got up or whatever, crying out, 'Ellie, come *home*!'

It was dark in the room. I put on the bedside lamp and checked my watch. Ten-thirty. I called her. The phone rang and rang. I tried the two-ring signal followed by extended ringing. Still no answer. Scared, or not home, or in bed with Number One, the young Jew. And who was Number Two, the Arab or the old Jew? And was the Greek employer seeded in the St Louis sex matches, and were there others...?

I went down to the Ford and got the can of gasoline. I'd brought the soft drinks to my room earlier. I emptied the soda in the toilet and filled one bottle with gasoline. I stuffed my handkerchief in the opening, tightly, leaving a tail as described by a freaky book I'd bought some years before, a book that had seemed a joke and created much talk and that I'd never dreamed I would actually use as a text, a guideline: *The Anarchist Cookbook*. I began to make a second firebomb; then realized it would stretch the odds too heavily against me to take the time to throw more than one.

I looked around for something in which to put the bomb. I finally wrapped it in a towel, and went down to the car and drove onto the parkway. Again, I got lost. It was dark and I'd forgotten my directions and I didn't have the head for reading maps now. I asked twice, and got to the Kingshighway exit. And from there to Ahmed's house. Eleven-thirty. Dark. But people were still on the streets.

Think, Nick. Plan it the way you plan a game. You shouldn't actually be doing this now, without having thought out all the angles beforehand. Think, Nick!

I drove to Lindell and a late-hours diner and sat at the counter and tried to think and didn't do very well. That view from Ellie's window kept getting in the way; Ahmed's hand moving boldly, confidently up my little girl's leg to her cunt...

I turned my head and looked out a large plate-glass window. A few blocks up Lindell was Alexis's shop. Tomorrow Ellie would be there. I could walk in as I had that first time. I could bring coffee and pastry and start all over again.

But that hand creeping up her leg. And Harvey-boo. No starting again. Not yet. And no copping out any more.

It was simple enough, the job I had to do tonight. I'd wait another twenty minutes, until twelve-thirty. I'd go down those stairs, light the wick, break the window, throw the firebomb inside, run to the car, drive back to the motel, and fly home tomorrow morning.

Simple, if no one on the street interfered, if no exceptionally bad breaks took place.

Simple ... but far from a foolproof plan covering all contingencies.

I just didn't have the head to sit down and plan games now! I had to *do* it! Do it, and get rid of some of the pressure!

I paid and walked outside. This was the bad neighbourhood Ellie had described; the going-black neighbourhood. I walked. No one on the streets. I didn't think I'd care if someone jumped me. Maybe a mugging, a bad beating, would stop me, force me to wait long enough to lose the insanity...

Two black men were coming toward me. Afro hair and black trousers and black jackets ... and wasn't that the way Panthers dressed? And if they hurt me, I wouldn't be able to fry Ahmed tonight ... and the thoughts I'd had a moment ago were bullshit, because I *had* to fry Ahmed tonight. Besides, I was afraid of being hurt without it meaning anything in terms of Ellie.

I turned and hurried back. In my car, the door locked and the engine catching, I saw the two blacks look at me as they swaggered by. They were laughing. They'd have laughed even harder if they'd known the truth ... a truth I'd realized just a moment ago: I would risk death, if it were in the fight for Ellie. Scout's honour. I would risk *anything*, in the attempt to win Ellie. But I was more afraid for my life, my safety, in all other areas, areas unrelated to Ellie, than I'd ever been before. I was *terrified* of anything that would take me out of the fight for Ellie.

I looked, and the two men were gone. I shut off the engine, took the keys, went round back, and opened the trunk. I found a jack handle and went back inside the car and drove to Ahmed's. I parked about ten feet before the basement entrance, left the engine running, took the firebomb from its towel-wrapping, got out carrying firebomb and jack handle, left the car door open, and walked, did-not-run, to the stairs. I looked up and down and around the street, saw no one, ran down the steps, reached the darkened window and closed door ... and found myself with hands full and no way to break the window and light the bomb and do what I had to do.

I froze for perhaps ten seconds. Then I put down both jack handle and bomb, got out my matches, struck one, and bent to light the bomb. The match went out. If only I'd thought to buy a windproof lighter! I struck another match, crouching over the bomb, and this time was able to keep it alight. The wick, my handkerchif, simply smouldered. I pinched out the spark, then turned the bottle upside down, allowing gasoline to seep into the cloth. I struck another match. Now the wick caught and flared, and now I had to move fast. But as I grabbed the jack handle with my left hand, the bottle with my right, and began to straighten, it seemed I was in a dream, moving in that frustrating, terrifying slow-motion ... only that was more bullshit, as Ellie would say, and I was in a situation where there was no time for bullshit! That bottle could explode in a few more seconds and Nickie, not Ahmed, would fry!

I smashed the window with the metal bar. The sound shocked me, it was so loud, but the glass broke well, half the lower pane falling inside. There was only a wispy half-curtain in the way, and I threw the bottle as hard as I could and turned and began to run up the stairs. I heard a heavy whoosh, and was illuminated by a bright flash, and then I reached the street. I ran to the car, got inside, and pulled away closing the door. Before I could congratulate myself, the Ford stalled. I was almost parallel with that basement entrance as I struggled to start up again. But the fucking thing had automatic gear, as did most rental cars, and I was accustomed to a stickshift, and I couldn't make the starter work no matter how many times I turned the key.

For one panicked moment I grabbed the door handle, ready to cut and run, feeling I had to get away before someone saw me, before the police came, before I was caught and stopped in my fight for Ellie before I'd really gotten started. Then I remembered that there was no clutch and that I therefore couldn't start in any gear.

I had to shift the lever to Park and start it there. I did, and the engine caught. As I shifted back into Drive, a man came running up those stairs; and as I drove off he reached the street and I saw he was naked and looking back down the stairs. Then I was at the end of the street and turning toward the parkway entrance.

The naked man was Ahmed. He hadn't fried. It had all been for nothing. He'd be back playing with Ellie the next time Harv was away. And I might still be caught.

I got lost again. But I didn't stop to ask for directions. I was finally beginning to think. And I was horrified at how many chances I'd taken. If there was ever a next time, I'd use my *Yiddisher kopf!*

Only when I was on Lindbergh, a few minutes from the motel, did something occur to me. Ahmed hadn't bothered to look around for his assailant, or even to cover his nakedness. Instead, he'd turned to look down the stairs. Was that a natural reaction – to see how bad the fire was – or was he looking to see if someone else had gotten out? And could that someone else be *Ellie?*

But Harv. She *lived* with Harv.

Or did he spend a few evenings a week with her? And was this one of the evenings he *didn't* spend with her? Or had he left town on business? *Anything* that could keep him away would give her the opportunity to join Ahmed, to continue the session I'd interrupted at her apartment.

I almost turned around to drive to her place and ring the bell and see for myself. I had to fight to keep going. I had to keep telling myself it was impossible ... or so improbable as not to deserve consideration.

I was in this thing to win, and I'd never be able to win if I fell victim to such fears and horrors!

And still I sweated. And in the room I turned on the television, but all that was on was a late movie. Maybe they would interrupt to bring a news flash. This was bound to be a big story, locally.

I wished I'd thought to bring my transistor radio.

I drank a water glass full of Scotch and put the towel back in the bathroom, and then realized it smelled of gasoline. And that the gas can was still in the rear of the Ford. And I had two pop bottles ...

The pop bottles were nothing; they sold by the thousands each day. I emptied them in the toilet and went down to the car, taking them and the towel with me. There wasn't a soul around. I emptied the gas into the Ford's tank; then drove slowly along Lindbergh until I saw a dark side road. I took it, and found a wooded spot with no houses nearby. I carried the can and towel in among the trees, put down the can, wiped it thoroughly with the towel and began to throw the towel away; then stopped. It had the motel name on it.

I returned to the Ford, and drove further down the road. At another dark spot, I broke the law by littering – wiped both bottles thoroughly, and threw them out the window, holding each with an end of the towel. Now there was nothing to connect me with that firebombing . . . except for the towel.

I tried the car radio on the way back; nothing but rock music.

In the room, I found I was trembling with exhaustion and wet with perspiration. I ran a hot tub, and as it filled I scrubbed out the towel in the sink. I sniffed it, and could smell no gasoline, and scrubbed it once again and hung it over the shower-curtain rail.

I mixed a large Scotch and water, and sipped it while I soaked in that hot tub. Everything drained out of me, and I was even able to discount the fear that Ellie might have been in Ahmed's apartment. And then I realized something startling, and wonderful : I'd broken a two-month stretch of agony tonight. I'd made mistakes; I'd sweated and feared; and Ahmed had gotten away, unhurt as far as I'd been able to tell. But I wasn't suffering the thoughts of Ellie being with other men; the thoughts that had tormented me continuously since the end of her month of forced abstinence following the abortion. And this with a failure. Imagine how good I'd feel with a success! Soon there'd be Harv. How fantastic *that* would feel! There's be no need for pills and booze then. There'd be peace . . . and then there'd be Ellie.

It was almost two a.m. when I got into bed. I leaned back against the pillows and took the phone from the nightstand and dialled Ellie's number. On the third ring, the phone was lifted. There were a few seconds of silence, which I didn't break. Then Ellie said, 'Hello?' and my heart jumped with relief that she was safe. 'Hello? Please . . . hello, *Nickie*?' My heart jumped again, in pain and pity, as I recognized the fear in her voice.

Smart girl, my little love. She knew whom to be afraid of.

I wanted to say something, to comfort her, to tell her how much I still loved her.

But I remembered Ahmed's hand moving into the black thatch between her legs, and Harv's underwear mixed in with her panties and those spotted sheets, and my few hours of peace came to an end. I hung up.

TEN

When I arrived at LaGuardia Airport the next morning, I checked the Manhattan Telephone directory. The number I had for Aaron Hoff was at his business address, and today was Saturday, and I wanted to get Harv's contract in the works *immediately*. I'd thought it all out on the plane; knew exactly what I was going to do in terms of protecting myself from suspicion, and in manoeuvring Ellie back to New York.

Aaron lived in Sutton Place, no less. The mob business must be a lot better than the garment business.

He answered, sounding sleepy. It was eleven-fifteen and, somehow, I'd never thought of Aaron sleeping late.

When I said, 'I want to discuss a zero...' he came fully awake and laughed to drown me out and said, 'Hey, jokes this time of the morning, and *on the phone*? You want to have some brunch? Meet me at The Eggery,' and he gave me the address.

He was in a booth, eating pancakes and sausages when I came in, lugging my flight bag. 'Been out of town?'

I sat down, putting my bag on the seat beside me. 'Yes, St Louis.'

He looked at me, shook his head. 'How long's it been since I last saw you? Five months? Six Months? Jesus, Nick, you've aged ten years since then!'

'That's why I'm here.'

'Order something and then you can tell me. Just keep your voice down. I got good ears. And don't *ever* talk about such things on the phone! I could have a tap on me.'

I ordered coffee. When the waitress said they served nothing alcoholic, I waited for her to leave and finished the half bottle of Scotch from the side pocket of my flight bag. Scotch doesn't go with coffee as well as brandy or rum or even bourbon for that matter... but I made do. Aaron said, 'Is it *that bad*?'

'It'll get a lot better if a gentleman named Harvey Cohen dies.'

I gave him whatever information I had on Harvey-boo; background, his home address, his spending nights at Ellie's address, his business background, his general description.

'No picture?' Aaron asked.

I shook my head, sorry I hadn't searched Ellie's place for snapshots.

'No sweat, Nick.' He finished his coffee, and caught the waitress's eye. 'Want to tell me anything more? *Why*, for example?'

'Just that while he lives, I die by degrees.'

'There's no other way of handling it? Say a quarter to begir with?'

'You trying to talk me out of it?'

'With a friend, yes. Because some people get attacks of conscience later and suffer, and why risk it if it's not absolutely necessary? Just want to make you think it over.'

'I've thought it over for months. There's no other way. It's me or him. He fast, or me slow.'

'A woman?'

I nodded.

'These things don't usually work out. What I mean is, if it's a divorce the client wants and can't get, of course the zero works out. Or a business partnership that needs dissolving. But eliminating the competition for a woman, not often. Mostly, the woman doesn't want that particular man, no matter who else is involved or not involved.'

'I can see that. It's just not so in this case.'

'They all say that. But you're a bright guy, Nick. An experienced guy. You should be able to accept a situation.'

I finished my Scotch-coffee, and tried to think of it Aaron's way, and couldn't. 'I've been talking against it myself for a month, Aaron. It's got to be done ... either through you, or by my own hand.'

'God forbid,' Aaron said piously. 'You're too smart for that, right?'

I nodded ... and wondered what he would think of last night and reminded myself to go to the big newstand on Forty-second and Broadway for a St Louis paper late tonight. The morning editions they'd handed out on the plane hadn't carried anything about the firebombing.

'All right,' Aaron said, after the waitress had refilled both our cups. 'It's twenty-five hundred dollars.'

'I thought it was two thousand?'

'That was some years ago, Nick. Inflation hits everything.'

'You'll want cash, I suppose?'

He nodded. 'If you've got more than one bank account, I suggest you take part from each, just to play safe. Not that a man in your position can't explain a sum as small as twenty-five hundred.'

I told him I planned to leave for Europe in about a week ... to pull myself together, and also to provide myself with an alibi, in case it was needed.

'You think it'll be needed?' he asked. 'You've been making public

275

threats?'

'Not public, no.'

'Threaten Cohen?'

'No, but I talked tough to the girl about what I'd do to him,'

'That's all right. Everybody does that. But not in front of witnesses?'

'No.'

'Can you leave for Europe, say, next Saturday?'

'If you want an exact day, yes.'

'Only so that I can pass it along. Then nothing'll be done until you're out of the country. It sometimes takes a while anyway, especially on an out-of-town contract. We don't have too much on Cohen. But as long as he shows up at his house, or the Ballwin address ... that's the girl's place, right?'

I nodded briefly.

'Then we'll have no real trouble. A scenario will be worked up and I'd guess in this case it'll be robbery rather than hit-and-run or suicide or anything too sophisticated. Because they'll want to check his wallet or identification before the actual hit. Robbery is always effective. You'd be surprised how many robberies are actually contract killings.'

'My name won't be bandied about? I mean, no one but you will know? I don't want to end up being blackmailed...'

'Nick!' Aaron was genuinely upset; he rocked a little in his seat. 'You know me better than that! Besides, that's not the way a big outfit does business.'

I had to smile. He didn't like it. 'If you want to end it here,' he began.

'I'd love to, but I can't. I told you, it's a matter of survival.'

He nodded, and relaxed. 'Looking at you, I can well believe it.' He lit a cigar. 'Frankly, Nick, I'm surprised, and disappointed. I never figured you for the type to play sucker for a broad.'

'Neither did I. We learn something new about ourselves every day, don't we.'

'Not me. I get all the gash I want, from teen-age tyros to madames who can do things with their cunts you wouldn't believe. And that's *all* I want. And not so much of that any more. I don't want to learn anything new about myself. It's dangerous.'

'I envy you, Aaron.' I meant it.

He shook his head. 'It doesn't figure, Nick. A man like you. The girls in your office ... a blind man can see how they look at you. And it's no secret you've been getting the best for years. How did it happen? Is she some sort of super-brain? Looks alone couldn't do it, not with you.'

'I don't know how it happened. She's no super-brain; far from it.' I paused to think. I never tired of this subject; never tired of trying to find out how it *had* happened. 'And while she's good-looking, I'm sure you could find as good or better on any street in New York ... though I no longer can.'

'Then what?'

'I think it's fucking.'

'How different ... ?'

'Very different. With her, it's more than it's ever been.'

'She got a golden cunt or something?' He laughed.

'Platinum, Aaron. for me. Diamonds and rubies.'

'And that's *all* it is, cunt?'

No use talking to him. He was like Ron, like everyone else I knew. Maybe there *were* men who would understand what I felt, but I didn't know them. To say, tbout Ellie and me, 'And that's *all* it is, cunt?' was like saying about breathing, 'And that's *all* it is, air?'

I smiled. 'A *mishigas,* Aaron. An insanity.'

He kept his eyes on me. 'Don't let it go past this, Nick. I mean, if this doesn't work ...'

'It will.'

He said he was going to have more coffee and read his paper. We would lunch Friday at Gatsby's, and I'd give him the money then. I was to call him if there was any change in my travel plans.

I left, caught a cab, and was home fifteen minutes later. I called Louise and arranged to come over at three. Denise and her boyfriend were there. I'd take them and Seth out to dinner.

I was just stepping into the shower when I thought I heard the phone ring. I cut the water to listen. Yes ... and I ran for the bedroom, but it had stopped by the time I got there. I waited a few minutes; then returned to the shower. When I came out, it was ringing again ... but stopped before I could even leave the bathroom. Probably Harold. He'd have a fit when I told him I was going to London next week.

I dressed, and began thinking that I should take Seth and Denise to see my mother. But it was almost two, and before we could drive up to Peekskill ...

I'd ask them to come along with me tomorrow.

The phone rang.

'Nickie? I've been trying to get you all day. Where've you been?'

'All day? It's not quite two. I slept late and went down for breakfast and played a little tennis and showered and here I am.'

'Where were you last night? I tried then too.'

'Went out. I'm taking your advice, little girl. I'm dating again. Not with pleasure, but still . . .'

'I called at three o'clock in the morning! And at five!'

'That's four and six here. I think I got back at about six-thirty. Real late night.'

Silence. Then, 'Are you sure?'

'Am I sure? Do you mean whether it was six-twenty or six-thirty?'

She laughed quickly. 'You were in St Louis, weren't you? C'mon, honey, admit it.'

'Are you insane? If I was in St Louis, wouldn't I see you?'

Silence.

'What's this all about, Ellie? You're making even less sense than usual.'

'All right! I . . . well, I got upset and wanted to . . . just shoot the breeze.'

'So shoot.'

'Very funny.'

When she didn't go on, I asked the big question. 'What were you upset about?'

'Oh, some dumb things. My doorbell ringing and no one there. Phone calls with a crazy voice saying something about Fatah and another with no one answering. You *sure* you didn't . . . ?'

'Fatah?'

'Al Fatah, that Arab thing.'

'How come you know about it?'

'A friend of mine . . . well, Ahmed, you know, Charlie's accountant.'

'Yes, your ass-fucker.'

'I made that up. Anyway, he told me he was in it; just raising money, I think. What *else* can you do in St Louis?' Pause. 'Something happened to him last night.'

'Hope it wasn't minor.'

'Nickie . . . you couldn't . . . ?'

'Listen, I'm on my way out to see Seth and Denise. If you want to talk, all right. If not, I have something to say and then I have to go. And what I've got to say is specific, and important for both of us.'

'What is it?' Again she sounded frightened. Oh, yes, my little girl's instincts were sharp . . . but I surprised her.

'I'm going to Europe next Saturday. For the same reason that I went out last night. I'm trying to be reasonable. I'm trying to let you go your own way, as you want. I'll do a little business with a company in London that handles our line, and look up some friends. I've been there three times before, and always enjoyed it, and ... perhaps I'll be able to think more clearly.'

'Good idea,' she said, voice subdued.

'A better idea would be if you came along with me.'

'You ... you'd *really* want me to come?'

I kept myself from telling her just how much. But I was still the dumbshit, and I became hopeful and excited. 'You know I do, honey. We could have a ball in London! It's the most civilized, interesting, enjoyable city on earth. And the English countryside ... even this time of the year, you'd love it. We could visit the Cotswolds – rent a car and drive there, and all the way up to Scotland. From Glasgow, we could take a plane to Switzerland. Do you know you can sample German, French, and Italian culture, all in that one little country? Then we could to on to Copenhâgen, Oslo, Stockholm ...'

'Nickie, you know I'm working. I've got a life here. I can't throw everything away again.'

'Just three weeks. Make it *two*. You could talk Alexis into giving you two weeks; you know you could.'

'I *can't*. Please don't ask me any more.'

I took a deep breath. I had to play it cool; had to remember the real reason for my trip to London. But then again, the underlying reason, the true reason, was to be with Ellie, and if I could be with her sooner ...

'I understand,' I said. Yes, I understood. Her Harvey-boo would be unhappy if she left for two weeks. Her Charlie would miss those 'shots' at her ass, miss pawing her, and maybe he got more than shots and touches now. Yes, I understand ... but this time I had something to stop the trembling: Aaron Hoff and the scenario for Harv.

She still hadn't told me about the fire at Ahmed's apartment. I couldn't ask, but I could angle the conversation back to him.

'I'll write you; let you know where I'm staying. I generally choose a small place, like White's Hotel off Hyde Park. Maybe you'll change your mind and join me. You're sort of low now. Those phone nuts can bug a girl. But don't let it get you down *too* much. What can happen to you on the phone? Besides, he was talking about Al Fatah, not you. Or didn't you tell me everything he said?'

'All he said was, "Al Fatah won't triumph"; something like that.'

'Why should he call *you* with a statement like that? Unless, of course, you're very tight with this Ahmed?'

'I just see him once in a while.'

'You told me you didn't any more. Now you say you do.'

'I don't have to answer questions about my private life!'

'Right. But Al Fatah is a terrorist organization, and if you spend much time with its members, and the opposition decides you're part of it, well, whatever happens to Ahmed can happen to you.'

'What do you mean by *that*? You're threatening me, right? You're saying I'm going to be firebombed just like him!'

'Firebombed? He was *firebombed*? Jesus, Ellie, stay out of that kind of scene!'

'Nickie...' She was almost crying. 'Nickie, you're not ... Ahmed's apartment was firebombed last night. He just got out. All his things were burned up. He had a lot of Charlie's records there and he wanted to go back in and get them, but he couldn't. The fire department saved the building, but his place was totalled. And he doesn't have insurance. Charlie's mad as hell that Ahmed took the book home.'

'Guess he wasn't working during the day, the way he was supposed to.' Small laugh. 'Guess he was working on ass instead of books, right? So he had to do his day's work at night.'

'You sound *glad*!'

'I'm certainly not crying, baby. For two reasons. One, you've obviously been playing around with him. Two, I'm a Jew, remember? Bet you won't get Harv to sympathize much either.'

'Harv's not that way! He said it was *terrible*! He hopes the police catch whoever did it!'

'And I'm sure they will. Crime doesn't pay, and so on. Was Ahmed hurt?'

'He cut his foot running, and his hair was singed.'

'Well, let's hope they get him the next time.'

'That's terrible! He's the sweetest, gentlest guy! And there won't be a next time. He's going to Algeria where he has relatives in business. He says he's going to *really* work against the Jews now. And I don't blame him!'

'I'd better get going. Have to visit a little Jew named Seth. I'll call you at the store Monday.'

'And something else. You might as well know ... he thinks there's a good chance *you* did it! But he's too scared to tell the police. And no proof. But he said you sounded crazy enough, ...'

'So you've been talking about me? Harv thinks I'm an abortionist sonovabitch, and Ahmed thinks I'm an arsonist bomb-thrower. You paint a pretty picture of the man you care more for than any man in the world!'

'It wasn't that way at all! He asked where I'd been all those months, and I told him how I'd lived with you and how jealous you were.'

'While he was doing the books in the store, right? Goodbye, Ellie.'

'Nickie ... wait. Honey, you *didn't* have anything to do with it, did you?'

'Of course I did. And the next time you fuck around with a man, betraying my fellow Jew, Harvey-boo, I'll try to fry that bastard too.' I hung up.

It was working well; perhaps a little too well. I hadn't counted on her being suspicious of me. When Harv got it, the suspicions would be bound to multiply. But after Harv, I would work hard to convince her I'd had nothing to do with either attack. After Harv, I'd be all love and softness; open arms waiting to comfort.

Unless, of course, she was crazy enough to continue to resist returning to me. Then the pressure would begin to mount; then the muscle would begin to shove her back to me.

She called again. I'd been reasonably sure she would.

She had to convince herself she was wrong in her suspicions ... or say things that would protect her Harvey-boo.

'Nickie, I'm sorry I said those dumb things. I know you wouldn't do such a thing. I mean, in Miami that nut was trying to hurt us, but poor Ahmed ... and I don't even have anything to do with him, I mean, personally.'

I remained silent.

'Anyway, he's leaving Wednesday.'

'I'm sure you'll get in one more session on the couch before then.'

I'd slipped! In my anger at her lie, in my anguish at the memory of his hand moving into her bush, I'd slipped!

But she didn't pick it up. She probably figured I was speaking generically, of couches in general, not of *her* couch.

'I'm not going to see him, except maybe if he has to come to the store again. And I don't think he will. He's hiding out with friends. He's afraid to walk out on the street.'

'Awful.'

'Call me Monday, Nickie. I wish I could go to London with you. I miss you a little more each day, honey. Send me lots of post cards, and when you come back I'll visit you, I promise.'

'All right.'

'What's the matter?'

I hadn't played ping-pong, hadn't leaped to the joy-side of the net at her little handout of verbal affection. 'Nothing, except I'd like to see you *before* I go.'

'Oh, you'll be too busy . . .'

'I won't be too busy to fuck you! Everyone else does, so why not good old friend Nickie!'

'No one . . . you can't say things like that!'

'Goodbye.'

'Nickie, wait . . . I'm afraid . . .' She was crying, I didn't soften. She gave Ahmed what I wanted. She gave Harv what I wanted. But she wouldn't allow me to fly a thousand miles to spend a few nights with her. *To hell with her!*

I almost hated her enough to be free at that moment . . . but then she said, voice thick, 'If you want to come, all right.'

'You'll spend two or three nights with me, at my motel?'

'Well, I have to go home to *sleep.*'

'Why?'

'Liz has been staying with me.'

'Forget it.'

'Nickie, honest . . .'

'Honest?' I laughed. 'You forgot about honesty when you returned to St Louis.'

'Maybe!' she shouted. 'But so would you if you were *afraid* of someone! If I told you I'm over twenty-one and can be with whom I want and do *what* I want, just like your Ledya or Karen or cock-sucking married girlfriend, what would you answer? That you'd kill everyone who touches me? That you'd kill *me?* Do you say that to your other girlfriends?'

'I don't have other girlfriends. And you're not a girlfriend. You're my life. And we've been through this a hundred times. And yes, you can't tell me about other men in your life, because with you that means other men in your cunt. And what does Harvey-boo think about Ahmed and whoever else you're fucking?'

'He has nothing to say about my friends! Even though I see him a lot . . .'

'And live with him?'

'See him a lot! And he knows I go out!'

'It turns him on, I suppose?'

'He doesn't like it, but he allows me my freedom. I told you – Harv understands me better than you, better than anyone. He's *patient*, and he'll probably end up marrying me.'

'Thank you,' I said, sick to my stomach, 'for that one truth. But you're wrong. No matter what it takes, or how long it takes, you're coming back to me. Back to the dumbshit abortionist monster!'

'No way,' she whispered.

I said, 'Let's forget my visiting St Louis. I'll see you after I get back from Europe. The invitation to come to London still stands. Or you can join me when I'm there. But the odds are that I won't see you until after I get back. Maybe by then we'll both have calmed a bit. Maybe by then we can be what you want us to be ... friends.'

'Oh, Nickie, how I want that! And maybe later, who knows ... I mean, I never know how I might feel.'

'All right. Can I have a kiss?'

The little lip-popping sound came. I said goodbye. She said, 'Don't I get one?'

What did she need with lip-pops when she had all that cock in St Louis? But I sent it to her.

When I got to Teaneck, Denise and her boyfriend had left. Louise explained that a friend had come by with an invitation to a weekend party in Saddle River, and Denise had felt I'd understand. They wouldn't return until tomorrow night, and then it was right back to school. I probably wouldn't see her before leaving for England, because next weekend they were skiing in Vermont.

I didn't take kindly to it. I made Daddy noises about spoiled kids and having had to work my nuts off when I went to college; and Seth looked at me and said, 'You kidding, Dad?'

It made me laugh. 'Right,' I said, and hugged him.

Louise said, 'I know you won't mind if I leave. I stayed around just to say hello.' She was going into Manhattan to see her Philip and his son. 'Can you tell me how long you exptect to stay?'

I said until about eight.

'Then I'll be back at eight-thirty. Phil will probably come with me.'

I told her I was leaving for Europe next Saturday. She said, 'Have fun,' a touch of acid in her voice. She'd always wanted to travel, and for most of our marriage I'd been working too hard to take time off. Then she said, 'Are you sure it's the wise thing to do? I mean, with your mother the way she is? I'd hate to think she might pass away while you were gone. It's up to you, of course...'

I didn't take kindly to that either, and said there was no indication Mom was in danger of dying, was there?

'At her age, in her condition...' She shrugged.

'Then what you're saying is that I should sit around and *wait* for her to die. Perhaps hope for her to die so as to be free...?'

'I don't have to take your undergraduate psychology any more, Nick!' And out she went.

Seth and I played football in the yard, taking turns running pass patterns. He was getting damned good at throwing, but his catching still left much to be desired. He worked on it, until we were both pooped. Then we drove to the Forum on Route 4 for hamburgers and Cokes. I enjoyed watching the pretty blonde hostess, and wondered if I were finally beginning to loosen up with other women. But when she smiled at me, I understood what it was. She reminded me of Ellie. I was hungering for Ellie.

I asked Seth if he would come with me tomorrow to visit Grandma Leib. He said, 'Sure, Dad.' I said we would take our sneakers and sweatshirts and run along an aqueduct I'd spotted near the nursing home. No 'Sure Dad' this time; just a glum nod. Well, it was good for him; he'd thank me for it some day; and I needed his company.

I asked him what he thought of Phil, and of his mother marrying again.

He shrugged, but he wasn't at all upset; far less so than he was about running with me tomorrow. In fact. I felt he was hiding a considerable amount of enthusiasm.

'He's okay, Dad. You'd like him. He's in real good shape. Boy, can he throw a football! He played in college; he showed me his letter. And he has a neat car – a Mercedes sports coupé. It isn't too fast, but it looks great and he says it handles better than the Porsche in normal highway driving and city traffic. He had a seat built in back, so it holds four.'

I nodded. He added quickly, 'I like the Porsche better.'

I smiled to show him I appreciated his tact. We ate. A little later, he returned to the subject of Phil and his son. 'Chrisie's a nice kid. It's fun being a big brother.' He grinned. 'Boy, if I treat him like Denise used to treat me, the end!'

'What does Denise think of Phil?'

'She really likes him.' He mocked her voice: 'A real *doll*!'

From Seth's description, Louise had landed quite a hunk of man, and a successful lawyer to boot.

I was still at the house at eight-thirty, Seth and I having gotten involved in a TV movie and forgotten the time ... and in walked Louise and Phil. She covered her surprise, and chagrin; he came on calm and confident, and with good reason. He was as well-preserved a mid-forties specimen as I've seen, with modishly long hair and a bushy moustache, and I'd have hated to compete with him for any girl. To put it more specifically, and honestly, I'd have avoided introducing him to Ellie.

He greeted Seth with a smile and a shake of the hand; no patronizing talk or touches, and no tension or discomfort because of my presence. Seth, however, was far from comfortable, glancing at me every so often. I apologized for overstaying my leave. Louise said, 'Quite all right, Nicholas.' I said my goodnights, kissed Seth, and left.

I drove to the big newstand in Times Square and got a St Louis Post Dispatch. At home, I found the story on Page Two. It wasn't at all what I'd expected, and I wondered if Ellie had seen it. The headline read: FIREBOMBING OR BOMB FACTORY? The story stated that 'The apartment of Mr Ahmed Dahnoran on West Pine was totally destroyed in a fire started by an incendiary device. Firemen saved the building only after a long fight. When questioned, Mr Dahnoran said a firebomb had been thrown through his window, igniting the blaze. Neighbours, however, stated that Mr Dahnoran was a member of a clandestine organization and that he had occasionally been in possession of anti-Semitic leaflets and, some believed, explosives. Mr Dahnoran categorically denied both statements. He said the leaflets were anti-Zionist and applied only to the state of Israel and its supporters. He said he had never handled explosives. However, under questioning, he admitted he was a member of the American branch of Al Fatah, which police officials classified as an activist-terrorist group. An officer of the bomb squad said the firebombs called Molotov Cocktails were often produced by members of terrorist groups in their homes, and that they occasionally ignited by accident, as when in the presence of lighted cigarettes. Mr Dahnoran smokes, but insisted he was asleep at the time of the alleged firebombing. An investigation is currently under way. Mr Dahnoran has expressed a wish to emigrate to Algeria. Police had no comment, but a member of the District Attorney's office pointed out that there was no evidence on which to hold Mr Dahnoran. Neighbours feel an example should be made of those who use their private residences to carry on dangerous political work . . .'

That story, along with one of Dr Ron Levine's super-pills, sent me to dreamland with a minimum of bad thoughts. Of course, Ellie was with Harv. She was in his arms. And it still tore up my insides, even though the bastard's days were numbered.

I picked Seth up at ten the next morning and we drove to Peekskill. My mother recognized him as soon as we walked in the door, and tried to get out of her wheelchair. She couldn't of course. She looked down at herself, frowning, and said, 'I hurt my leg. Who knows when it'll heal, with such doctors. How are you, my *sheinah zeindele*?' Seth kissed her and said he was fine. She looked at me.

She kept looking at me, and I began to sweat. 'Are you feeling well, Mom?'

She sighed. 'Who he is, I don't know.'

Seth laughed; then realized she wasn't joking, and went pale. I said, 'Grandma is very tired.'

'I'm *not* tired. If I don't know people, they tell me I'm tired. You give me five minutes, I'll remember you. Rosie's boy?'

If it wasn't for Seth being there, I think I'd have walked out. It suddenly seemed too much. I know I should have been understanding and patient ... but she didn't know me and I didn't know me and who the hell was I anyway?

Words. Bullshit, as my little love would say. But my love had left me and my son was getting a great new step-father and my mother thought I was Rosie's boy and I was anxious to kill people and was this really Nick Leib?

Will the real Nick Leib please stánd up?

Two other guys were standing up somewhere – a businessman, and a father; a serious, successful toy maker, and a smiling, loving daddy. They were both phonies.

The real Nick Leib was in a room in a nursing home, looking at his mother, and not with joy or love or compassion; the real Nick Leib's face was a mask that hid all the evils of the world, the seven deadly sins, and prime among them was murder. The real Nick Leib was Mr Hyde. I hated him ... but I'd go along with him until death us did part.

Seth and I stayed with my mother for perhaps half an hour, and it was the longest half-hour of my life. She became sleepy toward the end, and I had an excuse to get us out of there. The nurse in the lobby asked how our visit had gone. Seth said, 'I don't think she knew my father – her son.' She smiled and patted his head and said, 'Mrs Leib's smarter than all of us. She'll know him next time. She knows me most days ...'

I drew Seth away from the patronizing bundle of bullshit who was speaking of my mother as if she were an infant. Fuck doctors, and nurses too!

We changed into sneakers and hooded sweatshirts in the men's room, and put our other clothing in the car. Then we crossed Oregon Road and climbed a fence and began trotting up a long, gentle incline. Seth talked at first, asking me about my trip to Europe, but then he concentrated on simply breathing as the incline grew steeper. And I was able to wash my mind clean of agony with pure physical effort. Afterward, we had lunch, and went to a movie in Teaneck.

I was back in the apartment at seven-thirty. I looked over my clothing, planning what to take with me. I sat down at the phone and called BOAC. I made arrangements to fly out on a 747 Saturday evening. I also asked if they would reserve a single for me at White's Hotel and bill me for the cable charges. Then I showered, sat down with a drink ... and wondered what the hell I would do with myself until Saturday.

I called Ron. I asked if we could get together tomorrow. He said he had office hours until four-thirty. Vera was going to be out with a theatre group. Would I come over for a drink?

Great. Tomorrow night was taken care of.

Now for Tuesday, Wednesday, and Thursday. (*Don't think of them!*)

Friday morning I'd take money from each of my three bank accounts – the two savings banks and the commercial bank where I had my checking account. Friday afternoon was lunch with Aaron, and the closing of the contract. Saturday morning was departure day.

I called Ellie at ten-thirty the next morning. She answered, saying, 'Alexis Men's Fashions.'

'Hi, it's Nick.'

'Watcha doing?'

'Nothing. And you?'

'Reading. Things are slow, so I can relax.'

'Wish *I* could. But memories ...'

'You know what happened to Ahmed? The goddam pigs picked him up yesterday and questioned him for three hours! They tried to make him say he was filling soda bottles with gasoline in his apartment and that's how the fire happened!'

'Maybe that's the way it was.'

'Oh, c'mon now!'

'How can you be sure?'

'Because I know him! Because in more than a year I never saw him lose his cool or really want to hurt anyone.'

'Just Israeli Jews and their supporters, right?'

'He never even went to the Fatah meetings! They stuck him with a few pamphlets and he threw most of them away. I *know* the guy, I tell you!'

'Only from the rear.'

She laughed a little. 'Funny *mans*. Anyway, he's leaving Wednesday; got his flight and all. He wanted me to tell you he was going and wouldn't see me any more.'

'*He's* the funny mans.' But he wasn't, of course. He was the smart

287

mans, the shrewd perceptive mans. 'Still, you'll be safe from haemorrhoids.'

'What?'

'Piles. Rectal swellings.'

'Will you *please* cut that out?'

I heard a voice then. She said, away from the phone, 'Just a moment, sir.' And to me, whispering. 'Well, gotta go now. Customer. If he buys something he gets a bonus.'

I could see some nice young guy looking her over. Would he make a pass? Would she be receptive? 'Ellie ... honey, no more.'

She laughed. 'Maybe now you won't ask personal questions.'

'Will you be at the store Saturday? I'd like to speak to you before I leave for the airport.'

'I'll be here.'

'Goodbye.'

'Nickie ... I didn't want to upset you. It's just that I really turned on.'

'I know, cunt!'

'For *you*, dumbshit! I've been thinking of you a lot the last few days.'

Since the doorbell episode and anonymous phone calls and fire-bombing. 'In what way?'

'You always ask stupid questions! *In what way!* If I'm thinking of you, that means I miss you and want to see you. When you get back from Europe. But I really gotta go now. Give me a kiss.'

I popped my lips. She whispered, 'The guy is standing too close. I owe you one.'

'Sure. Give it to him, along with his fuck.'

Little laugh. 'If I wanted to operate that way, I'd be a million-aire.'

'No, just a whore.' I hung up.

I was sick of her. She *was* a whore.

Ledya and Karen and Ruth did as much, perhaps more. It was just that Ellie had to belong to me, and me alone. I no longer tried to reason it away; no longer questioned it. It had become a fact of life.

I drove to Teaneck and Ron's home at four-thirty. His office was on the playroom level of the big three-level house. There was no one in his waiting room, but he came out of his office in response to the automatic door chime and said, 'Still at it. Read a National Geographic.'

'Got one with naked natives?'

He grinned. 'You should see the naked native inside.' He closed

288

the door.

A few minutes later, a tall pretty black girl came out, looking back at Ron and laughing. 'That part of the treatment?' she asked.

'Only if they dissolve the AMA next week.'

They both laughed. She left. I said, 'The doctors are restless tonight.'

We walked into his office; he sat at his desk and I sat in front. 'With good reason,' he said. 'That girl has a minor vaginal infection, and a major vaginal area.'

We kept it up a while, and I wondered that I'd ever enjoyed evenings like this. Words. Bullshit. Nothing.

After a while, we walked back through his examination room. I saw his drug cabinet, which he'd once said would keep a heroin addict happy for a month. He stored his more potent sleeping pills, samples from the various companies, there too ... and I was reminded to ask him for a good supply.

'Use up those I gave you last time?'

'Not quite. But I'm leaving for what might be an extended stay in Europe Saturday...'

He lectured me on 'this sudden and dangerous reliance on barbiturates' as he unlocked the cabinet's glass panelled door. I said I was already slackening off. He turned. 'That mean you're finally getting Ellie out of your system?'

'No, it means I'm finally getting into position to win her back.'

He got me two jars of twenty-five capsules each, showing a remarkable confidence in my will to live. When I said I was low on Librium, he added a jar of 100 25-mg tablets of a new product, 'supposed to eliminate tranquillizer hangover ... but don't bet on it'. He warned me that the sleeping pills were 'quite potent', and that I wasn't to exceed two in any twenty-four-hour period.

I was standing behind him, taking the jars as he removed them from the shelves, and I asked about the heroin in his cabinet.

'No heroin. That's a drug-addict's drug, not used by the medical profession.'

'You once said an addict could stay high for a month...'

'Morphine, Nick. Any heroin addict would be happy with morphine. It's taken the same way – by injection, either subcutaneously, or directly into a blood vessel—mainlining it, as the addicts say. Are you thinking of easing your tensions *that* way?'

I laughed. He didn't. He said, 'I know too many people, many of them doctors, who've resigned from life with morphine. Some end their lives with an overdose.' He held up a small hypodermic syringe. 'This is a stylet, a prepared hypodermic, containing a solution of one grain of morphine.' He lifted small plastic box and shook out a few white tablets. 'These contain one grain of morphine each. Dissolved in water and drawn into a hypodermic, they can float away your problems, for a while. Then they themselves constitute the biggest problem on earth, and one that is basically unsolvable. Six of these will kill any man.'

'Ron, I promise not to take anything stronger than pot.'

'Do you have any?'

'Not with me. Want to smoke some?'

'Do you?'

I shrugged. 'I can take it or leave it, far better than alcohol.'

'Not actually proven, but I'll concede the point. And roll you a joint upstairs.'

His Jamaican maid was off for the night, and we were soon settled comfortably in his living room with Tuborg beer, a joint each, Vivaldi on the stereo, and some of Ron's reminiscences of practising medicine on female patients in New Jersey. The higher he got, the juicier were the reminiscences.

'One little teen-aged tramp came for treatment of a staph infection over a period of three weeks, telling me to bill her at the end, and then admitted she didn't have a dime. She was standing in my examination room at the time, and put her hands on her hips and grinned in my face and said, "What are you going to do about it, Doctor?" I didn't tell her. I *showed* her. Shoved her down on the table and gave it to her for fifteen minutes despite a waiting room full of patients.'

'Was it good?' I asked.

'After I stopped being angry, damned good! And do you know what she did? Came back the next week, asking for another session on the table.'

'You sent her away?'

Ron drank beer. 'Pot always gives me a sore throat.' He coughed and drank again.

'You *didn't* send her away.'

'It was dangerous, I know, but I hadn't had a good piece in months, Vera being what she is. Maybe if we'd had children ... well, the kid just pulled down her jeans and lay back, smiling and waiting. It was even better that time.'

'You still see her?'

He shook his head, sallow face glum. 'She said she'd be back, but she disappeared. I checked the address she gave me ... no one there by that name. Little tramp.'

'Think of her once in a while?'

He nodded, took off his glasses, rubbed his eyes. 'Lovely body. Heavy breasts and narrow waist. Just my type. Goddam ... it was two years ago, and I still think of her. Not that I'm hungry for it any more. Vera's a little better lately. And that girl I met at the cocktail lounge...' His voice trailed off. He looked old, my forty-four-year-old friend ... my friend almost two years younger than me. He looked smaller and thinner and over-the-hill. He missed his young cunt. I missed mine.

I went home.

Tuesday, Wednesday, and Thursday ... how to describe them? I created a new game, just for Nick Leib. It was called, *Playing At Being Alive*. Simple rules that even a child – a sick child – can follow.

Nick Leib, hereafter referred to as The Player, goes down to the street. It's cold. He tells himself he will walk and the cold will shake him out of his sickness. As he walks, he talks. He says, 'I warned you, Ellie. You should have listened. You can't go around fucking other men. You're mine. I'm yours. You *must* know that!'

A young woman stares at him. He realizes he's been talking aloud, and bends his head. He loses a point.

The Player goes to the local supermarket, a small 'quality' place that specializes in home deliveries. He feels they charge far too much, but remembers how Ellie criticized him for being cheap in small matters. He shops for steaks, and his bill is thirty-one dollars and sixteen cents. The butcher offers to grind the tails of the porterhouse steaks into hamburger. The Player declines with a smile. He's far too careless of money for *that*, and gains a point.

On the street, he walks briskly, carrying his package. He has purpose now, to bring his package home. *Purpose*, all important to life! Then he remembers he is leaving for Europe on Saturday and has brought more meat than he can possibly eat before then. It will have to lie in the freezer for who-knows-how-long, all this expensive steak, all this clip-joint-priced beef. He is enraged, and loses two points.

Returning to the Starting Point, he enters the elevator and smiles despite two noisy boys kicking at each other's legs as they ride with him all the way to the sixteenth floor. He loses another point just before the door opens, when he snaps, 'Stand *still*, dammit!' The boys freeze, frightened. He strides out, and sees a man in the uniform of an airline pilot. The smile flashes back on his face. The pilot says, 'Hey!' and moves to block The Player from his goal, Home Base. The Player is forced to stop. The pilot says, 'How's Ellie?' The Player just barely retains his smile and insouciance, avoiding the loss of a point. Ellie never told him she gave her name to the jet-propelled lecher. He says, 'Just fine. Visiting with relatives.' The pilot says, 'St Louis, is it?' The Player gains two points with his smile and nod under those most adverse circumstances, and with good body movement and a friendly wave slips by the pilot and strides purposefully to his apartment. The key goes directly into the key-hole, despite a trembling hand, gaining him another point and putting him ahead, plus-four to minus-three. He closes the door, is in Home Base, an apparent winner ... but then he says, 'You fucked him, didn't you, bitch? That night you said you were joking about being in his apartment, the night you ran away from me in the garage and didn't come home until nine or ten hours later. You didn't go to the movies. You let him do what he wanted to do after he watched us on the terrace, when you spread your legs for him to see, teasing, preparing ... Ellie, whore, bitch!' And with a sinking to the couch and an entering into heavy trembling The Player loses *three* points and the game.

At night, the game changed. *Playing At Being Alive* became *Playing At Being At Ease*. The evening's entertainment was TV, pot, Scotch, food, and sleeping pills. Varying combinations were supposed to bring an attitude of relaxation in which The Player could score enough At Ease points to reach the hour of twelve or one, and the goal of sleep. On Tuesday, the goal was reached with relative ease. On Wednesday, it took rather more Scotch and pills than The Player cared to use. On Thursday, the game was forfeit when The Player broke the rules and called Ellie nine times, up until five a.m., the last time screaming into the phone, '*Answer* me! Please ... Ellie ... don't be with him,' and cried like the demented child he was.

I didn't bother sleeping at all that night. I showered at six and drank coffee and had a morning joint and collected my bank books and was the first customer at the First National City Bank, nine a.m., Friday. By noon, I was in possession of twenty-five hundred dollars in fifties and twenties, filling a large manilla envelope, which I placed on the table when I joined Aaron in Gatsby's. He stared at me and said, 'My God. I didn't really believe you when you said it was him fast or you slow. I was right. It's him fast or you fast.'

I laughed. 'Late night,' I said.

He didn't buy it. 'If any of my clients ever had the right to let a contract, it's you. Take it from an experienced observer, don't ever let your conscience bother you. I don't think you can last a month, the way you're going.'

'That's me,' I muttered, gulping my Bloody Mary. 'The boy-chick with *mishigas*, as you once put it.'

'Yeah, but I was speaking of positive *mishigas,* not suicide.'

We ordered. He ate and I drank. By the time we left, he had to steady me with a hand under my elbow and put me in a cab.

Saturday looked easy. I had breakfast with Seth and Louise and said my goodbyes. Louise promised to keep tabs on my mother, and to let me know how the children were.

I was back in the apartment at ten to twelve and called Ellie. Alexis answered, and said she was out sick today. I hung up without leaving my name, and dialled her apartment. No answer. I tried a one-ring signal, a two-ring signal, and a three-ring signal, then let it ring on and on, the morning's comfort fleeing, the insanity returning, muttering, 'Answer, you bitch, *answer*!'

I didn't want to say much. Just goodbye. But I *had* to say that. I didn't know if I could leave without saying goodbye to Ellie.

My flight departed Kennedy Airport at six. The limousine would pick me up at four-ten. I called Ellie's apartment every twenty minutes, until four. I was pretty well shot, pretty well into the pit, by the time I took my luggage down to the lobby.

At the airport, I called again, with the same results.

I was talking to myself as I went through customs. Ten minutes before flight time, I played a hunch and called the store. Ellie answered. And suddenly I had nothing to say. Nothing important. 'Thought you were sick?'

'I was, this morning. Ate pizza last night and it gave me diar-rhoea and bad cramps.'

'You never used to eat pizza.'

'Harv loves it ...' She stopped.

I still had nothing to say, or to feel. Harv was dead. 'Well, take care of yourself, honey. I'll be at White's Hotel. I'll send you the number, or you can get it from the overseas operator.'

'You leaving now, Nickie?'

'Yes, I'm at the airport. Couldn't get you earlier.'

'I cut the phone off at home. Guess I should have called you. But ... my gut was really aching.'

'I'm sorry, little girl.'

'I gotta get on a good diet, take vitamins the way you do, take care of myself. My stomach's been out of whack the last few weeks.'

'You never had stomach aches when you lived with me.'

She laughed a little. 'Just headaches.'

'You been taking any dexies, smoking much pot, dropping acid or any other poison?'

She was silent a moment. 'Well, not really.'

Not really. Which meant yes. Which hurt, but not too much, because the plane was waiting and Harv was dead and soon I'd be taking care of my little love again.

'Goodbye now, Ellie.'

'Goodbye, Nickie.' Her voice was very soft, very sad. 'I . . . I wish we'd gone to London together when . . .' She stopped.

I sent her a kiss. She sent me one. I hung up.

I had a three-seat row to myself. The huge 747 wasn't more than a quarter full. As soon as they started serving drinks, I ordered a double martini. Then I pulled up one of the arm rests, lay down, bent my knees over the arm rest that was immovable, and closed my eyes.

Always before, a trip to Europe had been something exciting, something wonderful.

It was still wonderful, because the muted roar and vibration put me to sleep, and kept me asleep until about an hour before landing. And then, despite a slightly drugged feeling from the past week of booze, pot, and pills, a wash-up, shave, and a breakfast gave me a newborn feeling.

And coming in over London for our landing at Heathrow Airport, I began to feel the magic of a different country, a different world.

And landing, and finding that Michael Archer of our London outlet had met me after speaking to Harold, and driving through those wonderful streets in his Jag sedan, and listening to his plans for a few business sessions and then a 'round of parties', and finally passing through Hyde Park, wreathed in winter mist, I began to wonder whether I wasn't losing the *mishigas*.

I made myself think of Ellie. I wanted her with me, certainly . . . but I wasn't sure I needed her the way I had in New York, to stay alive.

Could it change this fast? And what would happen tomorrow, and when I looked up a few high-flying birds, and when I went to Michael's parties?

My God, what if Harv was dying for nothing?

ELEVEN

Not to worry, the English say.

And I didn't, with the help of a tall, sultry, turned-on item named Sheila Aston whom I met my third day in London. It was at the first of Michael's 'round of parties', and the last for me, since

Sheila took a week off from her job as a promotion specialist and we went driving through the wet cold countryside, warming up at various pubs and inns. And I was making it with a degree of pleasure, if nothing approaching what it had been with Ellie. And it got better and better as the week wore on. And so, after five days in England, and three in Sheila, I placed a cable call from the Shakespeare Hotel, Stratford on Avon, and got Aaron at home.

'Can you stop the contract from being filled?'

'I don't think so. The soldiers are in the field.'

'Try anyway, Aaron.' And for whatever the reason, I still wasn't worried.

'You shoulda gone to England *first*,' he said, before hanging up.

Back in London, ten days after arriving in Jolly Old, Sheila took me directly from the garage where we turned in our rental Fiat, to Chelsea and a little old house jammed full of swinging people. There we smoked black Algerian hash (I toasted Ahmed with a puff), and drank French wine, and got so bombed that she went to sleep in a bathtub and I barely made it to a cabstand and my hotel.

The night porter gave me my week's accumulation of mail, before getting my luggage from the storage room and showing me to my new room. I undressed, got into bed, began to turn out the lamp ... then decided I would read my mail. Louise writing that all was well with Mom and the kids. Harold writing that he'd decided to go along with my hockey-revision of Flip-Chip, and that I might look into a new best-seller in the English game market. And wonder of wonders, a card from Ellie – eight cents postage due – stating that she'd received my letter and the enclosed art-reproduction cards from the Victoria and Albert Museum (sent my second day in London). She thanked me for them; she hoped I was having a good time; she was working hard; love, Ellie.

Very cool. I'd rather have received no mail at all. It broke the ten-day charm. I took a while to fall asleep, pot and wine notwithstanding, and then my dreams weren't very pleasant. In one, I was reading Ellie's card, and at the end, in a strong male hand, was written, 'Best Wishes, Harvey.' And when I turned it over, instead of the Gateway Arch was a wedding photo, Ellie and Harv.

It failed to wake me. What *did* wake me was the phone. My travel clock read five a.m., and I wondered if Sheila had finally climbed out of her tub.

'Hi,' I said, the affable American to whoever it was.

'Sonofabitch!' Ellie said, voice shaking badly. 'Crazy, *crazy* son-ofabitch!'

That's when I understood I *wasn't* the affable American, had never been the affable American, hadn't lost the *mishigas,* had simply become a champion at *Playing At Being Alive.* Because I knew what this call meant, and felt a warm flood of venomous delight, and wondered briefly how many people would feel the way I did. Perhaps the next big-seller from Kraus-Leib would be a game called, *Murder Man,* or *Come Kill!*

'Who *is* this?' I asked indignantly.

'I'll go to the police! Or have *you* killed! I've got tough friends too! One, he could do it with his left hand! And he'd like to. I've told him about you and he'd like to! Or maybe we'll get your bitch daughter, who can't be worth a shit if she's yours, you rotten, you dirty, you crazy...'

'Ellie? Is that you?'

Oh yes, unmistakably my little love; unforgettably the voice I'd tried to wipe from mind and gut. But now it was in my ears, and despite the things it was saying, it was still the high, sweet, childish voice that had fueled my obsession. And I was hot for her on the instant; forgot Sheila Aston on the instant; wanted Ellie, *only* Ellie, had to have her or die.

'... such a sweet guy. So good to me. So good to *everyone.*' She was crying now, unable to go on, breaking down in heavy sobs.

It was a chill winter morning and I was sitting up in bed with no pyjamas on and the room was, in the English style, unheated before daylight ... and still I was sweating. With excitement. With determination. Because now I had to play her carefully, reel her in, make her return to me.

'I'll pay you back!' she screamed, finding voice again. 'I swear I will!'

'What the hell's this all about?' I looked at the dawn-grey rectangle that was my window facing Hyde Park, and smelled the subtly strange odour of this city, so much cleaner a smell than New York's and thought I was some four thousand miles from St Louis and Ellie and a corpse I'd created by remote control. Unbelievable, but I believed it. I smiled, the spotted sheet, the dirty shorts mixed with her panties, the deep voice telling me to stop 'bothering' her ... all finally wiped out.

As I'd said in my Miami Beach sales pitch, what an underrated thing interpersonal violence is, at least overtly in our society. What a lie we live with that turn-the-other cheek horse-shit. How *true* to human nature is 'An eye for an eye'. How deep-down *satisfying* is the death of one's enemy! God, how good I felt!

I took a deep breath of cold morning air, and said, 'Either tell me book and pencil from his pocket. But for once she didn't look, didn't nod or smile or respond. For once she was totally uninvolved in other men. *A murder a day keeps the competition away.*

I waved. She saw me, and for one unguarded moment her face lighted, her hand rose, the beautiful dimpled smile came. Then the moment passed and she stopped the cart near the doors and turned to the tall youth. I was already on my way. I reached them in time to hear her thank him for helping her with her luggage. He said, 'Perhaps we could meet for a drink . . . ?'

I had my hands on her shoulders and was turning her and we were looking at each other and I took her slowly, gently, into my arms, so very careful not to create tension, just as I had the very first time I'd kissed her in the back of Alexis's clothing store. I kissed her the same way now, and it was as if we were alone instead of in the middle of an airport crowd, and I murmured, 'God, Ellie, it is so *good* . . .'

She drew back and turned to the tall youth. 'Thanks again, Larry.'

He nodded. 'You two taking the airport bus? It's right outside.'

I'd planned to. But he'd sit near us, and I wanted Ellie all to myself. I said, 'No, I've made other arrangements, goodbye now.'

He blinked, and went away.

'Same old Nickie,' she said, and picked up the smaller of her two suitcases. 'He saw how down I was on the plane and talked to me and played cards and he was real nice.'

'I'll be real nice too.' I couldn't wait to prove it, in bed.

We walked to the cab stand.

Riding through London, she looked out the window. I spoke of the age of this city, of the green belts, of the weather . . . and finally took her hand and murmured, 'I'm so sorry about what happened.'

She turned to me. 'Are you?'

'Please, honey, not that again.'

She looked away. 'Did you get me a room?'

'The singles were all gone. I had to take a double.'

'It figures.'

'Twin beds.'

She nodded, still looking out the window. 'The funeral was day before yesterday. His mother wouldn't look at me. Not that she ever liked me, but she wouldn't let me say one word to her. The sister came in from out of town, and she must have asked about me because later she came over and we had coffee together and she said her mother was in a state of hysteria and that's why she blamed me. I asked how anyone could blame *me,* even completely flipped out.

299

The sister said it was because Harv hadn't been living at home...'
She paused. 'No harm telling you now. He was living with me. He'd go home once or twice a week, but like you guessed, he was living at my place.'

I released her hand. She looked at me. I looked away, to indicate a pain and rage I no longer felt. She took my hand back. 'What difference does it make? He's dead. Besides, you and I .. just friends. And you have someone here, right?'

'Yes, but you're still the most important...'

'Sure, sure. But you've been fucking all over London. And the only reason I'm here is that you're sorry for the dumb cunt.'

'Listen, you were the one living with someone else...'

And we were off. And it was *good*, because she was jealous!

I changed the subject back to Harv's funeral. 'I still don't understand why the mother blamed you.'

'Because she felt he was running around at night, not staying home with his wonderful Jewish momma. Because, shit, how the hell do I know what goes on in her goddam head! I should stick with blacks and Arabs!'

'Been seeing Russ Doon?' I asked quietly.

She shrugged.

'You mentioned someone who could kill me with one hand. That Mr Doon?'

'He *could*, baby! He's six-two, broad as a bull, weighs about two hundred thirty, but still in great shape.'

'And you've been seeing him, sleeping with him?'

'Saw him a few times. Then after Harv got killed, I spent a day with him.'

'I suppose he simply comforted you, held your hand...'

She laughed. 'Russ?' She laughed again. 'Your English cunt would flip out if ever she had a man like *that*!'

'Better than Jews, huh?'

She laughed again. 'No contest, man.'

It was no longer good. It was no longer even tolerable. 'Is *he* important to you?'

'I don't know. We go back a long ways together.'

'He was the one who raped you, just before you came to live with me, right?'

She nodded. 'Tried to. Someone came along.'

'He gave you the pot that you gave to me, right?'

Another nod.

'And other drugs...?'

We were at the hotel. We put her bags in my room and went

down to the tiny bar and drank a bottle of wine. We returned to the room and she bathed and I looked out the window. I didn't know what I'd accomplished with Harv's death. Perhaps nothing. Perhaps worse than nothing, if she was going to remain apart from me and swing far and wide.

But this was only our first *hour* together.

I went into the bathroom. She was leaning back, eyes closed. I sat on the edge of the tub and stroked her breasts. She opened her eyes. 'The first time with Russ,' she said, 'was rape, I think I invited him to a New Year's party I threw at my apartment. It was such a noisy mess, I split ... ran from my own party. Russ asked to come with me. We'd both been drinking and smoking pot, and he'd caught me in the kitchen a few times and kissed me and put his hands on my boobs and under my dress. I always said to stop, but he was so strong ... I'd never been with a man that strong before. He could hold me absolutely helpless with one arm around my body, pinning my arms to my sides, and then do what he wanted with the other hand. Yet he always let go when I said to. And ... he turned me on, I guess. He's really beautiful. Dangerous, but beautiful. Anyway, we went for a drive, and he parked, and then he did it.'

'How?' I asked, my voice weak.

'Turning on, honkey?'

I thought I'd hit her. I got up and went to the sink and drank a glass of water.

'He got me on his lap. I figured a few kisses, all right. And I loved his strength. You know how I go for *builds*. Well, he's the king. Makes even Ahmed look like a girl.'

I stayed at the sink, rinsing the glass.

'I was on his lap and he got an arm around me and I was helpless and then he began to do things with his other hand. I asked him to stop. I was high and he was high, but I didn't want it ... not that way. He kept saying he had to have me, I represented something important to him, and he loved me and hated me and a whole lot of shit that made me dizzy. And he got my pants down and he got his fly open and he pushed it up and into me, sitting. I barely felt it. But he moved up and down and made all sorts of noises, and when he stopped, I was soaked with his come.'

I left the bathroom. I missed Sheila and her cool control of her life and appetites. I'd failed to return her calls, three of them, since hearing from Ellie. I wondered what was going on in the little house in Chelsea; the safe little house where I cared for no one and was pitched by everyone and was never hurt. I suddenly missed it.

Ellie came out in her white fur-fringed robe. She lay down on one of the twin beds and looked at me and smiled. 'I know you're dying to hear the rest. Later, Russ kept calling, but I wouldn't see him. I wouldn't even talk to him. And it stayed that way all through the time with Harv, and right up until I met you. That's about when Russ began following me. Once he grabbed me in my hallway, and I said he could come up to the apartment. There was a couple walking through and they looked upset at the black guy pushing the white girl up against the wall and I didn't want them calling the cops and getting Russ in trouble. I made him promise to keep his hands off me. I'm not sure he'd have kept that promise, except that he took a shot of H, right in my place, and got sleepy and talked about football and whites and how he hated blonde honkeys and yet he had to see me every so often, had to have me because I wasn't full of hate like the others and didn't have the thoughts and words like the others and he could relax with me, feel some love with me, yet at the same time work off his hate with me...' She shook her head. 'He was always talking like that. And I understood it. He was always quoting Eldridge Cleaver, and he gave me a copy of *Soul On Ice*, and I dug that too ... though it scared me.

'*Russ* scares me ... yet he's a great turn-on, and smart man. Almost as smart, and as rotten, as you, Nickie.' I began to answer. She said, 'Except he's hooked now, really gone on heroin. No hope there.'

'Yet you went to him after Harv was killed.'

'I went to him before too,' she said flatly. 'I went to him right after the month of no-fucking was up. I was never straight with Harv the way I was with you. I went to him and I went to Ahmed.'

'Straight as you were with *me*?' I laughed. 'How about that pilot? And Harv? And Studsy? And who knows how many others, including Russ and Ahmed on your St Louis visits.'

She was looking at me. 'I was always straight with you. Harv was the *only* one, and I never really felt anything much for him while I lived with you. After the abortion, I wanted to have some uncomplicated sex. Harv was, in a way, like you, always bugging me to be true, to marry him, to change my life, Russ and Ahmed were easy to be with.'

'Easy to fuck, you mean.'

'Yes. Ahmed easier than Russ. But still, Russ too. No plans. No telling me to become different, better anything but exactly what I was.'

'I thought Harv accepted you as you were?'

'More than you, but still ... you know the Jews. *Read. Think.* Get a degree. Get married. Not that *you* wanted to marry me ...'

'I asked you at the Plaza, didn't I?'

'And now that you know I'm a nigger lover?' She smiled her bitchiest smile. 'Still want me as your wife, Nickie?'

I nodded. I also hated her, but I didn't say it. She, however, could *feel* it.

'Bullshit. You don't even want to touch me now. You want to be with your English whore, right?'

I came to the bed and sat down and bent to her. Eyes wide and unblinking on mine, she let me kiss her. With that kiss, with the taste and feel of Ellie's lips, the block of ice in my stomach began to melt. I kissed her again, my eyes closing. I began to caress her, parting that white robe, fighting the memory of Ahmed's hand doing what my hand was doing. I lay down beside her. We kissed and her hand began stroking the back of my head. I slipped a finger into her. She was wet, and her legs spread. 'Nickie,' she said, and opened my fly and grabbed me. The fire consumed me. I said, 'Jesus, why not with anyone else?'

The phone rang.

I tried to ignore it. She let me go. 'Answer it, Nickie.'

'Why? Probably someone at the branch office ...'

'This time of night? Answer it. Or don't you want me to hear you talk to your English lady.'

I sat up and lifted the phone. It was Sheila. Ellie leaned close, pressing her ear to the receiver. Sheila said, 'What happened to you the last few days? You haven't been ill, have you, darling?'

Ellie drew back to smile a death's-head smile at me. '*Dahling*,' she mimicked.

'I have a visitor,' I said, 'I'll get back to you later.'

Ellie lay down and laughed. 'Oh you bullshit artist, you lying sonofabitch.'

'Is that a woman?' Sheila asked. 'I mean, am I interrupting anything? Just say so, darling. I don't want to embarrass you.'

'Yes. I'll get back to you.'

When I hung up, Ellie stood up. When I tried to grab her, she caught me with a vicious slap in the face; then ran to the bathroom and locked herself in. I stood outside the door and said, 'I love you, only you. I want to travel with you, get close to you again ...'

'Liar, bullshit artist, games-player!'

The last – games-player – reminded me of *Playing At Being Alive* and all I'd suffered, and I smashed at the door with my fists and shouted. 'You lived with Harv, fucked for Ahmed and Doon, and

303

you accuse *me*? Come out, you filthy whore!'

'No,' she said, voice icy cold. 'Not until you leave. Then I'm getting another room.'

'If I leave, I won't be back. I swear it, Ellie,' and I *wanted* to run now, wanted to lose the pain, the insanity this girl created in me.

'Fine. I'll be able to do a little sight-seeing, and after a week I'll go home and get back to work.'

I stood there another moment. 'Ellie, *please*.'

'It's no good, Nick. I don't want to be with you. I can't have sex with someone I don't want to be with, can I?'

I went to the phone and called Sheila's home. She said, '*That* was quick.'

I spoke loudly. 'Remember the Rembrandt Hotel?'

'How could I forget?' She laughed. We'd gone directly there from the first party, unable to wait for the longer trip back to my hotel; her place was out because of a roommate. 'The bar, Nick?'

'Yes. In fifteen minutes.'

'Give me half an hour. I'll pack an overnight bag.'

I got my small suitcase, threw in a few things, and slammed the lid. Ellie opened the bathroom door. She watched as I put on shirt, tie, jacket, and overcoat. 'Nickie...'

I grabbed the bag and ran. Sheila was waiting. Normalcy was waiting. Here lay madness.

And yet, in the lobby, I realized that her murmured, 'Nickie...' had been placating, frightened, a plea. My little girl had pushed her game too far and wanted to retract.

I got a cab and went to the Rembrandt. I was early, and had a drink in the bar ... and began worrying. Ellie was alone in a strange city. I had no right to leave her, no matter what she'd said.

And wasn't leaving her for Sheila insane since everything I'd done had been to get *Ellie* here? And since there was no way Sheila, or anyone else on this earth, could compete with Ellie?

I went to the phone in the lobby. I called White's Hotel, and asked for my room. No answer.

Sheila was waiting when I returned to the bar. We checked into the hotel as Mr and Mrs Leib. We had wine and small meat pies. She talked about her job. We went to bed. We made love. And all the time I was numb, dead, unfeeling.

She asked me what was wrong. I said I hated to admit it, but I was ill. She was solicitous, and at ten o'clock stopped trying for another go and tucked me in and kissed me tenderly and said, 'I'm beginning to care more than I should, Mr Leib.'

Mr Leib smiled and kissed her back and said, 'Goodnight, honey,' now a grand master at *Playing At Being Alive* ... because the numbness had given way to pain, to panic.

Half an hour later, I asked Sheila if she would get me an antacid from the Midnight Shop just down the street. As soon as she left, I called White's. Still no answer. Regret, guilt, anguish ... a lovely witch's brew joined panic.

Where was Ellie?

Sheila returned with a roll of Tum-like tablets. I ate two, and we again went through our tender goodnights, and she soon fell asleep. But I didn't. I lay there, wanting to get the hell *out*!

I told myself Ellie was in the lobby of White's, having a drink. Or she'd taken a little stroll to look around the city.

And met a man and was with him...

God, not that crazy shit again!

The night crawled on. And then the phone rang and I had it and the operator said, 'Sorry to disturb you, Mr Leib, but an emergency ...'

Ellie cut in. Ellie as I'd never heard her. Ellie laughing and crying and shouting. 'Mr and *Mrs* Leib have retired. *Cahn't* it wait until morning, miss? How *is* Mrs Leib, *dahling*? But she hasn't had *my* action. Oh yes, London is better than St Louis and New York for quick action. For *gang* action. You dirty bastard, I've done it and I'm sick and you did it, you did everything to me, from the day I met you ...'

'Where are you?' I asked, sitting up.

Sheila said, 'What is it, darling?'

I winced.

Ellie said, 'I went out for a walk and this wonderful guy talks to me and I say I don't really want company and he tags along and soon we're in a pub and he keeps giving me *lagers*, oh those lagers ... beers to you, bastard! But he added little whiskies on the side. And then we're at his place and even so I'm going to leave then he gives me another drink, fruit juice he says, and after that the world goes wild and I know I've been had. Acid or something. And he's saying how he's Australian not English and how he really despises the English and the Americans too, and it's like Russ, with the hate mixed in, only this one's as bad as you, bastard! This one's got a friend hid in another room and later I'm in bed, and then I'm being fucked, and when I look up the guy's got a moustache and Peter, the one that I'm with, that I thought I was with, he doesn't have a moustache ... and God, I know they've been ganging me, two of them, and I'm being used like the piece of shit I am, and maybe more than two, maybe three, because it seems another face, older, a man like the bartender in the pub, the one that put his arm around Philip and looked at me and they both whispered and I'm drunk and drugged and a dirty whore just like you said and you're with *Mrs* Leib and they're retired, *dahling*, you filthy killer, you did it to Harv, didn't you, and I'm so sick . . .'

'Where *are* you?'

'What do you care, dahling, I've probably got syphilis now and I've got something worse in my head, my head, it's killing me to know those dirty . . . my mother was right about me . . . about men . . . my crazy mother and *I'm* crazy . . .'

She *screamed*. I held on and begged God help her and help me, and when she began to weep, I said, 'Where are you?'

She kept crying. She said, 'Mrs Leib . . . and I'm a dirty cunt . . .'

'I love you, Ellie. Please, where are you?'

She hung up.

I dressed, shaking and sweating. Sheila had her back to me. She spoke in a carefully controlled voice.

'Anything I can do?'

'I'm sorry, no.' I wish there was. I wished she could make me care, and make me stop caring, and make me sane again. But she couldn't. No one could.

I took a cab back to White's Hotel. It was two a.m. When I saw Ellie sitting on the front steps, I said, 'Thank you,' and the cabby glanced back at me. I paid, and walked to her. 'Ellie, let's go upstairs.'

She was huddled into her maxi-coat, and raised her head. Her face was – how to put it? – disjointed. Her mouth sagged; her eyes seemed to look in different directions; her skin was loose and pallid. She breathed heavily, once, twice, then leaped up and screamed, 'Get away from me, you dirty bastard!' and walked to the street.

For a moment, I could only stand there. The night porter stepped out of the hotel doorway and said, 'You should get a doctor, sir. She's been walking around and crying and falling . . .'

I had no more time. Now she was running.

I'd almost caught her, when she cut directly across Bayswater, the broad avenue separating White's and a string of other hotels from Hyde Park. I had to stop, because there were several cars and cabs coming. She went right through their blare of horns. As I started across after her, I saw from the corner of my eye two men stopped and watching. They were hoody looking guys. But again, I had no time to worry about anything but Ellie. She was on the other side

... and what she did next defies belief, except that I saw her do it. She stepped up onto the high ledge, which in turn held a high metal fence with spiked tops, perhaps six feet from concrete to spikes, and wearing that long maxi-coat, and holding a shoulder purse by the straps, she *vaulted* over the fence.

Perhaps she did it in two stages, putting a foot up on a metal cross-bar and *then* vaulting, but I didn't see it. And even so, it was still incredible, because this was Ellie, who was about the *least* athletic girl I'd ever known, among the least agile people on earth. On her back, a champion. On her feet, no.

Yet over she went, and I had to climb that fence to follow, and it was a job, I tell you. Then I was crashing through bushes, calling her name. And then I came onto a path. There was a bench about ten feet to my right, and someone was lying on that bench; someone whose coat had opened to reveal white flesh beneath.

I ran over. Ellie was flat on her back, seemingly unconscious. Two buttons were torn from her coat, probably during that vaulting climb of the fence, and only the top button, just below her neck, was fastened. Except for grey suède boots, she was naked.

I began closing the coat, and heard voices. I looked, and those two hoody guys from the street were now on the path, just a few feet away, watching.

I closed the coat, but when I tried to rouse Ellie, it fell open again, and I grabbed it and held it and looked at the two men – boys, I now saw, perhaps seventeen or eighteen.

'Need any help, mate?' one said with a sly voice, an insinuating smile. He moved so as to get a better view of Ellie.

'She's had enough help from people like you tonight,' I said and I was getting up and I was going to go for them because who else could I go for, where could I find the Australian who had done this to my girl? I was going to try and kill them ... and one turned and walked away. The other, the one with the dirty smile, looked from me to his friend to Ellie, and, 'Maybe he's attacking her! Maybe...' But then I was on him, swinging, and he ran.

I hadn't landed once. I was still full of fury. I turned to Ellie, and she wasn't there ... she was disappearing into the bushes and trees and shadows. I ran after her. She went back over that fence in one leap, so help me, and when I began climbing over after her, I saw she hadn't even fallen to her knees, had landed on her feet with an assist from her hands, and straightened, and begun running back across Bayswater.

A cab coming toward her slowed. The driver stuck his head out and stared. I could well understand why, but I shouted, 'Get out of here!' and he accelerated. Ellie's coat was flaring open. It made a pretty picture, that flaring coat, those suède boots, that naked body. And God, the world was full of men who would want her and she was vulnerable, susceptible, always in danger ... and I couldn't stand it, had to get her for myself, safe, secure, together, married. And was it possible? And would we be safe, secure, together, even if married?

I caught her near a little hotel with a blue-neon sign. She screamed and struck at me, and another cab slowed. Soon, someone would call the police. And then many men would be looking at and talking to my Ellie; questioning her; desiring her ...

I was as insane as she was, only I knew it. I spun her around and slapped her face. She stopped struggling. I pulled her coat together and said, 'What happened to your clothing?' to get her to talking to me.

'Left it Peter's place,' she mumbled. 'Wouldn't let me out. Naked except for boots. Turned on by boots, Peter. Peter and his friend. *Friends* ... God, Nickie!' She threw herself against me, shaking her head and trembling. I led her back up the street toward White's, keeping that coat together with one hand. She said, 'Kept saying I was *imagining* other men. And with someone in the other bed laughing under the covers. And in the kitchen ... oh, God! I feel so dirty!'

'No,' I said. 'Not you. *Peter*. If you tell me where he lives ...'

'Don't know. Saw my coat on the chair, and when he went to the kitchen and laughed with the other one, I think the moustached one ... ran out. My coat and purse on chair. He came after me. Stairs. So many stairs. Got to street and ran into cars and cab stopped. Peter tried to grab me and I said, 'Call the police,' and the cabby got out and Peter went away and I came to White's and called you. But I don't want you, Nickie. It happened because of you. I want to go home. I want to go home to St Louis.'

I murmured soothing things as we entered the lobby. She suddenly jerked free of me, that coat flaring again, only now there was no one to see it. The lights had been dimmed and the place was deserted. 'You stay here,' she said, face full of hate. 'I'll go upstairs and you stay here. You can get another room. I asked. You lied. They have singles. Get one.'

I said all right, but I'd see her to bed. She said no, and went to the elevator. I got in with her. She glared at me, then searched her purse. She couldn't find a key. I didn't have a key. We arrived at my room, and she sat down on the floor, back against the door. I went down and rang the night porter's bell. When he appeared, he asked, 'How is madame, sir?

I said she felt better. He said there was a doctor on the next street who would come over.

I took down the name and telephone number ... 'in case I need it before morning'. Then I went back upstairs. Ellie had stretched out full-length on the floor. I opened the door, and began to lift her up in my arms ... and she came awake and screamed, 'Leave me alone! Get out of my room!'

As I half-pushed, half-carried her through the door, she screamed again, wordlessly, insane. Doors began opening along the corridor. I got her inside, and she shrieked, 'Out! *Out!*'

I hit her on the side of the head, with closed fist, not too hard. And grabbed her as she began to sag. I put her on the bed. She lay there, eyes closed, and said, 'Nickie ... I want to sleep.'

I got the coat off, and the boots. As I tried to roll her to the side and free the blanket, she put her arms around me and pulled me down. 'Hold me,' she said. 'Don't let me go.'

I waited until I thought she was asleep; then freed myself. Her eyes snapped open and she cried out. 'Nickie, don't go!'

I got under the covers and undressed, dropping my clothes where I stood. I got into the narrow twin bed with her and held her, breast to breast, face to face. She sighed, and her lips pushed against my chest. She said, 'Tighter ...'

I hugged her. She said, 'Nickie, love me, make me forget everything.'

I caressed her body. I tried not to think of Peter; tried not to fantasize his death by torture. And when her hand fumbled between our bodies and found me, and when her mouth kissed mine, there was no room for anything but love.

But she was still psyched out on the abomination she'd endured, and on the acid, or whatever it was Peter had fed her. Her voice suddenly sharp, she said, 'What's the matter, don't you want me?'

'Of course I do.' I tried to kiss her. She twisted her head aside.

'You're stalling! I can feel it! You're turned off by that gang fuck, and by Russ and Ahmed too. You think I'm a whore, don't you!' She pushed at me. 'Go away! I don't blame you. Don't put on any acts for me. I wouldn't want to touch me either, if I were a man. It's dirty down there, isn't it? It'll be itching and get sores ...'

I shoved her onto her back, held her down, ran my mouth over her breasts and belly. She said, 'You're acting!'

I let go of her arms and pulled open her thighs. I pressed my mouth to her. She pulled at my hair and cried out, 'Nickie, no ... let me wash!'

I'd have loved to, but I couldn't take the chance. If I stopped now, she would probably see it as a sign of rejection. I went ahead. She said, 'Please, Nickie, I'll wash, I'll let you ...' And then my tongue was touching the soft lips, the damp flesh, the little button. Her hand stopped pulling at my hair and began carressing it. I felt her body loosening, and was able to play with her thighs instead of holding them forcibly open. She began to shift, to squirm, to moan, to excite me with her excitement. Now I was no longer proving anything. Now I was able to slide down to the edge of the bed, put my face directly and more comfortably between her thighs, look up over her belly and between her small tits to her face, beginning to twist in passion ... but in a moment she said, 'Nickie, right now!'

It had never been easier getting into that tight little box; it was sopping wet. I slid in, and she raised her legs high, and I pressed down. I began to move. I was calling her my little girl, my little love, and saying, 'This is it. This is everything. This alone, with *you* alone.'

She said no words to match mine; no words of love. When I came, I cried out I loved her, I loved her, I'd always loved her. Then I went on, working for her climax, waiting for her cries, hoping for her words, which if they ever came, would come now. Her orgasm was a strong one, shaking her, bringing gasps and moans ... but the only words she said were, 'Christ, Christ, *harder*!'

We slept until almost two the next afternoon; then went down for eggs and coffee. We walked around London, through a steady drizzle. It grew dark and we took a cab to Soho and walked some more and found a rock club and danced. She tired quickly, and drank too much, and grew morose and irritable. We went back to White's and changed and took a cab to the Serpentine Restaurant in Hyde Park. Dinner lasted over two hours, and she grew more cheerful. The drizzle had stopped. We walked a while before returning to the room.

Whenever I looked at her, as we went to Buckingham Palace and museums and the Thames and the Cotswolds and drove over half of England and Scotland in the next five days, wherever we were, I wanted her. And each night I had her, in sagging old beds in country inns, and springy new beds in city hotels, exhausting myself upon her body, spasming, ejaculating, giving of myself until there was no more to give. And sometimes during the day, in our rented Cortina, I went down on her and made her come, and was as stimulated, as satisfied, as if I'd also come. We were always moving, eating, fucking, or sleeping ... no time for talking. Until the night we returned to London and White's Hotel and had dinner in our room.

We were on the couch. She was sipping a glass of wine and I was lighting a small cigar, when she said, 'You *did* have Harv killed, I know it. You can admit it to me now, Nickie. We're growing close again. I might even come back to New York to stay.'

My heart leaped. 'Really? I didn't think ... would you marry me?'

She looked at me. There didn't seem to be much love in that look.

'Maybe. But what about Harv?'

'Don't be foolish.'

She turned away. 'If you're not willing to tell the truth even now, you never will. And we can't have a marriage built on lies.'

'So I have to admit to murder before you'll marry me, is that it?'

'If you did it, admit it.'

'If I had, I would. But I didn't.'

She finished her wine. I poured another glass. She burped, and shook her head. 'You make my gut ache with your lies.'

'I didn't kill Harv and I still want to marry you. Do I have to be a murderer ... ?'

'Let's drop it. I shouldn't have said anything about coming back to you. It's impossible.' She turned to look at me again. 'Nickie, you *did* firebomb Ahmed's place. And you *did* have Harv killed. Who else would do it?'

'An enemy of Al Fatah, and a homosexual mugger. That answer your question?'

'And the abortion and leaving me so I met Philip...' She shook her head, and asked for another glass of wine, and then left it and went to bed. When I wanted to make love, she said she felt sick.

I tried to buy her a necklace at Harrod's. She refused it. We drove to Stratford on Avon. She loved the winter scenery, but didn't love the sexual action as much as before. She resisted it in the car, and shortened it in bed. I tried to buy her an engagement ring when we returned to London. She refused. I shouted at her in the street, and was shocked at myself, and explained that she'd been tightening up, *squeezing* me emotionally the past few days.

She said, 'I know. It's time to go home, Nickie.'

We packed that night. I took her to a little Italian place within walking distance of the hotel. After we ate, I said, 'I love you, but you won't give me a chance. Please loosen up, honey.'

She dipped bread in Marinara sauce. 'The vacation's over, Nickie. You go home. I go home. Maybe we get together again some day, and maybe we don't.'

'Not good enough.'

'Sorry. It's the best I can do.'

I finished my second litre of wine. 'I won't accept that.'

'Go back to your *dahling* in Chelsea.'

'That's Chelsea,' I said, and couldn't help taking her hand and kissing it and laughing. My little girl, my little love, my little nitwit. Chelesa! No matter what she did, what she said, it charmed me. 'That's your new nick-name – Chelesa. That's what we'll name the girl . . .'

She jerked her hand away. 'Okay, go back to your cunt in *Chelsea*. Or Ledya and Karen in New York.'

I shook my head. 'No more girls. Just a cruel little bitch. Just Chelesa McBaren.'

'You did it to Harv. I know it. That and the abortion and Ahmed and Philip. There's no way we can ever be together.'

I called the waiter. I asked for a bottle of wine to go. He put it in a bag; I paid the bill; we went out into a dry cold night. We walked the four blocks to the hotel in silence. She wouldn't even take my arm.

In the room, I tried to kiss her. She pushed me away, saying, 'Never again.'

I slapped her hard, and she staggered and sat down on the floor.

I said, 'You're right. I firebombed the ass-fucker's place. And I had Harv killed. To get you back. And I'll do it again, and again, until you're mine.'

She stared at me.

'Whoever you sleep with, I'll kill.'

She smiled.

'And if I have to, I'll finish with Liz.'

She put her hands behind her and leaned back and laughed. 'Good act, Nickie. Even the slap. But I don't believe it. You'd never admit it. You're using it, or trying to.'

I dropped down to my knees. I'd drunk too much wine and absorbed too much punishment. Everything was breaking free. '*Please* believe it. I can't stop now. It's a matter of survival, of self-defence. If I don't have you, I'll go mad, I'll die. So anything I do to get you back is simply a way of fighting for my life. Ahmed, Harv, Doon, whoever stands between us, is killing me. Don't make me go on, Ellie. Come back now, honey. Even if you don't care, it's all right. I'll make you happy, I swear. Seth will spend time with us; you know you love him. And we'll get a bigger place and a maid . . . anything. We'll visit St Louis often; see your family. Just don't

312

cut me out of your life as you did before. Just don't go back to Doon and Charlie and whoever else there is. Don't sleep with them ... *I can't stand it*! Don't make me crazy again, little love.' I took her in my arms and kissed her.

Her mouth was cold. Her body was stiff. I drew back. She was smiling a cynical little smile. 'Wow!' she said. 'What an act! If I didn't know what a sharp, lying bastard you are, I'd almost believe it.' She paused. 'Maybe I almost do.'

I knew now she was going to leave me, and I was terrified. 'Ellie, you seemed to be warming to me again last week. What happened?'

She was still smiling her cynical smile, that full lower lip pushed to the side. She looked so goddam cute, so goddam desirable ... so goddam unattainable. 'You really thought I'd believe it, didn't you? And get scared and do what you want. You threw the love shit in to make sure. But all you want is free cunt. Maybe you're a little guilty about the abortion, but you don't know what love is. You couldn't have left me that night for Sheila if you knew love. *Harv* knew. Waiting for me while I lived with you. Never raising his voice. Never complaining. Not really dating either. Just *hoping*. But *you*? The great Nick Leib? The make-out artist?' She laughed. 'You just don't like to be rejected. Admit it! Admit it! Admit it!'

I stood up. 'It *was* true, at one time. It isn't any more. I love you, and I've got to have you, and I'll kill whoever gets in the way. I'll kill until you know I'm telling the truth. And if you try to hurt yourself, I swear Liz gets it. There's no way out, Ellie. If I don't get you, I'm dead, so I have nothing to lose.'

She shrieked laughter.

I met her gaze. I didn't back down on the melodrama ... because I'd spoken the truth.

She kept laughing, but she was pushing it now. When she stopped, she said, 'A crazy lie. Using a robbery ... who'd ever believe ... ?' Suddenly her face twisted and she screamed, 'If it *was* true, I'd kill you! No matter how long it took! I'd get a gun, a knife, hire someone ...'

I went to the bathroom, locked the door, drowned her out by filling the tub. I took a long hot bath, and heard her moving around, and then heard nothing. I grew frightened that she'd left, and leaped from the tub and ran dripping into the bedroom. She was sitting in an armchair, reading.

Later, I got into bed with her. She didn't resist my love-making; neither did she help much. I don't think I made her come. I tried to go down on her, but she said, 'Nick, enough.' It was her tone of voice that did it, more than her words.

We lay there a while. I said, 'I'm going with you to New York, St Louis, or Hades.'

'That Hell?'

'Yes, St Louis is Hell.'

'Funny *mans*. How about some wine?'

'I want to talk. I want you to know exactly...'

'In the morning. Now I want wine.'

I got the corkscrew from my toilet kit and opened the bottle. I poured wine into water glasses and sat at the edge of the bed. 'To us,' I said.

She sipped. I drank. And that's the way it went; she not quite finishing the one glass. I finishing the bottle.

Which is obviously what she wanted. I went out like a light ... and she was able to leave the room early the next morning without my hearing. When I got up, it was ten-thirty, and she and her luggage were nowhere in sight.

I checked the desk. Madame had left instructions I wasn't to be disturbed.

I went back to the room. I looked for a note. Nothing. I waited, hoping she'd come back, not willing to believe she would leave me this way.

I ordered a bottle of brandy and breakfasted on that and my spleen. At twelve-thirty, the phone rang. I lunged for it.

'Nickie, I'm just boarding the plane.'

'Come back,' I said, beginning to shake.

'I'm already through customs and everyone's boarded and I didn't want you waiting all day. Forget me, Nickie. It's ... too sick, too mixed up.'

'Come back, Chelesa. Don't do this.'

'Live your own life. I'll live mine. Don't try to come after me. I meant what I said. I have some very tough friends. I half-believe you did it to Harv. If I ever *really* believe it...'

'Come back.' I'd stopped shaking. I'd stopped hoping. But I hadn't stopped feeling, and the pain was impossible. 'Come back, whore!'

'See? You don't want me; not really. Not if I'm a whore.'

'You *are* a whore, and I *do* want you.'

'Let me alone! We've had it!'

'Come back...' But she'd already hung up. 'Well,' I said into the phone, 'that is too bad for both of us.'

I flew out at five that evening. I went to bed when I got home, and with the aid of three pills stayed asleep for almost twelve hours.

Then some food, a shower and a shave, and it was eight p.m. of Saturday, February twentieth. I phoned Aaron. No answer. I phoned Teaneck. Seth answered. There was music, voices, laughter in the background. I asked what was going on. Phil and another two couples were there. I chatted with Seth about the trip, and said I'd try to see him tomorrow.

I called Aaron again, and again no answer.

I called Ellie's home. No answer. It was now eight-twenty; seven-twenty in St Louis. The store was open late Saturdays. I called there. A male voice answered. I asked for Ellie. He asked who was calling. I said, 'Russ.'

Ellie got on. 'Hey,' she said. 'You're pushing hard, baby. I told you not until Monday.'

'I'm pushing harder than that, Chelsea. He's dead if you don't get on a plane . . .'

She hung up. I'd expected it. I dialled the number again. The male voice answered again. I gave myself a Western drawl as I asked for Ellie.

She said, 'Yes?' cautiously.

'Will you talk to me for a minute?'

Silence.

'Is there no way I can make you understand what I feel?'

'Say I believe you. Say you love me. But say I don't love you, not even a little. Isn't it over?'

'You said I was the most important man in your life. You said it only a month ago. And six months ago you were telling me I was your one and only love. It can't *all* have disappeared.'

'Maybe it hasn't. I don't know. But you can't force me. You have to give me time.'

'I've given you time. I can't stand being apart from you any more.'

Her voice dropped to an intense whisper. 'C'mon, stop that shit already! You know you can go out tonight and fuck almost anyone you want to! You know you're a champ at that! Maybe I want to become a champ too. Maybe after I swing, I'll be able to see you again and we'll take another look . . .'

'No. I can't let you swing. I can't let you have other men. I *can't*!'

'Then fuck off, you crazy bastard!'

Again she hung up. Again I dialled. This time she answered herself. As soon as I said, 'Ellie,' she said, 'I've got a store full of people. I'm not going to take any more calls.'

'Not even from Russ?'

315

'Watch it with him, Nickie. He's not Ahmed or Harv. He doesn't give a shit about anything. If he ever gets his hands on you . . .'

'I'm going to kill him.'

She hung up.

I called Aaron again. No answer.

I dialled St Louis information, and asked the telephone number of a Mr Russ, or Russel, Doon. I got it, and his address. Both seemed familiar. The address was in my book, copied off the back of Doon's business card, which I'd found in Ellie's purse after she returned from Claire's wedding. I then went to the desk and got out my stack of phone bills. Doon's number was on the August bill. I'd placed a question mark next to it, and remembered that Ellie had said it was *Claire's* new number.

A moment of insane rage, and then I shrugged. The lie would be wiped out, along with any betrayal, when Doon died. And now I hungered for his death! Now I added the stories of drugs fed my little girl, and rape . . . and I couldn't wait! I dialled the number.

The ring sounded seven times. I was about to hang up when a blurry voice answered, 'Yeah, who is it?' He sounded half asleep.

I was silent.

'C'mon, mother, say something!'

I cleared my throat.

He hung up.

I dialled again. It rang perhaps ten times, and then he said, 'All right. We'll play guessing games.'

I waited.

'Gainer? That you, mother? I'm not going to pay for that shit. I told you. It was corn starch more'n anything. I never got off the ground. You send any friends around, I'll *wipe* 'em, hear me? And then I'll come for *you*.'

I spoke in as hoarse and rasping a voice as I could manage. 'Gainer sending *me*. You dead.' I hung up.

That might keep him off the streets, and away from Ellie, until I could contact Aaron. Doon lived close enough, on Waterman Avenue, to walk the two blocks to Lindell and probably to the store. He was in a good position to meet my little girl during and after work; waylay her, seduce her, force her . . .

And then I thought, What if she'd simply used him – a lie, a torment, a threat – knowing how jealous I was?

Slim chance, after answering the way she had when I gave his name, and after calling him as far back as August while living with me. But a man's life hung on that chance.

What I needed was to be certain; to *know* who she was seeing,

316

not just to guess at it.

I called St Louis information again, and asked if they could read me a listing of Private Investigators from the Yellow Pages. The operator was a doll, and said one had a large ad on the page, stating, 'Twenty-four hour service.' I said that would serve my purposes, and asked to be connected. She said I'd save money dialing it direct. I thanked her. She had a sweet young voice. Perhaps one day a sweet young voice would turn me on. Right now, nothing turned me on but the thought of isolating Ellie from every man in St Louis.

I spoke to a Mr Deterwiller. I explained that I wanted Miss Ellie McBaren followed.

'Put under observation,' he said.

'Yes. All day and night. For a week.'

'That's three eight-hour shifts. Cost you . . .' He mumbled. 'Take it for two weeks, you get a reduction. Cost you one hundred ten dollars a day. Otherwise, a hundred thirty. And even two weeks is barely enough in establishing a subject's pattern of behaviour.'

'All right. Two weeks. Can you start right away? Tonight?'

'You have to come in and give a week's fee in advance. That's seven hundred seventy dollars.'

'I'm in New York, but I'll put a cheque for the full two weeks' costs in the mail right now. Air mail.'

'Better still,' he said, 'wait until morning, and send us a bank cheque or postal money order. Send it air mail Special. That way we can get going as soon as we receive the money.'

'No way to start tonight.'

'Would you work for a voice on the phone, Mr Leib?'

He'd made his point. I'd get a blank cheque for fifteen hundred and forty dollars out at nine a.m. Expensive . . . but at last I'd *know* what she was doing, and with whom.

I called Ledya. No answer. I called Karen. No answer. Of course, this was Saturday night. I went down and started up the Porsche and took a ride on the F.D.R. Drive. The lights of fabled New York, Imperial City, spun out alongside my windows. It didn't help. I'd take Ellie in Marfa, Texas, over being without her in New York, London, Paris, anywhere. In fact, I was *Playing At Being Alive* being *that* cool about it . . . because I wanted to cry for lack of her right this moment.

I went to a bar on Third Avenue and had a few drinks and ignored a *zaftig* Puerto Rican hooker and watched television. I called Aaron from the phone booth. He answered. When I asked if he wanted to join me, he said, 'No, thanks. I've got a friend here.'

'Listen, I may want to get up another contract.'

317

'I once told you, business in person, *not* on the phone.'

He was decidedly cool; *rude* was a better word.

'What's wrong, Aaron?'

'I warned you, didn't I? These things with women rarely work out.'

'Yeah, well, let me come over ...'

'My friend, remember?'

'Breakfast tomorrow?'

He sighed. 'Nick, Nick.' Like my old mother. 'The Eggery. About ten.'

I went home and did what I'd done in the bar – drank and watched television. At one a.m. I called Ellie's apartment. She answered. I said, 'I want to come to St Louis. For a week. We'll spend a few evenings together. Nothing heavy. Just to get reaquainted.'

'No. And I can't talk now. I have company.'

'Not Russ. He has to wait until Monday, right?'

'Right.'

'A new one. Let me guess. He's tall where Harv was rather short. He's blond where Harv, and of course Russ ...'

She hung up.

I called back. I let it ring, but she had that cut-off switch.

Aaron was late the next morning. I was on my third cup of coffee when he came in, looking very much like an amiable bear in a black coat and black Astrakhan fur hat.

'*Oy, vay,*' he groaned, divesting himself of outer clothing. 'I can't handle these young girls any more. This one's a go-go dancer. I get her some smack, and she thanks me too goddam much.'

'Should have asked me over to help.'

He gave me a level look. 'I thought of that. But then I figured you weren't interested.'

I smiled. He gave his order to the waitress. I said, 'I'm not ready to give the final go-ahead, but the man is named Russ Doon ...'

'St Louis?'

I nodded. 'An ex-football player. His address ...'

'Doon? A spook? The one with the rape cases, the dope cases?'

'I'm not up on his narcotics convictions.'

'He's playing with your girl?'

'Probably.'

'Then let her go. Anyone plays with *that* black bastard, she's not worth shit.'

I controlled myself. 'I'm not *sure* she plays with him.'

'Either way, I won't handle it.'

'Why?'

'I once told you, public figures are out.'

'You call Doon a public ...?'

His food came. He began to eat; then stopped. 'I'll level with you, Nick. I also told you we do business only with reliable people. You're no longer reliable.'

'My money's as good as it ever was! I could pay for *fifteen* contracts on half an hour's notice.'

'Not the money. You're acting like a *mishugana*. And even if we killed fifteen men for you, you still wouldn't get the girl. It's obvious by now. Tell you what I'd do if I were you. I'd get rid of *her*, not the men ... but before you ask, no, I won't handle it. You might as well try it yourself. You're no damned good to Harold, your kids, or anyone else the way you are.'

'Listen! I paid you to rub out a worm and you did it! That makes you an exterminator, not my father confessor! Keep your goddam...'

He was holding up his hand. 'I'm sorry, Nick. You're right. I never should have given you advice. Would you like me to move to another table?' He began to get up.

I sat there a moment, breathing heavily. Then I shook my head. I was ashamed. This man was a professional, and saw things clearly. I too had once been a professional. Now I was a madman. 'Maybe what you ought to do,' I said, 'is accept a contract on *me*. The girl, or one of her friends, will want one, sooner or later.'

He was eating again. He said, mouth full. 'Well, you're not a public figure, Nick,' and smiled his shark's smile.

I visited Seth, and later went over to Ron. He gave me another jar of sleeping pills. I was going through the stuff like an addict ... but how else to sleep?

I drove up to Peekskill to see my mother. In the corridor of the home, an overweight nurse told me that 'Katie isn't very attentive today, and it might be best if you returned another time.'

I said I'd driven all the way from New York and would like to see her anyway.

She hesitated, mouthed a few cutesie platitudes about the old as if they were children – 'If she has a good feeding, she's more likely to respond, and she didn't eat well this morning' – then led me to the room.

I went in alone. Mum was sitting in her wheelchair. It was placed beside a window with a good view – the long hill, scattered clumps of trees, a pale blue horizon flecked with tiny white clouds. But she wasn't looking out the window. Her head was down. Her old head. Her grey head, the hair shockingly thin. Her head that trembled continuously. She was looking at her hands. She was turning them this way and that; work-worn hands; veiny, age-spotted hands.

'How are you, Mum?'

She didn't look up. She didn't answer.

I drew a chair close to her and sat down. 'It's been a long time since we talked.'

She examined her hands with total attention.

I considered leaving.

What if I never saw her again?

I tried to talk to my mother. I talked about the few good things I could remember from the past – college, business, the night Denise was born, when my mother danced a crazy jig, singing, 'A *maideleh*, a *maideleh*!' celebrating her first grandchild, her first girl child.

And then I talked about her marriage. I said I understood she wasn't to blame, Dad wasn't to blame, they just hadn't been right for each other. It had been the same with me and Louise. No one's fault. But I'd gotten out in time, I said. I'd found someone to love. It would all work out for me.

She turned her hands this way and that.

I found I was breathing hard, sweating ... as if running. I said, 'You know you wasted your life, don't you? Again, not your fault, not his fault. But you *wasted* it! And ... you know how it affected me. I saved my children from that. Even Denise; she never saw me like I saw Dad ... *listen to me!*'

She never stopped turning her hands, examining them.

I stood up. I was gasping for breath. I didn't know what was wrong with me, but I felt my brain was about to explode. 'I'm going to be happy now, Mum. I wanted you to know that. I hope it makes you happy too. I'll bring Ellie ... my wife here some day. Soon, Mum. You'll like her.' But she wouldn't. If she were herself, she wouldn't. And it enraged me, because her tastes had influenced mine, had made me reject my little love in so many ways, and now it might be too late.

'I'm going, Mum.'

She kept turning her hands.

I went to the door. My knees were shaking.

She said, 'You be a good boy, Wallace.'

I turned. She was smiling at me; not Kate Leib's sharp, dangerous smile, but an empty, foolish idiot-grin.

'*It's Nickie!*' I screamed.

She nodded, retaining the idiot-grin. 'Be a good boy, Nickie.'

I took hold of myself. She was sick. She'd get better. I'd bring Ellie to her, and they'd make cautious conversation. I'd bring our first child to her, and she'd sing her celebration of another grandchild.

I didn't believe it. Ellie was lost to me. I had to give her up. There was nothing else to do.

And I didn't believe that either.

I said, 'I will, Mum.'

She said, *'Zei gesundt.'*

'Thank you, Mum. You too.'

She said, 'But your father, that devil...'

I left.

On Tuesday I called the private investigators. Deterwiller wasn't there, being chief of the night shift, but a Mr Cranwell said my cheque had been received Monday afternoon and an 'operator' put on Miss McBaren an hour later. I could call for reports, but I would have to identify myself with a case number. That number could not be given over the phone; it was being sent to me with a receipt for my cheque.

'You mean I can't call tonight...?'

'I'm sorry. How can we know who's calling, even right now? Assuming your *are* Mr Leib, the client who sent us the registered cheque, you wouldn't want someone else calling and getting information you paid for, would you?'

I said no and goodbye. It was Monday. Ellie had told the voice she thought was Russ Doon's that he had to wait until Monday. She'd be with him tonight.

I ate. And then I vomited. I sipped hot milk and tried not to think of Ellie and Doon, and began gagging on the milk.

It was really impossible to live this way!

I thought of all those pills Ron had given me. I had a jar and a half, more than enough to send me into an endless sleep.

Nice phrase, endless sleep. No more anguish. No more visions of Ellie being drugged, fucked, abused by a corrupt, criminal junkie who resented her being white; who had raped her once in his car and attempted it again near her apartment house; who had fed her drugs; who was big enough, strong enough, and smart enough to have achieved superstar status in the National Football League; whose powerful arms would be holding her helpless again tonight ... and worst of all, whom she *wanted* to see.

'We go back a long ways,' she said. She dug his body, she'd said. He was important to her, she'd implied.

After being with a specimen like Doon, what would she think of *me*?

Could she love me, desire me, after Doon and her athletic Ahmed? Or was I now totally unimportant, even slightly ridiculous ... ?'

Oh God, oh God, oh God!

I got the revolver and held it and thought of St Louis being only two hours away. Ellie and I, only two hours apart. I'd show her the gun and she'd finally believe and she'd realize it was stupid to let people die, perhaps she and I included, when she could solve it all by opening her arms and her heart to me.

I awakened the next morning full of disgust for myself. Gun, hell! If I shot anyone, there were ballistics and registration numbers and paraffin tests ... and even more important, the police would *know* there was a murderer running around, someone they could capture. And if Ellie said anything, they'd come right to me. I had to find a way to be safe, even if she accused me.

I created a game called, *Kill Doon.* I worked it out in my mind, and then sat down and worked it out on paper. I went back to it after breakfast, and was satisfied. All I needed now was six grains of morphine.

But perhaps it wouldn't be necessary.

I surprised Harold by showing up at the office the next two days. On Thursday, I finally got my case number from St Louis. I called the investigators immediately, and spoke to Cranwell. He said, 'Yes, we've got a report in progress. Want me to read it unit by unit? Pretty dry, and you'll get it at the end of the two-week period anyway. I could hit the highlights.'

'Yes, the highlights.'

'Monday, February twenty-second, six-thirty p.m. Subject joins male, Negro, about thirty-five, in Pancake House, Lindell. Seven-ten, they leave and drive in subject's car to apartment house, Waterman Avenue ...'

They'd entered apartment 1-C on the ground floor. It belonged to Russ Doon. She'd stayed there until a little after two a.m. When she emerged with Doon, she was 'dishevelled, weeping,' and Doon had 'shoved subject into her vehicle and driven it himself'. He went to the parking lot of the Pancake House, where he got into another car and drove away. Ellie had then driven home.

On Tuesday, she'd gone to an apartment development in Clayton and spent four hours in the home of Mr and Mrs Grebes – Gina and John. Afterward, she'd driven to her apartment, where she 'apparently retired alone.'

On Wednesday, she hadn't gone to work. She emerged from her apartment at noon in the company af 'a male, Caucasion, about fifty-three to fifty-five, short and balding', who had arrived half an hour before. In the man's Cadillac, they drove to a clothing shop in Ladue – Alexis Fashions For Men. Then they drove to her place of employment, Alexis Fashions For Men, Lindell branch. The operator entered the shop as a customer, and was handled by a salesman, 'Male, Caucasian, twenty-eight to thirty, tall, light hair. Subject and companion remained in back room for some five minutes, and then left. Companion was called "Mr Alexis" by salesman.' The operator followed them back to Ellie's apartment where they remained for two hours and forty minutes. Alexis then left; but he returned within the hour carrying 'bundles and packages, including flowers. He remained in subject's apartment until eleven-ten that evening, spending a total of eight hours and five minutes alone with subject, including the earlier two hours and forty minutes.'

'That's it, Mr Leib.'

And that was enough. I had a drink and walked around and practised speaking until I was certain I could keep my voice steady.

I called the store. Ellie answered. I said, 'Not much fun with Russ Monday night. Or *too* much fun. You looked pretty bad when you came out of his place to drive back to the Pancake House. But Charlie made *all*-better yesterday, didn't he? Driving you to the Ladue store, and then back home for that long, long session. I thought the flowers were a nice touch.'

'How did you . . . ?'

'Was Liz at Gina's Tuesday night? How's the baby? I think you should see more of them and less of Doon and Alexis, but of course, Doon and Alexis won't be around very long, so perhaps you should see them while you can.'

'Where are you?' She was controlling her fright, or anger.

'You can answer that for yourself. Just look out the window, Chelesa. Just look over your shoulder when you leave the store. Just look out your bedroom window when you go to sleep tonight.'

'Bullshit! It's a trick! You're trying to scare me! But it won't work!'

'Still have that picture of Harv on your dresser? How about his pipes on the nightstand? I love your dinette, especially the mobile hanging from the ceiling, and that cornucopia . . .'

'Nickie, stop.'

I stopped.

'What . . . you wouldn't really . . . ?'

'Doon will be dead in a week. Charlie a week or two later. And

323

Liz, well, I don't want to think of that yet.'

Silence, with heavy breathing.

'Of course, you can stop it all now by flying here tonight.'

'No!'

'How about tomorrow? We'd return to St Louis in a few weeks and drive back in your car. We can get a U-Haul and bring whatever furniture...'

'Never! You can kill the whole fucking world and I won't come back to you! No one's going to force me...'

'Don't shout. It's not necessary. I believe you. I'll just call every so often. I'm sure you'll want me to call just before Liz...'

'Lies! You had someone tail me, but you never killed anyone. You don't scare me. Russ'll murder anyone who bothers him, *or* me! I'll tell Charlie and he'll hire a bodyguard...'

I hung up. It felt good hanging up on her at that moment. She was frightened. It was no longer a matter of my loving her and she either loving or not loving me. It was now a battle of wills. Mine against hers. It wouldn't end until she was back with me, or I was dead.

Good! There'd be no more sleepless nights; no more grovelling.

I called my lawyer and arranged to see him later in the day. I wanted to check my will ... and make a change. Ellie was to get ten thousand dollars. By the time I met with Mort, I'd raised it to twenty. He made a suggestion, and I acted on it immediately. It saved paperwork on the will. I simply took out twenty thousand dollars' worth of savings bank life insurance with Ellie as beneficiary. It settled something that had been bothering me for some time now: what would happen to her if I died. And the possibilities were increasing that I might ... though I didn't plan on it. Still, I went to see Seth, and phoned Denise, and phoned Mort with a few more questions Friday morning. He finally said, 'All these questions about probate and access to safety deposit boxes ... Is there something I should know, Nick? A bad medical report, for example?'

'Just touching all bases, Mort. The way I live...' I gave him a laugh.

'Are you sure? Because if there's a real need for putting things in order, I suggest we examine your investment situation.'

'No need, Mort. Sorry I bothered you.'

He wasn't convinced. He wanted to meet me for lunch on Monday. I said I'd call him ... but I'd be in St Louis by then. Either Doon or I should be dead by then.

I called Ron's office. As I expected, the recording of his voice said, 'Dr Ron Levine does not have office hours today. In case of an emergency, call Dr Ira McReedy at the following number...' I then dialled Ron's home number. The Jamaican maid answered. I asked for Ron or Vera. She said they were away for the day; again as I expected. Ron never spent Friday, his day off, at home.

'I have to drop by and pick up something I left in his office.'

She began to say she couldn't allow anyone in.

'This is his friend, Nick Leib.'

'Oh, Mr Leib. Yes, I'm sure it will be all right.'

And it was. She let me in the front door and I strode toward the back stairs, carrying my attaché case. 'Don't let me interrupt your hard-earned day of peace and quiet,' I said, and went down to the examination room. There I stopped, waiting to see if she would follow. She didn't. To make sure I wasn't interrupted, I closed the door, pressing the lock button.

Now all I needed was the key to the drug cabinet. I looked in Ron's desk. I looked in a table drawer. Well, I'd figured I'd probably have to break in anyway. That glass didn't look too thick ... but first I tried the door.

Good old careless old Ron! Open and the keys lying on the first of two shelves.

I was smiling and chuckling ... and suddenly wondered what the hell I was so happy about. It wasn't as if any *real* problems had been solved. But then again, nothing, absolutely nothing, had gone my way for so long that this seemed a good omen.

I found the box of stylet, the pre-filled hypodermics containing one grain of morphine each. I removed six, putting them on the table ... then looked at them. Six separate injections? It would take too long; give Doon six opportunities to catch me off guard.

I found the morphine tablets and shook out eight. A man that large might be able to survive a normally fatal dose. I took two of Ron's three hypodermic syringes, and put back all but one stylet. The stylet would be the *coup de grace*, if one were needed. But my mind began to question it even as I placed it in the attaché case along with the envelope of tablets and the hypodermics. An autopsy might reveal an additional fresh puncture in the arm and raise some questions. Of course, showgirls on heroin shot it into the backs of their knees, where the tracks were less obvious ...

Patience. Patience. I was as anxious and excited to put all this theory into practice as Seth had been to translate my descriptions of various rides into experience before his first visit to Palisades Amusement Park. And, in truth, I felt it would be just as much fun. God, to destroy someone fucking, and mistreating, my little girl! What could compare to such satisfaction, such pleasure?

325

I began to leave; then made myself stop and think over what I'd done. Ron might not notice the loss of one stylet or the eight pills for quite a while, perhaps not at all, if he kept no accurate count of the items. But he *would* notice the loss of two of his three hypodermics. And the maid would mention the visit. If he put the two together, he'd have to assume I'd taken the hypodermics ... and then he would certainly check the drugs and suspect a loss.

I shrugged. Ron would never allow his suspicions to lead to an accusation. He might question me, but I'd deny everything. After all, he examined me regularly. He knew I wasn't on H! I'd say I'd come to his office looking for a gold cuff-link, or tie-clasp, or some such iten, lost the day he'd given me the sleeping pills.

When Doon died, Ron might or might not read about it. It wouldn't exactly be earth-shaking news. And why would he put together the death of a drug addict in St Louis with what had happened in his office? And even if he did, he was my friend and wouldn't allow it to go beyond speculation ...

I realized I was risking everything in the primary stages by rationalizing points of danger. I had to give Ron an alternative to thinking of me in connection with anything else that might later occur to him. So Nick Leib, game maker and game player, gave the problem a few minutes of intense thought.

It was a simple matter to use my clasp knife on the frame and jamb of the door from the street to the waiting room. I also scratched up the tongue-lock mechanism and left the door slightly ajar. I wiped my prints clean of all surfaces in good old detective story fashion, and went back to the examination room. I took *all* the stylets and morphine pills and put them in my case. I left the cabinet door open, wiped all surfaces clean as I had on the front door, and went back upstairs. I thanked the maid and drove along Route Four towards the George Washington Bridge. But I turned off onto the Palisades Interstate, and drove to the first Hudson lookout. Cold as it was, there were two cars in the parking area. One pulled away as I got out with my attaché case. The other still held its occupants.

I walked quickly along the path and through the copse of trees to the rock observation ledge. No one around. I opened the case, took out all the extra stylets and pills and threw them over the rail into the river. Then I drove home to pack.

I felt good. I felt I was operating logically, not as I had with Ahmed.

The phone rang at four o'clock. Could Ron have returned home this early? I walked over, and hesitated. I hadn't planned on speaking to him until I returned from St Louis. Of course, I didn't have to answer . . .

I picked it up on the seventh ring.

'Nickie? You always answer fast. What're you doing?'

I sat down. She sounded like my little love again. 'Thinking of you. Missing you. Wanting you. The same old thing.'

'I miss you too. I'm sorry I was such a bitch . . . but you said all that crazy stuff and . . . Nickie, I think someone's following me. I couldn't get a look at him. In the car a few times, I thought maybe it was you. But you're in New York. Are you having me watched?'

'Yes.'

'Really? *Are* you! How dare you! I could call the cops!'

'I'd deny it. Planning anything with Doon or Charlie for tonight?'

'If I am, it's my own business. I can do whatever . . .' And then she stopped. 'Nickie, why do we always fight? I don't feel . . . well, mad at you any more. I've been thinking of England. We *did* have some fun. And if that business with Philip hadn't happened, if you hadn't left me for Sheila . . .'

'I left you because you said you couldn't sleep with someone you didn't even like.'

'All right! I was pushing you. I have a right, don't I? But, Nickie, let's not fight *now*. Would you like to see me?'

The ping-pong game again.

'Yes. Do you want to come here?'

'I can't. Mr Alexis . . .'

'I think you can call him Charlie now. After spending all that time with him in your apartment, fucking, sucking . . .'

'Your goddam detective tell you that too? Well he lied! No one can see inside my . . .'

'They've got equipment you wouldn't believe, not to say understand. Sophisticated bugging and scanning devices. And yes, he did tell me you went to bed with Alexis. And I've got details . . .'

'Nickie!' It was a wail. 'Honey, I was *scared*. Russ was crazier than usual Monday and I thought I'd never get out of there alive. I don't have anyone, really, with Harv dead and you in New York . . .'

'Then you admit you make it with Charlie?'

'Don't put such words in my mouth! I . . . he begged me . . . he was so kind, so gentle. He's been paying my rent, buying me things. It was the first time, I swear. And it wasn't really . . . well, not like with *you*.'

'Better, huh?'

'Nothing's ever been better than you, you sonofabitch, and you know it!'

'What about Russ, who you said was better than any Jew?'

'I was trying to hurt you. Russ is ... well, strong and all, but he's freaked out, real sick. And no one goes as long with me as you, makes me feel as much as you. It's not really making love with anyone else, don't you know that, Nickie? Maybe we don't get along in other ways, but you must know we're the greatest in bed.'

I said, 'Yes,' with gratitude, joy, relief. It was of extreme importance to me. It might even save Doon's life. 'Will you stop seeing Russ, and Charlie?

'I've got to see Charlie, he's my boss.'

'You know what I mean. Stop ... sleeping with them.'

'They didn't *sleep* much, baby!' She was laughing.

'Don't joke about such things! You don't know what it does to me!'

'Maybe I do. Maybe that's my one way, my only way, to make you feel what I want you to feel.'

'Too dangerous, Ellie. If I don't have you all for myself, I can't live. *Will* you stop seeing Doon and Charlie? Will you stop seeing every man but me?'

'With you in New York?' Her voice was playful, bitchy, angry, and tender ... but she wasn't taking me seriously.

'I'll come to St Louis.'

'First stop having me followed.'

'No, Ellie. First I come to you.'

'That's pressure! That's forcing! I told you, Nickie, no matter how much I care for you ...'

'Stop there, please. *Do* you care for me? It's been so long since you said anything loving.'

Silence.

'Ellie, I love you. There are no female counterparts of Russ and Charlie in my life.'

'But *dahling*, won't Sheila visit you soon? And has Ledya died or something?'

'I don't see anyone. I *won't* see anyone. It would be better for both of us if I did, or could. But I can't. It's all you now, so give me something to hold to, little girl. *Tell* me, Chelsea.'

'Nickie, I can't just ... too much has happened. And Harv ... you *didn't*, did you?'

'Ellie, answer me. If you care, tell me. No questions until after you tell me. No talk about anything until after you tell me! *Tell me, dammit!'*

'You're screaming again! You *order* me to tell you I love you! Who the hell ever heard of anything like that. Can I love someone who wants to kill all my friends? Can I love someone who screams at me and has me followed and says he'll kill my baby sister. Can I?'

'You'd better,' I said, knowing it was the wrong thing.

'I'd *better*?' Heavy breathing. 'I'll call you again in a day or two. Maybe then I'll be able to tell you my feelings. They're not simple, honey. They're mixed up, but ... I care. Of course I care. Just let me *breathe*! Stop that man from following me. And let me alone ... no pressure! I'll call *you*. And when I'm ready, I'll tell you.'

'I'm sorry,' I said, and I was, but not very. This was old stuff. I no longer had faith in it. 'If you'll let me come to St Louis, if we can get together, if you'll let me stay with you for some time, all right. Otherwise, no.'

'You can't possibly pressure me! And you can't come here now anyway; I've got to settle things in my mind. I won't live with you just because you say I have to! And ... I'm losing the feeling I had when I called, Nickie. I felt I ... I loved you ... a little.'

My heart was jumping all over the place, but I stuck to my point. 'Then let me come to you.'

'Give me a month. Maybe two or three weeks. Then I'll have my mind made up. Then I can tell you yes or no.'

'I'd like to.' And I would have. But how to get through two or three *nights*, knowing about Doon and Alexis, not to say two or three weeks? And she'd probably stall even then. I just wouldn't be able to live that long. 'But I can't. It's got to be *now*.'

She shouted so loud that I had to hold the phone away from my ear. 'I'll fight back! I haven't ... because I don't really believe ... but if I believe, if you *make* me believe ... Nickie, look out! I've got Russ and Russ's got friends, *bad* friends. I've got Charlie and Charlie's got money and friends all over St Louis. I'll hurt you! I'll *hurt* you, you bastard!

'All right. Hurt me. But remember, if I die, then Liz dies. That's the protective contract.'

'Liar! Liar! Let me alone! I'll kill myself!'

'And I've already told you that there too Liz gets it.'

'I can't even kill myself? You think ... my life is *yours*? You think...'

'Yes. You put it perfectly. Your life is mine. My life is yours. Anyone who gets in the way is *kaput*. That's not like Copasetic, little girl. That's the end.'

329

She sighed. Her voice weak, she said, 'Nickie, Christ, I'm not feeling well. Can't you let me alone?'

'No. And I don't think you really want me to.'

Long pause; then, 'Maybe you're right. Who knows? Sometimes I wish you were dead. Other times, I wake up crying because you're not with me. Who the hell knows?'

'Last chance, honey. Can I come to see you?'

'In a month. If you take that tail off me.'

'Goodbye.'

'You won't?'

I hung up.

I waited. She didn't call back. I continued packing. I put my revolver and a box of fifty rounds in the attaché case; then I was finished. I could take the gun, because I was driving.

TWELVE

I drove from New York to St Louis in slightly over thirty hours. I napped at the side of the road twice, not pushing myself, and arrived at the Forest Park Hotel Sunday at three a.m. I'd called ahead for a room, and was soon in bed. I fell asleep quickly, knowing I was only a brisk walk from both Doon's apartment and Alexis's store.

I slept until twelve-thirty, the longest, purest night's rest I'd had in months, no pills or booze needed, thank you; then I went down for brunch and a walk. I thought of Ellie being only moments away, but resisted temptation, and turned into Forest Park. The weather was cold and wet, but I felt fine. Later, I ate a sandwich, bought a few things in the drug store across the way from the hotel, and went to my room. I left word with the switchboard I was to be called at eleven p.m., and lay down. And slept heavily, dreamlessly, until I was called.

Addicts, in their attempts to prevent blood infections, boil the water in which they dissolve their heroin crystals. Doctors use sterile liquid solutions to dissolve morphine for injections, or use stylets, which are germ free. I wasn't concerned with such delicate matters. My 'patient' wasn't going to survive to become infected. I simply used hot water from the tap in the bottom of a water glass, dissolved the eight tablets, and tilted the glass to fill the syringe. I wrapped a hand towel around syringe and stylet, along with the extra syringe I'd taken in case of malfunction or breakage, put my revolver in my overcoat pocket, and was ready for the evening's entertainment.

I phoned Doon's apartment. He answered, even more sleepily than before. 'Yeah, who is it?'

'Billy-May, please,' I drawled.

'No fuckin' Billie-May here.'

I went down, carrying my case, and walked seven blocks to Doon's address. I whistled softly, enjoying the exercise. Damn, but I felt good! Not the slightest bit uptight. It was almost midnight and the neighbourhood wasn't the best, decidedly shabby in spots, and on one corner a group of three black youths stared as I approached and I heard some mumbled 'Fucking Whitey' remarks as I passed, but still I felt fine. That gun was in my pocket. That solution to the Doon problem in any case ... and possibly to the Ellie problem as well, if she finally realized there was no way to go but to me.

Of course, when I finally reached the address, a four-storey brick building that was in better shape than most in the area, I began to sweat. And after walking through a bright lobby, and down a poorly lit hallway, I found I was breathing heavily and gripping the gun much too tightly. I took several deep breaths, looked up and down the hallway, and stepped close to the door marked 1-C. I put my ear to it. Nothing. I began to step back, to think ... and knew I was stalling. I pressed the bell button. There was a two-tone chime, and footsteps came toward me; heavy footsteps. Now if he would only open the door. If not, I'd have to say Ellie had sent me, and see what results that produced. Just as long as he opened it a *little*, so I could shove the gun in.

The door opened wide. I guess I'd expected a monster, a pro-football superman, a hulking beast, a huge black bogeyman.

He *was* big. Not that tall, or at least not that tall for his width. He was rather meaty, almost fat, but the hands that half-raised themselves when I drew and cocked the revolver were long, lean-fingered, almost delicate. His face was strong, but also long, also fine. Only his eyes fit the monster picture; small and sleepy and bloodshot. And mean. Oh, yes, those eyes looked at me in decidedly *mean* fashion. But then again, they were seeing a man holding a gun.

He backed up. 'Gainer wouldn't send Whitey. It doesn't figure.' Then he smiled, and almost destroyed my ability to do what I had to do. A wide, strangely innocent smile revealing a three-tooth gap in the upper front, a loss almost generic to the profession of football. Mr Doon had obviously put his bridge away for the night, and he was wearing nothing but red-and-blue striped pyjama bottoms. 'You must be the one Ellie talked about. Nick, right?'

I nodded, and stepped inside, and saw the pictures. The living room ran lengthwise, mostly to the right of the hall door. The closest wall was straight ahead, about six feet away. Scotch-taped to this wall were a dozen photographs, Polaroids, in colour. Three rows of four each. A blonde girl. Nude. Alone, and with a black man. And that black man was now a dead man; I could shoot him and not worry about the consequences!

I said, 'Back!' and he looked at my hand on the gun and went back fast and hit the couch and sat down. I looked over his head at the pictures. Ellie. A dull stare in all poses. A drugged look, or a *forced* look.

Doon said, 'Don't squeeze it any more, man!'

I eased up on the trigger, and put my case down.

The second and third row of pictures were with Doon. All the classic pornographic poses. Fucking. Sucking. Being eaten. On hands and knees, a black hand shoving a vibrator up her. Bent over a chair, being beaten with a strap. Over his lap, being spanked. One with a banana in her. One getting it standing. And the last with her hands tied to the head of the bed and he kneeling over her, shoving it in her mouth.

'She dug it, man. No muscle, hear?'

'She isn't smiling,' I said, and had to clear my throat. 'She's suffering. You can see it.'

'Suffering? She had some pills in her. She sees me once a week, sometimes more. We got a thing, maybe not everyone can understand it, but the races meet in us. We go a long way together. You understand black–white...?'

'You don't have to lecture me on Eldridge Cleaver,' I said, and stepped back and bent carefully and opened the case. 'I've read him. I accept him. But he isn't fucking Ellie.'

'She important to me,' he said, looking at the case but not able to see inside since the lid was blocking his view. 'I'm important to her. I know you got a thing for her...'

I took out the hypodermic.

He laughed. 'You think I'm going to let you put that in me?'

'Just to make you sleep. Either that or the gun.'

'Sure, sleep. Only I don't wake up.' He began to rise. 'Well, you're gonna hafta...

I jerked the gun straight out, tightening my finger on the trigger, *wanted* to shoot now and splatter blood all over that wall, wanted to drown those pictures that were shaking my mind. I told myself to hold on, but I was going to shoot... and then he sank back.

'Okay, you love her. I love her too. My own way. You ask her. Call her now. Phone's in the bedroom. Go on. She'll come over.

We'll talk. I mess her up some, sure. She messes me up in a different way. But like I said, we're *important* to each other! We got a right to each other! I got more of a right to her than you! Least I *know* what's pushing me. Black boy needs a touch of white thighs. *Needs*, because all the goddam ads and all the goddam movies and TV say white is beautiful. And you, Jew-baby? Need a blonde *shirksa*? Well, I still got more right than you. The Jew's fight is over. You can get what you want. But blacks...'

I said, 'Shut up.' He was confusing me. He had a little truth, and I didn't have the time to explain that it was age and youth, more than Jew and Gentile, that was *my* surface reason for loving Ellie ... and that surface reasons were of no use in explaining what I now felt. I'd need a lifetime *with* Ellie, to find out what it was ... and that's exactly what I intended to get.

And that's why I couldn't let my rage at those pictures push me into using the gun. Because then I'd be caught. Because then I'd lose my lifetime with Ellie.

I stood up, the needle in my left hand. 'Lie down on the couch. Stick out your arm.'

'What's in the hypo?'

'What you like.'

'Then why you giving it to me?'

'Because I want to put you away for a while, search this place, maybe mark you up...'

'Shit!'

'I've got a plan,' I said, wondering how I could approach him and knock him out ... and then realizing that a bruise on the head would create suspicion. 'A plan to make sure you never see Ellie again.'

'I'll see her as long as I live. You damn well better know that.'

'Because you love her, right?'

'Right!'

'And that's why you put those obscene pictures on the wall?'

'They're only for *me*.'

'Anyone comes into this room...'

'You wouldn't've come in without the gun. I put 'em up before bed. To go with the high. To fly with. Because she don't come to see me much. Because I scare her sometimes. Because, you mother, she won't live with me like she lived with you and with that other Jew bastard. And now her boss, that old Greek, is moving in...'

He gasped, wet his lips, and sank back, seemingly sick. He was raging, just like Nick Leib. He was agonized over his competition, just like Nick Leib.

333

I began to lose the will to kill.

But I *had* to do it! If no longer for hatred of this man and what he'd done with my little girl, then to prove to Ellie there was no way out; to make her understand I'd kill right down to the last lover, the most important member of her family!

I stood there, the gun in one hand, the needle in the other, and how to get that needle into him without coming within reach of those powerful arms? How to kill him without using the gun and throwing away my own life or freedom?

I talked, afraid he would begin to understand and come at me. I said, 'You love her, and you let someone take pictures of the two of you that way. Maybe you let the guy have her . . . ?'

He hunched forward, fists clenched. 'Self-timer, you dumb fucker! You think I'd let anyone see my rabbit that way?'

His rabbit. His pet name for my Chelsea. The hate was returning. The need to kill was returning. But *how*?

He'd sunk back in the couch again. His head nodded, almost as if it were too heavy for him to keep up. And now I noticed his eyes; they weren't mean, they were *dilated*.

Of course! He was on something. He'd even said so a moment ago – the pictures were up on the wall 'to go with the high. To fly with.' He'd taken something, hopefully a fix. With luck he'd grow very drowsy; perhaps fall asleep; or pass out under tension . . .

'Your rabbit,' I said, and laughed. 'You think she's *your* girl?'

'She is! She's been, and now she is again! My girl! If I was white . . .'

'If you were straight. If you were normal. If you weren't a brutal junkie who pushed drugs on her . . .'

'No difference,' he said, spittle flying from his mouth. He kept wetting his lips. His chest was heaving. 'No fucking difference, because she wouldn't . . . no difference.'

'She would, if she loved you. You know it. She doesn't have that kind of block. But you know what you are. And you know you're finished. And she knows it too.'

He was shaking his head. He rubbed his eyes, said, 'I'll kick the habit when I'm ready.'

I lifted the needle. 'It's what you want. It's a *lot* of what you want, but maybe you can survive it.'

'Go away, man, too dumb.'

'And even if you don't, it's the way you'll go, sooner or later. And maybe you really want it sooner.'

He rubbed his eyes. He wet his lips. 'You're . . . putting me on. No one kills for a chick. I couldn't . . .'

'But I can. For Ellie. That's why she's *my* girl.'

He closed his eyes. His head sank back. He seemed to be falling asleep. And then he looked at me. 'You kill Cohen?'

I didn't go into the subtleties. I nodded.

'You're crazy, you know that?'

I nodded again.

'Okay. You win. I won't see her. Give you ...' He rubbed his eyes with both hands. 'Word, man.'

I said, 'All right.' He was peering at me, as if having difficulty focusing. I bent and put the needle back in the case. He closed his eyes, then forced them open. I shut the case, tinkering with the snap locks. His eyes closed again. I rose slowly, lifting the case. His head fell to the side; he breathed heavily.

'I'm leaving now, Russ.'

He mumbled. He didn't move. But it could be an act. If I came close and he jumped me, I'd have little chance ... except by using the gun, and then I'd blow my future.

I waited. He seemed out. I put the case back down, opened it, and took out the hypodermic. 'Russ, wake up!'

He breathed regularly.

I decided to test him. I went out of the room. I passed through a kitchen to a lighted bathroom and paused in the doorway, listening, my hand sweating on the gun. Better to find out now, than when I was bending over him.

I was about to return, when I saw the equipment on the closed toilet seat: bent spoon, empty hypodermic syringe, length of rubber tubing. Yes, Mr Doon had definitely had himself a fix before I came. And that rubber tubing was something I'd forgotten.

I stuffed it into my pocket, and walked slowly, carefully to the kitchen. I stayed back from the corner, and edged forward until I could see the couch.

He was still there. He hadn't moved.

I went to the couch. I jabbed the gun into his stomach. He groaned, but didn't jerk the way a conscious man would.

I put the gun down behind me, checked on whether I could reach it easily, moved it further back. I put the needle on the couch, and tied the rubber tubing around his right biceps ... and he moved. I lunged for the gun. But he'd merely shifted weight; fallen further to the left, into a semi-reclining position. I tightened the tubing, rubbed the arm, tried to find a vein. He was dark brown not black, but it was still hard to find ... and then I saw the track marks, the needle marks, high on the forearm. I decided to go right in on an old mark. I took the needle, stuck it in, depressed the plunger, drew it out.

What if I'd overshot the vein, pierced it through and discharged the morphine into the flesh?

He couldn't live! He would accuse me! I was registered at the hotel and Ellie would join me in the accusations and he'd say I'd admitted to killing Harv...

I took out the stylet, found another track mark, stuck it in there.

I removed the tubing from his arm and dropped it on the couch, as he might have after coming from the bathroom where he'd taken his fix. I put everything else back in the case, and looked around, trying to remember what I'd touched in this room. Nothing, actually.

I looked at those photographs. I went to the wall and took them down, and went through them, twice. I began to turn on...

Doon moved and moaned. I jumped back, fumbling at the case. He was breathing heavily, and fell over on his left side. I decided to take the gun away, to be safe.

He made a choking sound. I backed away, levelling the gun. He rolled off the couch and crashed to the floor, landing on his back. His hand tossed once, twice. He opened his eyes, and his mouth, and then he went limp and loose. His chest heaved shallowly. Then it stopped. It heaved again, irregularly. And stopped again. His arms and legs jerked. His chest heaved. Now I wished I'd saved a few of the stylets I'd thrown into the Hudson. If he recovered, I'd have to use the gun.

No, I wasn't thinking. A pillow over his face...

I jumped a good foot into the air as the phone rang.

It kept ringing, incredibly loud, it seemed. I watched Doon. His chest was barely moving. The phone rang ... and it was twelve-twenty and who would be calling him?

Ellie?

I had to know.

No real risk. I'd soon be leaving here. I'd simply listen; then use the pillow.

I went to the bedroom. There was enough light from the bathroom across the hall for me to see the phone on a bedside table. I picked it up. Ellie said, 'Russ, you all right?'

I grunted.

'You've been shooting again, haven't you?'

I cleared my throat.

'Russ? Are you sick? Russ?'

I hung up.

They were important to each other. She was important to so many men, my little love, my little whore. And still I had to have her.

I picked up a pillow and returned to the living room. Doon lay very still. I bent close. His eyes were rolled back; his breath had stopped.

I put my ear to his chest. No heartbeat.

I returned the pillow to the bedroom, wiped the phone with my handkerchief, went back to the living room. I put the Polaroid shots and the gun in my overcoat pocket, then ran the rubber tubing through my handkerchief and dropped it back on the couch.

I looked around a last time.

The phone rang. I waited until it stopped, counting an interminable twenty-two rings, then used my hankerchief to open the door. I looked up and down the hall. Empty. I stepped out, wiped the outer knob, and walked along the hall and through the lobby.

It was twelve-thirty, and the streets of this transition neighbourhood now seemed terribly dangerous. Gun or not, I was afraid. I'd done what I'd come to do, and I wanted to get back safely to my room. I couldn't face anything more tonight . . . but I had to.

The three black youths were still on that corner. I crossed over to the other side. One began to come after me, saying to his friends, 'It's a better neighbourhood on the other side. Whites live there.'

I walked more quickly. When I glanced back, his friends were also crossing and he was close behind me. He said, 'Hold it, man. Let's have a cigarette.'

I stopped and pulled my gun. He did an abrupt about-face and walked away, waving a hand in the air and sing-songing, 'I'm giving up smoking 'cause it kills your lungs.'

I watched as he reached his friends and they all entered a building; then I walked on. At a deserted corner, I dumped the contents of my case down a sewer, and continued on to the hotel.

In the room, I stripped off my clothing, intending to shower. Instead, I looked at those Polaroids, and dialled Ellie's number. She answered on the second ring. 'Yes?'

I gave a deep sigh.

'Russ?'

'Sorry, it's Nickie. Just wanted to say goodnight. And to tell you I decided to buy a Polaroid camera. They're great. You don't have to send film away to be developed. Each shot is developed right in the camera. That makes it possible to take, well, *naughty* pictures. Know what I mean? Hey, Ellie, you still there?'

'Yes.'

'Maybe you'd consider posing for a few with me? No problem about who takes the pictures. I'll get a self-timer. Ellie? Why don't you answer? Don't you like the idea?'

'Nickie, where are you?' Her voice was shaking, frightened.

'At a phone booth near the cottage, honey. But let me go on. If you agree to do a few fun poses with me, we can mock up a spanking scene...'

'Give me the phone number. I'll call you back.'

'Why? The connection's fine.'

'I ... I have to go to the bathroom.'

I laughed. 'I'm through talking now. Goodnight.'

'Nickie ... I'll let you visit.'

'Thanks, but I've changed my mind about that. You come to New York, for good.'

Silence.

'Goodnight now, love. I'll call you again tomorrow. Maybe you'll say yes then.'

She began to answer. I hung up. I showered, and looked at the pictures, and masturbated. And then wondered at myself for being able to pull off looking at Ellie and another man. When I'd first seen those pictures, they'd driven me insane.

But of course, Doon was dead. I wasn't looking at pictures of Ellie and a threat to my future with her. I was looking at Ellie and a dead man; a man I'd made dead myself.

I looked through the pictures one last time, and tore them up, and flushed the pieces down the toilet. I went to bed, and slept beautifully until ten-thirty Monday morning. Again, as after fire-bombing Ahmed's place and learning of Harv's death, I'd experienced release from anguish, a period of comparative peace. It was broken when I phoned the private investigator.

Ellie had worked Thursday morning, then gone to a 'medical building' on Kingshighway at one p.m. The operator had followed her to the office of an internist, Dr Walter Roesch. She'd remained in the office forty minutes, and 'emerged with male Caucasian, forty to forty-five, tall, grey-haired, holding his arm. They proceeded to a restaurant down the steet, and spent an hour in close conversation. Male held subject's hand for long periods of time...' The operator was later to determine from the receptionist that the man was Dr Roesch, and Ellie had visited him often in the past month. They'd lunched together several times...

Another one. No end to them. She made lovers of all the men in her life, from those who checked her books to those who checked her diarrhoea. And I thought of Shebsia pulling her dress up and

338

her pants down, and Ron with his 'little tramp'.

She returned to her apartment, where she was joined at four p.m. by Alexis. He'd stayed until seven.

I'd called her at the store that morning. Afterwards, she'd held hands with the doctor, and fucked for Charlie.

I began to sweat.

On Friday, Ellie had worked until one-thirty, then driven to a four-family house in a section of South St Louis not too far from her old neighbourhood. She entered the ground-floor rear apartment, listed to Mrs Mary McBaren. Ellie's mother. She remained until three and emerged with a 'female Caucasian, young, fourteen to sixteen'. Probably Liz. They embraced, and Ellie had then driven to an address near Washington University, entering the apartment of a Mr Jerry Perlmade. Claire's husband. At that point I began to hope she was going to spend at least *one* innocent day. The hope vanished as Mr Cranwell went on.

At eight, Ellie left Claire's and drove the few blocks to the Tenderoin Room, a fine hotel restaurant. At ten, 'she emerged on the arm of her employer, Mr Alexis'. They'd driven to her apartment. Alexis had remained two hours and forty minutes, and left alone.

On Saturday, she had worked from two p.m. until nine p.m., 'then left in the company of the salesman who is her co-worker'. They had dinner at an inexpensive steak house called the Red Brick Inn, and drove around in the salesman's Plymouth sedan. 'Subject showed signs of nervousness, awareness of being followed.' She kept looking around when entering and leaving the car, the restaurant, and after they parked near the clothing store, where she'd left her car. 'Nevertheless, subject and male companion engaged not only in conversation, but in what appeared to be various forms of intimate sexual play.'

Oh God. No end. *Or was she doing it to let me know there was no end?*

Yesterday, Sunday, she had spent almost all day alone in her apartment, 'emerging toward evening to drive to the Tenderloin Room. Operator entered and dined, observing subject and her employer, Mr Alexis, at a nearby table. Subject seemed agitated. Alexis showed signs of affection, touching her hand, her face, once kissing her.' They then went to her apartment 'in their respective cars, where he spent the night'.

I asked if it were possible to find out if Charles Alexis were married. It was, for 'a slight additional fee'. I said to go ahead, and that I'd call tomorrow for an up-to-the minute report. Cranwell suggested I allow two or three days to pass so the information could

339

be 'collated'. I said sorry, I didn't have two or three days.

I ate. I tried to nap ... but the shakes, the sweats, the anguish, the rage, the hatred, the need to be with Ellie, was back.

I watched the six o'clock news on television. No word of Russ Doon.

I called Ellie at home. No answer.

I went down for dinner. As with most of my meals lately, I left just about everything on the plate. But I put away three martinis. I returned to the room, beginning to get the panicked feeling. No cause, I told myself. Once she hears about Doon ...

I tried her home. No answer. I was sorry I hadn't tried her earlier at the store. Of course, I could drive to her home, use my key to get in ...

But no, that would blow my cover.

I called her every half-hour until midnight. She was with Alexis, or Dr Roesch, or her 'co-worker', or a new man. She was fucking, sucking, coming. She cared nothing for me, nothing for any one man. She was a whore.

So what else was new?

I watched the late news. Doon had been found by 'a girlfriend' who had tried to phone him several times Sunday night and Monday morning. 'Gaining entry to his apartment at noon today, she found the body, called the police, and left before an ambulance arrived. A doctor pronounced the controversial ex-football star dead, victim of his well-known addiction to heroin. The police surgeon stated that pending results of an autopsy, the cause of death will be listed as overdose of a narcotic agent. Police are still trying to learn the identity of the woman who phoned them.' The newscaster went on to recap the life of the 'once-fabled running end who set National Football League records ...'

I called Ellie's apartment. No answer.

I called the private investigators, asking if the information on Charles Alexis was in. It was. He was married, had two daughters, had not been living with his wife for approximately two weeks. He had taken an apartment in Ballwin, and appeared to be in the process of securing a divorce.

I asked where his address was in relation to Ellie's.

'About ten minutes by car ...'

I phoned her. No answer. For the best, perhaps, as I was shaking, raging, and would probably have made very little sense.

And I thought of something else. The detective following her knew she'd gone to Doon's apartment this morning. Was that privileged information between agency and client, between them and me,

340

or would Ellie's name soon be plastered over the newspapers as Doon's girlfriend'?

I couldn't call them andd ask to have the information suppressed, because I wasn't supposed to know it until they told it to me.

I phoned her again, a little calmer, thinking how to handle her accusations on Doon. Probably best to backtrack a bit at first, give her some room in which to manoeuvre emotionally. If she was to return to me, she would have to convince herself I wasn't a total monster.

I called again, and again. And thought of Charlie, and that young salesman. And began to sweat, to tremble.

At one a.m., my phone rang.

'Hello, Nickie. It's Ellie.'

'I've been calling...' And then realized *she* had called *me*, and I was supposed to be in New York.

'How did you find out?'

'After Russ, I decided to call around. You stayed at the Forest Park when we first met. So I asked for Nicholas Leib, and there you were.'

Her voice was dull and dead. She sounded strange.

'Yes, heard about Doon on television. Too bad he didn't do it three years ago, before meeting you.'

She said nothing.

I said, 'Arrived a few hours ago,' playing the cover game, wondering why I'd never thought to use a false name.

'You've been there since Sunday, early. The desk told me.'

'Here's something the desk can't tell you! If you care anything about Charlie, you'll stop seeing him! Him and everyone else!'

'All right.'

For the second time in the last minute I was caught by surprise. 'I mean it, Ellie!'

'I know you do. I'll start looking for another job.'

'Why bother? You're coming back to New York with me anyway. And don't start that business about forcing...'

'I won't.'

'You mean ... you *are* coming back to me?'

'I guess so.'

That dead voice bothered me, worried me. But then again, it probably reflected surrender.

'Can I come over now? To help you pack?'

'If you want. But ... would you give me until tomorrow? About one or two in the afternoon? I've got to ... tell people, make arrangements. I'd really like a few days...'

'Tomorrow, at two.'

'All right.'

That strange voice. That dead voice. Such complete surrender. I couldn't believe it. 'Do you mean it, Ellie? Because if this is some sort of trick...'

'What else can I do, Nickie? What's left?'

For a moment I had nothing to say. For a moment I was stricken with guilt. Then, 'Ellie, it was all because I loved...'

'I know. I'm so tired, Nickie. I'll see you tomorrow.'

'Goodnight, Chelesa. I love you, honey.'

'Goodnight, Nickie.'

She hung up. I sat there with the phone in my hand. I didn't know what to feel. It wasn't Ellie who had surrendered to me. It was a stranger. A dull, dead stranger.

But later, in bed, the joy began coming, in spite of that voice. The joy made me get up and pace around the room. I had a drink, not to put myself away, but to celebrate tomorrow and my reunion with Ellie. And when I went back to bed, the joy helped me fall asleep.

In dreams, the strangeness of that voice returned to torture me. Ellie dead when I came to help her pack. Ellie lying in a coffin, nude, surrounded by leering male mourners. I got to her, pushed them away, shouted I'd kill them all, every last one. And she said, 'What else can I do, Nickie? What's left?'

I awoke to daylight, afraid that she was going to kill herself. I ran to the phone, and by the time I reached it the nightmare had dissipated. She couldn't risk suicide; not with what I'd said about the contract on Liz. She wouldn't anyway. She knew now how much I loved her.

Not that she could be certain I'd killed anyone. In time she wouldn't believe I'd done anything wrong at all.

And what *had* I done? Given Ahmed a hot-foot. Paid a man to have Harv killed, without being certain it would actually happen, and then tried to abort it at the end. Helped a doomed junkie to a somewhat quicker death than he himself might have managed.

I washed and dressed, and only then called her. No answer, but it was nine-thirty, and she could be on her way to the store to tell Alexis she was quitting. I went down and had coffee. And then I called the store. A man answered. He said, 'Ellie won't be back until after her vacation.'

My heart began to pound ... but she might have explained her leaving with *me* that way. 'This is rather important. I have to locate her. Family business. Mother taken ill this morning.'

'Gee, I wish I could help you. I'd give you her home number but she's not there. I got a call from Mr Alexis at my home last night saying Ellie wouldn't be around for a while. He said I was to hire an assistant and clear it through his Ladue manager.'

'Why not through Charlie himself?'

'Because, well, he's gone on vacation too.' Little laugh. 'Coincidence, right? If you want to check with the Ladue manager ... ?'

I called immediately. Mr Blaylock was perfectly sympathetic, but could offer no information as to when either Ellie or Charlie would return. 'And I don't have a clue as to where they might be. He called me at home last night...'

I got my coat, and my gun, and ran down to my car. I drove to her place, and was stopped by a cop for doing ninety in a fifty-mile zone, and tore up the ticket as soon as I was on my way again. I didn't get lost this time. I didn't ring or knock this time either. I let myself in, shouting *'Ellie!'*

The place was empty. Her luggage and most of her clothing was gone.

Ellie and Charlie had run away together. That crap last night, that dull voice, that surrender – just to throw me off guard! Just to give them more time!

I went to the phone. I was shaking. I was sweating. I had to call her. And there was no way. I pounded the phone with my fist. No way!

Then I said, 'The detective agency! They'll be with her. Anywhere she goes, they said, they'll be with her. And I'll be with her by tonight. And then there'll be no Charlie. And if I have to, yes, there'll be no Liz! If I have to, there'll be no *anyone* for that bitch!'

I was shouting. Nothing she'd ever done had hurt me as much as this. She preferred that pawing, sickening bastard to me! The man she'd mocked as a peeker under dresses, a seeker after feels, was now preferable to her Nickie!

I went to the bathroom and washed my face. I didn't look in the hamper; I didn't dare.

I went to the kitchen and there was two beers in the refrigerator and some bourbon in a cupboard and I poured equal portions of both into a water glass and drank it down. I walked around, to regain some modicum of control. Then I went to the bedroom and her vanity, and sat down and dialled. She'd soon find out...

I spoke to Cranwell. At first he tried to act firm about not having enough to report to me. When I *insisted*, he was evasive about what he did have. 'No point giving disturbing information when it will probably change in a day or two.'

I said, 'Oh God, you've lost her, haven't you?'

'Well ... yes. But it's expected, once a subject suspects being followed. And Miss McBaren obviously spotted our operator a few days ago. We changed him, twice, but to no avail.'

I was dizzy. I was sick. I didn't know where Ellie was. I couldn't live not knowing where Ellie was!

'We'll pick her up again at job or home, Mr Leib, never doubt it.'

'Not unless she returns to job or home.'

'Eventually...'

'Eventually hell!' I screamed. 'I want to know where she is *now*! I want to be able to get to her *today*!'

There was a moment of silence. 'If you wish to terminate the contract, it's all right with us. We'll refund on a pro-rated basis.'

I took hold of myself. Without the detectives, I was finished. I said, 'I'm sorry. You're right. But I think we'll have to operate in a different way now. She's probably with Charlie Alexis, her employer. We'll have to look for him as well as her. And simply watching their homes and places of business won't be enough. Any chance of doing something to the phone at her mother's place? And to the phone at Alexis's stores?'

'You mean tap the lines? I'm afraid that't illegal.' He paused. 'And far more expensive than you might think.'

'I'd pay it.'

'It could run to a thousand, perhaps more. And that only for the initial work and a week of monitoring.'

'Whatever you say.'

'And if it took several weeks, a month, at an additional five hundred a week?'

'All right.'

Long pause. 'Could you come to our offices in the next few days? It'll be neccessary to do some paper work, have you sign certain documents that will at least assure us you won't turn around and accuse us of operating without your consent and approval.'

'Why would I do that?'

'Entrapment is fairly common in our business, Mr Leib. You might be a federal agent.'

'I'm sure you'll check me out in the next day or two.' I gave him my business address.

He said. 'Thank you. But still ...'

I was tempted to say I'd be there later today, but decided against it. 'I'll be there tomorrow morning.'

'Fine. I'll see you then. In the meantime, I want you to know

344

you aren't being charged for the shifts since she lost us Sunday night. There's be a rebate...'

Sunday? Then they hadn't followed her to Doon's ... and she might have called me from a thousand miles away last night! Or three thousand! Or five! She might be in Europe, Asia, South America with Alexis! She might be gone forever...

I covered the mouthpiece and fought for control.

'... spot check her home and business address once a day,' Cranwell was saying. 'Alexis's residence too. The fee will be kept minimal.'

I uncovered the mouthpiece. My voice was a little hoarse, but I managed to speak normally. 'Would you mind telling me how she lost you?'

'No great trick losing a tail, Mr Leib. After all, there's just so much an operator can do. He can't enter homes with her. In this case, she drove to Mr Alexis's place at two a.m. Sunday night ... rather Monday morning. The operator parked where he could see not only her car and the front entrace, but the one rear door to the building as well. What he couldn't see was a window on the opposite side, and she obviously climbed out there and was picked up by someone waiting. Alexis's Cadillac is gone. Her car was still there this morning.'

'How can you be certain she's not hiding in Alexis's place?'

'We have our methods, Mr Leib. If there was any chance she was still there, I'd never have admitted she lost us. Our operator was able to enter the premises with the custodian the next morning – yesterday, that is. No one there, and every indication that Alexis had left on an extended trip.'

'You'll get on the telephones right away?' I asked. 'There's enough money left of my old fee to cover at least part of the cost.'

'Yes. We'll have operators moving in as repair men as soon as possible.'

After I'd hung up, I said, 'Why worry over a few days, Nick? A week or so? Life goes on, right?'

Except that my life *wouldn't* go on. It would stop dead...

No, that too was wrong. Stopping dead wouldn't be bad. Being unconscious, unaware, unfeeling, wouldn't be bad. It was the *thinking*, the fantasizing Ellie's lovemaking, the fearing never seeing her again that would kill me.

¶I left the apartment, and tried *Playing At Being Alive*. I walked briskly. I planned a few more days in St Louis, and then some trips. The Ozarks. Chicago. Perhaps even Los Angeles...

After visiting Cranwell in the downtown offices of V.E. Investigations, I stayed in my hotel room, night and day, for two weeks, fifteen days to be exact. I walked a little at night, despite the desk clerk warning me about 'crime in the streets'. No one tried to rob or kill me, though my insanity was such that I'd have welcomed the action. I had an occasional meal out, though I rarely ate more than a few mouthfuls, and I couldn't wait to get back and check with the detective agency. I bugged Cranwell and Deterwiller to the point where they put other people on the line to say they weren't in. Their reports were the same each day: 'The monitoring continues without results.' I phoned Teaneck twice, speaking both times to Louise and Seth, and once to Denise, explaining I was away on business. I didn't speak to anyone else. I watched television and drank and took tranquillizers and sleeping pills. Room service got much action from Mr Leib. Once, a bellhop asked if I wanted 'company'. I said, 'Later, perhaps,' and tipped him heavily. I thought how nice it would be to have a lovely young blonde come up and screw me into placidity. But when I finally gave him the go-ahead, the girl was dark and plump and while far from ugly, nothing at all like Ellie. I turned her away at the door, saying there'd been some mistake.

My phone rang Monday morning at nine-thirty. I was in the bathroom, shitting my brains out. I'd had diarrhoea for two days running ... running hard. I ran again, hitching up my pyjama bottoms.

'Mr Leib? Cranwell. We've found them.'

I sank down on the chair.

'Alexis called his Ladue store Friday, and was told he had to sign certain papers left by his lawyer. He said he would let the manager, a Mr Blaylock, know whether he'd be in town Monday for the signing. He also said to leave the papers on a desk in the office, and this sounded as if it were worth a few days' surveillance. We put a man on the Ladue store, and it paid off. Alexis drove up, alone, at seven-thirty this morning, went inside, stayed about ten minutes, came out carrying a Manilla envelope, drove to a mailbox, posted the envelope, got onto Highway Two-forty-four, then headed west on Interstate Seventy. He drove some forty miles, turned off ...'

I asked him to stop while I got paper and pencil. I began to write down directions. Alexis was about an hour's drive from me, in a motel off the main highway.

'I gather we should stop the monitoring service, Mr Leib?'

'And the surveillance. Immediately.'

'Our man's due to call in within the hour. He'll be off by' ... pause ... 'ten-thirty. Your billing, on all services, will terminate as of then, and the refund mailed to your home address.'

'Thank you. I apologize for my nervousness. Excellent service.' And I was dashing for my clothes.

The motel was not one of the national chains. Far from it. A green frame building, one-storey and barracks-like, it faced the road and held at most twenty units. Across the two-lane blacktop was a diner. There was nothing but flat, reddish-brown fields in all directions, and the highway about a mile and a half south. Ellie and Alexis were obviously trying to remain hidden here.

I went to the diner, checking carefully through the window before entering. It was small, very chrome-shiny, and very empty. I sat at a window booth and ordered coffee and whole-wheat toast from a cute black waitress with a classic ass ... the kind of ass I liked. Make that *had* liked. Now there was only one ass, one cute girl; and that was love and that was sickness and it should only happen to Hitler, as my mother used to say.

I checked the time. Five to eleven. The tail should be off by now.

I drank the coffee and forced half a slice of toast down my throat. And felt the diarrhoea hit. I went to the bathroom. I stayed about ten minutes, and when I came out ordered more coffee. And looked out the window and saw Charlie Alexis walking from the motel, wearing youthful Scotch-plaid trousers, suède half-coat, and narrow-brim hat. The door stayed open behind him ... fifth door from the left, I noted. I watched Charlie, then saw another man come out of the room. He was big, burly, crew-cut, brown hair, wearing a short Mackinaw. He had the look of an ex-boxer, or ex-cop. He walked about ten paces behind Charlie.

I went to the counter, where the cute black girl was shelving cups from a tray, and gave her a dollar and said, 'That'll cover it. Is there another way out of here? I think my wife had me followed.'

'Well, through the kitchen, but we're not allowed ...'

I put another dollar in her hand, and said, 'Please.'

She motioned me around the counter. I ran, because Charlie was crossing the road. We went through swinging doors into a kitchen. Two men were working there, and neither looked at us, and then I was going out a back door and down three wide concrete steps. I moved away from the door, but didn't go around the building so as to see, or be seen from, the road. I waited, counting seconds in my head, until I felt I'd waited five minutes. Then I walked south, in the direction of my car, but not along the road. I stayed in the field until I reached the bend, never glancing back. Then I crossed the road to my car.

I picked thistles off my trousers, U-turned, and headed toward the

347

highway. There'd been a large shopping centre about five miles back.

The exit off the highway was marked, 'Shopping & Services'. I entered a side road, and then the enormous parking lot. It was eleven-twenty. The supermarket was jammed, and so was the parking area closest to it. I parked a little further west, near a five and dime, and went inside and bought a pair of gloves from a rack – brown, cloth with leather backing, a dollar and twelve cents. I put them on as soon as I came outside, and walked to the parking area near the supermarket, and began to stroll up and down the rows of cars, looking inside.

Many were unlocked, and I could jump ignition wires, and time was short since I wanted to get back to that diner before Charlie left it. But I hoped for a key. And saw the teen-aged girl drive up in the Javelin hardtop and jump out and run for the supermarket.

I walked over. The door was ajar, and the key was in the ignition.

I got inside. Automatic, of course, and she hadn't bothered to put it in Park. I did, with experience born of Ahmed's hot-foot, and started and drove ox.

I was back at the bend in the blacktop road in five minutes, but didn't stop there. I'd been planning this game since heading for the shopping centre. I was facing in the wrong direction for what I was going to do. I had to go past the diner – and with luck get a look at Charlie – and turn and position myself facing south; facing the diner, and beyond the diner the entrance to the highway.

I went past the diner, and there was Charlie at a booth, bending over and spooning something into his mouth. And there was his bodyguard across the table, looking out at me. Lucky it hadn't been the other way around, with Charlie looking out, though he probably wouldn't have recognized me in a moving vehicle.

I went about two hundred feet down the road, and U-turned, and parked on the shoulder. I left the engine running, and put on the radio, and wondered if the girl would return to look for her car before I returned the car to the parking lot. Either way, I would make it.

I listened to rock music, and thought of that night in Miami when I'd forced the punk off the road. This was going to be far less sporting, though the bodyguard might give chase. If he did, it all depended on how fast he could get into a car and come after me. If he came quickly, then it was going to be a tougher game to win.

But the more I thought, the more I felt I was in excellent shape, even taking into account my desire, my absolute *need*, to finish

Forest Park Hotel.'

She drew the robe closer around her, as if cold.

'Are you finished playing games?' I asked. 'Are you coming home with me, or do I have to kill that salesman you petted . . .'

'I knew I was being watched. I wanted to give you something to steam about. Eddie's just a nice kid.'

'They're all nice kids to you. The doctor, for example. Walter Roesch, tall, grey-haired, forty to forty-five?'

She shook her head and laughed, and the laugh was bad. 'Oh, I'll see *him* all right. Not for a while, but I'll see him. Or whoever you get to take his place.'

I grew frightened. 'Are you sick? Really? But all that lunching and hand-holding . . .'

'He liked me. He pitied me. He tried to make me feel I wasn't going to die. And up until the exploratory, he believed it and I believed him.'

'Exploratory? But when . . . ?

'You killed poor old Charlie for nothing. He couldn't even get it up for me the last week . . . no, nine days, since I left the hospital. He was stuck with a *body*; I mean a dead body. But still he promised to be with me and he promised to take care of Liz, to help her out, maybe a job after high school, maybe even send her to college, and I had to be with *someone*, didn't I?'

It had been so long since I'd really eaten anything and my guts were crawling and my head was spinning and I *wouldn't* let her go on, I *wouldn't* believe what she was saying. And so I stood up and clenched my fists and said, 'Why didn't you come to *me* if this is true? And it isn't, it's another trick, you whore, you bitch . . .'

She was opening her robe. She was naked. That body I'd hung-ered for was changed. There was a raw-looking scar, about five inches long, started close to her belly button, running down almost to where her pubic hair had been, but no longer was. She was shaved and scarred, my little love. She'd had an exploratory, just as she'd said.

I sank down on the bed.

She smiled that bad smile, looking at me. 'See why I didn't come to you? Who cared about Charlie turning off. But the way *we* used to be . . .' She shrugged. 'Bullshit. All of it.' She sat with her robe open and looked down at herself. 'The doctors opened me up, took one look, and closed me again. Metastasized, they said. It means the cancer's all over. No hope. Six months. Eight at the most. And the last months won't be nice, baby.' She looked at me again. 'So it was all for nothing, wasn't it? Big joke on you, Nickie. You can leave

351

now. It's okay. I know you, Nickie. I can see it in your face...'

She was crying. I was crying with her. I went to her and kneeled at her feet and kissed her thighs and bent my face into her lap and tried to kiss her sex. She said, 'Go away! Butcher! Liar! It's bullshit! Bullshit!'

I kissed her hands. I drew her up out of the chair as she shouted and wept. I pulled her against me, and she gasped. I let go, saying, 'Did I hurt you? Did your stomach...?'

She shook her head. She stared at me, and came up against me, and we kissed, and her hand went between us and touched me, exploring my hard on, making sure it was there. Then she came at me in a frenzy, tearing at my clothes, ripping down my pants, pulling down my shorts and kissing me, licking me, squeezing me. On the bed, she spread wide, and plunged me into her. I told her how much I cared, and she said, 'Fuck me! Fuck me, Nickie! When you fuck me everything's all right!'

I fucked her. And everything *was* all right. And how wrong she was about my having killed Alexis for nothing. Eight months or six months or two months – *that* was what I'd won with his death. And that was all I wanted, because that was all that was left.

Later, I asked her to say she loved me.

She sighed. 'That crap again? Well, maybe a little.'

I began to get up. She pulled me back down, kissed me violently. She put her arms around me and hugged me to her. She burrowed her head under my chin. And made everything all-better.

'Nickie, Nickie, thank you.'